I0666201

Queen of Diamonds

An Amber Farrell Novel
Book 7 of the Bite Back series

by
Mark Henwick

Published by *Marque*

Series schedule, reviews & news on
www.athanate.com

Bite Back 7 : Queen of Diamonds
ISBN: 978-1-912499-25-0

Published in February 2021 by Marque.

Mark Henwick asserts the right to be identified as the author of this work.

Author's Notes

Asian names:
Throughout this series, I use the Western sequence (First, Middle, Last Name) to depict names, so as to match with the majority of characters in the books. Most Asian societies would use Last, First, Middle Name.

Continuity:
The Bite Back series is a continuous story rather than a string of episodes. It's not advised to start anywhere but at the beginning, with Book 1, Sleight of Hand, and read through in order.

There are three novellas between Bite Back 5 (Angel Stakes) and Bite Back 6 (Inside Straight). Two are set in Michigan and explain the background to House Lloyd (The Biting Cold & Winter's Kiss), and one is set in New York (Change of Regime). It's not essential to read them before Inside Straight, but they do provide much more information on the side stories that feed into Bite Back at this point.

Acknowledgments

Joe, who talked to me about how to really take out a whole fortified building.
Alejandro, who corrected some of my Spanish. Any errors are mine.
Mayumi-san, who provided the names of the swords.
My alpha/beta readers.
My editor.

Denver
Chapter 1

The setting sun is too big, too red, and it paints the streaming clouds with the color of drying blood. Long shadows creep along the boulevards of the city, dark and thick as crude oil. There are things moving in those shadows.

We didn't have much time.

It was coming nightfall in the City of Lost Gods—the heart of the spirit world, a place spilling over with uncontrolled and unpredictable power harvested from every religion, myth and cult ever to have existed on Earth. It also housed every deity we'd ever worshiped, including ones I wouldn't want to meet in a dark alley, here or anywhere.

My Adept team and I had stayed too long; hell, we shouldn't have been here at all. Spirit walking—'projecting', in the new language of the Adepts—into the City was crazy dangerous.

But it was also a place that touched every part of the human world. Anywhere people were using spirit power, there was a reflection of it here.

That knowledge lay over the City like a fallen spiderweb. It took the form of connections. It could be physical appearance, patterns, proximity, paths.

If you had the ability to see—and the experience to interpret what you saw—you could gather all kinds of intelligence about who was using large amounts of power, and where, and sometimes even what they were doing with it.

What my House and my coven had learned over the last seven weeks painted a chilling picture of an evil power that grew more dangerous by the day—much more than anyone had realized.

If what we were seeing was right, then Luc Matlal, the leader of the Basilikos Athanate, was getting ready to make a move that could destabilize the entire paranormal community throughout North America, and threaten the delicate negotiations towards a peaceful Emergence of paranormals into human society.

We'd known he had his own plans for Emergence, which including ruling over paranormals and subjugating humans, whom he considered to be *marai*—human cattle.

We'd known he attempted to seize power wherever he could find it, first trying to subvert the Athanate Assembly, and then engineering the kidnapping of Tullah to snare her dragon spirit guide Kaothos, and use her potentially world-breaking magic for his own ends.

We'd known he was using ancient Aztec rituals to raise power, in blood-soaked workings designed to spread his influence like a cancer through Athanate, Adept and Were, from his base in Yucatán, up through the rest of Mexico and into North America.

What we hadn't known was how close he was to success. It was only today that we'd found the last pieces of evidence linking a large, powerful set of workings, with tentacles spreading through Mexico and up into El Paso, where my husband and co-alpha, Alex, was working for the Were's Southern League.

Even more worrying, it reached all the way into Louisiana, where the co-alphas of that League, Felix and Cameron, were stalled in their attempts to convince the local Were packs to join us.

Now we knew why that was.

We didn't have all the details—not enough to take to the Athanate Assembly as proof. But together with our on-the-ground, real-world intelligence about the activities of the Mexican Were and their ties to Matlal, we had enough.

We'd had our strong suspicions for weeks, and had used that time to lay plans to break the reach of Matlal's network. Now, we had to move.

I had to move.

That was, assuming I could talk the head of Panethus, Skylur Altau—or his Diakon—into allowing me to leave Denver.

"We need to go." That was Flint, one of the two young, handsome, Native American shaman-Adepts that had recently joined my House, and were, with me, part of the new Denver coven.

I was running point for Flint and Kane on this spirit walk, because we worked well together like this. My projection into the City was a hummingbird: small, vibrant, moving quicker than the eye could follow. Kane was Coyote, Flint was Raven: their spirit animals.

Flint was right, time was of the essence—both in leaving the City of Lost Gods, and moving on the intel we'd gathered.

And yet I hesitated.

Partly, because we were sure we didn't just happen to find all the information we'd gathered today. Like everything else we'd learned about Matlal here in the spirit world, we felt we'd been led to it. And that eerie yet familiar sensation was crawling over me again, making my neck prickle and my scalp itch. Out of the corner of my eye, I thought I saw a shadow slinking through the ruins of the City, dark and sinuous as a jungle cat.

Of course, when I turned to look, there was nothing there but empty, derelict buildings.

More and more often in the last weeks, I would think I saw the shadowy cat—a panther, maybe, or a leopard. Or I'd get a half-imagined glimpse of a man watching me from afar, his cloak stirring in an invisible wind—but when I looked for him straight on, I saw nothing.

Whenever I was here, I could feel something watching. Waiting. Giving us—giving *me*—hints of where to look and how to view it. Feeding me enough crumbs to form that horrifying picture of what Matlal was up to.

It was true knowledge, as far as we could tell, and it was desperately needed, but I couldn't help but feel that those precious crumbs were also leading me, like a mouse following cheese, straight into a trap.

"Let's *go*," Kane—Coyote—said now. "This place is freaky enough in the daylight. No *way* do I want to be here after dark."

He was right, and yet there was something…

Amidst the ruins, when I'd turned to look for that shadowy cat, I'd half-glimpsed a building in a sort of park that had decayed into a swampy jungle. From what I could see above the trees, the design of the building looked Nahuatl. Aztec. A typical stepped pyramid with a temple on top.

"Over there," I said. "See the pyramid? Maybe it's something else to do with Matlal."

"Last one," the Coyote snapped. He was obviously antsy, but I'd stopped paying attention. The temple pulled at me; it *wanted* to be found.

I darted through the trees, dodging trailers of parasitic moss and always flying from cover to cover; there were predators in this City, above and below. The Raven kept watch looking up, and the Coyote looking down.

Closer, I saw the ziggurat was damaged. Swamp trees were locked in a contest with the lowest steps, root and branch winning slowly against hard rock. Foliage was creeping up the sides. At the top, the stones of the temple had once been rich with carved detail, but time had eaten them away until they looked pockmarked.

The City could somehow repair buildings, but this one looked as if it had been forgotten.

"There's nothing here," Raven said.

"Just a quick look inside," I replied. I could see the same ruin he saw, but I definitely *felt* something here. Like a sound below audible range, like an unexpected bump under a searching fingertip, like a feeling of something familiar that refused to surface.

Huitzilin, the temple breezes whispered. *Huitzilin.* Hummingbird in Nahuatl. It was calling to me. It wanted me, and not the Coyote or the Raven.

That low sun was shining straight in through the gaping mouth that formed the door of the summit temple, and that light was so bright I couldn't see clearly into all the shadowed parts.

It made them alluring. Mysterious.

I slipped inside in a blur of iridescent wings.

The carved designs in there were better preserved. Beautiful stone jaguars twisted around each other on the walls, slinking between representations of the Nahuatl gods, who in turn seemed to writhe up all the way to the ceiling.

There was a huge statue of a god on the floor, posed as if resting cross-legged against the west-facing wall. The upper half was a monstrous shadow, hinting at a huge, ornate headdress. The lower part was aflame with the light of the setting sun.

"Enough," Raven called out, voice as harsh as his spirit animal.

"We're here, we might as well see some more," Coyote countered. "Get an ID on this one. See if there's any connection to Matlal."

As the sun was floating down into the cloudy tumult of the western horizon, its light was inching up the statue's body, revealing exquisite workmanship. A patterned cloak draped from the shoulders. A jaguar pelt crossed the hips, its rosette markings exquisitely inlaid with matte stone. A hand almost seemed to move, as if reaching out toward the light. The wrist was encased in an ornate bangle which dripped feathers.

The statue's bare stomach emerged from shadow, rippled with muscle, stone flesh made red as blood by the setting sun. Above that, the beginnings of a chest plate appeared, ornamented, also edged with feathers.

There was a sound outside, a raw noise as if the City groaned, followed by a rattling like dry bones. We'd heard it before, but we had no idea where it came from or what it meant, other than it was time to bug out.

Raven and Coyote had had enough. I could feel them pulling at me, but the design in the center of the statue's chest plate was just becoming visible. Yet it remained dark, sucking in the light and giving nothing back. A circle of night, the surface as deep and insubstantial as space. A stirring, movement beyond, a call—

"Back! Now!"

But I'm falling, falling forward into that eternal circle of darkness, because something calls to me from its depths...

"Amber!"

I struggled to open my eyes, feeling like I was swimming up through murky water. When I finally surfaced, I saw a face inches from mine.

It was Gabrielle, a young and gifted Canadian Adept, trusted lieutenant of Gwendolyn Enkeliekki, who was both Hecate of the Northern Adept League, and leader of the new Denver coven.

Gwen and Gabrielle had become allies and friends as well as teachers of my wayward, newly discovered Adept powers.

I suspected they also wanted to keep an eye on my equally wayward, newly discovered Shaman-Adepts, Flint and Kane. Shaman-Adepts were viewed with suspicion by traditional Adepts—meaning, considered to be rogue. Gwen had softened her stance toward them after they helped save her life, but I still suspected she thought they'd teach me their wicked, lawless ways if she didn't keep a close eye on them.

I also called them rogues, but usually while I was struggling not to laugh at what they told me they thought of the Northern Adept League's rules.

Right now, Gabrielle was looking worried. So were Diana, Tullah, and Gwen, who were pressed in behind her.

Even my irrepressible rogues looked a little worried. Apparently, unlike me, they had popped right out of the spirit world without a problem.

"It was difficult pulling you out," Gwen said. "What happened?"

I blinked, unsure. "Nothing, really. We'd finished our intelligence mission and were coming back when I saw an Aztec ziggurat we hadn't mapped yet. It... pulled at me, like some of the other things our little helper has shown us."

Gwen's lips tightened at that. She and Gabrielle both strongly disapproved of putting any trust in our unknown information source, however good the intel turned out to be.

I went on, "There wasn't anything in there, though—just a statue of an ancient god. The carving was amazing—it looked almost real. And the way the setting sun lit up the carvings was spectacular."

I frowned, trying to bring details to mind. There was something... The chest plate. "It was the chest plate that really struck me, though," I said. "The ornamentation seemed familiar, somehow."

I shook my head. It was already fading, beginning to feel unreal.

"I thought I heard it call me," I added. "Huitzilin. Hummingbird. Didn't even know I knew the word."

The others looked at Flint and Kane, who shrugged.

"We didn't feel anything," Kane said.

"Or hear anything, apart from the usual rattle," Flint said.

"Just the usual feeling about wanting to know about these places," Kane added.

"And wanting to get the hell out because it was getting dark," Flint finished.

"Interesting," Gwen said.

Kane began to write up notes on the whiteboard that covered one wall. The building would be called 'Temple 132' until we could identify the god it had been dedicated to. He scribbled a brief description, and that it had seemed to single me out.

"It was odd. That statue. Out of place." Flint was rubbing his face, probably feeling disoriented, as we all did after a spirit walk. "A stepped ziggurat with a temple on top is classic Aztec. The outer carvings are Aztec. The outside looks weathered and worn. But *inside* the temple it looks new, and that statue isn't Aztec. Those patterns—diamonds, lines and triangles like that—are more recent. It's like an artist's reinterpretation of an Aztec subject."

"That *is* odd," Gwen said. The others nodded agreement. We were becoming experts on the City of Lost Gods, and anything new we treated as a warning that some gods were not as forgotten as others.

But that was an issue for another day. I said, "This is all very interesting, and I'm sure it warrants further investigation, but it's not what we need to be focusing on right now. We found what we were looking for on our mission today, and it's not good."

That silenced everyone. Kane wrote a big question mark next to Temple 132, and then everyone looked at the second wall, where we had several white boards containing everything we'd learned about Matlal and his operations, through the spirit world and through our own real-world intelligence efforts.

At the top of the middle board, Gabrielle had drawn a staring eyeball with the tag alongside it: 'mysterious help'. Then, later, she'd added horns because she was sure whoever or whatever it was, it was evil.

I wasn't sure I'd go that far, but I didn't fool myself that it was altruistic, either. It wanted something; we just didn't know yet what that was.

Briefly, I reiterated what we knew so far and then filled in the final bits of information from today. Most of the Were down in Mexico had allied themselves with Matlal, his strongest supporters being the northern packs from Chihuahua, Sonora and Baja. Though they weren't yet a super-pack, they behaved like one, and it was centered around the town of Villa Ahumada, where an alpha by the name of Mauricio Gálvez had his headquarters in a fortified ranch he'd named Astilla de Luna.

Gálvez was a dangerous psychopath. In the same way a fish rotted from the head down, he'd corrupted those packs. They'd become heavily involved in the trafficking of people and drugs, and they'd copied behavior from the worst of the criminal gangs they competed with. Pack members needed to commit serious criminal offenses to show their loyalty. They terrorized and murdered the communities they lived in.

They were also working against the Athanate Assembly and the Southern League of Were. We could trace their attacks all along the border states.

We'd always suspected that the level of organization and power involved had to lead back to Matlal. As of today we'd traced the final connections in the spirit world—making it one continuous stain of corrupt power that had spread from Yucatán to Mexico City, through Astilla de Luna, and up into San Diego, El Paso. And now Louisiana as well.

Even worse, we'd confirmed that what Matlal and the hardcore remnant of Basilikos were doing down in Yucatán involved a way to harness some of the City of Lost Gods' powers for their own uses. One effect of that had been to somehow anchor the City in close proximity to our physical world—so close that it was now almost impossible to spirit walk without landing right in the middle of it, whether you wanted to or not.

That use of the power was insanely dangerous in and of itself. More immediately worrying was that he was feeding that power into some kind of working based at Astilla de Luna and the results were being seen as far away as California and Louisiana.

We had to move now, before the power reached its tipping point. We had to destroy the working, and gather proof that it led back to Matlal—that he was pulling the strings behind everything the Mexican Were were doing.

More important, we had to accomplish that in the physical world—gather evidence that the Assembly and the Adept League would have to take action on. Maybe even get the Were and Adept Leagues to formally join the Assembly, instead of arguing about it, as they had done for the last seven weeks.

The rest of the paranormal world had left me alone for that seven weeks. Mostly. The time had been incredibly useful on many fronts, and I was grateful, but it was over.

But the next step was going to be tricky.

The Athanate Assembly was delicately balanced at the moment.

House Correia of the Hidden Path held the presidency, but the real power sat with the two opposition groups: Panethus, led by Skylur, and the Empire of Heaven. Correia had re-formed her political party from Basilikos into the Hidden Path after expelling Matlal. Unfortunately, a lot of those supporting her in her position were actually still really members of Basilikos, and under Matlal's command. While it stayed this way, the Assembly was in a stalemate. Correia couldn't command the entire Assembly. She couldn't even call the Assembly. She was trying to run the functions of Athanate government as committees, but even that had limited success.

Matlal and Basilikos were deliberately and effectively preventing any progress.

In the meantime, Emergence crept closer on a timescale Skylur could no longer control.

Short of huge and improbable shocks like the Carpathians coming out of their isolation and changing the balance in the Assembly, we needed *something* to be done. The Assembly had to realize the threat Matlal posed, cease their political maneuvering and present a united front for the paranormal world when Emergence broke. Even nearly united would be okay.

I was the one who had to do that *something*. And it seemed it could be put off no longer.

As if on cue, my Diakon, Yelena, and my immediate boss, Bian, walked in together.

Yelena spoke first. "Big, bad wolves, they want to talk finally."

She meant Felix and Cameron. When they'd left for Louisiana at the New Year, they'd said they would call me when they needed me.

After what we'd seen in the spirit world, I was unsurprised they'd decided that time was now.

However, there was someone I needed to talk to first. I looked at Bian.

"I've already told Yelena they're going to have to wait," Bian said. "We have ten minutes before the scheduled call from New York."

I felt the emotion in the room change. We'd laid our plans for just this moment, but putting them into motion was something else.

We had to stop Gálvez and Matlal, but it was going to be a bloody, dangerous business—and it began with me convincing Skylur's Diakon that I needed to be set free from the restrictions that currently surrounded me, without telling her what I was actually going to be doing.

We all turned to Diana.

She looked tense, but she nodded. "I think we have learned enough through the spirit world. We cannot wait any longer. It's time."

I made to leave with Bian, but Diana held up her hand. "I am concerned with the evidence that the trail of workings in Mexico can now be traced all the way to Louisiana," she said. "It seems too coincidental, with Felix and Cameron requesting Amber's presence there just now. Gwendolyn, I think we need someone in Louisiana immediately, *quietly*, to investigate any unusual workings or Adept activity. Amber can handle problems in the Athanate and Were communities, but if there were Adept problems as well..."

"The strongest coven is Lafayette," Gwen said. "It would be the obvious place to start. But I can't go. Bryn and I can't leave Kaothos yet. It's too dangerous."

Tullah frowned. Much as she appreciated what Gwen and her Valkyrie spirit guide, Bryn, had done, she and Kaothos were of the opinion that they had to be ready to stand alone soon.

Gabrielle spoke. "The first step would be to discover if they've been infiltrated or influenced by Matlal's people, like the Denver coven was. As long as they haven't, then recruit them to help in the investigation. I can do that."

Gwen said sharply, "That's dangerous work, especially for a lone Adept."

"It's up to you," I said to Gabrielle and Gwen. "It would mean a lot to have you at my back, assuming I manage to get down there."

Gabrielle and I had grown close in the last couple of months; I respected her power and loved the excitement and enthusiasm she brought to everything she did. I'd also begun to see her as part of my House. I was sure she had the Adept capability to handle this task in Louisiana, but I also knew Gwen was right. It was dangerous work, and she was young and inexperienced.

Gabrielle exchanged glances with Gwen, and then said quietly, "I know what you're risking. You're doing your part to keep Matlal's plans from coming to fruition, and I need to do mine."

Gwen gave a short nod. "Very well."

I could tell she wasn't happy about it, though. She treated Gabrielle like a daughter, or maybe a favorite sister. She was almost as protective of her as she was of Tullah and Kaothos.

"I'll get the next flight," Gabrielle said.

Gwen wasn't finished, but she changed subjects. "Are you absolutely sure about the part of your plan where you keep Skylur in the dark? From what I understand, according to Athanate law, all actions taken by you—and your House—are regarded as his responsibility."

Diana smiled. "Keeping Skylur in the dark is more difficult than you might imagine. We need to make sure he has complete deniability in front of the Truth Sensors of the Assembly. He knows I'm here, and he knows much of what's happening, so he'll know we're going to do something about it. Something he'll be able to use in the Assembly, while truthfully denying he ordered it. In the meantime, his attention is better focused on Emergence."

Gwen nodded again, still frowning, still unhappy, but she made no further objection. I gave Gabrielle a hug and wished her luck, and headed out with Bian for our conference call.

I wouldn't be talking directly to Skylur yet. As soon as we'd reported the success of rescuing Tullah and the return of Kaothos, he shut himself off, leaving explicit instructions that we were to talk to his Diakon, House Flavia. She was the one we had the call scheduled with.

Diakon to the head of Panethus, and yet she described herself as *Basilikos*. She was so set in her ways, she even refused to call herself Hidden Path, the more acceptable name House Correia had taken for her political party. Flavia remained Basilikos, and proud of it.

Skylur had also explicitly put Flavia in charge of Bian and me, but without telling her everything that was going on in Denver. She knew nothing about the trick we'd pulled in Los Angeles, rescuing Kaothos under the cover of Diana's 'death', and she only knew the bare minimum about the dragon.

And we had no authority to enlighten her.

Given those difficulties, and considering what I needed to achieve in today's call, this was going to be one bitch of a conversation.

Chapter 2

I guess I didn't really expect Diakon Flavia to be on time, but the image of the empty chair on the videoconference screen was still irritating, especially now when so much was at stake.

Bian snorted and took the opportunity to kiss me.

As my direct boss in the Athanate hierarchy, she could demand my compliance, but of course I responded enthusiastically. At Christmas, Bian and I had finally acknowledged the simmering attraction and genuine feelings that had been between us since we'd first met, though she'd insisted she wouldn't take it forward until Jen and Alex were here and we'd talked to them about it. In the two months since, that meeting hadn't been possible to arrange. And yet, for someone who delighted in breaking rules, she'd stuck to this one strictly. She'd also stuck to Skylur's restriction on taking my Blood, though I knew that both forbidden fruit tempted her. I could hear the surge in her Blood every time we met, let alone kissed like this.

"Mmm." She broke the kiss and straightened her sweater where it had somehow gotten pushed up. "It seems you've fully recovered from our last training session. No lingering aches and pains?"

"Pains? No. Aches?" I smiled and tried batting my eyelashes. "I guess I'll have to live with those a while longer." I sat up and sighed. "And if we can swing this, I guess that's the last training session for a while."

"We have to swing it," she said.

Diana insisted that we follow all the protocols so Skylur could deny knowledge of my mission. That meant we had to at least try to get Diakon Flavia to allow me to leave Denver on a pretext, and if she refused…

The problem was, the entire state of Colorado was in an Athanate quarantine. No Athanate allowed in, none allowed out.

The real reason was to protect the knowledge that Diana was alive from getting out. Even if the Diakon of the Empire of Heaven already suspected it, making it public—and thus effectively announcing to the world that we'd tricked everyone and he'd fallen for it—would be seen as an insult to the Emperor, and the unspoken agreement between the Empire and Panethus to run the Assembly would break.

However, the excuse given to the rest of the Athanate world, and Diakon Flavia, was that the quarantine was to allow for a controlled test of whether my infusion reduced the period and severity of crusis, and whether that ability was transferred.

Which meant the quarantine applied most specifically to me, and this conversation had to pretend to be about the experiment, which Diakon Flavia had control of.

I felt my jaw clench at the tide of frustration rising in me, as it often did when I had to confront Athanate politics.

Sensing my emotions, Bian squeezed my thigh just as Flavia appeared on the screen.

"Livia Flavia, House Flavia, Diakon Altau," she said.

Her voice wasn't harsh, but gave the impression of strength beneath the smooth tones. Her face, framed with straight, dark hair, was sharp, with an uncompromising hardness in her eyes and mouth. Those eyes told me she was intelligent. And that she *knew* she was being lied to.

As I'd already guessed, this was going to be one hell of a conversation.

We went through the formal Athanate greetings. She and Bian had spoken before, so it wouldn't have been such an insult to skip them, but we were being deliberately polite.

She finished with: "Altau insists we should be less formal, so please call me Livia."

Bian and I murmured our names back and she fixed her eyes on me.

She'd been speaking in Athanate up to that point, and she continued in the same language. "I have Bian's weekly written reports, Amber, but please don't just update me on the project. I want to hear a complete overview of how it's going, in your words."

I took a breath and answered her in Athanate.

"To reiterate the background: my own crusis was unusual. It appeared to be put off for a long time after I was infused, and then, when it started, it passed quickly. It also appeared that a member of my House finished crusis almost immediately after a secondary infusion of my Blood through biting me. Skylur said that, when the time was right, we'd need to check whether my infusion reduced crusis in all cases, whether there was a delay in starting, and whether those characteristics were passed in turn."

I paused, enjoying her surprise at my ease with the language. The last few weeks had been surprising to me as well. We'd been exploring the advantages of my Carpathian eukori, and it was amazing how easy it had been to learn the Athanate language by being linked through an enhanced eukori to my teacher. I'd had lessons every day with Diana, Bian or Pia, and was now fairly fluent.

I went on: "There's a lot of scientific aspects that we've been discussing about protein strings in blood, the way they mimic DNA and the way they fold at the molecular structural level, creating different Athanate characteristics. Some folds are dominant and some recessive, like genes, and they can sometimes be passed on through infusion. Do you want me to go into that?"

"I've read some of the reports on the investigations," Livia said. "Led in part by Savannah, another one of your House kin. What a surprising, remarkably versatile and useful House you have, Amber."

"Thank you." I smiled at her. I didn't want to get blindsided by a charm offensive, but it was nice she was making an effort.

"But to answer your question, no," she went on. "Please stick to the results of the experiment."

"Very well. The major point to note is that there was a fundamental difference between the first two infusions and the remainder."

Livia interrupted. "Yes, I understand that Scott and Mykayla are the only hybrids—Athanate and Were mixed. Do you know why? Did you try something different with them? Did it feel different?"

It was difficult to tell from her expression what she felt about hybrids. Likely not positive; the more conservative among the Athanate thought hybrids were abominations, and she was so conservative she wouldn't even compromise on the name of her creed.

"No, no, and no," I answered her. "Scott manifested first as a werewolf, Mykayla as an Athanate. Within a couple of weeks they'd both become hybrid. The only difference between them and others that we can think of is that I'd accepted Scott into my House, and Mykayla and I have been close for a while."

Bian stirred beside me, but Livia spoke first. "*Close.* Is that a euphemism?"

Even more than English, Athanate had the ability for words to be used with different meanings.

"No," I said. "Mykayla and I haven't had sex."

Bian smiled, and spoke before Livia could. "I think Amber instinctively regards Mykayla as part of her extended House. Trang and Farrell are becoming very closely integrated as Houses, and we're talking about formalizing that."

Out of sight beneath the desk, Bian's knee nudged me again.

Right. Play along.

Livia raised an eyebrow. I would have sworn she'd caught that look from Skylur.

"I'm effectively acting as one of Amber's Diakons," Bian explained. "And Amber's Diakons are effectively acting as mine."

She was right. All the Athanate that would have comprised Bian's House had been given their own Houses by Skylur. She had had no one except kin and Aspirants, and Haven was full of Ops 4-10 and wolves in training. So, as I'd progressed from infusing Scott and Mykayla to infusing Bian's Aspirants and volunteers from Ops 4-10, we'd called on Pia to look after them. And while that was happening, Yelena, Julie and Keith were helping Bian with her security tasks. David had taken over interfacing with local authorities for matters like accounting and taxes, which Athanate Houses did carefully to ensure they remained hidden in plain sight, attracting no unnecessary attention.

Livia's other eyebrow had joined the first. However closely they might work together, the suggestion of *integrating* two Houses was unusual. And unless I'd suddenly developed amnesia, Bian and I hadn't discussed it at all.

Not that I was complaining.

I could guess what Bian was doing—effectively telling Livia that I was not just a new Athanate House with peculiarities and potential, but actually integrated with an existing House. What was more, not just any House, but one that had provided Altau with one of his previous Diakons. So, not to be treated casually. Bian wanted to show her support for what I was working to achieve in this conversation.

"Oh. And are you two sexual partners, then?" Livia asked.

"Not yet," Bian said. "Not until both Amber's kin are back in Denver. We're still waiting impatiently for that."

"Ah, yes, yet more versatile members of House Farrell." Livia's lips thinned. "I can't promise when you'll get Jennifer Kingslund back. That's up to Skylur, and I assume it will depend on when he feels it's appropriate to take back control of his human businesses. As for Alexander Deauville, I understand he's down in El Paso on werewolf business, so I can't speak to that either. How frustrating for you."

"We'll have to speak about it," I said, maneuvering the conversation the way it needed to go, at the same time feeling uncertainty.

Why had Livia mentioned Jen?

I understood why Jen was so valuable to Skylur. She'd taken over control of his sprawling mass of companies and reorganized them in preparation for the changes that Emergence would bring. She had to be in New York for that, but apart from obviously missing her, I hated the thought that Jen was somehow under the control of House Flavia. It felt as if it gave Livia a measure of control over me.

But she waved off my attempt to divert. "Please, finish the briefing."

I brought her right up to date. Every other day since New Year's, I'd infused a new Aspirant. Half came from Bian's kin, and the other half from former Ops 4-10 members. Twenty in all. For each of them, there had been a short delay, then they'd gone into crusis and they'd emerged safely. The delays and the depth of crusis had been variable, but both far below the expected norms for Athanate. The proof of which was that Pia had been able to mentor all of them without difficulty.

These stark facts were what Livia wanted to hear from me. It was hard to push aside the blizzard of sensations that swept through my memory as I spoke. The tension before each infusion, the uncertainty, the mounting excitement, the unbelievable immediate pleasure of biting and finally the longer, more profound pleasure from knowing I'd successfully infused another person.

"So, in a matter of weeks," Livia said as I ended, "you've made it possible for House Altau to establish at least another couple of Houses, or bolster existing ones. From the sound of it, you could even increase that to one infusion a day."

While I bit down on my retort, Bian answered smoothly, "Not really the outcomes that are under discussion, Livia. In the meantime, you can appreciate why we're suggesting an integration of Houses, given that half of these new Athanate were my kin, but were infused by Amber."

My jaw was still clenched at Livia's words. I was *not* going to become some kind of Athanate breeder, locked away in Denver, infusing Aspirants for Livia to dispatch to the corners of the country.

"And the hybrids?" Livia asked.

I snapped my focus back and shrugged. "They had a bigger change to overcome. It took longer, crusis was harder and they've had more to learn, but they're successfully hybrid, and they're not going rogue."

"So they're safe?"

"Safe?" I huffed and let my teeth show, wolf style. "Never. But they're no more likely to snap at you than any other Were, and no more likely to want your Blood than any other Athanate."

I took a calming breath. "It's time to close the first phase and proceed with the second."

Livia's eyes narrowed. "Explain."

Not so much of the charm offensive now.

"The purpose of this project was not for me to stock up the country with new Athanate," I said. "It was an experiment to test my infusion. We've shown I can infuse people successfully and that it reduces the time and danger of crusis. That part is over. The second step is more important: to determine whether my new Athanate have inherited the ability to infuse others in a similarly short time. It's time for that second step."

Livia sat back.

I'd just issued a challenge to her authority. I needed to re-emphasize it. "In fact, my part is over for the moment," I said. "The quarantine no longer applies to me."

Her expression didn't change. "The reason I was late for the start of this conference today was I received an urgent call from Felix Larimer." She fixed me with her stare. "He wants you to go down to Louisiana."

I cursed silently—bad timing. Now she'd think my reasoning was being coordinated by the werewolves.

"So there can be no confusion about this," Livia continued, "I told him you would be available when I said you were. The experiment you're conducting is vital to Panethus. It's been ordered by Skylur and he's put me in charge of it. You will remain in Denver, and what you call the first phase of the experiment will continue until I say it ceases."

One: she'd caused a huge problem for me with Felix.

And two: there was no other way to progress now.

Buckle up, Tara muttered in my mind.

"I don't answer solely to you, House Flavia," I said. "Or to House Altau. I've given Skylur my oath, and through that, you have authority over me. But I was appointed by him as syndesmon to the Assembly, to ensure that the integration of Were into the Assembly did not fail through misunderstanding. The fully convened Assembly can dismiss me from that position, or Skylur can debate my interpretation of my responsibilities with me. My assessment of the situation is that my role as syndesmon overrides any further need for me to remain in Denver, so I will be going to Louisiana. I will be acting on Panethus' behalf as much as the Southern League. If necessary, I'll discuss my reasons with Skylur."

She was furious, but her control was absolute and her voice remained level and reasonable.

"This is a particularly bad time to be interrupting Skylur. I can understand you may resent me, but your actions aren't serving his interests."

"I disagree."

Her eyes flickered to Bian. In other circumstances, the obvious response for her would have been to demand for Bian, as my superior, to punish or imprison me, pending judgment. Bian had taken the same oath to House Altau and Skylur that I had. An absolute oath. Except when it wasn't.

Livia was aware now that Bian's earlier comment about integrating Houses had been intended to put down a marker that she entirely supported me and would refuse Livia's commands.

Never give an order you know will be refused.

"It's now clear to me you intended this from the outset," she said. "You'll get your talk with Skylur, but it may not work the way you anticipated. Remain there."

She left the range of the camera.

Chapter 3

The first to return to the videoconference room in New York wasn't Skylur or Livia. It was Skylur's head of security.

I'd heard about her, and Bian had shown me the files.

Naturally, she looked like she was in her twenties or thirties, but I knew she was old. Maybe five or six centuries. Before Skylur had moved to America, she'd been his *pelea*. The word originally came from the name of a piece of ritual Athanate shield armor, a guard that covered the whole left shoulder and arm, segmented like a lobster shell. 'Pelea' was also used to mean a dedicated bodyguard. *Close protection*, we used to call it in Ops 4-10.

Remember her name, Bian had told me. *Maia Kiriani. Be wary of her.*

She was tall, with short brunette hair, lovely brown eyes, and a look that could freeze nitrogen. She moved like a gunslinger in an old Western film—the guy in the black Stetson. She even got the clothes right—black, head to toe.

Maia deliberately stood in front of the camera, silently looking at me. Making a point. Then she moved back to allow Livia and Skylur to sit.

"Bian, Amber," Skylur said, and we murmured hellos back at him.

I was shocked at how tired he looked, and he saw that.

A ghost of a smile crossed his face.

"Yes, I'm extremely busy, Amber." He sighed. "I know you will have a valid reason for forcing this conversation to take place, so let me see if I agree with you."

"On the surface, this is all about what you can tell people," I said, carefully not looking at Livia. "You can tell them I've achieved what needed to be done in the first phase of the infusion experiment, so my leaving Colorado doesn't mean the quarantine is lifted while the second phase takes place."

Skylur's lip twisted. What I'd said was correct, but he knew me well enough to know it wasn't enough on its own for me to be refusing his Diakon's orders.

"The Southern League wants me in Louisiana, and my status as syndesmon makes that a valid public reason for leaving Denver and going there."

He could read between my words. "Which means there's an underlying reason."

I took a deep breath and launched the strategy.

"Yes. You need the Athanate situation there to be fixed and you can't do it. You probably don't even want to order it. Your Diakon certainly can't do it. You need someone to do it for you, acting without orders and without it being done openly. I am that someone."

Livia twitched. Skylur looked angry, but he waited for me to lay it out.

"When you took down the Eastern Seaboard association at the Assembly in LA, you hit them twice. You took away their metaphorical head when you persuaded House Prowser to withdraw from the association. She was their intellectual driver, the one who could justify their position in debate. Then you forced House Ibarre into a position where he had no option other than for him and his team of advisors to commit *korheny*, dying so you would spare the remainder of his House. With that, you took the metaphorical heart out of the Eastern Seaboard association."

"Take away the head or the heart, and there's not much left to fight," Livia said.

"Wrong, but I'll come to that," I replied. "You moved Naryn to New England, to adopt the rest of House Ibarre, along with the mantle, domain and territory of Boston and Portland. That move, the association could accept."

Livia knew what was coming, but at a glance from Skylur, she kept her silence.

"You moved to New York. No problem with that either, but then you chose a Basilikos Diakon," I said. "*I* understand the reasoning. And if the Eastern Seaboard association still had House Prowser, she might have been able to rationalize it for them."

"*Former* association," Livia said. "Not only does the Eastern Seaboard association no longer exist, I remind you that all the principal Houses have given their oaths, in person, to House Altau."

"The association members still talk to each other," I said. "And among the members of my 'surprising, remarkably versatile and useful House', I have people who can snoop on private conversations."

That shocked her into a moment's silence.

"Not enough for proof," I said, holding a hand up. "Not even enough to justify an open investigation. But enough to be clear that what's left of the association is being driven by what you could call the metaphorical gut. The unthinking reactionary part."

"One of the Houses gave their oath and is now backing out?"

"No," I said. "Because House Labastide in New Orleans never gave you her oath."

"They're just a sub-House of House Wingfield in Atlanta," Livia said. "They were barely in the old association, stuck out there on the Gulf."

"Eastern Seaboard is just a name," I countered. "Labastide in New Orleans was as much an integral part as House Prowser, even though Prowser was 'stuck out' on the Upper Peninsula in Michigan."

"Amber's right. Being at the edge of their territory doesn't disqualify them. In fact, the most dedicated members of any association are often those at the edges. You should never ignore sub-Houses, Diakon." Skylur's voice was quiet and his eyes stayed on mine. "But that was my fault. In giving the old association some dignity by not requiring every sub-House to give an oath, I allowed enmity to fester."

"And you can't rethink your original decision about oaths now," I cut in before Livia suggested it. "Firstly, it would look like weakness. Secondly, you've just made everything *much* worse by giving Naryn a second domain, in Washington DC."

"How did you know..." Livia stopped. "You eavesdrop on *our* communications?"

"No. And no need to, either. House Elicott in Washington has been sending angry updates about the 'invasion' of his domain to all the members of the former Eastern Seaboard. I'm sure he's complained to you as well."

"It's not a permanent domain," Livia said. "He's been told—"

Anger got the better of me and I interrupted her. "House Flavia, I suggest you employ another assistant. One fluent in Athanate tact and diplomacy. One who will *explain* rather than *tell*."

Skylur raised a finger. I backed down. He was right.

"I apologize, Livia," I said. "That was out of line. You are under considerable stress, and it's easy to criticize from the sidelines. I'm playing armchair quarterback."

"You know the real reason Naryn's in Washington, then?" Skylur asked.

My stomach clenched. We didn't *know*, here in Denver, but we'd guessed.

"Emergence?"

Skylur nodded. "Agent Ingram has decided that he cannot delay any longer. He and Naryn are working together to introduce Naryn to his bosses. It's happening," he said, and his simple words made it a real thing, an almost physical pressure on me. "There's no more time for maneuvers and preparation. Wherever it is we're at, that's what we're going to have to go forward with."

"How long before it comes out? Before ordinary people know?"

Skylur smiled. "That's going to be driven by the government. We're already leaking, deliberately, to segments of the population we think will be receptive. Some of that you already know. As my Diakon and I agree, your House is indeed 'surprising, remarkably versatile and useful'."

In this case, I assumed he was talking about Dominé. An initiative started off by Jen had Altau Holdings investing in setting up franchises of Dominé's Club Vasana in major cities. 'Blood Orchid Vampire Nights' were becoming famous. Except now, there were actually vampires attending and on the lookout for kin. There had been Werewolf Nights, too. There had even been a hugely successful Chanting and Spiritual Healing Night at the San Francisco club where the local Adept community had been astonished at the number of people with latent abilities they'd been able to recruit.

"I will speak directly to House Elicott in Washington, and soothe his fears," Skylur said.

"I don't think that's enough to quiet the resentment in the association, given the association's starting position is we shouldn't be emerging at all."

Skylur nodded, conceding the point.

"The extent of any potential revolt needs to be assessed," I went on. "The best place to do it is at the House who appears to be the most conservative and reactionary. That's Labastide in New Orleans. You can't go down there without setting the rest of the old association on fire. Livia or Tarez going down there for a 'courtesy call' would achieve the same result. I have a reason to visit, completely unrelated to Athanate politics. If I'm in the New Orleans area, I would be expected to stop in and introduce myself."

Skylur was silent for a minute, sitting back and thinking. Livia watched him, and Maia watched me from the back of the room.

I wondered if the pelea had any politics or opinions outside of complete loyalty to Skylur. She'd been the resident, long-established House in Seattle when Skylur had moved to New York. One call and she'd given up all that to be his bodyguard.

Were they lovers?

I wasn't sure I was brave enough to ask.

"Yes," Skylur's voice broke into my thoughts. "The first phase of the experiment in Colorado has reached a satisfactory conclusion. You should not have to be involved in the second phase, and your pressing business as syndesmon takes precedence over remaining in Denver."

He was *not* ordering me to go down and investigate House Labastide in New Orleans, in case anyone ever asked him if he had. Especially in front of the Assembly, with an Adept Truth Sensor standing beside him.

For the same reason, I was *not* going to tell him exactly which route I was going to take to Louisiana. I wasn't even going to think about it. The important thing was that I had permission to openly leave Denver for a reason entirely justifiable in front of the Assembly. Focus on *that*.

But Skylur hadn't finished. "The position of syndesmon provides autonomy, but it also requires that you must be able to justify your actions to the Assembly, and argue the benefits your actions and those of your House bring to all the parties involved. All of those actions, since taking up that position."

That made me twitch. He knew I'd broken quarantine to save Tullah, and therefore I'd assumed I had his tacit approval. And the quarantine was a House Altau order, not an Assembly order. But now he seemed to be implying, or warning me, that all House Farrell actions might become a matter for the Assembly.

I wondered if he already knew how much I'd broken the quarantine. I'd not only left Colorado, I'd left the country. I pushed the thoughts away in case something showed on my face.

"The Assembly is not impartial," Skylur said. "You know this of the Athanate. Do not believe that the addition of Were or Adept will make it any more impartial. Be prepared. To build the case you will be called to make, the best foundation is success, and the more spectacular, the better. A partial success or a failure leaves fertile ground for might-have-beens to grow."

Anytime I had Skylur's full attention on me, I'd found it unnerving. Some of that was his sheer presence, the weight of his eukori. That should have meant that he was less unnerving in a teleconference. I reminded myself I was looking at nothing more than pixels on a screen, but my hindbrain refused to accept that. Even if I suspected he'd deliberately lightened his lecture by making a joke about growing beans.

"You must be able to face that examination alone. I am sure you will be a light in the dark, and hold high the marque you bear."

To truly benefit Emergence, I had to beat the enemy, and then beat the political machinations of the Assembly. Just surviving wasn't good enough. Unless my success was obvious, he might need to make me stand alone for what I'd done. I'd started my planning suspecting as much, but it was chilling to have him confirm it to me.

He'd closed with a formulaic Athanate blessing, but his eyes told me it was intended as it was said.

Livia missed the subtext.

"You're attaching a tremendous weight to the analysis of one junior Athanate House, who's not completed even a year in Athanate society, and who's been restricted to Colorado since the end of the Assembly in Los Angeles," she said.

I hadn't been restricted to Colorado, but that wasn't the point. Livia was right. I wouldn't have had the feel for Athanate politics that was needed to come up with this assessment.

Skylur was looking at me, and he knew the truth of where the analysis had come from—Diana.

I shrugged. Telling Livia that Diana was alive was up to him.

Livia *knew* something was being kept from her. I didn't think it was a good way for Skylur to work with his Diakon, but I'd probably provided enough forceful opinions for one day.

But it was as if he could read my mind. "You're right," he said to me. "It's time to bring Livia fully on board. I'll do that. You probably have some urgent organizing to complete. Bian, Amber."

The screen cleared.

Bian let out a long sigh.

"That went *way* better than it might have," she said, slipping back into English.

"You and Diana prepared me well."

I got up and paced. I had the familiar pre-operation feeling from my days back in Ops 4-10. Restlessness. Tightness in the stomach. A narrowing of vision.

I took my cell and called Yelena.

"It's on. Everything. Go."

"Yes, Boss. Plane will be ready in a couple of hours."

"Okay, but we stick to the plan. We leave tomorrow at four-thirty in the morning. I want to be landing at dawn."

"I will make sure that's passed on."

She didn't just mean internally. She would post a flight plan. She would ensure it was known that I was flying, when and where I'd be landing. Not New Orleans, but El Paso.

She ended the call, and I could imagine the members of my house sprinting into action. Everything had been planned. They'd see to the final preparations. For once, all I had to do was show up at Centennial and get on the plane.

But however prepared I'd been, now that I had the green light, there wasn't going to be enough time for all the things I wanted to do before I left. Needed to do.

But there was time for some of them. One in particular, with honesty and openness, without all the subterfuge.

As Bian began to stand, I swept her up and dropped her butt down on the conference table.

"Oohh?" She managed to make a sound that was questioning as well as encouraging.

She was wearing one of her loose college hoodies. I pulled it away from her neck and set to kissing every rosette of the leopard skin tattoo that I could reach.

"Whatever are you doing?" she murmured.

"You'll work it out in a while."

"I thought we were waiting until Jen and Alex..." Her breath caught as my lips brushed against her pulse.

"For *that*, we are," I whispered.

"Oh? Ahh! Phase one complete." Her voice faded into sighs and her hands slid up my back, pressing me to her, holding me against her throat. "No longer any restriction on Blood for you. Giving or receiving."

"None at all."

I kissed the edge of her jaw, her cheek, her lips. Had to be careful; both of us had our fangs out.

"I hope you won't regret this," I said between kisses.

"Never."

Athanate being Athanate, there was no doubt some ceremony Bian and I would be expected to go through. No time for that now. I knew what would be enough for the moment.

"My Blood is yours," I said. "Blood for Blood."

"Blood for Blood," she responded. "My Blood is yours."

One of us had to go first, and I pressed Bian's mouth against my throat. Flesh parted exquisitely to her fangs, with the melting pleasure of desires long denied.

She *pulled* my Blood, and my vision clouded as every other sense soared.

After the long weeks of training with our eukori open to each other, there was no longer any border between Bian and me. We were seamless: one heart, one breath, one desire.

One Blood.

Chapter 4

I held off calling Felix until I had an excuse to keep the conversation short.

I knew that he and Cameron wanted me in Louisiana primarily to run a ritual for the halfies. But it was likely that there was more to it than that. I had members of my House down there with the alphas: Nick Gray and Ursula Tennyson, my two were-bears, and Olivia Todd, the werewolf halfy I'd first helped change in the ritual down in New Mexico. They'd kept me updated on the situation in Louisiana, although I hadn't talked to them today.

Felix and Cameron knew about the situation in El Paso and the other border pack territories. They knew the Mexican packs were causing trouble, even as far as Louisiana and the other Gulf Coast states.

I wasn't sure if they realized that things were hitting a crisis point, but what I didn't want my alphas to do was give me a direct order to go down to El Paso and 'fix it'. I needed to provide them with plausible deniability in exactly the same way I needed it for Skylur, in case something went wrong.

"Alpha," I opened with, as soon as Felix answered. "I apologize about the misunderstanding with Diakon Altau."

"This Assembly isn't worth our time if the snakes keep thinking they're running the entire show, and Were needs are trivial," he growled. "How will it benefit us if you're following everyone's orders except ours?"

"I understand your frustration," I told him. "As co-alpha of my own pack, and as part of the League, my instincts are to head straight out and take care of my Were business. But as syndesmon, I have to take the larger view."

The background noise changed on the cell, and I knew Cameron was now listening as well.

I went on. "We all have to be part of the Assembly—the League and the Confederacy; Panethus and Basilikos. As the Southern League, you *have* to be there, because the Assembly is going to be making decisions that affect all paranormals, whether you're there or not. We, as Were, need to be heard, so we also need to persuade the Confederation to join as well, if for no other reason than to make sure they're not working against our interests. And I need to keep on good terms with the Athanate, so that they listen when we talk."

"You've made that argument before," Cameron said in her rich, late night voice. "But then the Altau Diakon tells us that your Altau oath overrides the authority we have as your alphas. Respect needs to go both ways."

"She's wrong," I said. "I got through to Skylur and I'm going to be coming down to Louisiana in my role as syndesmon."

"He agrees his oath takes second place to your duty to the Assembly?" Felix asked.

I could lie for an easier life now, but it wasn't worth it.

"We didn't discuss a general case. He's accepted it in this instance."

"Kind of him," Cameron said.

I wasn't fooled by the softness of her voice. I could tell she was completely pissed at Skylur, and I was going to have to smooth her ruffled fur when I got down there.

"If I could suggest, alphas, that you get the Heights to spend more effort on Diakon Flavia."

All diplomatic! Listen to you! snarked Tara.

Felix thought so too. He snorted, but it was Cameron who answered.

"Some of your suggestions *are* working very well, Amber. Maybe not so much in El Paso."

She was referring to advice I'd given them back at the beginning of the year. The bits that had gone well were the relocating of the Heights pack from Los Angeles to New York. Their alpha, who still called himself 'Heights' in the LA style, had leaped at that. He was one of the very few werewolf alphas that seemed to relish the political scene. It was necessary to have the Were represented permanently in the committees that the new president, House Correia, had set up. The Heights was ideal for that.

As a second step after moving the Heights, Felix and Cameron had also allowed Billie to expand her territory from the Belles' original downtown location in LA to include the old Heights territory, as I'd also advised. Billie had gone several steps further. She'd pulled all of the southern California packs, from LA right down to San Diego, into one super-pack, loyal to the League. That had made Felix and Cameron *very* happy.

But I'd also advised on organizing things down in El Paso, and *that* wasn't going so well—mainly due to Matlal and his influence on the Juárez pack, over the border in Mexico.

When Caleb and Victoria Oaken, the old El Paso alphas, had challenged Alex and me, we'd killed them. The laws of the challenge meant the El Paso pack had become ours. The plan was to move the El Paso pack to

Denver. Fine, in concept, but they were a large pack, well integrated into the El Paso community. What was more, the city itself couldn't be left without a pack, because that would leave an open door for the Juárez pack. They'd move in, with their murder and terrorism and criminal enterprises, right smack in the middle of where we were establishing the Southern League.

Alex had been sent to manage the move of El Paso wolves to Denver, and I'd suggested to Felix and Cameron that Zane move one of his sub-packs from White Sands into El Paso, which they probably would have done anyway. But I'd also said that Zane, Alex and both packs should work together in the handover, despite rivalry between them.

At the time, it was one of those clever solutions to lots of problems, but seven weeks later, constant attacks and harassment by Juárez had brought progress to a near-halt.

Now our spirit world intel had confirmed that neutralizing Juárez wasn't enough. We had to go further. Luckily, that was exactly what I'd been building a plan for. I just couldn't tell Felix and Cameron until it was done.

"It's partly El Paso we wanted to talk to you about," Felix said. "but more about the whole situation with the Mexican border packs. They're causing a lot of trouble, and I can't believe it's not coordinated. Almost like they're forming their own association because they think the League threatens them."

I made noncommittal noises. My alphas were intelligent and experienced. It would have been dumb to expect them to *not* notice what was happening.

"Not just the trouble on the border," Cameron said. "And not just the involvement with drugs and trafficking, although that's certainly bad enough. One of the problems we're having here on the Gulf Coast is there's less pressure on the packs from the problem with halfies."

"They don't have halfies?"

That shocked me. As I understood it, the growing number of halfies—Were who'd been bitten but were unable to change to wolf form—was a problem throughout North America. Since halfies usually died within a few years of being bitten, it was of deep concern to all the Were.

"No, they have them," Felix said. "But they're growing their packs from singles and small groups making their way here. We think a lot of those are coming from Mexico."

"And they don't *smell* right," Cameron growled.

That was disturbing. "Do you think another Adept—one in Mexico—has figured out a ritual similar to mine?" There really wasn't any reason why they couldn't, I reasoned. It was just that it was more of a shaman-Adept thing, and there were few shaman-Adepts left. Most of them didn't get involved with Were. "Or is it just Were defecting from the packs that have gone criminal, not wanting to be involved in that activity?"

"They haven't said," Felix said. "They don't seem to *want* to say, which is part of the problem. But it also means that we have less to offer them, as potential members of the League, if they don't have as strong a need for the ritual."

"Now, we know you have resources in Denver," Felix said. "We need to get any information you might have uncovered on the situation."

Not until my mission was complete.

"I'm sorry, alphas, but I'm just arriving at my sister's house." I took a breath. "Yes, we have been investigating, and I have a lot to show you, but it'll be easier to do it face to face, down in Louisiana. Right now, I'm preparing my trip and I need to tell my sister I'll be away."

"She's pregnant, isn't she?" Cameron said. Her voice changed. "You need to make sure she's taken care of while you're gone. We understand. We can talk more when you get down here."

"Absolutely," I said. "As soon as I see you. I'll call soon. Bye." I ended the call and turned the cell off. I was walking a razor-thin line, and I hoped I was making the right decision, asking for forgiveness rather than permission.

A lot of forgiveness, if things went the way I intended.

"You've got some kind of bite on your throat," Kath said as soon as she'd opened the door.

Ah. Yes. The marks of Bian's fangs would heal in another couple of days, but they had to be pretty obvious at the moment.

I shrugged and followed her inside. Emergence was nearly here, but I still couldn't tell her anything about paranormals.

Kath and Taylor were living in David's old house, just a twenty-minute walk from Manassah and within easy reach for me.

Things *had* been getting better. The first few visits had been like walking across eggshells, and conversations had been slow and awkward. But just showing up, every other day, drinking coffee, meeting Mom here, and not talking about anything in particular seemed to have calmed everything down.

There was Tamanny as well. We'd rescued her from the Los Angeles end of the same appalling people-trafficking business that the Chihuahua, Sonora and Baja packs were still involved in.

When her mother had died, Jen had formally adopted Tamanny, but Jen couldn't be here, and it wouldn't have been appropriate for someone so young to live at Manassah, with my House—including all our complex emotional and sexual relationships—headquartered there. But a strange solution had offered itself. Tammany was living here, and Kath had effectively adopted her. Then, because Tamanny was here, some others from Manassah came visiting regularly. Dante was around every day. Kath liked Dante. Dante brought Tove. Even more surprising, Kath liked Tove, too.

It wasn't for me to say anything about it, but the most damaged people in my House were drawn here, finding comfort in helping my sister, without making it obvious what they were doing. And thinking of it that way, I saw it applied the other way around as well; Kath was helping them heal.

But now I was arriving after Tamanny was asleep, neither Dante nor Tove was here to support me, and I was about to break the pattern.

"You're going away again, aren't you?" Kath said as we sat down.

My sister had always had a sixth sense about me.

"Yes. I'm sorry. It's important," I said.

"Always is. And you can't tell me what it is."

"No. I can't yet. But I believe that'll change soon."

Whether the truth that would come with Emergence would help was another matter.

"It was such a long time. It's been, what? Seven weeks? That's some kind of record, isn't it?"

I wasn't sure what to say, but then she chuckled. "It was getting tense, like waiting for the other shoe to drop. I'm kinda glad it's happened now. We can relax."

Taylor came over with cocoa for all of us.

"Hi, Amber." He sat down on the edge of the sofa, next to Kath.

The man did relax with other people here—Dante told me so—but still not with me. However, despite not being comfortable with him, I thought he was partly responsible for Kath settling down as much as she had, and I was grateful. He'd stopped his career to look after her. He was committed to her, even if he couldn't actually say it outright or show it in a way I understood.

"Amber's going away," Kath said.

Taylor licked his lips. "Can you tell us where?"

He'd worked closely with David. Taylor knew some of the kinds of things we were involved in. It was Taylor that had analyzed enough of Weaver's business deals that we'd been able to guess where he would be hiding when he'd kidnapped Tullah.

Taylor had also worked closely enough with us to realize I wasn't lying when I said it was dangerous and bloody work. Or to hold out much hope that I'd answer his question.

"South," I replied, because even if I didn't think Taylor was spying, I wanted this information out there. "El Paso tomorrow. Then New Orleans."

"Alex is in El Paso, isn't he?" Kath wrinkled her brow. "What's in New Orleans?"

"Trouble. Things that need fixing. I can't—"

"Say any more. I know. And you can't say when you'll be back either."

I nodded.

We were quiet. Not exactly one of those completely comfortable silences, but nothing like as bad as I'd expected.

There was a noise from Tamanny's bedroom and Kath stood quickly.

"Nightmares, still?" I asked.

"Not so many now, but yes."

We hugged. For the first time in ages, I hugged my little sister and I didn't want to let go.

"Take care. We'll all miss you. See you when you get back," she said.

As I stood watching her walk to Tamanny's bedroom, I had a strange vision of us together as if the events of twelve years ago had never happened. Just two sisters and best friends. It was like a photograph we were posing for, looking toward the camera, arms casually around each other's waists, laughing. The image seemed to float, as if beneath water, but then I saw the surface wasn't water, but black stone, polished to a gloss.

What?

"Amber? Are you okay?"

Taylor touched my arm and I jerked.

"Sorry," I said, and shook my head. "Dreaming with my eyes open."

We sat back down.

"I was asking what you thought about everyone changing so much. I don't mean just Kathleen and Tamanny. Your friends, Dante and Tove. You."

I snorted. "And you. Yes, I guess we all have. Seven weeks, give or take, without everything we do being driven by other people's problems."

"Indeed." Taylor nodded, his gaze full of questions about me he still didn't quite have the courage to ask.

I wondered whether Taylor shared all those questions with Kath when they were alone, and what Kath said.

I drained my cocoa. "I have to go."

I arrived back at Manassah twenty-five minutes later.

There was a present waiting for me in the living room.

Wrapped in black silk, loosely tied with a scarlet ribbon. There was a strange weight of purpose about it. It was about twenty inches long in total. The silk fell away from an ornate scabbard, and a gentle tug opened it to reveal twelve of those twenty inches were a gleaming, hand-forged blade with a distinctive wave pattern in the metal.

A wakizashi. The short companion sword to a samurai's katana. I suspected I knew which one it was, and if I was right, it was priceless.

Bian's elegant note, in Athanate, was rolled around the handle, tied with a red ribbon.

> *You'll find our southern cousins are all die-hard Athanate conservatives. In those circles, it would be impolite to wear your pistols when you meet to introduce yourself. A blade is much more in keeping, and as you have found out in training, a short one can be devastating in confined spaces. Even better, they will have studied your files and they will assume you cannot wield this blade effectively.*
>
> *You have been a good student, my love. If they compound bad intentions with that assumption, I am sure it will be their last mistake.*
>
> *Put the burdens of Denver aside. Your House is my House, my House is your House, and I will perform your responsibilities, Athanate and human, House and family, Were and Adept, to the best of my abilities.*
>
> *You must concentrate on our plans in the south.*
>
> *This blade is called Nekotsume: Cat's Claw.*
>
> *We do not own these swords; they are only in our keeping.*
>
> *This one is in yours.*
>
> *With my heart.*
>
> *Bian*

El Paso
Chapter 5

Next morning, when Alex met me in the terminal at Doña Ana airfield, just outside El Paso, his eyes had already gone wolf gold in the early light of dawn.

We hugged. I'm not small, but I felt comfortably lost in his hot embrace. And yet, I could feel the tension in his body, as if he'd start growling with anger any second.

"What have we got?" I asked, my voice pitched low. The anger was catching.

"You were right," he said, words hard and clipped. "They're here. Looks like it's set for the road out of the airport, just before it hits the highway."

Juárez had set up an ambush for us. I'd anticipated this—hoped for it, even. It was why I'd had Yelena leak the flight plans.

"How many?" I asked.

"Can't tell. There are a couple of stolen eighteen-wheeler rigs there, with enough space on board for dozens of people. Much more than we thought."

"Won't just be people. They'll have to have trucks or cars."

"Then maybe six trucks in all. Say three or four people per truck. Twenty-four total?"

I frowned. That *was* more than I'd expected for an ambush. And if they were going to use those six trucks inside, that was a lot to hide or dispose of afterwards. I wondered what they'd planned for a getaway. They could hardly ride the stolen rigs across the border to Juárez.

Zane joined us.

In contrast to Alex's strength and size, Zane looked almost skinny. His black hair was tied back from his honey-dark face and his different-colored eyes looked thoughtful and assessing.

"You could just fly to another airport," he grunted.

I couldn't and he knew it. He was pushing me, alpha-to-alpha, and I had to respond in kind.

"Where's the fun in that?" I forced a smile.

Despite their control, both men were tense, on edge, adrenaline pumping. Right where they should be.

"This is what we wanted," I reminded them. "What we need, even, to strengthen our position with both the Were and the Athanate. An in-person leadership challenge is one thing, but to try to assassinate three alphas from ambush, in someone else's territory? That breaks all our laws and traditions, and it requires—hell, it begs for—a response. They're playing right into our hands, so we better get a move on before they get suspicious and call it off."

Doña Ana wasn't a big commercial airport. The terminal building wasn't designed to hold more than a couple of dozen people, and the parking outside was limited to twenty vehicles. It would be difficult to hide an observer there. But across the way was an air museum with lots more parking, and as we left the building, I could see at least one car with someone sitting inside, despite the hour.

What a surprise.

I sniffed. I didn't know the scent of the Juárez pack. I could taste El Paso and White Sands on the breeze. El Paso would become the Deauville pack when we finally got them moved to Denver, and White Sands was the pack that would replace them here.

There was Zane as well, of course. His marque was distinctively Albuquerque, close to the White Sands scent. There was Alex. And my team from Denver—Yelena, Julie, Keith, Mykayla and Scott. I could have picked out my marque across a crowded taco festival.

No other paranormal scents.

The Juárez lookout in the museum parking lot could be human, a PI hired for the one job. Or the pack might have been using any one of a dozen ways to prevent their marque from alerting us.

It didn't matter.

I turned my attention to our vehicles.

As per my instructions, Alex and Zane had picked us up with the appearance of minimal security, in a twelve-seat van with tinted windows and a battered-looking pickup truck as escort.

The vehicles been complete scrap when we acquired them. In a way, it was a shame that they weren't expected to last the day, because the pack down here had done a good job of fixing them to my specification. They rode low on their axles, but not so much it would tip anyone off that they were armored and much higher performance than they looked.

It was a chilly morning, below 50, and the casual jackets we were all wearing looked completely normal. Hidden beneath, we wore Kevlar vests and I was feeling like Baked Alaska—hot and cold in different parts.

We spent a minute loading luggage and greeting our escort—four El Paso and two White Sands. This group of werewolves had been specifically chosen to give the appearance of calm at this point, but I could smell the adrenaline starting to pump in everyone.

"Time to move," I said.

If our estimates were right, our numbers gave the ambushing Juárez pack about a two-to-one advantage, but they weren't expecting us to be prepared. They certainly hadn't realized that this wasn't their ambush, but ours.

We loaded up and left, the van at the front. Julie was in the back of the pickup, the rest of us in the van, unpacking weapons that had been delivered to El Paso earlier.

Hidden behind the darkened windows of the van, I slipped on my comm set and had everyone call back their status.

"There's a car exiting the museum parking area, ma'am," said the guy riding shotgun in the pickup. "Chevy Impala. Dark blue. Staying a couple hundred yards back. Two inside, I think."

Could be a coincidence.

Could be humans taken on to do the surveillance without knowing what was planned.

"All units, that blue Impala is *not* a target, unless it comes after us when everything kicks off. We are *not* killing bystanders or people who we aren't *sure* are part of the Juárez pack."

A chorus of acknowledgements came back.

We took the left turn out of the airport, toward El Paso. Long, low commercial properties lined the right-hand side.

"Where's the feed from the drone cam?" I asked.

One of the El Paso pack swiveled a laptop so I could see. High above the two stolen rigs, a small, quiet drone flew. Its picture was jittery as morning thermals pushed it to and fro, but I could still see men unlocking the rear doors.

Ramps came down.

In one trailer, I could see the nose of a truck edging forward. Tall grill with a blue oval. Ford. Black paintwork.

Complete stereotype: the police would take one look at it and write this off as drug cartel related.

Good.

I couldn't see what was in the second rig. I didn't like that, but I didn't want the drone to get closer and be spotted.

"Watch that second rig," I said and pushed the laptop back. "I want to know the moment anything comes out."

"All units," I said into the comms, "we have at least one truck visible in the rigs and it looks like they're going to time it to hit us just before the intersection with the highway. Wait for my signal. We play dumb until they commit."

The wind funneled between a couple of buildings and kicked up a dust devil that spun ominously across the road in front of us.

The choice of place for the ambush made sense in one way. The intersection was away from the commercial buildings and most of the potential witnesses. There was also a choice of roads, for them to escape afterwards.

On the other hand, the drug cartels' favorite black pickups kinda stood out. How on earth were they expecting to get away?

It was only a few seconds, but it seemed endless, stretching taut as a piano wire, before everything happened at once.

A shock to my Were senses as they were flooded with a hunting Call from the Juárez ambush.

"Trucks on the move!" the watcher called out. "Two. Three. Four."

There were flashing blue lights on the pursuing truck dashes, as if they were unmarked police vehicles.

Oh! Theoretically great distraction, but ruined by the Call.

"All units, they're going to come up behind us," I said. "Bring them on. Floor the gas."

"Motorcycles!" the watcher yelled. "Second rig. Dozens of them."

The Juárez pack had made a decision that turned out to be smart and dumb at the same time. Dirt bikes made for great escape options. They were lousy for attacking armored vehicles.

"Hundred yards behind, piling it on," shouted the lookout from our trailing pickup.

"All units, on my mark, make the wall. *Go!*"

Both our vehicles screeched to a stop in a chatter of anti-lock brakes and a shriek of tires, both parked across the road, partially blocking it.

Julie came up into a low crouch on the bed of the pickup, resting her rifle on the side. At the first shot from the attackers, she fired. Big, heavy bullets took out windshields and the Juárez pack's heads behind them. More of us joined in. Bullets slammed into radiators, ricocheted around engine compartments.

Two of the trucks collided in the middle of the road. A third, undamaged at that point, slammed into them from behind.

The fourth came on.

Alex had stepped out between the van and the pickup, an RPG already tight against his shoulder.

There was a bright flash as the propellant booster lit off, a second as the rocket fired and then a third as the last of the Juárez trucks exploded in a fireball. RPGs had gone out of favor with the army for use against tanks, but they did just *fine* against civilian trucks.

The motorcycles were something else.

A swarm of thirty had left the rig. Half had veered off when they saw the danger, some had actually been caught up in the destruction of the trucks, but nine came on. They had people riding bitch and trying to fire guns at us. Hopeless—no stable platform. They'd left the road, engines screaming like angry hornets, spurting trails of dirt into the air as they swerved and swooped on us from the sides of the road toward our front and back.

Where we weren't armored.

But even where we didn't have armor, we still had weapons they weren't expecting. Zane and Yelena leaped out of the van to empty MP5s on full auto. Keith and Mykayla racked and fired shotguns as I braced myself with a two-handed grip on my Mk23 to pick off riders.

One down.

Two.

Then, as quickly as it started, the survivors were racing away across the desert, crouched low over their handlebars, leaving us with smoke, dust and a stink of burning drifting across the road.

A couple of the Juárez pack had made it out of the trucks and were sprinting back toward their colleague in the distant Chevy.

"Want me to take them, Boss?" Julie said, rifle tracking the fleeing figures.

"No. Time to go."

The van was already moving while everyone was clambering in.

"Hide the gear," I said. "Anyone injured?"

"My pride," said one of the White Sands, holding up his automatic. "Damn thing jammed. Didn't get a shot off."

We laughed abruptly. The sort of post-action laughter I recognized from Ops 4-10. A sudden release after facing death. Relief.

As it had happened, it had taken less than two minutes from the first shot and we hadn't even picked up a bullet hole.

The Juárez pack had lost around fifteen members.

And I wasn't finished with them, or Gálvez, or Matlal. I wasn't nearly finished.

Chapter 6

Alex and Zane wanted us to go straight to meet our packs.

"I gotta call on the Athanate House first," I said. "They knew nothing about what was going down this morning. It would be bad to let them find out through other means."

"Snake courtesy in front of pack celebration?" Zane frowned.

My Blood was still hot. I bared my teeth at him.

"Courtesy, which means in this case not screwing up relations between pack and House."

I cooled off quickly again. It wasn't Zane's fault that the local House were from the ultra-conservative end of the Athanate spectrum.

"I'm sorry," I said. "I'll be there later, and we'll celebrate then. Just so long as you remember, there's much more to do."

Alex snorted. "Not worth arguing, Zee," he said, clapping Zane on the shoulder.

Zee? Besties, huh?

There were things I planned for, meticulously, and things I made up, more or less on the spot.

When I made it, Alex and Zane working together had been one of my better on-the-spot plans. I'd really needed Zane's help to get Tullah back. I thought the situation in El Paso could be handled better.

But in among the clever solutions, I implied some promises of a *personal* nature while the balance of my mind may have been disturbed.

I wasn't sure how to handle that.

Alex's and Zane's alpha dominance had increased with their rank in the super-pack that the Southern League had become, and any two alphas working closely together boosted each other. On top of that, they still had a werewolf aura of ferocity from the ambush clinging to them.

Dangerous bad boys.

Hot enough to melt metal at fifty yards.

Top woulda said shut up and play the cards you're dealt, when you're dealt them, Tara said.

Yup. Play this hand first.

And this hand was now all about Athanate.

Alex and Zane dropped us off at the gates to the exclusive Pointe Hills community, which bordered the western side of Franklin Park.

And they left us with the pickup, making us look like poor hick relatives come visiting.

I allowed myself one roll of the eyes, where no one could see me. Appearances mattered to old Athanate, but it couldn't be helped. Showing up was more important than what you looked like when you did it.

I'd emailed ahead, so I was expected. I called the number I'd been given on my cell.

"Hello," a voice responded. Female. Hispanic, quiet.

"Amber Farrell, House Farrell," I said.

"Isabel Cuarón, Diakon de Socorro," she replied. "Be welcome, House Farrell. The gates will open. Take the second road on the right, Rocky Pointe Drive, and then we are the sixth house, about a half-mile up. I will meet you."

We passed through the gates and took the right road. Yelena drove slowly between the mansions. She didn't show it, but she was frustrated not to be able to test the performance of the supercharged engine the pack had shoehorned into this old truck. Maybe later.

I turned in the seat and said to the others, "Best behavior, guys."

Scott nodded soberly and I didn't need to worry about Yelena, or Julie, or Keith.

Mykayla was smirking.

"I'm serious, Mykayla. We have to do this, but these border Athanate are old-fashioned. The three of us hybrids," I indicated Scott as well, "we're abominations to them. And as for having a Carpathian as my Diakon..."

"Is appropriate for Carpathian House." Now Yelena was smirking as well. "And her answer was welcoming when you first emailed her."

She had a point. Diakon Cuarón's email had sounded eager for my visit.

Probably just old-fashioned politeness.

"If *you* don't want to, and you think *they* don't want you to, why visit with them at all?" Mykayla said.

"Because they're old-fashioned and it's important to pay your respects when you enter any House's domain. More important than what they might think about us, or how little we want to do it."

"And..." Julie prompted.

"And it shows that we will honor Athanate rules," I responded, "even while on Were business. They talk to each other, these Houses."

"Which will be important when we visit New Orleans," Julie finished, bumping Mykayla with her shoulder.

We had hidden all our firearms in a locked box beneath the rear seat.

Julie passed me Nekotsume from my gear bag, and I experimented with slipping the scabbard underneath my belt buckle so it lay across my waist.

It made me feel ridiculous, so I handed it to Julie to pack away again.

Yelena turned into a shingle drive which ended in a perfect circle surrounding a lawn with a single, shapely boxwood topiary in the middle, and a border of herbs. The whole drive looked like one of those Zen gardens, not a stone out of place, raked every morning and evening. And after every visiting car had left.

Cherry trees wept pink blossoms along the drive. Behind them were ranks of neatly trimmed pine with the occasional floating willow and spring-blossoming aspen.

Impossibly pretty.

I grimaced.

I was reasonably sure that the pickup didn't leak oil or worse, but our truck looked massively out of place here. The quicker we were in and out, the better.

Not to mention, there were things to be done on the other side of town.

We crunched to a halt, and I opened the truck door.

The air was heavy with the scent of lavender and sage, thyme and rosemary, mixed with flowers I couldn't see or name.

Contrasting, but looking very much part of the whole image, the mansion in front of us was a blend of styles that spoke of sunlit Mediterranean influence and hard Athanate practicalities. It was an inverted U shape, with wings that stretched towards us, forming a three-sided courtyard in front of the main doors. The windows of the main section facing us were all tall and arched with weathered stones. They looked like they'd been stolen from old European monasteries. Wavy terracotta tiles of contrasting shades covered the roofs. The building's wings had pencil-thin spruces planted at intervals along their walls, to contrast with the pale cream color and break up blank spaces. Yew and boxwood topiary, trained into perfect spheres, seemed to float above their deep shadows all across the courtyard.

Beautiful. Shockingly bright-edged in the sunlight.

But beneath...

Like the impenetrable shadows under each sunlit tree, there was a feeling of darkness below this mansion. A waiting, a tension. Like coming into a room and seeing an empty coffin. The floral and herbal scents that came to me seemed woven around with despair.

Don't like this, Tara said. *Don't want to go inside that house.*

The others sensed it, too.

Julie handed me Nekotsume again, and this time it didn't feel wrong to slide the scabbard underneath my belt.

The path from the main door descended in wide, lazy steps of apricot-colored flagstones, and down that path walked a woman I recognized from her file. Deceptively delicate. Dark eyes that seemed too big for her face. A mane of black hair cascading down her back. She wore a tailored blue blazer over a light and elegant summer dress.

The Diakon herself had come out to greet us.

If she thought I looked odd in rough modern clothes with an antique sword at my waist, she didn't let it show.

"Welcome, House Farrell."

The voice on the phone.

We embraced in the Athanate fashion, the lamia, bending forward to kiss each other on the neck, the traditional Athanate greeting designed to allow us to assess marques and gauge the other's emotional state and intentions.

For all her poise, Diakon Cuarón was stretched taut as a violin string, and her eukori was locked down.

As we parted, her nose wrinkled, but that could have been the stench of nitro coming off me from firing weapons. Or it could have been the unmistakable wolf part of my marque.

A good reminder that this entire Athanate House might see me as a monster.

I turned. "These are the members of my House that are accompanying me on this visit to your city. My Diakon, Yelena Vylkove, her kin, Julie and Keith Alverson, and my ehvasi, Edward Scott and Mykayla Smythe."

"Ehvasi," Cuarón breathed.

I had deliberately chosen the Athanate word to indicate that they were Athanate infused by me.

Her eyes held theirs for a long moment.

"The rumors are true, then," she said, her mouth becoming firmer. "Welcome. Please, come in, take refreshments with me."

She led us back up the path toward the grand arch of the front door. She'd left it open, but my sun-dazzled eyes couldn't see into the hall.

My back twitched with that someone-looking-at-me feeling, and glancing up at the wings of the mansion, I saw shadows move behind the windows.

"Will House de Socorro join us?" I asked.

My fingers moved rapidly in the secret hand signals I had created for my House after seeing the Albuquerque pack use them.

Windows. Watchers. Danger?

Yelena dropped a pace back. Mykayla and Scott moved up and flanked me. Julie and Keith spread wider.

"Alvar... House de Socorro is... indisposed," Cuarón said.

"Diakon." I stopped abruptly, making her turn.

Cuarón was at least two centuries old, and I suspected from Bian's files that de Socorro was about a century older. For Panethus Athanate of that age, there was little reason to be 'indisposed', except for the death of a kin.

"We were here to pay our respects and make a report of trouble among the packs," I said. "We won't intrude on your House's distress."

Something was wrong at this beautiful mansion, and I didn't want to be drawn into whatever Gothic horror was unfolding inside.

Cuarón's eyes widened as she took in the way we were spread out, the way Julie and Keith were ceaselessly scanning the windows of the building.

"I apologize, my honored guests." She clasped her hands and bowed her head. "Things are not as they may seem. No harm will come to any guest in our house, to any of you. I so swear, on my Blood."

She lifted her head, swallowed once and then tilted it back, offering her throat.

Her skin had taken on a sudden sheen of perspiration.

And as tightly as her eukori was clamped down, I could sense the battle of emotions inside her. I tasted sorrow. Fear. Even anger. And a cold determination that was frightening in its intensity.

I'd come directly from fighting the Juárez pack. I still had the lingering traces of adrenaline and elethesine in my system from that, and they had ramped back up at the suspicion of threat here.

Combined with her emotions and the offer of her throat, that potent mix made a response rise in me. An ache in my jaw, a hunger that was probably visible in my eyes.

I took a deep breath, forcing the hunger to subside.

I am not an animal. I have control.

Instead of biting Cuarón, I reached out and took her hand.

"Let's go inside and tell each other what the hell's going on."

Chapter 7

She led us to a marble-tiled sunroom more luxurious even than Manassah's. In contrast to the gloomy hallway, it was flooded with light. The air was sweet with scented flowers, and a small fountain played in the middle of the room.

Cuarón summoned a maid, who arrived in a hurry.

"Gina. Ice water, coffee and tea, please."

Gina was visibly upset and wary of us. She rushed off.

Kin.

Not abused and certainly not frightened of the Diakon. This *was* a Panethus House, and they were sworn to Altau. Even without Cuarón's Blood oath, we should have been safe here, but there was clearly something going on.

Cuarón refused to discuss it immediately. Her earlier emotional turmoil was under control, and the only remaining thing I could sense was that determination. It lay there, under her poised manner and small talk about our journey—the flight time, the comfort, the convenience of having an aircraft.

With the drinks on the table, she turned to me.

"House Farrell, you mentioned trouble among the packs and I sense from you there was violence this morning."

I put my coffee down.

At last.

"There was. We flew into the airfield at Doña Ana, and we were ambushed as we drove toward El Paso. There was a gun battle near the junction with the highway that goes down to the Santa Teresa border crossing."

I could see the questions race across her mind. An overt battle between paranormals in her domain. Investigations. Risk. Agiagraphos rules.

Of course, the supreme Agiagraphos guidance, to keep the Athanate hidden from humanity, was going to be broken by Emergence soon. It was up to Skylur or the rumor mill to tell her that.

I held up a hand.

"This was strictly pack business. The Juárez pack attacked us. There were no injuries on our side, and no close witnesses."

"What about injuries on their side?"

"Several dead. They planned their attack around four trucks, with dirt bikes to chase down any of us that tried escaping off the road. Those trucks of theirs made it look like it was drug cartel rivalry."

I fed her the details carefully, emphasizing again that it was their attack on us. That the Juárez pack had seen an opportunity to take out three alphas and expand their territory across the border. That I suspected this aggression was encouraged and supported by the Basilikos Athanate faction from their headquarters down in the Yucatán.

I was very careful not to even think about the fact that we'd deliberately leaked our travel plans with this outcome in mind.

Or that this morning wasn't the end of it.

Whatever else was going on, she was a thorough and conscientious Diakon. Only when she was finally satisfied she knew everything she needed to know and had assessed all the potential ramifications for House de Socorro did she turn to what had happened in Athanate El Paso.

"It started in many places," she began, losing some of that poise I had been admiring. "It started with the best of intentions. Where it has ended..."

She got up, unable to sit, and paced the floor.

"Last year, we received strongly worded advice from House Altau to make contact with the local packs, to create an alliance of sorts with other paranormals."

She turned her face to me, but the angled morning sun hid the expression of those huge dark eyes in deep shadows.

"There was only one within our domain, the El Paso pack, and we met with their alphas, Caleb and Victoria Oaken. These meetings went well, all things considered."

Yelena's lip twisted. "Means not well."

That almost raised a smile from Cuarón.

"Please understand how difficult this was. I will give you this information as a token of trust: guesses underestimate House de Socorro's age. He is not three hundred, but six. Close to seven."

Even Yelena blinked at that. Supposedly immortal, many Athanate died from conflict, and those that were older seldom left the domains they had matured in. Six-hundred-year-old Athanate in America were *rare*.

"It was those times," Cuarón continued, "the troubled times of his birth, that formed him. The closing stages of a war for Iberia that had lasted even longer than Alvar de Socorro has lived since then. Under the tumult of that war, alliances between paranormals came and went, and could turn on a look, a word. It was a long and bloody history, but it's enough to say, he emerged as House de Socorro with a deep distrust of werewolves."

"Did the El Paso pack ever give cause to confirm that distrust?" I asked, trying not to be shocked by the age of her House. Or that she'd actually told us outright. Older Athanate *never* discussed their age.

She shook her head.

"So, when news came that Alex and I had killed the Oakens and gained their pack," I said, "what was worse, that they'd died or that I didn't?"

She dropped her head. "A searching question, House Farrell. The answer, I am afraid, is that it was your survival that disturbed him more."

I stood up, feeling more tired than angry. "Thank you for your hospitality, Diakon Cuarón. I will not distress this House further with my presence. Luckily, my pack business will be concluded rapidly. I expect I'll leave El Paso tomorrow."

"No. Please, you don't understand at all."

Her control faltered and I sensed her eukori again—dark with fear.

I didn't walk out, but I remained standing. I was sick of justifying my existence to old-fashioned Athanate. If her House couldn't even bear to come down and meet me, I had much more important business on the other side of town. The only reason I stayed was I guessed this mess wasn't Isabel Cuarón's fault.

But I was so wrong.

When she moved, it was with the speed of a striking snake. She came straight for me.

Yelena was the quickest to respond. She was poised to kill Cuarón when the woman dropped to her knees and grabbed my hand.

"Please listen." Her voice broke. "I cannot ask forgiveness. I do not expect forgiveness. All I have done, I have done for this House. All I have left, all I can ask, please, I beg of you, with all my heart, is to help this House."

"What the hell?"

"Alvar does not take change well. For him to finally accept the El Paso pack, only to have the alphas swept away and replaced by... by a hybrid..."

"By an abomination," I said. "That's what you were going to say, wasn't it? That's what he thinks of me."

I tried to get my hand back, but her grip was fierce.

I could feel her tears wet against my skin.

"Yes. But it didn't stop there. The whole pack was moving. A new pack started to move in. Outsiders. While you remained in Denver to test your infusion."

"And create more abominations."

"Yes. Please listen, House Farrell. It was not only you. There were also the instructions from House Altau. But not from Altau himself. From a Basilikos Diakon raised up by House Altau over us. Understand, Alvar can change. This unsettling of his mind will pass. He will accept the new ways, but he cannot change quickly. I know it. In time. If you only..."

"If I what?"

"His favorite," she started to say. "The best of our Aspirants. Carrizal Ribera. One of his oldest kin."

"You're not making sense, Diakon Cuarón," I said.

But Yelena understood, from all the hints that had been dropping. "House de Socorro infused Ribera, yes? He infused him while he was suffering *etropia* from the changes around him."

She used the Athanate word for a lingering anger-madness that the sufferer could not see in himself, but which colored all his thoughts and actions. And could communicate itself to an Aspirant during infusion. The worst possible starting point for the already dangerous crusis.

Understanding crashed in on me. "So there's a risk Ribera isn't going to survive crusis. And you want me to save him?"

"It is no longer a matter of risk," Cuarón whispered. "Carrizal is restrained now."

"He's gone rogue?"

"Is too late, then," Yelena said bluntly.

"No." Cuarón refused to accept that.

"What makes you think—" I began.

"I heed the stories I hear, House Farrell. When I first saw this PackChat, this private social media that the Were use, I thought it a toy, a diversion. Then I thought it a subtle political tool for the Southern League's growing ambitions. It is that and more. Now I use it to understand what is happening that Altau and the Southern League do not broadcast in their information."

She took a deep breath.

"They never speak openly on PackChat, but I stitch together the truth from hints. You went rogue, House Farrell. They say you went rogue, and you came back and now you've proved your infusion works. Your ehvasi are stable."

"Yes, I went rogue, but it took others to bring me back. My infusion doesn't heal."

"They say David Thaler proves it does."

PackChat had a *lot* to answer for.

David *had* become dangerously unstable during crusis, and after I'd allowed him to feed on me, the crisis had passed and he'd finished crusis faster than anyone had believed possible. He'd been completely stable ever since.

But that didn't mean I could cure someone infused by an old, powerful, half-insane House.

I shook my head angrily. "That's really stretching it. It didn't happen the way you think. And anyway, it's not as if House de Socorro is going to let me have access to Ribera."

Cuarón didn't answer, but my words created an explosion of emotions beneath the sorrowing surface of her mind: hope overwhelmed by fear. Fear and guilt.

"Oh, God! Where is de Socorro? What have you done, Diakon Cuarón?"

Chapter 8

This is madness.

Carrizal Ribera hadn't gotten to the foaming at the mouth stage, but I could feel the uncontrollable tumult in his half-developed eukori.

In better times, he was probably a good-looking man. Not right now. His skin was sallow, his eyes feverishly bright.

He was securely tied down on a bed. He'd stopped struggling for the moment, but Yelena had his head in a grip like a vise, so he couldn't move his fangs and tear my flesh. I was letting him bite my wrist because there was *no way* I was taking his fangs in my throat, restraints or not.

Plan A was to try to re-create what had really happened with David. Contrary to PackChat rumor, what made the difference to David had been my Blood, not my infusion, so I was going to let Ribera take as much as possible without me actually passing out, *if* it showed signs of working. He was pulling hungrily, but the pleasure I usually got from being bitten wasn't there. Ribera wasn't enjoying what he did, he was just driven to do it.

It made me feel soiled.

Worse, although he was quieter, it was quickly becoming apparent that my Blood on its own *wasn't* working.

Time for Plan B; I linked with Yelena and sank my senses into Ribera's eukori.

I was no skilled guide, no *xenagia*, like Diana, but I was all Ribera and House de Socorro had.

If we could find some key part to the structure of his madness, and break that, it might dilute the effect that de Socorro's etropia had had on him. It *might* reverse the slide into rogue.

The first touch under that tumult of eukori was worse than all the unpleasant sensations from him feeding on my Blood. There was a shrieking emptiness to it, a foulness, a hopelessness. The worst thing was that there was enough of Ribera left for him to understand the horror that he was becoming, and there was no disguising that he was on that slope. Yelena and I could feel the horrific siren call of Blood-craze.

The deeper we got, the worse it became. Yelena and I had unusually strong eukori from being Carpathian, but that wasn't going to be enough.

I wasn't going to use Scott and Mykayla. They were here to prove to me what stable little hybrids they were in normal situations. Even given the expanded interpretation of normal for my House, this was way beyond that.

I didn't want to try and link to Ash. Diana had advised me against revealing that capability. Enough people thought I was an abomination just for being Athanate-Were. Hell, enough thought I was dangerous just for being Carpathian. I wasn't going to top it off with being a dark witch as well.

How to fix this ourselves?

It started with the best of intentions, Cuarón had said.

De Socorro was already unstable when he'd started the process of infusing Ribera, otherwise he wouldn't have tried. Ribera's crusis had pushed de Socorro closer to the edge. Close enough so he decided that to save Ribera, it would be best to link with him through eukori. If he'd paused to think it through, he must have reasoned that a six-hundred-year-old Athanate would easily be able to guide an Aspirant through crusis.

But the problem was inside de Socorro, and connecting with Ribera had made it worse. It gave de Socorro a channel for the confusion of his etropia, an easy path to sweep all the conflicting emotions aside. Now there were two of them, their increasing madness mirrored, each mentally feeding off the other.

At the point de Socorro had decided to infuse Ribera, it had been Diakon Cuarón's duty to inform Skylur that de Socorro's balance of mind was disturbed.

Skylur hadn't been available, and there was no doubt in Cuarón's mind what would have happened if she'd reported the matter to Diakon Flavia—a *Basilikos* placed in authority over her. I was in no doubt either. Livia would have come here and immediately executed de Socorro to save the rest of the House.

As Cuarón hesitated, the situation slid from bad to worse: de Socorro had tried to use his eukori to guide Ribera through crusis.

If she'd reported it *then*, Livia would have executed both de Socorro and Ribera, but still the rest of the House would have been saved.

But again, Cuarón had hesitated, out of misguided love and loyalty, and de Socorro began to slide into true madness.

Eventually, with the fate of the whole House hanging in the balance, in her despair, she'd latched onto the one possibility that presented itself—that I'd emailed and said I was out of quarantine and I would be visiting her city.

In any rational analysis, she had to know that she was almost as crazy as them, but she'd separated and confined de Socorro and Ribera. She'd imprisoned her own House. With violence.

The shock of it still reverberated through the House.

Athanate laws of the Agiagraphos were clear. Any Athanate who managed to overcome their Blood oaths were criminals, but there was a special place of revulsion reserved for Diakons who betrayed their master, and Houses who turned against their master.

The moment she'd put her blind faith in me and imprisoned de Socorro, Cuarón was damned by the Agiagraphos, and double damned by the interpretations others would put on it.

And I was trapped in this craziness. Trapped by her appeal—*I beg of you, with all my heart.* Trapped by the thought *I* was going to be blamed for this if de Socorro fell, whether I helped or not. Trapped by the damage this was going to do to Altau, if I didn't fix it.

If I succeeded beyond all expectations, de Socorro and Ribera and the rest of the House might be saved.

If I failed...

Hell beckoned. Ribera would fall into madness, dragging de Socorro along, and through him, the rest of the House as well.

Stop concentrating on failure.

Forward. One step at a time.

We needed to fix Ribera first, as the easiest step. Then de Socorro. Then the rest of this screwed-up situation.

To help fix Ribera, Yelena and I needed someone strong. What we had was Cuarón. She was slightly stronger than an average Athanate of her two centuries, but not by much.

I'd warned her earlier I might need her help and now, I touched her eukori. I could sense the shiver that passed through her, but she didn't close down. She allowed me in, and I pulled on some of her strength to support me.

It helped, a little.

It hindered, too. Because with Diakon Cuarón came an echo of everyone else in the House. Everyone. And in the strange auditorium of eukori, I could hear ripples of the Blood-craze and a flood of guilt coming from all around us.

We turned against our master.

It shocked me to my core, all over again.

The whole House, each individual Blood-sworn to Alvar de Socorro, had turned against him, forced by their Diakon. That it was all motivated by their love for him didn't lessen the impact. That he was sliding inexorably into a rogue state, dragged by his link to his favorite, didn't excuse their action in Athanate culture. Not even that his link to them would drag them with him.

The Agiagraphos was absolute. Inflexible.

They were depending on me, the *abomination*, to fix it and then hide the evidence.

It wasn't even as if I were an expert. Their faith in me was from an entirely false image they'd gotten from rumors.

I'd just had seven weeks of intense experimentation with eukori. I knew my strength and Yelena's and now I had a feel for Cuarón's. But there was no clear map of what to do. Eukori shared sensations and emotions. We'd sense things from Ribera and the three of us would unconsciously form some way of representing that in our minds. Then we'd have to visualize a way to change what we sensed, force that to happen and hope that effect was transferred accurately into Ribera's mind.

Almost immediately, rising from the depths of the ocean of shared eukori, I glimpsed the monster we fought, and realized our step-by-step plans weren't going to work.

Physically separating Ribera and de Socorro hadn't broken their eukori link.

And it wasn't Ribera's crusis infecting de Socorro with madness anymore. This was now all driven by de Socorro.

The image we saw was as if they were dancing, spinning around and around each other to music only they could hear. To both of them, there was only the other.

It was sick, and yet they gave off a sense of contentment which rose up like a mist around us all.

What better than to dance?

All is bright. All is as it is meant to be.

Come with us. All will be well.

See? We are whole and perfect.

Join us.

Dance.

Sensations like Blood rapture soaked into us. The bliss, the afterglow of pleasure, the pure and swirling satisfaction.

It would have been so easy to let go, and float down in the gentle spiral.

All of us. De Socorro, his whole House, Yelena and me.

I could feel the others in the house drifting down around us like leaves.

Yelena and I had to fight back with everything we had.

Unable to break my mental focus to talk, not even for a single minute, my fingers fluttered in our secret sign language for Scott and Mykayla.

Get guns. If we fail. Kill all rogues. All. Even me.

Cuarón steadied herself and joined us in trying to prevent other members of her House from falling into the dance.

We needed to communicate that it wasn't like that. It wasn't glamorous and peaceful and dancing. It was a mindless hunger for Blood. It was a desire so strong you could never quench it, never escape the hold.

Not giving and receiving, but just *taking*.

Never escape...

And with that thought, I managed to change the image we were sharing. Not two dancers, but two suns, circling each other, tearing the life force from each other, consuming each other, unable to escape from the force that dragged them closer and closer to mutual annihilation.

That's more like it.

Cuarón's eukori pushed forward. She was familiar to the rest of the House. She gathered them. Drew them back. They'd follow her to safety.

Leaving Yelena and me with de Socorro and Ribera.

De Socorro was aware of me now, and who I was. I could sense his revulsion, and that was fine. Hate me. Whatever it took to shock him out of the daze that was allowing Ribera's crusis to overcome him.

No, that would have been too easy.

The imagery of dancers and suns dissolved, and I saw de Socorro as his House saw him. A face staring out of history. I shuddered. He looked to me like one of those fanatic priests of the Inquisition: a thin man, strong features dominated by intense eyes beneath thick brows.

He was imprisoned only a couple of rooms away, and I could hear when he started screaming in Athanate.

"Abomination!"

His grip on Ribera loosened.

"Because of you, whore, I have no House," he shouted. "Altau whore! Wolf whore! Sub-human animal."

Yelena was coaxing Ribera away from the precipice.

"You have polluted his Blood!" He noticed Ribera drifting away from him. "You cannot have him!"

His eukori fastened on Ribera again.

"Can fix this," Yelena said, her voice blurred with the effort. I felt her prepare to withdraw. She could be in de Socorro's room in seconds and Ribera would be free of him forever.

"No! Please!" Cuarón said. She'd managed to force all the others out of the merged eukori, and she was back to help us.

"Then you two break his link to Ribera," I said. "Or this won't work."

I concentrated on de Socorro.

His power of eukori was strong. Not strong like Carpathian, but the strength of ages. Six hundred years. It had a depth. An immovability.

Even with three of us, nothing was working.

I needed to try something different. I could feel Tara stirring, beginning to rise. My eyes going wolf. The visual projection the others saw of me in eukori started to blur.

"Abomination," de Socorro called out, but his voice was weaker. "You have made an abomination of him too. Come, Carrizal, it's better like this."

In our spirit-world of eukori, Tara shouldered me aside. I felt myself change, my skin catch fire, and a howl exploded from me.

Tara didn't push or pull de Socorro—she attacked him straight on, jaw gaping, fangs hunting on his vulnerable neck.

All of them were shocked, even Yelena, but she recovered quickest.

Pulled the spirit-Ribera away from de Socorro.

Cuarón made herself a barrier between de Socorro and Ribera.

Which left me alone with him.

No longer distracted by Tara, he recovered himself and reached out, but found he was alone now. Without a boost from Ribera's eukori, he couldn't get past me, Cuarón and Yelena.

To his unbalanced mind, all that mattered was that he'd lost Ribera, and his own Diakon had helped. No doubt about who to blame. Me.

Instead of struggling against me, he fastened his eukori to mine.

"I will have my revenge on you," he shouted. "You are the corruption in the body of the Athanate. You have taken them from me. I will take you from them."

And his mind slithered down, dragging mine with it.

Strong as I was, I couldn't hold him. The madness itself gave him strength, more than he'd lost from Ribera.

No time for anything else. In desperation I reached out.

Ash?

But everywhere around me was a darkness, and I couldn't feel the Irish soultree.

De Socorro's laugh echoed around me as I slipped inch by inch into that final emptiness of insanity.

In that void, the darkness compressed, sucking in the light and giving nothing back. It became a circle of night, the surface deep and insubstantial as space. Shapes moved in it. A voice called to me as all outside sound and movement ceased.

Use this strength.

Use this power of chaos and madness.

Look into the void and see.

You are the stronger.

That circle of night became like a black mirror, reflecting my startled face, and then the surface broke and shadows in the shape of jaguars and snakes reached out. I could feel them all around me. I heard voices raised. A thousand, a million voices, united in prayer or worship. A sound like thunder, a sound that shook the earth itself.

And I *could* move back.

Even with de Socorro's eukori hanging on to me.

Whatever lost god I'd found—or been led to—in Temple 132, he was lending me power.

Back. Back!

Away from that monstrous void de Socorro pulled me toward.

Up. Faster and faster.

Blinking in the light. Swaying, with Yelena's hand steadying me. Cuarón looking on, open-mouthed. Ribera reaching out to grip my hand. A long moment of silence from de Socorro down the corridor, and then the sound of his weeping.

"I was not mistaken," Cuarón breathed. "You've saved us. You are no abomination."

Ribera spoke, surprising all of us.

"Either we are all abominations," he said, his words faint, but his eyes clear. His head fell back, exhausted. "Or none of us are."

Chapter 9

The sunroom was no different from earlier, but the whole building felt changed.

As if there were more oxygen in the air.

Ribera was now in one corner of the house, and de Socorro in another. As far apart as they could be. Neither had tried to re-establish a eukori link to the other, which I took as a tentative good sign. The recovered de Socorro was still cursing and calling me an abomination. *Meh.*

He was no longer sliding into madness and dragging the House with him.

That was what counted.

I took a couple more swallows of ice water and started to get up slowly.

"You are pale, House Farrell," Cuarón said. "Carrizal took a lot of your Blood. Must you leave? We have been poor hosts. I would be greatly honored by the opportunity to thank you with our belated hospitality and to give you time to recover."

She gathered herself, like a horse before a steep jump, and switched to Athanate.

"I extend to you the freedom of the House," she said.

I blinked. Pia told me that the phrase was sometimes meant these days as a polite greeting. A token offer. But for an old House like de Socorro, it meant more: that I could choose any of their kin to satisfy myself. Or, within boundaries, any Athanate member too.

It wasn't something she would offer lightly, and that made it something I couldn't politely refuse.

The elephant in the room was that the master of the House wouldn't make that offer to me, and Cuarón knew it. She was going against his wishes, again.

The other thing that made it unattractive was that, however politely or freely offered, I imagined the Blood of this House was going to forever taste tainted to me.

"Thank you for this offer," I replied in Athanate. "My business with the packs is urgent, and it cannot be delayed as much as I might wish. Too much hangs in the balance."

Speaking Athanate makes you a diplomat, Tara whispered in my mind.

Shut up, sis, I replied.

Cuarón hid it well, but I knew she was disappointed. She wanted the chance to redeem the House in my eyes.

What could I do?

I needed to get going, but I also needed to *not* burn my bridges behind me. *And* I needed agreement from her that whatever werewolf business I got up to was not going to be considered anything to do with House de Socorro.

More than that, over the course of this morning, I'd come to consider her something special. A Diakon in a cast-iron conservative House had thrown aside her preconceptions and the whole damned Agiagraphos rule book to try to save her House, all for her love of de Socorro.

I liked her, even if I hated her master.

Aloud, I went on, again in Athanate, "I would like to take a token in hope of future friendship. Let there be the gift of Blood between us."

Her eyes went wide. "Blood for Blood," she murmured the traditional response, and added: "With all my heart."

She led me to a flat-topped seat that allowed us to sit side by side, facing opposite directions, and slipped her jacket off.

I hadn't thought through how awkward it would feel. Taking and giving Blood is as intimate as sex. I'd only met Diakon Cuarón this morning. We hadn't worked up to this. Absolutely the opposite. I hadn't even had the opportunity to get to the 'call me Amber' stage.

She sensed my hesitation, and spoke in Athanate, turning around the traditional love declaration that kin made.

"You have been a light in the darkness," she said. "I give my Blood with love."

It startled me how quickly my jaws responded with a sudden ache and rapid manifestation of my fangs.

She kissed me. A polite kiss, no tongues, but her lips brushed my fangs and made them sing with pleasure.

Then she slipped her arms around me and guided me to her throat.

Her pulse beat against my lips, her marque filled my nose and I stopped worrying about manners and names and the attitude of de Socorro. My fangs slipped through her skin, seeking her Blood.

I *pulled* and she groaned with our shared pleasure. Despite my fears, it erased the sour sensation in my mind from Ribera earlier.

I wanted more, but in the space between heartbeats, I felt Tara holding me back. This was a formal, symbolic exchange of Blood. An Athanate level more than polite, less than intimate. I was not feeding. However much I wanted or needed it.

With a sigh of reluctance, I let my fangs slip out and I licked her neck, sealing the wounded flesh. Every touch still tingled with pleasure.

I sensed a complex folding of emotions from her. Not exactly amusement at my awkward contest between desire and restraint. Not exactly a promise that this could be more, later. Maybe more a feeling that she would keep to forms now and nothing was really out of the question, sometime. Maybe.

All things considered.

I stretched my neck. Felt her breath on my throat. The touch of her lips, her tongue. The way my neck muscles loosened in response. The first, almost hesitant breaking of my skin and then the rush of pleasure as her fangs sank in and found my artery. Followed by the exquisite *pull* as she took my Blood.

So brief. Her tongue again, sealing my wounds.

We held each other, breathing heavily, partly for support and also partly to prolong the after-glow of delight in sharing Blood.

Yelena cleared her throat. "Alex is calling."

"Duty," I said. "There are likely to be repercussions from the events this morning. I need to make sure that the El Paso werewolves stay ahead of that and minimize any disruption."

Cuarón nodded.

I went on, "I need House de Socorro's understanding that my actions will not be regarded as infringing on your Athanate mantle or domain. It's purely a werewolf matter."

She nodded again, and I was sure she understood there was more than my words said.

"My master being indisposed, it is within my authority to grant that agreement. I wish you well in your endeavors and hope somehow, at some later stage, we will be able to meet at leisure." She held my gaze, also seeming to be saying more than her words. "But you must go now. I understand duty."

"I believe you do, Diakon Cuarón."

She smiled. "Isabel, please. We're overdue to change to less formal address."

I laughed. "Amber."

She escorted us to the door, and we passed out into the courtyard.

She seemed genuinely sad that we were not able to stay and she ended the Athanate farewells quietly. "You have written on my heart, Amber Farrell, House Farrell. Others will know this."

Yelena gave me my cell back, then put me in the rear seats between Keith and Julie. She drove us away.

I locked eyes with Scott and he nodded, his face determined.

"Airport first," I said, while texting Alex that we were okay, but we'd be a while yet.

Julie and Keith offered their wrists for me to top up after I'd been bitten so greedily by Ribera.

It wasn't as awkward as it would once have been. Being squeezed between my ex-boyfriend and his wife, both of whom were kin to my Diakon, and enjoying their Blood didn't seem so bad any more. The last few weeks had made me a lot more Athanate, and I'd taken Blood from both of them before.

They had changed too. It was a lot harder to make Julie blush, and I hadn't managed it before we were pulling into the drop-off zone at El Paso International.

We all got out and everyone else hugged Scott.

Diana and I had planned this attack against the Mexico Were with flexibility and options at several points. I'd made it plain to Scott that I had to have him with me in at least one major action before agreeing to let him go to the fight he chose. He'd done well enough in the ambush.

"You still have choices," I said to him. "You can stay with me. You can take the flight back to Denver. Or you can go to Los Angeles, like you volunteered."

We'd joked about how eager he was to visit LA, ever since he'd met Billie and the Belles at the challenge in Denver. I saw him start to say something along those lines, but then he pursed his lips and his eyes went distant. There wouldn't be time for that before bullets started flying.

"Not really, Boss. I know it's going to be dangerous in California, but it's not something you wouldn't do. Or aren't going to do, in fact. And more dangerous than staying with you?" He smiled briefly and shook his head. "I look at the life I've lived: a hundred and fifty years longer than everyone I grew up with. Good years, too. I haven't been a complete dilettante; I've supported my House and I've been responsible to them, but I've never given anything back to the wider Athanate community. That's not right. We can't be uninvolved while Emergence breaks. We can't leave it up to someone else. I believe it's time to start being a full member of the Panethus community. If that means dying for the cause in California, then I'm ready. Although I have every intention of living for the cause."

There was nothing I could say to that, so I hugged my ehvasi, my Athanate offspring, and let him go find that flight to LA and the danger that waited for him.

It was time for me to prepare my part of the offensive, here in El Paso.

Chapter 10

The El Paso pack owned a dusty old brewery building, up against the railroad and close to the interstate junctions in the industrial end of downtown.

The contrast with the upscale Pointe Hills community where de Socorro lived couldn't have been greater. But even if I'd kept them waiting much longer than planned, the welcome was warmer.

Mainly.

There was a selection from both the packs, around forty werewolves in all, including the half-dozen that had been with us at the ambush.

The brewery had been closed a while before the pack bought the premises, but there was a lot of beer around today.

Drinking that beer helped, and this morning's good news helped even more. I was happy to see the two packs together here, mingling as if it were the most natural thing in the world: the old El Paso, and the White Sands, who were soon to be the new El Paso pack.

The first part of the reason I'd come down to Texas was to see for my own eyes if Alex, Zane and I had really managed to get it through some thick werewolf skulls that we were just parts of one super-pack.

It looked as if it had worked. It wasn't one pack on the left and the other on the right.

Alex and Zane deserved most of the credit. They had put together deals where businesses and houses were passed from the outgoing pack to the incoming at a mutually agreed value, which would enable White Sands to move in easier, and help the old El Paso to make a new start in Denver. The two packs had gotten used to working together on that level.

The other way they worked together was the old pack teaching the new pack all the tricks and traps of running the werewolf side of El Paso. That was more complicated and it was taking *way* longer than we'd thought, mostly because of interference and incursions from the Juárez pack.

A second part of the reason to be down here was to fix that, and in fixing it, achieve something for all of Emergence.

The third part of the reason to be down here...

Even if they'd never met me, the El Paso pack knew I was their alpha. There had been some pushback on Alex, and one actual challenge, but he'd quickly established his authority. I was more of a gray area. There was a difference between a pack *knowing* I was an alpha in their minds and *feeling* it in their bones.

I got a welcome, but there was no mistaking it had an edge to it. A testing, a sense of a push, to see what I'd do.

Well, they were about to find out.

I made my way through to Alex, who hugged me, to a chorus of wolf whistles. I gave Zane a quick hug too, and they both gave me a rundown on what they'd been able to monitor through police radio chatter and pack contacts in the force.

"Over to you to tell them the details," Alex said, and gave me a hand up onto a platform made from a board over a couple of old aluminum kegs.

More whistling and a lot of suggestions that I was overdressed.

"Settle down, boys and girls," I growled.

They weren't easily going to become *quiet*—they were excited werewolves after all—but when I could make myself heard without shouting, I kicked off.

"Early this morning, before most of you had your first coffees, I flew into Doña Ana with five members of my House." I pointed at where Yelena and the others were standing with Alex. I added as if it were an afterthought, "Members of my House makes them members of your pack."

There was a self-conscious growl of welcome. Not grudging, but the thought of Athanate and hybrids and humans being *pack* was still difficult for many of them.

Yelena smiled lazily and got a couple of whistles.

"I was met at the airport by Alex and Zane..."

I paused to let them cheer their alphas.

"... and another six of you."

I pointed to the group, who were standing together. The packs knew there had been no injuries on our side, and they were still pumped up, so I let them cheer their fellow pack members as well.

"We were ambushed. Two of their trucks collided with each other when their drivers were shot. Another one crashed into those two and the last one got cooked by an RPG."

Some stomped on the ground, some punched the air and yelled. They understood that the pack couldn't mobilize all of them at once, but every single one of them wanted to be in on a spectacular action like this.

"Then came the dirt bikes. Twenty-eight in all, as far as we can tell. Fifteen or so got real smart and turned around right away. Four or five got caught in the blast or the wreckage of the trucks. Nine had the balls and stupidity to attack and only three of those got away. Overall, maybe twenty escaped. Police reports say there were ten injured and about the same number dead.

"Police captured fifteen, five of the ones escaping and all ten of the injured. The prisoners aren't talking, but some of them are in criminal databases and they're all pretty obviously from across the border, so the police are calling it a drug cartel fight that spilled out of Juárez and went badly wrong. They're saying they have no clues to what happened to the intended victims."

Laughter and back-slapping.

"Not a scratch, boys and girls. About $20,000 of costs fixing up that van and truck. Maybe $5,000 on extra equipment and ammunition. For a dozen of us, a morning away from what we should be doing. That's the complete cost. Now, is that a good return?"

They thought so, very loudly.

I let it all die down. A few of them noticed I wasn't exactly pumping the air and hollering. I could feel a slight unease leak into the celebrations. The Call lost its stomping, cheering celebration. Some puzzled expressions were forming.

Good.

I let a touch of bitterness leak into the Call.

"We gave the Juárez pack a shock all right. Set them back... maybe a couple of months. Maybe three."

It quieted down, and the atmosphere had shifted. They exchanged uncomfortable looks.

Someone called from the back, "If we'd put more wolves into the ambush, we'd have taken more of them down."

"Maybe," I half agreed. "But then maybe there'd be El Paso wolves in police cells now. The more wolves in the fight, the more difficult it is to wrap it up cleanly after."

"So what do you call success?" a belligerent voice asked.

"Not having to do it at all," I responded.

Feet shuffled, and looks were exchanged again. Uncertainty crept into the Call.

This is the fire-breathing alpha we heard about? Doesn't want a fight?

"Alex and I were challenged back before New Year's," I said. "And when we defeated the Oakens, Felix and Cameron said the El Paso pack would move up to Denver and White Sands would come in to replace it."

Sullen silence, especially from the El Paso. The Oakens had been popular alphas. The challenge and the aftermath had been accepted, but this cut close to the bone.

Even Alex and Zane, who knew where I was going with this, had gone stony-faced.

"Where are we on that move? I got twenty-three wolves come up to Denver," I said. "All of them cubs."

"It's not easy," someone shouted.

"It never is. Each one of you has some good reasons. Your house, your friends, your job, your special circumstances." I made sure I swept the crowd from end to end. "But *all* of you have one reason in common."

"Juárez," muttered someone down front. Not even someone I'd paid to feed me the line. *Good man.*

"Yeah," I said slowly, my voice raising. "The Juárez pack. As I hear it, time was when the El Paso and Juárez packs were good neighbors. I heard, even up to thirty years ago, Caleb and Victoria Oaken would cross the border for a meal with the Juárez alpha. That a phone call could get a Juárez pack member a pass to spend a weekend in El Paso."

The room had gotten tense. Some of the werewolves here would remember those times.

"It's a long way from that to a Juárez team trying to assassinate your alphas in your territory."

A pack growl started simmering from the back.

"The El Paso pack isn't the one that changed that. You don't prey on humans. You don't cross the border to kill as part of an initiation into the pack. The Juárez pack does that. While you continue on being a good and responsible pack, they have become the opposite. It's built up over time so you've started to think this is normal for packs. It's only when you have to plan to pass the territory on that you realize what an issue it's become. You can't resolve all your individual problems, because day after day, night after night, you're working on keeping the Juárez pack in their own box. You're working on transferring those defensive skills to the White Sands, because there *is* no El Paso pack if Juárez regards this as their territory."

Anger. I could feel it in their Call. El Paso and White Sands combined.

Anger. Because the truth hurts.

"They *know* there's a handover happening. They *know* you're caught up in it. They're exploiting it. Just like they'll exploit White Sands' unfamiliarity after the change."

More anger.

"You have your victories. Out there in the darkness on the Devil's Ridge, or the alleys of Chihuahuita. Good victories all of them. Ever stop to count how many you've lost?"

The anger grew.

I dropped my voice and got them leaning closer. "And those victories. How good do they feel? Because you know, inside you, that for every one of them you take down, there are two next month."

There was real, deep-seated anger now.

"The Juárez pack outnumbers us," I said. "We're good citizens who work in the human economy and pay our taxes, live by a code. The Juárez pack trades in drugs and they traffic people. Sex trafficking and human misery have made the Juárez pack rich. Rich enough in terms of money that they'll shrug off losing trucks and dirt bikes today. And they're rich enough in terms of new cubs they'll replace today's ten dead and fifteen in prison, and they'll do it in a month."

"We need to call in other packs to help us." I could see the woman who suggested that. She was old El Paso and right in the front. "That's what the League is for, isn't it?"

I shrugged.

"You're right, it *is* kinda what the League's for, but it's the wrong answer. If we call the Tucson pack, who's protecting their territory? Ask Zane how many times Albuquerque's had to go help them out because of the Sonoran pack raiding across the border."

Silence.

"If we call Big Bend, the Coahuila pack will move in and there'll be hell to pay getting rid of them." I met eyes and stoked the anger in them. "So, wrong answer."

"What's the right answer, then?" someone shouted.

"First you gotta ask the right question," I said. "We know all about how rich they are and where they get their money from. What don't we know?"

The woman in the front again: "Where they get so many cubs from?"

I pointed at her.

"*That's* the right question. All the cubs for all the sub-packs in Chihuahua and Sonora and Baja, including Juárez, come from one pack headquarters. One ranch near Villa Ahumada called Astilla de Luna. The ranch owned by the Chihuahua alpha, Mauricio Gálvez. That much we know. Which only leads to the next question: how are *they* getting so many new werewolves?"

"So what's the answer?"

I lowered my voice. "The answer is we go and find out," I said.

Forty puzzled and angry werewolves looked up at me.

Their Call was a storm cloud of confused emotion, full of power but directionless. It was time to give it the direction it needed, a channel, so that all that power could be put to work.

I raised my voice. "We're not calling on the Tucson or Big Bend or Albuquerque packs. We're not even going to take all the werewolves we've got here in El Paso. We're going to go with volunteers from this group right here in this brewery. You." I pointed at them. "We're going to meet with some of those cubs you've been sending up to Denver to train, who are waiting in Juárez right now. We're going to take part together in an operation. A real, military-style operation."

Forty shocked faces.

"And when we're finished," I shouted, "there will be no Juárez pack, and there will be no headquarters at Villa Ahumada."

I leaped down off my platform and started shoving angry werewolves to make my point.

"Because while I'm still co-alpha in El Paso, Juárez doesn't get a pass to *ambush me* in *my* territory. Chihuahua doesn't get a pass to set up a pack in the other half of *my* town. They don't get to murder people and traffic people and sell drugs."

That got the howls building. This they liked.

"They don't get to attack the Southern League. They don't get to attack the Assembly. They don't get to force us onto the back foot the whole time," I yelled as I shoved a few more. "Because I'm tired of it. I'm tired of dancing to their tune. I'm tired of changing our plans because of things they do. I'm tired of not having my husband and my pack back in Denver. I'm tired of Basilikos urging the packs across the border to make trouble for us. I'm tired of it all, and I'm going to make it stop, right here, right now."

They were all howling at me now.

Some of them shoved me right back, which was werewolf encouragement.

Their anger and mine blended now, and I let it all flow into the Call.

"This morning, we ambushed the ambushers. Tonight, we hit them in Juárez. We hit them at Astilla de Luna. They've been biting us for too long. It's past time, wolves, *long* past time. Now, we bite back."

Chapter 11

Ride the shock wave.

That had been a favorite of my old instructors in Ops 4-10, Top and Ben-Haim.

It meant when you hit the enemy, you kept hitting them, faster than they could respond. Hit them a second time, just as they realized you hit them the first time. And a third time, and again. And again. Until they came apart and there was nothing left to hit.

Following that through to the end would mean hitting Basilikos all the way down to the Yucatán, because Juárez linked to Villa Ahumada, and I knew Villa Ahumada linked through other sites, tributaries, growing like a river, all the way down to Mérida at the tip of the Yucatán peninsula, where the Basilikos headquarters were.

Roll all of them up in one pre-emptive strike.

I sighed. If only we could. All the drugs that would never hit the streets; all the women and children who would be saved from trafficking. Eliminating Matlal's corrupt influence in the paranormal community, hopefully making Emergence safer for everyone.

The emotion I'd raised in my speech was still running high among the pack, to the point that I was having trouble keeping my own emotions under control. My wolf was angry about this morning, and the desire to hunt and kill raged in me.

But I had to keep control; I couldn't allow mission creep. We would hit Juárez in a few minutes' time, when everyone was in position. If that went well, we would race 75 miles south and hit Astilla de Luna before they knew we were there. Over in California, Annie, Scott and Billie would do the same for the Baja pack.

That was it—the limit of our reach, however much I was itching for more. And however much Zane was demanding we hit Sonora. I'd let him propose a plan, but however well things went, we couldn't keep ahead of the shock wave.

From where I was parked, I could see the lights burning in the windows of the Juárez pack headquarters. Pack members kept arriving, forcing the guard to leave his post and unlock the gates every five or ten minutes. The pack were jittery, not because they knew they were being watched, or they suspected anything else would happen tonight. But getting hit like they had been this morning had rocked them back.

Good.

It wasn't the whole pack here, just the alpha, his lieutenants and the werewolves who were getting included in the plans to 'retaliate' against El Paso. I could feel the rage building in their Call, while we kept ours quiet and dispersed.

It was worrying that pack members were still arriving. I'd counted twenty-three individuals in the time I'd been sitting here, and I couldn't see how many were already inside. How well armed were they? What sort of weapons would they have inside, and how quickly could they reach them?

There was a point at which I'd have to call off the attack, but I didn't want to do that unless I absolutely had to. We needed to stop Matlal here, and at Astilla de Luna. It would also be a bad move for Alex and me to make as alphas. After winding up the pack like we had today, werewolf sense said we *had* to go through with it or lose control of them.

To our advantage, the Juárez pack didn't *seem* to be expecting anything. Outside of the ten-foot chain link fence, and the guard in his gatehouse, there were no visible security measures. The police and the drug cartels both gave them a wide berth. The El Paso pack? They would reason that was the other side of the border. They *knew* El Paso never crossed into Juárez. This was Juárez territory, and no other werewolf would dare come here.

Dumb.

But the HQ did have some protection. Nothing in comparison to the fortress that was Astilla de Luna, but some.

The Juárez HQ was a warehouse at the edge of the southwestern industrial zone. The front of the building had a concrete dock five feet tall, for loading and unloading. There was a huge dusty space in front of that for rigs to turn around and back up. There were rows of empty trailers parked, blocking my view of the loading dock and the car parking space at the side of the building.

If it were me, I would have increased security at the same time I sent the ambush out, purely on the basis that if I punch someone, I should expect them to try to punch me back.

I was gambling they didn't expect it.

There was a hush of static on the TacNet, and then Rita's voice, calm and light: "Backdoor. Drone up."

Alex woke his tablet up and tapped the drone feed icon to open the bird's eye view of the warehouse.

It came to rest, hovering about a hundred feet right above the flat roof. Point one—no guards on the roof. *Good.* Point two—no *armed* guards on the loading dock, just one guy stalking up and down in frustration at being left out. *Good.*

The parking lot was shown clearly. Full, but it only had twenty spaces. At the average for the number of people inside each car since we arrived, that meant there were about sixty werewolves inside.

"Gate," I said. Hadn't had time to come up with a better callsign. "Backdoor, do a slow circuit."

The drone slid out to the west and then followed the line of the fence until it arrived back where it had started.

There were an additional six cars, parked wherever there was a space between trailers. Another eighteen werewolves maybe.

"Say eighty in all," I murmured to Alex. "That's close to no-go."

There were eleven of us in front and ten behind. We had some reserves, but if we called them back, that would blow the Villa Ahumada leg of the operation.

"Maybe more. With an unknown number of them armed, and we have no idea what weapons they have," he replied, frowning.

"Every single one will have a handgun," Zane said, from the seat behind us. "And I bet there'll be shotguns in that building."

I nodded absently. We'd been over this before. Handguns didn't worry me much. Shotguns were more concerning, but only if they had them where they could get them in a hurry.

Rita had been down here preparing the strike, and so I knew the layout of the offices above the warehouse. If they were having such a big meeting, there was only one room they could be in, and even then, they'd be spilling out into the corridors.

I keyed the TacNet again. "Gate, rig situation query."

"Rig rolling now," the answer came back from Yelena. "There in ten."

"At last," Alex said.

"Rig, advise any further delays," I said. "Frontdoor, sound off."

The team responded. Everyone was in place, ready and listening for my calls.

Nothing to do but wait.

Zane leaned forward from the back and breathed over my neck.

"So, mi corazón, tell me something," he murmured.

As long as it was only mildly distracting, I didn't mind him teasing me.

Alex just snorted.

"For you, guapo, anything."

"I see you finger-talk with your cubs and House," he said.

I snorted. "Stole it from you. Guilty as charged, but y'know, it's kinda handy."

Alex looked sideways at me. "Was that a joke? Handy? Really?"

We all laughed.

"Not my point," Zane said. "It's not our finger-talk. It's just that you didn't finger-talk two months ago and now you all do. On top of that, two months ago you got sent some no-account El Paso cubs..."

Alex growled, and Zane raised his hands. "No offense intended to your cubs, but the reason they got sent up to Denver is they weren't doing anything good down in El Paso. Am I right?"

Just the three of us in the car and the TacNet transmit was off. Alex's jaw worked, but he nodded.

"Those same no-good cubs are working with Rita, who has *no* time for fools, and they've been here a week playing James Bond like they were all born wearing tuxedos and drinking martinis."

"People get better," I said. "Good training."

"Bullshit. Not even two months. This training you got going in Denver isn't just training."

Alex and I exchanged looks.

"Your ears only," I said.

"Can't give you that if Cameron gets on my case."

"Tell her I asked to be the one to talk to Felix and her about it. Soon as I catch up with them in Louisiana. Same as everything that happens here tonight."

Zane looked like he'd tasted lemons, but he nodded.

"Okay. Imagine a combination of werewolf Call, Athanate eukori and Adept aura."

Zane frowned. I understood; it was a leap, like it had been for us.

"Fighting involves a lot of muscle memory." I scratched my head. It was easier to *do* than explain. "Language is the same sort of thing, based on associations. You have one person who's good at one thing, you can create an environment with telergy, I mean Call, eukori, aura all mixed. An environment that supercharges the ability to teach other people skills."

I shrugged. "We learned a bunch of things. The cubs and I can speak Athanate now, and I speak better Spanish. On four legs we fight like cougars, thanks to Rita. On two legs, they fight like I do, like Ops 4-10 troops do—"

"Shit! You making a pack of supersoldiers?" Zane said.

"No," Alex said. "Difference between training to fight and doing it for real—"

"And it's not just for us. I'm going to get Felix and Cameron to start the process of training trainers for the whole League. Get this for everyone—"

"Rig," hissed the TacNet. "On track. In two."

One more pickup of the Juárez pack with five people inside had arrived while we'd been talking. Eighty-five, or possibly as many as a hundred Juárez werewolves, against twenty-one of us, but with surprise and weapons on our side.

Decision time.

I pressed transmit. "Gate. All ears: we are green to go. Green to go."

Chapter 12

About half a mile behind us, an anonymous pickup pulled out in front of an eighteen-wheeler truck. Another quarter mile, it happened again. Moments later the little convoy loomed up in our rearview mirror and I pulled out in front.

The pickups behind us were dirty, dusty. Unremarkable to the casual eye. The middle one had a rack above the cabin with a pair of searchlights for night hunting mounted on it.

My pickup was the biggest, with a massive, full width bull bar protecting the grill and lights. It had an engine that made the sort of sound you felt in your belly.

Less than a hundred yards to go, I stomped on the gas.

"Gate. Lights out," I called on the TacNet.

In the pickup behind us, Mykayla pressed a switch and a small explosive device went off in the utilities conduit in front of the warehouse. Every light in the building went off.

Here's hoping their shotguns are behind electromagnetic doors.

However much the boredom of the wait, thinking calm thoughts, listening to music and spreading out had helped keep our Call below the level of notice from the Juárez pack, that was gone now we were heading in.

Hunt!

I could feel the surge of our mixed El Paso-White Sands-Deauville Call and the shock registering in the Juárez pack.

Too late.

The tires howled as I swung across the road and aimed at the double-width gates.

I wasn't sure whether it would be the rusty hinges, the old chain or the padlock that gave when I hit it with a three-ton pickup going flat out. It was all three. The gate burst open and flew away.

The other pickups followed me in while the eighteen-wheeler stopped in the road, blocking the entrance and anyone's view of what was happening.

We skidded to a stop, lined up facing the loading dock.

The middle pickup's hunting lights came on, blinding anyone who was looking for us.

The lone guard on the dock had retreated through one of the steel-shuttered bays. He'd left it open.

We'd already left the pickups, and all eleven of us vaulted onto the dock outside of the beams of the searchlights.

Shots came from above us, but they were aimed at the truck that everyone could see. They were from handguns.

Mykayla and I hurled half a dozen short-fuse grenades through the open bay.

As the last grenade exploded, Zane and Alex raced in front of me, their shapes looking like something out of nightmares with the bulk of the weapons they carried.

The ground floor was a maze of yellow-painted racking and gantries. We weren't interested. Thanks to Rita's research, we knew the layout. We knew where to go.

I beat the others to the metal mesh staircase on the west side. Sprayed it with bullets from my MP5. Made it to the landing. Mykayla and others fired from the sides.

Eight or nine Juárez werewolves died trying to come down those stairs.

The others were smarter.

They wanted to wait until we emerged on the office level.

My team leaped up to join me on the landing. All five of my remaining grenades flew through the opening to the office floor and bounced along the corridors. These were stun grenades and when they went off, we had hands over our ears, eyes shut and faces down.

The Juárez pack didn't.

Werewolves hear and see much more than humans. It's a strength. Right up until someone uses it as a weakness.

Time to ride the shock wave.

Zane and Alex shouldered me out of the way and were through the opening before the echoes of the explosions had died.

They had flamethrowers.

Compressor, nozzle, tank, trigger. Simple to make and terrifying to face.

Whole corridors filled up with flames. As I sprinted behind them, firing at anything that moved which wasn't us.

Out of ammo. Eject, replace magazine.

Someone inside had gotten the shotguns. Blasts sounded above the sinister whoosh of the flamethrowers. But Zane and Alex had already moved on. The rest of us were crouched low. Three bullets down each corridor. Shoot and move.

Behind us came Martin, from the White Sands pack. He still had grenades. He hurled two down each corridor.

Then we all crouched, and as the flames died, the new explosions rocked the offices. Glass shattered; carpets, tables and partitions burned. Figures, some alight, struggled to get away.

It was like a vision of hell. No surprise that they were running.

I'd left them what looked like a way out—the emergency stairs on the side of the building, leading to a back door to the compound, which opened onto waste land.

A pack's Call was its strength. But tonight, it was the Juárez pack's weakness. The same Call that could urge the whole pack into a hunting frenzy could also spread shock and panic.

They ran. Down the emergency stairs, flames reaching out to catch them. There was a gate, a restriction. Some of the Juárez pack went crazy with panic and killed each other to get away. Some climbed the fence. They boiled out onto the dark waste land.

Where Rita and nine of our best snipers waited with long rifles and infra-red sights.

I left it to the others to chase the Juárez pack out.

"Mykayla!"

She ran to join me. We leaped down to the warehouse level and sprinted to the east wall. Measured ten yards south along the wall from the main middle gantry. Slapped explosive packs against the cinderblocks. Retreated.

The wall blew out, leaving a hole five yards wide.

And on the other side stood a fuel tank.

Mykayla had a steel pipe with a sharp end. It was specially treated so that it wouldn't create sparks as I hammered the end until it pierced the tank. Fuel started to spray from the pipe into the warehouse.

I switched on a timer-controlled explosive and dropped it where the fuel was spreading.

"Gate. Rig," I said into the TacNet, "go, go, go. Green on phase two."

"Rig rolling." Yelena's voice was flat. She was upset not to be with me in this attack, but she knew the bigger one was coming at Astilla de Luna, and she would have a major part in that.

The eighteen-wheeler pulled away.

On the other side of the access road she'd been blocking, there were ranks of low, cheap houses. They all had walls and shutters, grills and gates. I'd worried about them at the beginning of planning, but Rita had been scouting the site. She told me that nothing short of the destruction of their houses would get people who lived there to come out after dark if they heard weapons fire.

With the truck and trailer blocking the way, there had been no casualties, no unexpected witnesses.

"Gate." I panted into the TacNet as we ran. "Backdoor. Situation."

"Confirmed alpha and five lieutenants, all down. Pack tried charging some of us. They hit the claymores. They're all running now."

Hunt. Kill!

Our joint pack's Call echoed in the night, strong even against the Juárez pack's blind, screaming fear.

An unexpected wave of darkness came over me for a moment; I wanted to chase them, and kill them all. I had to force it aside.

"Let them go," I said. "Cease fire unless attacked. Watch for us. We'll be out in two. Be ready to roll."

"Pushing it," Mykayla panted as we ran back through the warehouse. There were fires burning on the office floor, and we could smell the stench of the volatile fuel behind us.

But Alex and Zane had split their tasks, and had them nearly complete.

Zane was already at the back door. Alex and five others were just finishing a run through the ruined offices, picking up cellphones, laptops, backup devices.

One more objective: the server room.

"Amber!" Urgent calls to get out.

I tore an array of drives out of the biggest rack. No time for more.

We all ran to the back gate.

"Go. Go. Go."

I was last out. A massive, fiery thump from behind me, and I was hurled through the door onto the dirt outside.

The warehouse and all three pickups at the front of the compound were ablaze.

It would take the rest of the night before anyone got inside that building.

Trucks skidded to a halt and hands hauled us into the back.

"Casualties?" I panted as we sped off.

"Nothing from the backdoor group, but we lost Vaughn," Zane said. "At the back door. Too quick to put his head out. Dead before he hit the ground. Body in the other truck."

A White Sands werewolf. Not Zane's immediate pack, but I could feel the pain in his voice, and in the Call of the White Sands.

"I'm sorry," I said. "Any others?"

"Bunch of us caught some pellets. Couple are bleeding. No es nada. Mykayla's helping."

I twisted around to look.

My hybrid ehvasi, coming out of the fighting with all her adrenaline and Athanate elethesine pumping, was still able to function rationally and calm down enough to help heal wounds.

She was handling it better than I would have at the same stage.

Of course Zane had said it was nothing, but some of those wounded weren't going to be able to be involved in the attack on Astilla de Luna. I needed everyone there to be at their best. We were down to the bare minimum for an attack, and the ranch was a fortress.

I collapsed back on the flatbed as the truck jolted onto the tarmac and picked up speed.

I estimated we'd killed at least three quarters of the Juárez pack in the compound. Maybe sixty. The whole pack numbered a lot more, near six hundred according to our estimates, but the alpha and most of his seniors were dead. Their headquarters were a blazing ruin. The survivors would remember. And even the ones who hadn't been there would live looking over their shoulders: in addition to recon for the operation, Rita had stolen a drug shipment from the Sinaloa Cartel, and left evidence that would point here.

If the Juárez pack ever troubled El Paso again, it would be a long, long time.

But... *only* if I made sure there wasn't another ready-made pack that Mauricio Gálvez and Matlal could send here. Only if I made this crushing defeat in Juárez no more than a warm-up for the main event in Villa Ahumada.

Chapter 13

Never lose sight of any vital part of the operation.

That had been one of Top's maxims, and he would have been laughing at me.

We were splitting up into our teams for the second phase of the night when Mykayla handed me a cellphone.

"Problem," she said.

"Alpha?" I recognized the voice on the cell. It was Briana, the cub I'd put in charge of what I thought was the easiest part of the operation, the dragnet. Their job had been to check the five locations in the city that the Juárez pack used for their sex trafficking operation. Five teams, five soft targets. Take out any of the pack that was there and rescue the kidnapped women and children. Hand them all over to the one team assigned to get them back to their homes, the remainder of the teams to join in phase two. An important task, but an 'easy' one.

Briana had gotten the honor of leading because she was smart, strong and steady. I wasn't getting that from her voice now.

"Tell me," I said.

"Team 3. Still in place. Refusing to meet and hand over. Wants to talk to you. The rest of us are at the handover location. What do I do?"

"Hold the line," I said to Briana, and waved to Julie, who was getting ready to drive me. "Julie, we're detouring. The house on Parque Bartolomé."

Julie grimaced. "Tight timeline, Boss."

We piled into the truck and sped away.

"Any other information on Team 3?" I asked Briana.

"No, alpha."

"Okay, you hold in place for the moment." I frowned and thought about distances, and being well out of the way before the Juárez police got a grip on the situation at the burning building, and keeping on the schedule I'd set for the attack on Astilla de Luna. "If I don't call before, you go fifteen minutes from now. Understood?"

"Yes, alpha." Huge relief in her voice.

"The rest of the teams okay?"

"Yes, no problems, but they're getting edgy."

"Give them the time limit, and they'll calm down. It's uncertainty that spooks people in situations like this. Any casualties?"

"None, alpha."

"Good. Well done. Call Team 3 and tell them I'll be there in five."

I ended the call. We were already most of the way to the house next to Parque Bartolomé.

Lots of things could go wrong, even in a supposedly easy operation. The cubs had been trained for this type of hostage situation by Ops 4-10. They had the added benefits of their paranormal abilities. But no operation was really easy until it was finished, and I had put a hard limit on the time the teams could spend.

Team 3 consisted of two of the cubs I'd had trouble with at my first meeting. Connor and Rebecca. I'd nicknamed Connor 'Mr. Surly', but he'd done enough since then to earn his way past that. At that same event, his girlfriend had taken a swing at me, and quickly been very sorry about it. She'd also earned her way back in.

They'd both gotten to the stage where I trusted them enough to put them in a team and give them an objective in this operation, and I hated thinking my evaluation had been bad.

Still... *something* had gone wrong.

Julie slowed as we came around the corner.

The house was ahead, on the left. Like all its neighbors, it hid behind gray concrete walls and a heavy steel gate. The top layer of those concrete walls had broken glass embedded in them. Every window in the house was covered by a steel shutter. Apart from weeds there was not a single plant to be seen. Above the house, a tangle of telephone cables swayed in the hot wind.

The gate was open and I could see Team 3's truck had been parked inside. A blinding yard light was on, but there was only darkness showing through the house's heavy window shutters.

We turned into the drive.

I could hear music from the neighbors, but the house in front of us was silent. I could already smell blood.

Keith checked his watch. "Want us with you?"

I shook my head. My gut told me this wasn't that sort of problem. I had to deal with it as the alpha, using my authority. And I had to make it quick.

I walked past the truck into the dazzle of the yard light. They'd been watching for me. The door creaked open as I approached.

A fetid breath of air wafted out. Hot. Humid. Sour. Under the blood and death, I could smell the marque of my werewolves, woven through with the odor of adrenaline and fear.

Although a team of two couldn't really provide much of a Call, I got an echo of *hunt* and *kill* from them. What surprised me was the sense of *pack* I felt as well.

The inside was dark, lit only by angled beams of the yard light stabbing through the horizontal shutter grill, sharp as razor slashes. A dirty ventilator fan with an unoiled bearing marked time with a faint squeal every time the blades completed their circle.

The first room was a bare kitchen. There was blood on the floor. The stench of sickness and death hung like a fog in the air.

Connor stood way back, on the other side of the kitchen, by the inner door, hands at his sides and head down, radiating submissiveness. He was a storm of emotions—his heart racing and his lungs laboring to get oxygen. Above all, he was scared of me, as any pack member who disobeyed an order from the alpha should be. In pack rules, I had the power of life or death over him, and he knew it.

I let my silence grow until it pressed on his shoulders like the weight of sin.

"Alpha," he whispered.

"Were my instructions unclear?"

"No, alpha."

"Then what happened?"

"We got here and found three of the Juárez pack, holding four kids prisoner. They..." He swallowed. "The kids..."

I shook my head. I didn't need to be told how the pack had treated their victims. I didn't *want* to be told. I needed my head clear.

"We killed the Juárez pack," he finished. "The kids are... okay."

Meaning not okay, not really. His position and body language told me the children were in another part of the house with Rebecca. I walked forward. "So what's the problem?"

He remained blocking the door. He trembled. There was sweat running down his face and he couldn't meet my eyes.

"Alpha. The kids..."

I was standing right in front of him now. I could taste the fear in his body, and beneath it, an anger he was having trouble controlling. Despite his control, he was a finger-click away from going wolf.

"Look at me, Connor." He raised his eyes reluctantly, and I grabbed his jaw so he couldn't turn his head away. *"What* about the children?"

"Our info was wrong for this group. Not kidnapped," he said. "They were *sold*. By their families."

I *reached* then, with my eukori. Just instinct. Athanate and wolf mixed. I didn't think it through. It was *not* what I needed to be doing, but I locked into him and sank through his emotions. The excitement of the hunt, the frustrated need to suppress their Call so the Juárez pack wouldn't be warned, the sudden frantic explosion of the fight. And then the horror as they understood what had happened to these children.

I took from him. I took some of that anger, because I had a place and a use for it, and he did not.

Then I swore, let him go and moved to push past.

He put his hands out to stop me.

"You can't send them back, alpha." He jerked back as if touching me had electrocuted him. "Please."

He bared his neck. A werewolf does not lay uninvited hands on an alpha. A werewolf does not tell their alpha what she can or can't do. "I'm sorry." He steeled himself and stammered on. "Rebecca and I... we can't have kids."

What?

I frowned. No werewolf or Athanate can. I was too focused on the children at first, then I caught up.

"You want to *adopt* them?"

He started to say *Rebecca*, and caught himself. "Yes. We want to, alpha."

I swore again.

This time when I pushed past, he didn't try to stop me.

I followed my nose through the darkness in the house.

Rebecca and the children were in an empty storeroom at the back. As I made my way there, my wolf nose told me I'd passed the room they'd been kept in, and the room the Juárez pack used as a bedroom.

Not just a bedroom; a 'training' room for their captives.

I crushed the anger down, down into the place that Ash had helped me build. A better strongbox, a place where I could tap into that power when I needed it. I didn't need it now. I needed to *not* be angry.

They were huddled together on the floor of the storeroom, Rebecca in the middle, each child clutching a little corner of her.

Rebecca was whispering words to them, feeling panicked and helpless, unconsciously giving off a Call of *pack*, trying to comfort them the best way she knew how.

In the darkness, I was only another monster.

My wolf eyes could see them from the heat of their bodies, but they could barely see me at all, except as a shape that blocked out what jagged illumination came into the house from the yard light.

Decision time, Tara said.

We couldn't leave them here; there was nowhere in Juárez that was safe. We couldn't send them back to the same people who'd sold them.

I knelt down.

There was no decision to be made about *what* to do, only how to do it.

I needed a lot more work on my Spanish, but I could do this.

Estoy aqui para ayudarte...

"I am here to help you, and everything will be all right," I said in my softest voice, keeping it simple. "You are safe now. Rebecca and Connor will be with you. They will take care of you. They will need some of our friends to help. Our friends are good people too. Do you understand me?"

My Athanate glands were putting out *trust me* pheromones, but there was a limitation on how much that would work in situations like this. The connection these children felt with Rebecca was more powerful than anything I could achieve, short of compelling changes in their memories.

It would be a blessing. The words formed in my mind, and that wasn't Tara speaking.

Deeper darkness formed in front of me. It took all light, even the heat of their bodies, and compressed it into a circle of utter nothingness. Yet, inside that circle, I could sense a shadow of myself, a mirrored darkness.

The voice spoke again: *As you help them, let me help you. Open the way. Reach for me and I will come.*

I heard a tiny cry from one of the children, and the mirror of darkness was gone.

Even though they couldn't see me or whatever strange manifestations crowded my mind, they could sense something wrong.

"Alpha?" Rebecca breathed.

"Get Briana on your cell," I told Connor.

He handed me the device. The light of the screen against my face must have made me look like something from a horror show. I couldn't help that.

"Briana? The women and children you have there. Are there any that have been sold by their families rather than kidnapped?"

"No, alpha. I've spoken to every one of them while we waited—"

"Good work. Different situation here. Send Grace and Dominga to Parque Bartolomé. The rest of you go to your assigned tasks."

She repeated the instructions back and I ended the conversation.

This operation was already short of troops. Now I was going to lose four more. The possibility to call everything off pressed into my mind.

But calling it off meant none of it would have any lasting value. Skylur's warnings echoed in my mind. The best foundation to persuade the Assembly would be a spectacular success.

Destroying the Juárez pack would not qualify. They were just a unit. The proof I needed about Matlal's involvement would be at Villa Ahumada.

And left alone, Mauricio Gálvez, sitting in the fortified security of Astilla de Luna, would form another pack and send it to Juárez. They'd find a new headquarters. They'd buy new houses and trucks, and in six months' time there would be another group of terrified, brutalized children like this.

"Señora?"

It was the oldest of them. A girl. The least terrified, which meant she could actually speak, even though her whole body was trembling.

I put my arms around her, very gently, aware I was not a comforting figure at all.

She didn't pull away.

"Tía Rebecca dice que debo decirte," she whispered, hiding her face against my neck.

Aunt Rebecca says I must tell you...

She spoke quickly, stumbling and crying. I lost bits of what she said, but the story I understood.

The horror of realizing she'd been sold. The long drive in a truck.

El palacio blanco en el desierto...

The white palace in the desert. My stomach sank. They'd been to Astilla de Luna.

They were kept in the cellars for *el Grande*—she had to mean the alpha— to sample before sending them onwards.

La bruja reina del pantano...

Something about they were being sent to the witch queen in the swamp, but before I could ask about that, she started to speak about Rosa. An older girl, who'd been with them. Had tried to comfort the youngest. To protect them.

Ella era muy valiente...

She was so brave. She wouldn't do the things *el Grande* told them to do.

I bit my lip and tears ran down my cheeks because I knew how this would end.

I didn't want to hear about this, but I could not refuse. I sat there in the dark and listened, because I had to. Because it was important. I needed to bear witness. I needed to be the one she passed this burden to, not like a link in a chain, but like working a thread into a weave. We were not as weak as the weakest, but strong, and we were strong because this bound us together in anger, all of us, against the monsters that walked the earth.

Ellos nos hicieron ver...

They made us watch. And at the end...

La arrojaron al pozo...

They threw her somewhere? Into a mine shaft? No, a pit? A pit of animals?

Keith's voice came from behind, interrupting us. He came in with Grace and Dominga. Partly to remind me that there was a clock ticking.

There was nothing more I could do here, and justice for what had happened to these girls would come from a successful strike on the ranch at Villa Ahumada.

A successful strike needed me.

In hard going, take one step at a time. One of Ben-Haim's little sayings.

I kissed her hair. "Fuiste valiente para sobrevivir. Será mejor ahora."

You were brave to survive, I told her. *It will be better now.*

I briefed my team of four cubs. They were to get the children across the border to safety, and protect them at all costs. We knew about some tunnels that the Juárez pack had used. If that way wasn't safe, then they'd have to take them down into the wilds and I didn't care if they had to carry them across the Rio Grande, so long as they made it.

They could call other members of the El Paso pack to meet them on the other side.

Then they were to take the children to Denver, and Bian would hide them all in Haven until we worked out exactly how we were going to make this up front and legal.

The darkness threatened to wash over me again, and for me personally, the rest of the operation tonight gained another incentive.

Revenge.

Chapter 14

"Billie?"

"I'm here, girl."

Fifteen minutes after leaving the house at Parque Bartolomé, and I was trying to touch base with every part of my operation.

Behind the breezy California voice on my secure cell, I could hear pain.

"How bad?"

"Three dead," she said, and that pain came through even clearer. "Two from the San Diego pack, and... and Suri."

I remembered Suri. Smaller than her fellow Belles. Tough, wise-cracking woman. So good at working with the pack's Harleys, they joked she'd been born with a wrench already in her hand.

I closed my eyes. "I'm sorry, Billie. For all three. I liked Suri."

"Had to be done. Price to be paid for things that need doing." She took a deep breath. "Tijuana pack is gone. Just gone. They won't be selling drugs and girls in San Diego anymore. That vamp Annie of yours, she an' the rest of your soldier spooks, they is *good* at what they do. Those freaking cubs, too, along with your handsome hybrid."

My 'soldier spooks' were a squad of Ops 4-10 on loan from Bian. The 'freaking cubs' were half the former El Paso cubs we'd been training at Haven, and at his insistence, they were led by Scott, my 'handsome hybrid'.

Annie was also ex-Ops 4-10, and as Billie had pointed out, she was now Athanate, one of my ehvasi. Officially, not mine, but Billie clearly didn't agree.

Annie was supposed to be at Haven. She was supposed to be part of the experiment to see if she could infuse others this quickly, and whether she could transfer the same benefit of reduced crusis she'd received from my infusion.

I'd tried arguing with her, much good it did me.

"Speak more later, Billie," I said, "but I'm on a tight schedule, and I need to talk to my vamp Annie now."

"She here."

Billie handed over the cell.

"Good job," I said. "Well done."

"Your plan," Annie replied. "Hit fast, hit hard. Worked."

I snorted. "Colonel Laine's strategy and Top's plan, just amended by me for this enemy. You good to go for phase two?"

"Truck's ready to roll."

"You could leave it to the rest and head back to Haven..."

"Talked about this, Boss. I'll stick to the plan. I'll be back at Haven tomorrow night, and no New York-based Diakon is going to know any better. It's *you* who should be staying out of harm's way. *You're* the one who's got to be there to argue with the brass about the political reasoning behind these attacks."

Ehvasi were sometimes referred to as the Athanate children of whoever infused them, but my experience was that any supposedly sweet childhood period was replaced by argumentative adolescence. None of my ehvasi had a problem arguing with me, not even mild-mannered Scott.

"The political argument delivers itself, if I get the proof it needs from Astilla de Luna," I said. "That's the main objective, getting the proof. That needs me."

She snorted. "Political arguments never deliver themselves, and even after they've been delivered, they need to be hammered in, hard. *Your* job, Boss."

I snorted back at her. She had a point.

I knew proof from Mauricio Gálvez's pack headquarters would show Matlal's involvement in territorial disputes of werewolves all along the border. It would show the eventual aim of that was to destabilize the Athanate Houses that shared that territory. It would wake the packs up to the importance of making alliances with each other *and* their local Athanate. It would show the involvement of the packs in drugs and sex slaves. It would make those Basilikos-influenced werewolf packs a legitimate target for combined attacks.

It would overcome the arguments of those Athanate who suggested the werewolves shouldn't be in the Assembly. It might even make the Confederation, the super-pack that stretched along the Rockies from Wyoming northwards, realize that they needed to join the Assembly.

And it would be justification for the attacks tonight. For the risks. For the deaths.

But Annie was right. I was the person in a position to make sure the message got through to the Were *and* the Athanate *and* the Assembly.

I changed tack. "How's Scott?"

"He did well," Annie said. "I'd pass the cell for him to talk to you, but it seems some of the Belles have taken him away."

I laughed. I could hear Billie in the background. "Tell her we keep him a while, before sending him back."

"Send the rest of them back. And tell Scott to call Amanda. I gotta load up now."

"Good luck with the Chihuahua pack. Don't let them bite your ankles."

"Very funny." I ended the call.

Annie and her team should be all right in Baja. Their second mission tonight was much simpler than mine, and would only involve Annie and a couple of ex-Ops 4-10. They had to travel down to the Baja pack's headquarters outside of Ensenada, and drop some mortar shells on it. Quick and easy job, more of a demonstration. No contact. In and out. Everyone back in San Diego before dawn.

I debated making one more call. I needed to speak to Gwen and Diana, but the mission clock was ticking in my head. No. Yelena would be less than thirty minutes away from Astilla de Luna now. I couldn't stretch this schedule.

Julie, Keith and I were at Juárez International Airport standing beside a de Havilland Twin Otter. It belonged to a recently formed company called TransAdentro that flew small, legitimate courier packages between Albuquerque, El Paso, Juárez, Chihuahua and Mexico City on a regular basis. Its usual route happened to pass right over Villa Ahumada.

The Twin Otter was a versatile little aircraft. It could carry freight or passengers and land on short runways. It was sometimes used as a medical evacuation aircraft.

It also made a great plane for skydivers.

Chapter 15

The flight wasn't long, but I had enough time to check on the status of the operation. I wouldn't use the TacNet until I called for the attack to start. Instead I watched a small overview display that Matt, our tech genius who was also Tullah's boyfriend, had managed to create. Yelena, Rita and the cubs were relaying their position to our 'base' unit—a cub with a laptop in a motel in Villa Ahumada. That information was transmitted in micro-bursts by a highly illegal and encrypted transmitter to my laptop.

It showed Yelena had turned west off the main Juárez-Chihuahua road and was already out of the town of Villa Ahumada. Rita and the cubs had overtaken her and were hiding in position around the remote ranch, just out of range of infra-red sensors.

The copilot came back from the cockpit.

"Five minutes," he said.

Right on time.

We edged our way around the cargo boxes and unsealed the door. The slipstream howled as the copilot slid it back and locked it into place. Outside, the wing navigation lights glowed, casting a red glaze on the underside of the port wing. The scattering of little lights that was Villa Ahumada slipped beneath us. Most of the land was an unrelieved black mass.

I took a last glance at Matt's display on the laptop.

There were limits to his ingenuity. He couldn't crack all the Chihuahua pack's communications in real time, but he *could* monitor their volume and source.

The arrow showing calls between the ranch and the Juárez area had been steadily growing. Now it jumped, and the display showed several people in the ranch were calling cell numbers that we'd previously logged as belonging to the Juárez pack.

With the Juárez alpha and lieutenants gone, it had taken over two hours for the first report of the attack to come through, and another hour for the Chihuahua alpha to be told. Now he was waking up people and asking questions, trying to work out what had happened and who had done it.

The shock wave had just hit them. A little early, but not enough for them to get any benefit from the information.

A jury-rigged green light came on beside the door.

I strapped on my helmet, switched on the electronics and spoke on the TacNet.

"Valkyrie above. Hammer, Anvil: sitrep."

Rita: "Anvil. All in place and ready."

Yelena: "Hammer. All on board. Is good. Gate in two minutes."

"Valkyrie. We are green to go."

They acknowledged, the copilot gave me a thumbs-up and I threw myself out into the night, fifteen thousand feet above the ranch of Astilla de Luna, Keith and Julie close behind.

Not flying. Falling.

My instructors in Ops 4-10 had drilled that into me and made us remind each other before every jump.

I spread my batwings to keep the speed sensible and began a spiraling descent toward the ranch. I had the full HALO kit in addition to my batsuit and brake. Colonel Laine had 'liberated' a Cyclops navigation system from Ops 4-10 before they closed it all down. The Cyclops display was a pale green, with a series of diminishing hoops dropping out of the sky. I had to guide myself through each hoop to land exactly where I wanted.

My heart skipped a beat.

The last time I'd fallen through the night in my batsuit, looking through the Cyclops, it had been the Hacha Del Diablo beneath me, and I'd been hours away from the deaths of the rest of my team.

For a second, I was back there, falling into the lightless jungle.

I cursed and shook it off.

Concentrate.

I was already down to ten thousand feet above the ground.

Seen from that vantage, Astilla de Luna was an ugly, squat, H shape. The two wings were living quarters, comprising palatial penthouses above open, colonnaded patios and comfortable barracks. The central building contained the communal areas, with offices and meeting rooms on the top floor, elegant living rooms, libraries and dining rooms on the second floor. The marble-tiled ground floor was for security and utilities. The basement... well, we knew they had game rooms and storage areas down there. Prison cells.

And something they called 'lugar de entrenamiento' — the training place, or simply 'horno' — the oven.

I shuddered.

Above ground, for all the smooth, white-stone walls and luxurious appearance, Astilla de Luna was built like a fort. There was even a military-style lookout post on the flat top of the central roof, disguised as some kind of ventilation shaft.

It *was* a fort. Every wall had been built with a double thickness of heavy brick. All the windows, even the huge ones looking out over swimming pools at the back, were bulletproof glass. Anyone trying to rush the ranch, from any direction, would quickly find that every corner of the building had a machine gun emplacement. These were hidden in boxy structures made to look like part of the design, and we'd seen through a covert drone's camera, when they ran one of their training days, that they could be accessed in a couple of minutes.

There were patrols throughout the grounds, day and night. There was a guard on the entrance off the main road, half a mile from the ranch. If that wasn't enough, there was another, heavier barrier on the long drive, sufficient to stop a car, and a thick, low wall surrounding all the buildings, about a hundred yards out.

One of those patrols, day and night, walked the extensive boundaries of the ranch. That lookout post was in use 24/7/52. It was impossible to sneak up on Astilla de Luna. Impossible to break through their lines of defense.

And if you *did* get in through all that? The place was full of werewolves.

You'd have to be crazy to attack Astilla de Luna.

Five thousand feet. Less than thirty seconds left.

Those guards in that rooftop lookout post might be watching the more distant gate. If they were, they'd see an eighteen-wheeler rolling to a stop at the barrier. But nighttime deliveries were not unusual here. The man on the gate would know about it, or he'd call in.

Maybe those lookout guards would have another cigarette. Maybe they'd take a quick drink from the bottle they'd smuggled up there. Maybe they'd listen out on their radio to hear if it was something interesting being delivered.

Sometimes, if they did their jobs well, they'd get to play with the goods.

They needed some incentive to be vigilant, because nothing ever happened to relieve the tedium of nightly guard duty at Astilla de Luna. After some stupid criminals had tried sneaking in just after the ranch had been built, there hadn't been a single incident. Even the drug gangs gave it a wide berth.

Everyone knew it was a bad place. Locals didn't call it by its name. Whether they realized the truth of their words or not, they called it

Nahualcalli, the House of Werewolves in the old Aztec language. They kept away from it.

The protection extended even past the borders of the property. If you stopped your car in the vicinity, the police would show up and move you on.

So the guards in the lookout tower were relaxed. The big canvas screen they used to keep the sun off during the day was hinged and folded back out of the way. There was a slight breeze, and they were ideally placed to catch it at the top of the building.

And there was simply no reason they would *ever* think to look up.

One thousand feet. Five seconds left.

I could see a cigarette glow.

My wolf eyes made out everything I needed. The Cyclops had done its job. I switched it off.

To keep the noise to an absolute minimum, I timed it so my parachute was fully deployed a hundred feet above the lookout tower, with one second of descent left.

Chapter 16

People don't appreciate that even with a parachute, you still arrive in a hurry.

There were two guards. I hit the first at the top of his back with both boots; the combined energy of me and all the equipment I was carrying transferred to his spine. I could feel the crack and I knew he wasn't getting up.

The second guard had good reactions and he might have been a problem, but Tara manifested as I landed.

No one expects a wolf on fire.

She tore the guard's throat out before he could scream, and disappeared again before his dead body hit the floor.

There were muffled thumps as Julie and Keith landed on the roof, twenty yards either side of the lookout tower.

I swiftly wrapped up the chute and batsuit. Took off the Cyclops and tapped the TacNet.

"Valkyrie," I said. "In the nest."

"Hammer. Through the gate," Yelena responded. "One down."

"Anvil. Waiting."

I let Julie and Keith do their job while I looked out toward the road.

How was this going to go?

Yelena's rig was rolling down the half mile of drive.

Sixty seconds.

The guards at the inner gate would be trying to contact the guard at the outer gate, and getting a voice blurred by static. They'd make out 'entrega'—delivery.

Forty seconds.

The rig was going faster. Now the guards would be getting a confused 'no lo sé' from the guy on the main desk. They'd start to be feeling something was wrong.

And despite all the warnings to keep it down, the El Paso/White Sands' Call was starting to be felt. Werewolves would be waking up inside Astilla de Luna, confused and sleepy.

Thirty.

The noise from the eighteen-wheeler was rising. The engine was gunned. The front looked odd.

Panic.

The pack Calls started to rise.

On one side: *hunt!*

On the other: *danger!*

Twenty seconds.

The guards were halfway good. The heavy, inner gate barriers came down in a hurry, and one guard went out and started urgently waving at the rig to slow down. A searchlight came on and in the glare, the front of the rig racing toward them must have looked even more odd.

Ten seconds.

No doubts about it now. The eighteen wheeler was going flat out and that front... a cowcatcher? Like on an old-fashioned steam train? And the cab? Hidden behind metal?

Five seconds.

They started to fire at it.

Which was the signal for Julie behind me to hit the trigger and blow their electric substation right off the roof.

All the lights went off, including the guard station searchlight.

And then the eighteen wheeler smashed through the gatehouse and thundered up the long flight of steps to the main entrance of Astilla de Luna like an angry god returning.

The rig came to a stop in the courtyard of the building, and the trailers' sides blew off to reveal the payload.

Yeah, you'd have to be crazy to attack Astilla de Luna.

Or very, very serious.

Our first surprise for the defenders was a remote operation naval gun made by the Italian firm Oto Melara. It lifted up on a turret behind the cab and lined up with the left-hand side of the building. It took a minute to traverse the building. Every second of that minute it delivered a 76mm shell as wide as a clenched fist, each weighing as much as a car's battery and travelling at a speed of 3,000 feet a second.

The walls were thick and all the glass was bulletproof, but that made no difference to the shells. The structure of the building might as well have been made of paper.

The shells penetrated walls, broke up, scoured rooms and still had enough power for the fragments to punch through-and-through.

Before that gun had even run out of ammunition, the next surprises took over.

Alex and Zane worked twin M2 Brownings on either side. Custom mounted, water cooled, firing half-inch rounds that were a mixture of incendiary and armor-piercing.

The structure of the buildings' wings just evaporated into clouds of smoke and spraying fragments. The machine gun emplacements were shattered before anyone reached them. For the pack inside, just waking into a hell on earth, there was nowhere to hide. The very walls around them were torn apart. The air they struggled to breathe was full of dust and flames.

The Chihuahua pack's call descended into *Panic! Run!*

"Anvil. Perimeter patrols cleared." As soon as the boundary patrols had heard the noise and turned towards the house, Rita and the cubs had pounced.

"Valkyrie. Descending." We needed to get down one floor.

"Hammer. Affirm." Alex and Zane continued working their M2s around the barracks. The central section was now off-limits for them.

We dropped one level from the roof to the top floor, where the meeting rooms and offices were.

Julie and Keith hurled grenades into the darkness and followed the explosions with MP5s ready.

Someone on the ground floor switched the power to the backup generators, which suited us fine—we cleared the whole floor in five minutes. Half of the small group who'd been there were dead before we entered.

Our target here was the server room.

It had been professionally built. It had fallback power supplies— batteries would have taken the load on the servers as soon as the main power dropped.

If any pack member in the building was thinking clearly, and had clearance on their systems, the servers would be purging themselves of data now, but there was no one here.

Julie slapped a shaped charge on the server room door and sheltered while the lock was demolished.

Keith and I covered the empty floor until Julie emerged with her misshapen grab-bag of every single hard drive.

"Valkyrie," I spoke into the TacNet. "Objective one complete. Descending."

"Anvil. Breakouts to north and west. Dealing as per Romeo Echo."

Rules of Engagement. My instructions were clear. Any small groups running away, the cubs could take them. If there was an organized retreat, they were to keep out of the way. We didn't have the numbers for a pitched battle. All we had were weapons and surprise.

"Hammer. Both wings done. Taking central ground floor."

Alex and Zane stopped the destruction of the M2s and rushed in through the front doors with Yelena and a small team of the El Paso and White Sands wolves.

Someone took out the emergency lighting, and we switched to flares.

Revealed in the harsh light, the living areas on the first floor were empty. Some rooms were, incredibly, untouched by the mayhem.

"Anvil." Rita's voice was choppy on the TacNet. "North breakout in force. Using ATVs. Organized. Pre-planned."

I swore.

Someone had been smart enough to have an emergency plan in place. Would that be Mauricio Gálvez himself?

Shit.

Killing him was one of the major objectives.

And revenge for Rosa.

"Do not engage, Anvil," I said between clenched teeth.

There was no response.

Julie and Keith signed this floor was empty.

"Valkyrie. Descending to ground floor," I said and checked the time. "Eyes open, everyone. Fifteen minutes and we're gone."

As we reached the ground floor, a squad of the cubs came running in from the west wing.

"Clear, alpha," their leader said, dropping a bag at Alex's feet before racing up the stairs.

Julie placed her bag of hard drives next to it and checked the cubs' haul. At least thirty cellphones. Every single one would need to be cracked and examined. I didn't care how cautious they were with their security, how encrypted their drives were, I'd soon have proof of exactly what went on at Astilla de Luna, and every person involved.

Zane emerged from the east wing, carrying a straight stick. He tossed it to me.

I snatched it out of the air, and felt the hairs come up on my neck.

Not a stick.

It was a bō, a dark wooden staff about five feet long, and tipped with silver. There had been plain bō used for centuries in the Far East as martial arts weapons. But this was different. These silver tips gave electric shocks. I'd seen bō like this before, in Taos, when I'd been caught by Mirela Tucek and her ninja nuns.

If House Tucek been here...

I suddenly knew who'd been in that breakout to the north. Tucek would never rely on the pack to protect her. She'd have always had a plan for herself or any of her followers who were here.

"Bodies?" I asked Zane.

He tapped the camera mounted on the front of his tactical vest. "None alive."

"Amber." Yelena's voice on the TacNet. "You need to see. Basement."

Chapter 17

The basement was a low, massive room with rows of doors off to the sides, but Yelena was standing near the middle. There was a circular, raised brick section there, about hip high. It was huge, about fifteen yards in diameter, and the opening was sealed with heavy-duty glass supported on iron beams. All arranged so you could look down into a lower room, without being exposed to what was there.

A lower room. A pit.

Darkness and a girl whispering through tears, determined to tell me, determined to bear witness, so I could bear witness in turn. So Rosa and her bravery would not vanish.

La arrojaron al pozo...

They threw her into a pit.

My stomach wanted to rebel, because there was a half-formed pack Call coming from the pit. It was frantic, chaotic, like the Call halfies sometimes tried to make when they couldn't change. It was full of fear, and threaded through it was a sickness.

Not any normal sickness. I felt the touch of workings sliding across my skin.

And I knew that sensation.

Dark magic.

It sang to me, but not a song I wanted to hear. Even the evil that had made up part of Ash, the soultree of the Threefold Spiral Coven, had not felt quite like this. There was a darkness here of an entirely different order.

Steeling myself, I made it to the wall and looked down into the pit. The only illumination came from Yelena's flashlight.

For a moment all I saw was black glass, sucking in the light and giving nothing back. A darkness with shapes inside it. The dark workings I sensed were *in* that pit, and they called to me. I shuddered.

"The training place," Yelena said.

There *was* movement in there. It wasn't my imagination.

The pit below was much larger than the viewing circle. It was full of bodies, most lying down. They were naked. Some were wolves, slowly changing back. One or two were on their knees, trying to get their feet under them. As I watched, one of those fell over and his whole body started shaking violently.

This was where the new wolves were coming from. This was Matlal's and Gálvez's answer to the halfy ritual. There were dozens of them down there, suffering. Dying.

"We've got to get them—"

Yelena grabbed my arm.

"Nothing we can do," she said. "Already dead. Is poison gas. A fail safe. Electricity goes off, gas released. Strong enough to kill Were, also strong enough for Athanate."

Her flashlight steadied on one motionless face.

The woman was on her back, eyes staring upwards, bloody foam from her mouth and nose covering her lower face.

All those people—and we couldn't save them. The horror and cruelty of it was unfathomable.

"Why?" I asked through numb lips.

"I don't know," Yelena said. "But we ask where all the new wolves come from."

I nodded. "It's here."

She played the beam around the pit. There had to be more than a hundred bodies in there. New bodies. And beneath them, older bodies, in layers. Some half eaten. The lowest layer had bare bones showing.

I still felt sick, but my mind had started working again, asking questions, trying to figure it all out. If they were new werewolves, why put them down there?

Why kill them if the building lost power?

Why was I sensing so much magic? When I did the halfy rituals, we raised power, the halfies found their wolf forms, and the magic dissipated. This was some kind of ongoing working.

"Tara?"

My twin sister manifested in her wolf form, standing on the viewing glass, her breath coming in a whine of distress.

They smell wrong, she said and disappeared again.

She was right. Buried in my reaction to the feel of the dark magic, there was another sensation. It wasn't the smell of the gas—I was sure the pit was airtight. It was a smell that hung in the basement from the times that the pit had been opened. It was like a werewolf marque. The Chihuahua pack had a marque that I'd been breathing during the attack, and it wasn't that.

It spoke to me of sickness, like the smell of gangrene, or...

A memory of something like it remained just out of reach, and I was distracted as a group of White Sands came down the stairs. I ordered some to search all the storerooms quickly, others to videotape evidence. The ones who managed not to start retching when they saw what was in the pit.

The clock was ticking. We had five minutes.

Whatever method Gálvez had used to create new werewolves quickly was so awful it killed many of the people subjected to it. And while they were being changed to werewolves, they were so monstrous and uncontrollable that Gálvez had them killed if the power in the building failed. This was a method that required ongoing magic, and something that gave them a distinct marque. And produced werewolves who joined in the behavior of the local packs.

There was no more movement from inside the pit.

Surely most had been victims rather than volunteers. Would there have been a way to repair whatever damage had been done to them, if we'd saved them?

I would never know. I turned away, sickened.

I was needed upstairs.

Outside, it was like a scene from hell.

Clouds of smoke and dust billowed across the courtyard and through the gaping holes torn in the building, lit up red by fires, white by flashlights and flares.

One team was in the final moments of disassembling the weapons on the rig.

Across ground covered in the rubble of Astilla de Luna, another team was unrolling cords to explosives that they'd planted on all the surviving load-bearing structures. We were not taking chances with electronic detonation signals tonight, and we weren't leaving this building standing.

A couple of helicopters circled in, searchlights stabbing down into the mayhem to check that the landing spaces marked out by flares were safe.

High-clearance off-road trucks were bringing in Rita's cubs.

Mykayla tapped me on the shoulder. "Team 7 in Villa Ahumada confirms the local police cars disabled."

I nodded. "They're done then, tell them to make their way home by their assigned routes."

Zane loomed up on my other shoulder.

"Santa Ana?" he asked.

That was where the Sonoran pack's HQ was situated. We hadn't had the time and people to hit it at the same time. It was a day's drive to the west, so Zane wouldn't have the advantage of surprise that we'd used here. We couldn't use the helicopters, because we needed them to get the rest of us back over the border. We'd run out of ammunition for the naval gun. We'd wrecked the rig.

There were a hundred reasons not to hit the Sonoran pack, and I'd tried to simply defer the decision when we'd been planning. Hit the two biggest threats and take that as a win.

But Zane's concern was legitimate. Even though the Sonorans weren't as powerful as the Chihuahua or Baja packs, they regularly attacked the Tucson pack, and that meant they were attacking the League. They had to be dealt with sometime.

More important, the sickness I felt—that we all felt—over what we'd seen tonight was burning inside of us. The little children, bought and sold into sexual slavery; the dying werewolves in the pit. All the atrocities that the Mexican Were, under Matlal's influence, were trying to spread into our territory.

They had to be stopped.

We'd already made some alternative plans that grafted Zane's additional objectives onto mine; it was time to set them in motion.

"I can take teams 3 and 5," Mykayla said. "All of them want to do this, but those are the steadiest. They should be enough, and if they're not, we'll still be a small enough group to back off and disappear."

I snorted. Six months ago, the focus of this girl's life had been raves. Well, that and getting horizontal with Bian. The last two months had brought a rush of changes and skills; not a new person, but certainly a changed one.

And the thing was, Zane needed someone to balance him out. *He* wouldn't back off and disappear if it were up to him. He'd think that would diminish his alpha authority. Maybe it would.

But if he had someone else to blame it on?

"You let Scott off the leash," Mykayla prompted me when I didn't answer immediately.

"I let him go with Annie, who has a sound tactical understanding and a feeling for risks," I replied. "Which of you two has that?"

Zane laughed and pointed at Mykayla.

"Make it small," I said. "The option we called Piano. The best four from the White Sands pack and eight from teams 3 and 5. Take the off-road trucks and cut cross-country to reach the highways. Hit them hard and fast tomorrow night. Get out within ten minutes. Hurt them, but you have no other objectives, except to get yourselves back home."

The pair of them trotted off, appropriating trucks and picking their teams, some of them literally just before they got into the helicopters.

"He'll spend the next day trying to get into her pants," Alex muttered as he came up beside me.

"As long as he's focused when it matters. Any other time, best of luck to both of them."

Alex smiled.

One of the helicopters took off, fully laden. The off-road pickups began to disperse.

The second helicopter was loading bodies. The TacNet had been whispering names in my ear. Three White Sands wolves. Four El Paso. Three of the cubs out on the perimeter. I'd wanted to hit Mauricio Gálvez's pack so hard and fast that we didn't take any casualties, but that was never going to happen.

Every name hurt, because there was nowhere else that list ended up but at my door. I'd planned this whole thing. Every death was my responsibility.

Sensing my thoughts, Alex squeezed my arm.

"It's a good operation. We're nearly done," he said.

I shook my head. "Not till we're home."

Yelena joined us and indicated with a jut of her jaw. "Last cubs in. And Rita."

Through the ochre clouds of dust and smoke, three figures emerged, walking from the dark perimeter into the harsh glare of the lights.

Two of them were carrying large bags. Rita sent them to the helicopter while she came on alone.

There was blood all over her, but I suspected none of it was hers.

She'd gone to her cougar. I could see it in the way she walked, the look on her face, the way her clothes had been hastily replaced.

She was holding something in one hand, letting it swing and bump against her leg, as if she'd forgotten she was carrying it.

But as she got nearer, she tossed it at my feet.

It was a human head.

"Gálvez," she said.

The alpha. He'd had a reputation for being strong in a fight, but I guessed that hadn't worked well against a were-cougar.

"He made a run for it," she said. "Had two lieutenants with him. Carrying bags of money. Got all of them. Only that group on the ATVs got away."

She was like this after fights—strangely disconnected from what was around her. As if the cougar had leaked into her and she needed to keep everything damped down until the killing fever was finally gone.

"You're with Alex and me," I said to her. "Helicopter ride home, departing now."

I put an arm around her and steered her towards the last of the helicopters. I left Gálvez's head in the dust. But I also left Rosa's bones in the pit. There were limits to what I could do in the time I was given.

We lifted off thirty seconds later, Rita squashed between Alex and me, her eyes closed and a slow peace descending on her.

As we raced northwards, there was the flash of a huge explosion behind us, and Astilla de Luna disappeared forever into dust and darkness.

Chapter 18

"Are you okay?"

Alex's voice was quiet compared to the noise of the helicopter, but our heads were close together over the sleeping form of Rita.

"No. Not really."

He didn't push, but my response wasn't enough. I owed him more of an explanation.

"We killed a lot of people," I said.

"Not a single one of them—"

"I know. Not one of them was innocent. All involved in everything Gálvez was doing. Also they wouldn't have hesitated if the roles were reversed. I know all that."

"Then what?"

"When I was in Ops 4-10, everything was clear. Us. Them. We had a mission and that mission was sometimes that we killed them. When I left, I wanted to put that behind me. Find other ways. This? It's a bit like being right back in the unit."

"A bit?" He snorted. "It's a by-the-manual Ops 4-10 operation. Deniability. Secrecy. Mission parameters. Objectives. Then plan, infiltrate, recon, prepare, strike hard and fast, get out even faster. Leave no one behind. You're even using the old Ops 4-10 border crossing procedures."

He was right. We were. Down to that last detail about getting home safely. Colonel Laine had quietly checked the old border protocols we had used, and found enough of them still in place. It was far from safe, and we couldn't assume everyone would just blink and look away, but no one was going to scramble a couple of F-16s to check us out.

In fact, the majority of the infrastructure outside of the detailed attack plan had been put in place by the Colonel. All of it based on what we'd used so often, before the unit had been disbanded.

We'd deviate from those Ops 4-10 procedures once across the border. Each helicopter had a target for a remote landing. Each landing site had a couple of pickups waiting. We'd all filter back into El Paso at dawn, and the helicopters would scatter to different places all over the south. Even the deviation was somehow like Ops 4-10 in style.

"It is," I agreed. "And it's like putting on an old jacket; familiar and comfortable, in some ways. But..." I hesitated. "Before, I was just following orders. I trusted the people above me in the chain of command to decide what targets to hit."

Alex snorted.

"I know. Some of them turned out not to be trustworthy. But the thing was, the decisions of whether and who to kill used to be above my pay grade. Now I'm making them, and…" I sighed. "It weighs heavily, that's all."

He touched my face gently. "I know. But I trust you. The others trust you too, or they wouldn't follow."

I leaned my forehead against his. His faith in me helped. I just hoped it wasn't misplaced.

After a little while I said, "But in answer to your question, I don't miss this life. I'll use the skills when I need to, when it serves a purpose, but I've moved on."

I shifted so my mouth was closer to his ear, so I was almost breathing my words. "My new life is so much… fuller. So much more satisfying."

He growled, and the sound reached deliciously into me.

Rita had woken as I moved and she'd heard that exchange. There was a chuckle, muffled against my shoulder, but she didn't offer to get out of the way. She was content where she was.

In a more profound way, so was I. She'd volunteered to move temporarily from the Albuquerque pack to Denver as part of a gesture from Felix and Cameron, but she wasn't going back now. My unusual House and pack suited her better. She had quickly become one of mine, katikia to House Farrell, lieutenant in the Deauville pack.

With everything going on, I hadn't tasted her light and spicy Blood in over a week, and my fangs throbbed with remembered pleasure. I pushed the thought of it aside. Not cool in the tight confines of the helicopter. *Not* a good idea in front of my husband at the moment, who had restrained himself since I'd arrived in El Paso. And whose eyes, I could tell even in the darkness, had gone gold.

We were back in El Paso as dawn shaded the eastern sky.

Our rendezvous was the El Paso pack's old brewery in the armpit between the interstates, and hard up against the railroad.

The pack had cleaned the offices, brought in tables, chairs and a bank of computers. The plumbing was connected and a row of showers had been installed. A quiet area had been set aside with cots.

Restraint was still the order of the day; I insisted there were no premature celebrations, despite pushback from the pack members. I had to explain that the operation wasn't over until everyone was back home. No beer, boasting and congratulations until I saw the last straggler was back across the border. That meant waiting for Annie to report back about Baja, and Zane to report about Sonoma.

I could have added that it wouldn't really be a complete success until I had the proof I needed to persuade both the Athanate and Were communities that Matlal and Basilikos were not only the enemy, but that their activities were more widespread than we'd thought, and an imminent threat to all of us. We needed to work together, and we needed to take the attack to them before they became powerful enough to do serious damage.

I still got glares for being a hard-ass killjoy, but I ignored it as I quietly debriefed every wolf who'd been with us, took their bodycam footage and directed them to showers and bed. Told them to wait.

David and Matt arrived an hour after I settled in for my vigil.

They caught the mood and settled down quickly with computers to start the process of pulling the information from hard disks and cellphones that we'd brought back from Juárez and Villa Ahumada.

Alex and I started reviewing the body cam footage, searching for anything we'd missed with our own eyes.

Incongruous take-out pizza arrived for breakfast. I rolled my eyes, but took a slice.

Someone noticed I wasn't pleased. Minutes later there was another delivery and we had to put tables aside for the spread of machaca con huevo, quesadillas, chimichanga, fajitas, enchiladas, burritos, chile sausages, eggs, beans and dishes I simply didn't recognize from a dozen different stores.

Coffee started flowing.

Werewolves stopped grumbling and gradually relaxed from the post-action high. They kept it muted, but as more kept arriving, the packs started to build a quiet Call of satisfaction.

Someone had put up a corkboard outside the offices with a picture of everyone they knew in the Chihuahua pack hierarchy.

At the top was Mauricio Gálvez, with a line through his picture.

Three of his four known lieutenants got lines through them. Below them, the Juárez pack: the alpha and all five of his lieutenants got lines through them. Where we didn't have images, we had body counts and estimates.

Annie called. All safe, and the Baja pack's HQ was a smoking ruin.

We started a second corkboard for Baja. Annie didn't have any information about anyone who had been in that HQ, but she gave me the figures on the earlier attack in Tijuana and confirmation of the death of the sub-pack's alpha.

More of the El Paso pack came in, men and women who hadn't been involved but wanted to know what happened. Some White Sands came in as well. A team assembled to work on cover stories for our deaths from the two attacks. Another to monitor chatter on the Mexican police channels. Another to check whether any questions were being raised this side of the border.

I got a message from Connor and Rebecca. They were on their way to Denver with the children who'd been sold by their own families. I'd already messaged Bian and put them in touch. I could rest easy on them.

In the afternoon, I showered and dozed, trying not to think too much about Zane and Mykayla in Santa Ana, who'd be working recon on the Sonoran HQ. I had given them a template for an attack which *should* be safe, but no plan survives contact with the enemy.

At 4 p.m., one of the El Paso lieutenants approached Alex and me with a cellphone.

"Alphas, it's Agustín Díaz."

"As in the alpha of the Coahuila pack?" Alex asked.

The guy nodded.

Alex looked at me. I waved him on.

"See what he has to say. He'll be happier talking to you."

Agustín Díaz wasn't the same as Mauricio Gálvez. As a pack, the Coahuila were strong. They'd taken over the territory all the way down to the Gulf, absorbing the coastal Tamaulipas packs as they did. They pushed and probed across the border in the Big Bend's pack area, but not like the Juárez pack. I didn't think they'd been influenced by Basilikos.

Díaz was also smart. As soon as he had news about Juárez and Villa Ahumada, he'd known who had to be responsible. He'd been well aware of the way Juárez had been attacking us. It seems we'd impressed him with the thoroughness of our eventual response.

He was making very careful inquiries.

Alex put him on speaker as the conversation unfolded.

Are you moving into Juárez? The whole Chihuahua territory?

Alex told him we had no such plans. For the moment. It would depend on how neighborly any new packs might turn out to be. Enough was enough, didn't Díaz agree?

Yes, Díaz did agree. The behavior of the Juárez pack had been shocking and obviously ill-advised. So...

Would we object if a new, strong pack was set up in Juárez? An old-fashioned pack. A neighborly pack. Not interested in crossing the border. A sub-pack of Coahuila.

Alex said we wouldn't, but pointed out that we had extremely close links with Big Bend.

There had been occasional minor difficulties in the park area, Díaz conceded. The exuberance of cubs, he assured us. Wouldn't happen again.

"We're very old-fashioned in the League," Alex continued. "We don't hold with trafficking or drugs. We respect the human society we live in."

I listened hard to Díaz's voice as he responded. I didn't think he was lying when he said the Coahuila didn't get involved in that sort of behavior. From what I could hear, he was almost offended at the implication.

Alex looked at me, if I wanted to say something.

"Señor Díaz, esta es Amber Farrell."

"He escuchado muchas cosas sobre usted, señora Farrell."

Yes, I bet he'd heard a lot about me.

I went on in my best Spanish: "It seems you're more like us than Juárez. Packs who share the same outlook should be more comfortable with each other. Form groups that understand the principles they share."

But the approach was too obvious. I couldn't catch everything he said, even though he said it politely. But I understood he wasn't willing to contemplate joining the League yet.

At least not for positive reasons. I had one more try.

"Being in the League is a defense against Basilikos."

His reaction to that was a whole lot more interesting, and I could only just keep up with the flow of Spanish as he got more animated. What caught me most was the word *rabioso*. Rabid. He was making a connection between packs who worked with Basilikos and the insanity of rabid dogs.

Not *delirante* or *loco*, but *rabioso*.

Why choose that word?

I was too busy trying to keep up with him.

At the bottom of it, he didn't want to back the League against Basilikos, and he was waiting to see how it came out. Maybe we were all doomed and the rabiosos would flood through everywhere.

His antipathy to Basilikos was making him talkative, to a degree.

I tried to counter his argument by saying the League was associated with House Altau and the League would form part of the Assembly in due course, but he stopped me dead. To him, the Assembly was Athanate politics and he didn't want to get drawn into it. He said outright that Basilikos wouldn't bother with the Were, other than to progress their fight against Panethus, so his best policy was to not get involved between Basilikos and Panethus.

Alex and I pushed back with Basilikos wanting to fight one enemy at a time, and that they would regard anyone not on their side as an enemy. But as the exchange progressed, instead of Basilikos, I said Matlal and got an immediate response.

"Enough," he said. "You're looking over my shoulder, all the way down to Yucatán. Maybe you're right, but for me, I look at Louisiana. Your grand alphas are there, trying to expand this League. I hear there are difficulties, yes? I hear many things, all the way around the Gulf Coast. There are difficulties for the witches too. Maybe even the vampires. To me, this is interesting. Should you not also be looking at Louisiana?"

I couldn't get drawn into discussing Athanate issues, but there was an obvious question: did he mean a particular witch? I asked it using the phrase that the trafficked girl had used. The witch queen of the swamp: *la bruja reina del pantano.*

"I hear many things," he repeated, slowly. "But I warn you, I do not know. Speak to your Athanate associates in New Orleans. Speak to the packs of Louisiana, with great care. Speak to the covens. I hear this, that these new wolves, these rabid ones... we have the witch queen to thank."

"Rabioso?" I asked. "No loco?"

"Rabid," he replied in English. "It is like a contagion. A werewolf may go rogue, yes. Loco. All can see plainly. The *rabioso*... no. It's in the blood, hidden, then too late. I don't trust them. I don't trust the smell. I don't allow any here. But maybe I am just old-fashioned. Or maybe the answers are in Louisiana. I hear many rabioso have gone to packs along the Gulf Coast."

That tallied with what Felix and Cameron had said—that the packs in Louisiana weren't as concerned about the halfy ritual. They were getting new members from other sources—most likely, Gálvez's pit.

But the 'rabioso' part of it was disturbing.

We'd reached the end of what he knew, and he wouldn't say any more. "I don't wish to be involved. Here, in our great territories along the Rio Grande, we will behave with respect towards each other. As the American children say: are we good?"

Alex looked at me and I nodded.

"We're good," Alex said. "Zane or I will call you soon. Maybe we can meet for a dinner."

I'd need to be in Louisiana long before that happened, which I regretted. A dinner with four alphas around the table would have been... interesting.

Díaz said his farewells formally, and added *cuidaos*. Take care. I had a feeling he meant it entirely literally.

The El Paso lieutenant whose cell we used for the call took it back thoughtfully.

"More movement out of the old stick in one call than years of talking at him," he said, and immediately stiffened. He'd just said something disrespectful about the Oakens, the former El Paso alphas. Some might have regarded that as disloyalty, despite the fact that we were now the alphas.

Alex and I ignored it.

"He thinks packs that work with Basilikos are rabid?" I asked. "Is there some subtle meaning there I'm not getting?"

Alex frowned. "Not just a madness, a sickness?" He shrugged. "Not exactly like going rogue. Contagious. Something that would spread through the pack."

I thought again of the sick smell in the basement at Astilla de Luna, the dark workings. Rabioso. It was all connected—maybe to this witch queen, whoever she was?

It was frustrating. We were close to something important, something that clearly needed investigation, but I needed to be in Louisiana to investigate it, and I had to finish off here first.

David, sitting a couple of tables away, broke my chain of thought.

"We're not getting much from the hard disks," he said. "The encryption needs more processing power than what we have here. But we're closer with the cellphones. Two points. First, even if we can't read it, there's a *lot* of traffic with Louisiana. Second, we're feeding the cracking software with words and phrases we think might turn up in messages. Y'know, common things that might be said. When Díaz started talking about *bruja reina del pantano*, I put that in."

"And?"

"*Lots* of hits. And while 'witch' and 'swamp' might be common words for them to use, a specific phrase like 'witch queen of the swamp', well, you'd think that would be an outlier."

"Can you crack the rest on that basis?"

"In time. It's not a straight replacement code or anything. Just because we have the vowels or strings of letters lined up from one word, doesn't mean that tells us the codes for those in another word."

Matt sat back and scrubbed his fingers though his hair.

"There's another word that comes up sometimes with 'reina'," he said. "'Diamantes'. Diamonds."

"Queen of Diamonds?" Alex said. "They're talking card games?"

David shook his head. "We tried that. No other common references to cards. Maybe 'Queen of Diamonds' is some kind of a title, and 'witch queen of the swamp' is a description."

Alex looked over at me. "I don't like where this is all pointing. Can you delay going down to Louisiana for a couple of days? Wait till I can come with you?"

"Even with no more interference from the Juárez pack, it's going to take you more time than that to do the handover properly. And even if it were only a couple of days, you know Felix will hear what we've done here in that time. I need to be face to face with him and Cameron to make them understand why we did this. I need to be on the road tomorrow. There's a lot of Texas to cross."

Chapter 19

The old brewery got quieter as the day ebbed away.

By sunset I realized I was leaking my tension into a werewolf Call that everyone else was picking up. I couldn't stop it. I knew that out near Santa Ana, Zane and Mykayla would have made their plans and be waiting for full night to fall. Maybe even waiting for the small hours.

The Sonora pack would have had a day to prepare. They would have heard about the Chihuahua pack in Juárez and Villa Ahumada, they would have heard about the Baja pack in Tijuana and Ensenada. They could draw a line on the map and see it passed right through them.

I stated to second guess myself on the decision to let Zane and Mykayla off the leash.

But then of course, Zane wasn't on my leash. He'd followed orders up to the point where we finished at Astilla de Luna. That was entirely in his interests. Maybe he would have revolted if I'd tried ordering him back, because Sonora was also in his interest.

None of their cellphones was active until they got back, so there was nothing I could do about it anyway.

Except worry.

Dinner came and went.

All the moving around and talking slowly petered out. We gave up on the offices and went down to the large room I'd used on the first visit, so that everyone could sit there and wait for the news to come in.

At 10:25 pm, a woman who was monitoring internet network traffic around Santa Ana raised a finger.

"Reports of gunfire outside of town," she said, and a chill settled over the pack.

She was the limit of surveillance we had. I hadn't ordered more for Santa Ana because I never really expected we'd add it onto our objectives. In Villa Ahumada, the central objective, Matt had come up with sneaky ways of monitoring call volumes and internet traffic right into the ranch. But in Santa Ana, we were nearly blind.

"Nothing about the police," the woman said.

Fifteen minutes later: "Must have been a false alarm."

We went back to waiting as the hours dragged by.

Maybe they'd decided against attacking the Sonora pack, and were already at one of the crossing points. Any moment they'd call and we'd laugh about it.

Both Alex and I had our cells on the table in front of us.

At 1:45 exactly, Alex's cell pinged.

Zane's number.

Alex snatched it up before I could, and hit the speaker icon.

"Hey, good morning! You shouldn't have waited up." Zane's voice, and at his irritating best.

"What happened?"

"They put up barricades on the road to the ranch, and they had guards with machine guns and shit like that. Not interested in sticking my arm into a hornets' nest."

"So you called it off?"

"Not exactly. My chiquita—"

He cut off. There was some noise in the background that sounded like a fist striking a body.

Zane came back: "My esteemed, excitable, hybrid snake-wolf colleague, Mykayla, proposed a strategy to achieve a good result under the circumstances."

"We poked the nest with a stick." Mykayla's voice came on. "By which I mean we took out a couple of guards with long shots and then ran. They were in two minds, so they split their forces. One group to stay and guard the ranch in case we were a diversion. The other to chase us."

"And you ambushed the chasers?" I asked.

"Yeah. Had the M2s all ready, set up with intersecting arcs of fire, and we planted explosives beside the road."

"A killing zone."

"Uh-huh."

Mykayla's voice was fading. Zane came back on.

"Worked. Then we scooted for the border. Used one of the tunnels the Tucson pack captured last month. We've left the trucks on the other side and wired them and the tunnel with the last of the explosives. Tucson are going to watch them for a couple of days. Anyone from the Sonoran pack stupid enough to mess with the trucks or take the tunnel will die. Otherwise we'll retrieve the trucks and then blow the tunnel anyway."

"Casualties?" I asked.

"Nothing serious. Very useful having a vamp along for stopping blood loss in an emergency."

The sound of another blow. Mykayla was going to keep violently pointing out when he was rude.

"Yes, about that," Zane continued after a pause. "I'd like to use this opportunity to borrow Mykayla. I want to learn more about this training you're doing with the cubs." He paused again. "I'm impressed. I want to roll it out."

I snorted. "Hold your horses. Take the points separately. If Mykayla wants the pleasure of your company for a while and feels happy to give you her insight into the training, that's okay with me."

Mykayla said something in the background that made Zane laugh.

"You do need to return to Denver, Mykayla, but a couple of days is not a problem." I heard an acknowledgment before I went on. "Now, about the training itself. The cubs are the result of an intensive two-month regime with input from all sides. Setting that up, like a kind of franchise, to train everyone in the League in a short time isn't doable."

"Yeah, got that," Zane said. "But even half of what they've done—"

"Finally," I cut across him, "it's up to Felix and Cameron to give it the green light. Don't talk to them yet. I'll call you when I'm in front of them, and you put your weight behind my request to roll it out in some form."

"Okay. Deal. So then... we'll be stopping off in Tucson and Albuquerque before getting back to El Paso."

"I'll be here," Alex said. "Amber will be in Louisiana."

We ended the call.

Alex shook his head. "Like I told you, Zane's going to spend half the time trying to get into her pants. I can practically hear him drooling."

I laughed.

"You think he's wasting his time?" Alex said. "I mean, that's one of the things that really turns him on: that sort of cool disinterest, but Mykayla..."

"It's true Mykayla was exclusively into girls, and she still puts out that vibe, but she's Athanate now."

"That makes a difference?" Alex stopped himself. "Silly question, 'course it does."

"Yeah."

The celebrations I'd held back all day were now taking off in the brewery. Really taking off. No one parties like a werewolf. They'd be dancing on the tables in ten minutes' time. Clothing would become optional shortly after that.

I knew I should stay and party with them, but I'd been up for more than sixty hours straight.

Alex also knew it. "Head on to my rental house," he said. "I'll drink a few with the pack and make sure everything here gets cleaned up, and all the evidence stuff gets sent up to Haven."

"You got it." I stopped and slapped my head. "Damn!"

"What?" He touched my arm and frowned in concern.

I leaned forward and whispered: "I forgot to pack my PJs. I'm gonna have to sleep *naked*."

His eyes went all gold again.

"Hurry home, wolf," I said and walked out, with my hips still talking to him.

He had a sprawling five-bedroom rented up near where the scenic drive skirted the south side of the Franklin Park foothills.

There were guards. A couple of cubs from the White Sands pack, fresh and eager to show their worth. Having guards meant Yelena, Keith and Julie got to go off-duty together and they piled into one of the larger bedrooms. There would be some horizontal celebrations going on.

"Sleep well," I called out through the rapidly closing door.

Rita grinned and nodded her head to the outside.

"The youngsters want to hear what happened. I'll give them the bare bones before I head to bed."

"Thanks." I left her and headed for Alex's room.

I made it from the shower to the bed. Just.

Chapter 20

I was having a wonderful dream.

One of those where I float on the water and feel the warmth of the sun spreading all over my naked body. Butterflies fluttered down out of a clear blue sky and landed on me.

Ah. Not a dream. And not butterflies.

Kisses.

"You smell like a brewery," I muttered.

"Well, that would be appropriate," Alex growled back from somewhere around my belly button, making my insides melt. "I'll go shower."

"Don't you dare stop, wolf." He nipped me gently in response. "Oh! What big teeth you have."

I gripped him by the ears, all the better to guide his kisses.

"What a big, clever tongue, too."

But not what I wanted right now.

I grabbed him and pulled him up the bed, tearing at his clothes, wrapping legs around him.

Didn't want the holding back, didn't need the careful lover this early morning. Wanted the rawness, the wolf in him. Wanted him to *take*. Wanted to get drunk on his uncontrollable desire for me.

Seemed that was fine with him. Too much time away.

Too much flirting, not enough—

Oh!

He was inside me. His weight on his locked arms. Looking down at me as I melted in the heat from his eyes.

Deep. All the way in. My back arched and I stretched my arms above my head, loving the response that got, loving the wave on wave of lust that I was causing in him.

Teeth on my neck. My nipple. So sensitive, it almost hurt. Wrenched a gasp from me.

Excited him.

Withdrawing slightly. Returning. Filling me.

None of the usual Athanate tantric stuff was going to work, and I didn't want it right now. Maybe later.

I reached, clutched at him, pulled him closer, wrapped myself around him, felt his arms unlock, close around my shoulders, his weight pressing on me and then we were moving together.

Fast. Urgent. Primal.

Muscles flexing under my hands. The glorious, slippery, sweaty bunching of his back and his butt, pushing my thighs apart, driving him into me, again and again.

A storm raced up on us. The world went dark and narrow, nothing but the desperate, frenzied pounding of our bodies, the soaring pleasure, sweeping us away, breaking over us. I screamed against his fever-hot skin as my climax exploded through my whole body.

We collapsed, trembling with the shock that loving each other always brought, and I chuckled, happy at the glorious, messy absurdity of it, the way it felt so right.

Content, satisfied as a woman, a wife.

Alex was already thinking of the other satisfaction I craved.

His weight still trapping me beneath him, he moved a little until my face was pressed against his neck, and I could sense his pulse beneath my lips, urgent with the racing of his heart.

He'd even learned a bit of Athanate. Bian had taught him an old-fashioned, courtly phrase.

"Feed, beloved."

Breath ragged with anticipation of Blood, I licked his neck. Before I buried my fangs in him, I whispered how I was going to make love to him in round two.

"Again?"

Much later.

We were comfortable, lying like spoons in the bed, and his interest in a *fourth* round was becoming obvious as it pressed against my butt.

I had no objection, but of course there was a tap on the door.

"Come in."

Yelena, with my cellphone that she'd stolen again last night.

"You sleep well?" she asked, smirking. She held out the cell. "Is Bian. We make brunch in half an hour for lazy people."

It wasn't too late for breakfast, but it was a subtle reminder about the time. However important this morning had been on a personal level, I was due in Louisiana. And I was in a race against rumors of what had happened reaching Felix and Cameron. I needed to be there to handle the flow of information and provide the context.

I'd messaged Haven and Jen a couple of times last night and promised to tell them more this morning, so it was hardly surprising they were chasing me.

"Gang's all here," Bian said on the cell. "Diana, Gwen, Tullah. Got Jen on a conference relay from New York. Spill."

Alex went off and showered while I greeted everyone and then gave them the more detailed highlights.

"A mixed result so far then," Diana said, as I ended. "Unequivocal success tactically, and yet the strategic aim of tying Basilikos into the policies of the border packs is still unproven."

I stated to disagree, but she went on.

"*We* don't need more convincing, Amber. We need something that will convince the Assembly, including the Were and the Adepts."

"We'll find it," I said. "David and Matt are heading back to Denver. The data extracted from the hard drives and cellphones is encrypted, but they'll crack it. We already have fragments."

"Time is not on our side." Diana paused. "Agent Ingram delayed as much as he could without compromising everything, but his boss at the FBI is going to be more difficult to persuade and much quicker to escalate. His boss' boss even more so."

"But there's a clear connection between Tucek and Matlal," I said. "Tucek and her House rescued him from the incompetents in the Hidden Path security teams, and took him down to Yucatán. There's evidence that some of her House were at Astilla de Luna, even if she wasn't."

"Maybe. Again, you don't need to convince me. As far as the Assembly is concerned, your 'allegations' about Tucek are untested. She has already insisted that to challenge her, we would need to convene a full Assembly..."

"And we can't convene an Assembly, with Truth Sensors, without potentially compromising the whole structure that Skylur and Diakon Huang have put in place to neutralize the Hidden Path and manage Emergence from the sidelines. Shit." I blew out a long breath.

Bian spoke. "Do we know who in Louisiana they were speaking to?"

"We didn't know last night, except that it wasn't with any of the comms addresses and numbers we have for House Labastide in New Orleans, or the other Houses in Lafayette, Baton Rouge, Alexandria and Shreveport. I'm not sure if things progressed from that; I've been... asleep."

I could hear the smirk in Bian's voice. "Are you there, Alex? Did she sleep well?"

Alex had returned, drying his body in a distracting way. He grunted and Bian laughed.

"Good morning, husband," Jen purred. "Love you."

"I love you, honey," Alex said, trying not to blush as he hurried on. "As for the analysis of data—nothing new. David and Matt should be back in Denver soon. They packed up last night and got a flight this morning."

"And I have to pack and head for Louisiana today," I added. "It's all very well concentrating on convincing the Assembly, but I also need to convince Felix and Cameron that what we did was justified, and not disrespectful of their authority."

Gwen cleared her throat. "Flying or driving?"

"I'm taking the Hill Bitch and another truck," I said. "Can't take the arsenal on a commercial plane, and Jen's Pilatus isn't available this week."

"I see," Gwen said. "How soon do you think you can check on Gabrielle? I haven't heard from her since shortly after she arrived in Louisiana. We knew communication would be sporadic; the Lafayette coven doesn't believe in using electronic devices, or even electricity, I believe. They're completely off the grid. But it's been a couple of days now."

That did worry me, especially in light of what Díaz had said about 'rabioso', and problems that might involve the Adepts in Louisiana, as well as Were and Athanate.

"I'll get out there as soon as possible," I assured her. "Text me the address."

Heading out to the coven's headquarters meant I would need to get off the interstate. Which meant I would need to talk to the Lafayette Athanate, House Broussard, as a courtesy. I couldn't remember much detail about them. Which meant I would need to read up on them before I arrived.

None of which mattered more than making sure Gabrielle was okay.

Bian stopped me from going down a rabbit hole of worry. "Scott and Mykayla..." she said.

"They'll be back, and they know they're expected to take part in the second phase of the experiment," I said. "They're... dallying. That's a nice word, isn't it?"

I heard laughter on the loudspeaker. Everyone had connected the dots as to why Scott and Mykayla wouldn't be back for a couple of days. Whether that was accurate in Mykayla's case would be something we'd find out later.

"I disagree," Alex said. "It's not dallying. I think it's vitally important."

"How interesting. Please explain, Alexander," Diana came back.

Alex looked at me. I had the beginning of an idea where he was going with this, but I gestured for him to go on.

"We all know what Amber went through during our 'Christmas vacation'," he said. "And whether or not that knocked something loose in her head, she came out of it thinking politically, thinking about how much stronger we could be, as a pack, if we had strong bonds with packs in New Mexico and California."

Strong bonds. I had to laugh. When Weaver had used a working on me that reduced my inhibitions, I'd contemplated climbing into bed with Zane and Billie, possibly at the same time.

But Alex was right; if I'd made it work, the increase in cohesion and the boost in dominance we'd all get from it would have been enormous. With Cameron away, Zane was in effect the alpha of the New Mexico packs, and Billie had moved into a similar position in southern California. That was some serious juice in Were terms.

Then I stopped laughing. Alex had a point.

"The Were and Athanate do have a feudal sort of structure," Diana said. "And a feudal lord would marry his daughters off to neighbors to cement alliances. Amber's ehvasi are achieving the same sort of political ends. Fascinating."

"Okay, folks." I brought the conversation to an end as Yelena waved at us through the door. "Enough, apart from me restating I have no ambitions to take over the Were from Felix and Cameron. If these connections make *their* foundation more secure, then that's a good result."

"We need more time to talk," Gwen said, and the others joined in with their agreements.

Gwen went on, "Specifically, we need to talk about Temple 132."

That last temple. The stepped pyramid. The obsidian breastplate. The other temples we'd investigated in the City of Lost Gods had merged into an indistinct memory, like half-forgotten dreams, but *that* temple hadn't.

And there was the presence in my mind that had helped me with de Socorro, and the image I kept getting of the dark, glassy surface that resembled the statue's breastplate. I was beginning to suspect that I'd received more help from our mysterious benefactor, and that he was connected with the temple, and that old god.

If that were true, then he could now reach me outside of the spirit world, which was disturbing.

I told them what I'd experienced.

Gwen's response was quiet and determined. "Don't do any spirit walking without me there. I'm going to go back in right now and check that temple. We need to know what we're dealing with. I'll call back later."

"At least you shouldn't need to use your aura today," Tullah said, but I could hear in her voice that she was concerned.

"Yeah. Today's agenda is a courtesy farewell to House de Socorro, a call on House Broussard, check on Gabrielle, get my ass to New Orleans. But first I have really important stuff like a late breakfast with *coffee* waiting. Promise I'll call again later."

Chapter 21

It was noon, and I hadn't called Haven back because the day felt like it was rushing away.

In fact, time on this trip had been rushing away. Was it only a couple of days ago that I'd been right here, at the gate to the Pointe Hills luxury community where House de Socorro lived?

We were ready to get on the road to Louisiana, but I had decided I should pass by House de Socorro and tell him we were leaving rather than just making a phone call. Try and settle any bad feelings.

Despite Gwen's worries and having to say goodbye to Alex, I'd been feeling good earlier today. On the business side, my visit to El Paso had been a success for the packs and House de Socorro. Seeing my husband... well, I ached in places, but it was the good kind of ache.

But now...

That good feeling was leaking away. I couldn't put my finger on a reason why. I heard nothing but the buzz of cicadas. There was a siesta-time look about the exclusive homes dotted among the hills and trees. The sun made deep shadows beneath trees and softened distant shapes with heat haze.

There was the same barrier gate across the road, the same number to call to get it lifted.

The same difficult-to-define feeling that things weren't right.

I was in the Hill Bitch this time, but she wasn't much of an improvement on the truck I'd last arrived in. Rita had set off ahead of us in that one, for us to catch up later.

I'd been careful with my Athanate manners for this visit, messaging ahead that I was leaving the area and wanted the opportunity to say farewell. I'd given a time and here I was, showered, dressed neatly... and uneasy again.

The response to my earlier message had been terse and unsigned, requesting I call the number when I was at the gate, as I had had to before.

Don't read too much into it, Tara had said, but she was feeling exactly what I was.

I called.

"Hello?"

I'd been expecting Isabel to answer, but the voice on the cell sounded like the maid.

"Amber Farrell, House Farrell," I said. "I messaged this morning."

It was foolish to see problems just because Isabel didn't answer the call. It wasn't her personal number, after all.

"House Farrell. Gina Robinson, kin-Costilla." It *was* the maid, and she sounded as upset as last time. The gate started to rise immediately. "Please come through. It's the second road on the right, Rocky Pointe Drive—"

"I remember the way, thank you."

I ended the call, angry for no particular reason I could point to.

"Problem?" Yelena asked as she drove through.

I shrugged, trying not to overreact. Something *was* wrong, but it could be anything.

"It was the maid who answered," I replied. "She sounds upset again."

Julie leaned forward. "House de Socorro wouldn't fall into the same trap twice, would he? Can't be him. Maybe Ribera has had a problem?"

Julie had given me Nekotsume just a minute before.

"Give me my HK as well," I said. "At this stage, I don't care if it's not polite."

Julie handed me the weapon in the clip holster. "You want us as backup?"

"Just Keith." I hummed for a moment and then added, "When we get there, go up to the top of the drive, turn around and park facing away. Leave the engine running and keep your eyes open."

Yelena frowned.

Julie and Keith quietly checked their Sigs.

I looked at the house as we approached along Rocky Pointe Drive. There were no clues to any disturbance. It was still the same carefully maintained, beautiful setting it had been. The sun was still casting those deep shadows which divided the gardens so precisely into light and shade.

Nothing looked out of place.

But Yelena didn't get to take us up the shingle drive.

The maid, Gina, had hurried down from the house, and she stood in front of the drive entrance, blocking the way. She looked distraught and scared in equal amounts.

"What the hell?" Julie murmured as Yelena slowed to a stop.

"Stay in the car," I said to Keith. "I don't think the maid is going to attack me with her bare hands."

Still, it was such a calculated Athanate insult, I could barely believe it. Gina wasn't Athanate. She was kin to someone called Costilla in House de Socorro, who I hadn't even met. To deny entrance to a visiting Athanate, and then compound it by sending kin to block the road? Bian had told me of petty insults like this that had caused century-long feuds between Houses and only ended when both Athanate involved were dead.

It wasn't so much the insult that upset me, but that de Socorro had made it.

I got out and made a point of feeding Nekotsume's scabbard through my belt.

Gina's eyes fixed on the sword and her face went even paler.

"House Farrell." She bowed deeply and her voice trembled. "I present my sincere apologies for this."

"I'd rather you told me what's happened than present apologies that I guess don't come from your House."

She bowed again and stared fixedly at the ground. "House de Socorro thanks you for your actions in his recent troubles—"

"I can't be bothered to exchange platitudes for you to relay back to House de Socorro, when he has started by insulting me. Did he order Diakon Cuarón not to meet me? Did she accept that?"

She shook her head, and I saw the movement dislodge tears that ran down her cheeks.

"Then I'm going to talk to her." I made to move past her.

The maid collapsed to her knees, folding like a dropped coat.

"No. Please. She's not there," the maid whispered.

Something was very wrong here. Boosted through Yelena, my eukori reached out and tasted nothing but sorrow from inside the house; a grief so profound I didn't want to probe any deeper.

Of course Isabel wasn't obliged to wait around for me to show up. No doubt she was a busy Diakon.

But why was the house filled with grief?

"What happened?" I asked. "When will she be back?"

Gina shook her head again.

"She's dead, House Farrell."

"What?"

It was like a punch to the stomach.

The maid covered her face in her hands and sobbed. I reached out. My touch on her shoulder made her flinch, as if she expected me to harm her.

I knelt beside her.

"Tell me what happened," I said.

Through the tears, she stuttered. "We imprisoned our House..."

"You saved his *life*."

"There is nothing in the Agiagraphos that justifies our actions," she said. "All our lives were forfeit."

It felt as if the ground had opened up beneath me.

Surely, she couldn't mean...

But she did. "Diakon Cuarón offered her life as korheny, as sacrifice of Blood in payment, to plead for the lives of the rest of the House."

I stood up. The world went darker. I couldn't seem to get enough oxygen.

The maid bent forward from kneeling to rest her weight on her hands. It was bizarre, as if she expected me to cut her head off or something. And that she would accept it because it was recognized in the Agiagraphos.

Anger at her and everything about House de Socorro burned the shock out of my system.

"And House de Socorro took that," I shouted. "He took her korheny rather than admit the whole thing was *his* fault. Rather than spend one moment thinking about whether any book could possibly give him the answer to every situation. Rather than offer his *own* life as korheny, which would have been the right thing in this case."

"Boss."

A hand rested on my arm. Yelena had gotten out of the truck and she was standing beside me. Scared I was going to do something I would regret.

She was right. Wolf and Athanate sides of me both hated House de Socorro with a poison that burned like acid in my gut. My vision had locked down until I was barely registering anything other than the path that would take me up to the front door, and inside, to kill de Socorro.

An obsidian darkness descended over my sight, and yet I could see through it. Shapes moved within that darkness and I could tell what they were. I could see the building with walls tottering, door and windows made into great gaping holes that were flooded with fire and pouring out smoke. Like Astilla de Luna.

I can do this. I can will it and I can make it so. I hunger for it.

I shuddered.

I couldn't go down that path. It wasn't the whole House, however weak they were. It was de Socorro. I ran a hand across my eyes, refusing to look at that dark, siren promise of destruction. That offer of power had come on me so quickly. The same source that had helped me save de Socorro would now help me kill him.

I didn't dare go in and confront de Socorro right now, or I would use that power.

Yelena had helped Gina to her feet, and wiped her cheeks with a tissue.

It gave me a chance to get myself under control. To concentrate on turning my anger ice cold.

"You're a messenger, sent by a coward, Gina. It's not your fault. But you *are* a messenger. Fine. I have no platitudes to give you to pass back to de Socorro. I don't think he's fit to be House, let alone fit to have a domain as important as El Paso. The Were community will reject him, and I doubt House Altau will ignore that in these times."

I wasn't sure how much was getting through to her, but I went on.

"I'll leave this household to its grief today, but warn de Socorro to look for sanctuary in Ireland. Tell him to look now. If for some reason Altau does not act against him, he should not consider himself safe. If I ever come across him face to face, I'll call him out. He can go check his precious Agiagraphos; he cannot deny me, or he will be outcast. Tell him, I will call him to the Last Place of Judgement, and there, I will kill him." I grabbed her. "Tell him that, word for word."

Chapter 22

We were an hour outside of El Paso, on I-10, before anyone spoke.

Keith asked me what I'd meant about the Last Place of Judgment.

I was driving, because if I didn't have that to occupy me, I might have gone back and challenged de Socorro regardless.

"It's Athanate history, bound up in their precious Agiagraphos," I said. With Diana and Bian as tutors, I had used my 'rest' in Denver to the maximum. I had a good working knowledge of the Agiagraphos, the important rules that governed the Athanate, and the legends that had formed it.

"A long time ago, sometime between the collapse of the Bronze Age and the start of the Iron Age, Athanate made one of their many attempts to find peace between Athanate and humans. They gathered together and made a city-state called Itrexia, on the shore of the Caspian Sea. That was where they started compiling all their individual versions of the Agiagraphos into the official version everyone refers to today."

I'd fallen into the rhythm of speaking that Diana used, when she talked about these things.

"Part of that lore included a very Athanate way of ending disputes, a method of last resort, by dueling."

I quoted the ancient Athanate saying.

Beyond emotion, there is reason.
Beyond reason, there is logic.
Beyond logic, there is faith.
And beyond faith, there is only iron in the Mandaviran.

"The Mandaviran, also called the Hero's Circle, or the Last Place of Judgement, was a sacred arena with a sand floor. A place for a formal duel when all other methods of resolving disagreements had been exhausted. Iron meant traditional weapons. For protection, they used a *pelea*, which was segmented armor that covered one arm from the shoulder to the hand, like some Roman gladiators had, much later. For attack, the *kinirak*, a sort of sword. Instead of a simple hilt, the kinirak has a brace along the forearm and a handle that stands up at right angles to the brace, so your grip does not bend the wrist. The blade actually starts from the brace and then curves in front. It's about a yard long in total. The brace is strapped in place along your arm."

There was silence as I drove on.

"There are no Mandavirans now," Yelena said. "They were only consecrated by the king of Itrexia, and there is no Itrexia, no king."

"Maybe. But there are still the rules. There is still the challenge, the duel, the pelea and the kinirak. It's all there in the Agiagraphos, for those that think the book must govern all their actions."

"Are you good enough?" Yelena was my instructor in hand-to-hand. She knew exactly how good I was at that, and the answer was still not as good as her. In the same way I was not as good as Diana with the old weapons.

But only the very, very old Houses still practiced for the Mandaviran. It was an oversight that Diana had seen, and it was Diana who had trained me, blade to blade, with my learning boosted by eukori.

"I am not good, but I'm good enough," I said. "House de Socorro probably never practiced with pelea and kinirak. I don't care how many advantages he might think his centuries give him, I will kill him."

"I get you're angry..." Julie started.

"I'm angry at de Socorro. I'm angry at myself. I'm angry that I made such an effort to obey the manners laid down in the Agiagraphos because it gives weight to that book at exactly the time it has to be thrown aside. I'm angry that old Houses can't see that. We're literally tearing out the most important rule in the Agiagraphos—that Athanate hide their presence from humanity—and yet Houses think that rules formed thousands of years ago have relevance today. *More* than relevance. His House saved his life. By the Agiagraphos he should be condemned, but he interprets it in a way that it's everyone else's fault."

Silence for a minute but for the growl of the engine and roar of the tires.

"I'm angry because it's my fault. If I had called Diakon Flavia, de Socorro and Ribera would be dead, and Isabel would be House Cuarón. The Athanate House of El Paso would be strong and flexible. But Isabel put her trust in me, and I allowed her to. So she's dead, the House is ruined and Skylur has to find someone to replace de Socorro."

"It was her decision to avoid calling Flavia," Julie said.

"Yes, she showed she could work without going by the Agiagraphos, and now she's dead."

Julie started to point out my argument was circular, but Keith stopped her.

"Not your fault," Yelena said.

"Tell Isabel that."

That was stupid. I couldn't even think straight so I stopped talking.

A mile later we reached the turnoff for the town of Fort Hancock. I'd told Rita to wait for us there because we were going to divide ourselves between the two trucks and drive through the night.

It was also time to cool down and call Haven.

"Gotta call home. Entertain yourselves," I told the others after we'd filled up the gas.

They had a choice between a couple of stores that looked to be big on chiles, and Angie's Restaurant. Probably also big on chiles. They took the restaurant, promising to get me something to eat on the road.

It took a long half-hour of talking to Diana and Bian before my anger subsided.

"I will call Skylur," Diana said. "It may take a little time, but he will respond to me. He'll replace de Socorro in El Paso."

"Who's available?" Bian asked. "We're stretched."

"That's Skylur's decision, but we could move one of the northern Louisiana Houses. Hamelin in Shreveport, for instance. Or Adair in Amarillo."

Whichever one, it would be a wrench, as complex a process as moving the former El Paso pack to Denver, and exactly what we didn't want to be happening at the same time.

"It would be easier if de Socorro died and the next most senior in his House took over." The words were out of my mouth before I could stop them.

"Not a good precedent." Diana closed that direction of conversation. "It will be Skylur's problem soon. We need to update you on what we've learned from your trip to Mexico."

"The pit in Astilla de Luna," Bian moved on smoothly. "It looks like you were right—that's where the new pack members were coming from. It's some kind of mass production."

"But forced, and using Adept power?" I couldn't imagine what kind of working would produce that result, or what Adept would want to do it.

"It seems so," Bian said. "It's known that strong Adepts can make a working that will increase the infusion power of Were prions. So instead of a drawn-out process of incremental infusion, you get a one-time hit. The problem is there's no adjustment time, and it almost inevitably ends in the new Were going rogue."

"What's 'almost inevitably' in actual numbers?"

"More than ninety-nine out of a hundred."

"So you're saying literally hundreds would have to be fed into the pit—"

"Unless they've found a way to improve the odds."

I felt dizzy. The memory of the pit forced its way into my mind. The inhuman way that people must have been forced in. Victims' bodies on top of bodies on top of bones, but not *thousands*. And there had been dozens of almost-werewolves who had died when the poison gas was released. The numbers didn't add up. It was sickening to try and think logically about the charnel house.

"Gálvez must have found a way," I said. "But he wasn't an Adept."

"It's not something Gálvez did on his own. David says there's evidence in the cellphone communications that the working came from Louisiana. A gift or an exchange. From the conversations, it sounds like he wasn't using it in the 'best way', whatever that means."

"From Louisiana? You mean from the witch queen in the swamp?"

"Yes. We can't tie down who or where, but it's looking more and more as if lots of things come back to her, whoever she is."

If, *if*, we were right and this all tied back to one person, then we were looking at something bigger than Gálvez's operation. If Gálvez was only carrying out instructions—badly, according to the communications—then whoever created this process was a bigger threat by far. Blowing up Astilla de Luna wouldn't have put an end to this plan. What if the next pit was deeper inside Mexico, that much more difficult to reach, that much more efficient?

Was this Matlal in disguise? Vega Martine?

Why disguise themselves? Why the level of communications to Yucatán, if it was Matlal in Louisiana? Same for Vega Martine and Mexico City.

Bian agreed, but there was nothing more we could do without David finding some major security breach in their communications, or me finding something in Louisiana.

I was about to close the conversation when I remembered: "Gwen wanted to talk," I said.

"She's busy," Bian replied. "She and the Lost Boys are having an intensive on that temple you were speaking about last call."

With Flint and Kane always referring to Gwen as Wendy Witch, Bian had come up with 'Lost Boys' for them, and it looked as if it might stick.

The others returned from the restaurant bearing food, so I ended the call and we got back on I-10.

I'd started this morning with a sense that I'd surely achieved the bulk of what I would need to on this trip. An ambush ambushed, two dangerous, military-style ops across the border, the threat from Villa Ahumada all but eliminated, boxes full of proof about what had been going on, House de Socorro's emergency fixed, the handover of the El Paso pack organized.

I had thought that all I had to do in Louisiana was run a ritual for Felix and Cameron, and smell out whether House Labastide was a problem for Skylur. And, of course, explain everything I'd been doing to Skylur, Felix and Cameron.

Now everything I'd done seemed only to identify the real task that lay before me. The other tasks hadn't gone away, and it was clear Louisiana was going to be anything but straightforward.

I still didn't really have a clue.

Chapter 23

It was midnight. Damn, but there was a lot of Texas. We'd swapped drivers three times and we were still an hour short of Houston.

I woke from a troubled sleep in the back of the Hill Bitch, with dreams of an Ops 4-10 extraction gone bad, flares lighting billowing smoke around the LZ and a sense of danger looming out of the darkness.

"What's wrong?" I said. I was still hearing the thud of helicopter blades.

"Nothing—"

Yelena's response was cut off by a beam of light flashing down, illuminating the whole truck.

She swerved, stomped on the gas. The light clicked off.

"Steady," I said, hand on her shoulder. "If they wanted us dead, we'd be a smoking ruin right now."

Anyone who could find us on I-10 and pick us out with a spotlight could hit us with a missile.

And they could contact us if we had our phones turned on. With Yelena driving, I actually had mine and hers in my pocket for once. We'd agreed to turn off the cells while we tried to sleep in the back of the truck, turn them on only at handovers.

I turned mine back on and it immediately beeped. *Skylur.*

"My apologies, Amber. Your cell has been off and it has been an interesting few hours. Please take the next exit. There's an empty truck stop off the ramp. We'll meet you there."

Julie and Keith in the truck behind followed us down to the truck stop, where we parked.

As Skylur had indicated, there wasn't anyone else there.

We got out warily as the big black Bell 429 helicopter sank down fifty yards from us.

Even before it actually touched down, a figure opened the door and flowed out onto the concrete, like some predatory animal. Maia Kiriani, Skylur's pelea. She was followed by three others, all of them in black and equipped with compact FN P90 submachine guns. Two of them had night vision goggles attached to their helmets, and they were scanning the area in slow, wide sweeps.

Maia turned and nodded. Skylur stepped out as the Bell's rotors began their wind-down.

I let some of the tension leak from my shoulders and finger-talked the others to stand down.

We met halfway. I was a little surprised to be greeted with the formal lamia, the Athanate neck-kissing gesture.

It told me he was on edge, which I guess I could have figured out anyway.

"Walk with me."

We made a strange formation: Skylur and me, then Maia and Yelena just behind us and to each side. The rest spread out. Maia's team had training and they clearly didn't regard us as potential enemies, so they coordinated with Julie, Keith and Rita to form a wide defensive perimeter.

"Quite a display," I said. "Has something spectacular happened?"

"'Something' is attempted with regularity," he replied. "Maia's caught most of them early, but we're out here with a reduced team."

I looked around at the empty night.

"In the middle of nowhere, at a truck stop you couldn't have picked before figuring out where we were, and I suspect you've told no one where you were going. I doubt you arranged the transport with your credit card. So, apart from calling me on a secure and encrypted channel, you should be invisible to enemies."

"It's the 'apart from' that concerns my security," he said. "We're not the only ones who crack communications. But that's not what I'm here to discuss."

I waited silently as we took a few more paces across the concrete slabs. His meeting, his opening.

"When we last spoke I urged you to be in a position that you would not merely be able to justify your actions before the Assembly, but to be able to do so from a position of considerable and spectacular success. Diana spoke to me about the net effect of your military operations in El Paso and Mexico, and about the contemptible actions of de Socorro."

So far, so good. An implication that he supported my views about de Socorro. That was a long way from agreeing with what I'd done, but better than him not agreeing.

He went on, "We didn't spend much time on your activities south of the border, but I have a team who can piece together your actions from the mayhem in your vicinity. Do you feel you have achieved the level of success I suggested you would need?"

"Yes. And no."

His smile skewed.

At his urging, I gave him the rationale Diana and I had formed, and then an overview of the military planning that Colonel Laine and I had come up with. He waited until I rounded off with a return to the basis of my thinking: "In a fight, one on one, with an opponent of considerable skill and strength, you need to avoid traps that exist at a higher level than physical skills." I was aware I was lecturing someone who would beat me in any fair fight. "It's the same for leaders in a war. You need the mind to be both narrowly focused and widely aware. And you can't fight from the back foot."

"You're saying Panethus has been on the back foot? Too narrowly focused? Merely reacting?"

"Diana and I thought too widely focused. A few setbacks against Basilikos were worth less than a setback to Emergence."

He nodded. "I agree with you. As Maia said to me a while ago, if I did not have you, I would have needed to invent you. I suspect Felix and Cameron think the same. You give us both plausible deniability and a reliable weapon." He smiled again. "Thank you, Amber."

We walked a few steps more.

"Diana will send me the detail, and it's my decision that there's already sufficient in there to say that it was a sanctioned operation, if anyone asks. Tell me about de Socorro. I want to hear it from your point of view."

I forced myself to relive the events of my two visits to the house in the Pointe Hills community, trying not to second-guess any of my decisions.

"De Socorro will be removed," Skylur said. "You're right; you should have killed him and let Diakon Cuarón take over. I would have supported that. You've done well in a difficult situation. As to the rest of it—the whole Mexican operation... tactical success but strategically incomplete."

"The proof will follow. Basilikos was *all* over this."

"I believe you. In fact, I will send people to Denver who may be able to assist in decryption."

"That would be good, thanks."

We turned and began the walk back along the concrete lot.

"But even before we crack the comms," I said, "it looks like someone in Louisiana is the key to all of the troubles."

I had begun to wonder what Skylur had come all this way for. Not to hear my report.

Skylur laughed briefly, then fell silent for another minute.

It was quiet here. The lights of vehicles moved on I-10 and the sound of their engines seemed lost in the darkness, disconnected.

"Your rescue of Tullah over what was supposed to be a Christmas vacation exposed you to even more new experiences. Revealed new abilities. Even some ability in Athanate diplomacy."

"Hmm." I wasn't going to rise to his teasing.

"And you and Diana and Colonel Laine are right, we've been on the back foot. Your operation will give us justification in front of the Assembly to prepare an offensive of the Ops 4-10 kind. Though its timing will have to be determined by the progress and demands of Emergence."

"As always," I muttered. Even with the rider that we'd only do things that didn't damage a successful Emergence, his acceptance of my actions and acknowledgment of the case was huge. Why did I feel like I was being softened up for something?

Didn't have long to wait.

"To do that," he said, "I need Ops 4-10 expertise."

I misunderstood what he was saying. "I need to be in Louisiana."

"Which is why Colonel Laine and Vera are on a plane to New York as we speak. His knowledge and insight will be vital, both in planning aggression against Basilikos *and* in planning defenses against humanity, should that need arise during Emergence."

As quietly as we were speaking, Yelena heard that and I felt her angry reaction.

"If that's some kind of apology, it should be directed to Yelena," I said. "As you well know, the Colonel and his wife are her kin."

He grunted.

"I'm not apologizing to her because I'm not suggesting separating them. It wouldn't be wise to turn up in New Orleans with a Carpathian Diakon anyway. House Labastide is ultra-conservative Panethus. So it would be especially unwise if that Carpathian had also spent time with Basilikos."

"Stop right there, Skylur! You can't take my Diakon away. And she was only with Basilikos as a spy for Carpathia."

I knew, even as I said it, that was a bad point.

"Hardly a reassuring argument," Skylur said. "A Carpathian *spy* as a Diakon."

I changed tack. "Well, how about this for an argument: *I* am a Carpathian House. I'm the heir to House Chrysos, the Golden House, the lost House of Carpathia. Labastide can suck it up."

But Skylur was having none of it. "I would really keep that quiet, on the slim chance that Labastide knows enough Carpathian history to recognize the name of one of the most aristocratic of Carpathian Houses. But enough, it's none of these arguments that dictates why I need Yelena in New York. Why I need a loyal Carpathian by my side, alongside a loyal Basilikos Diakon. Why *Emergence* needs it."

"What then?"

"In absolute secrecy..."

I nodded. Of course it was. What the hell was going on?

The cold wind buffeted us, and Skylur stopped walking. He turned to face me.

"A ship has arrived in New York from Odessa, with the very highest ranking Houses on board. After centuries of silence, Carpathia has finally come to talk to the rest of the Athanate community. Through us."

Chapter 24

I was still stunned as I watched the black helicopter lift and turn away into the night.

New Orleans will be a different challenge from El Paso, Skylur had said. *On top of finding this witch and running rituals, there will be old-fashioned Panethus Athanate politics. Hugely sensitive. Tact and diplomacy. Yelena and her former Ops 4-10 kin would not be the best team you could have down there. Use Pia for the politics, and the Adept members of your House.*

So that helicopter was carrying my Diakon, Julie and Keith away to catch a jet from Houston to New York.

Yelena had required a direct order from me to comply, and she'd refused Skylur's offer to elevate her to a sub-House of Farrell.

"I am Diakon Farrell," she'd growled.

She'd gone, worried for me and worried about what she would have to do in New York, but she'd gone, eventually. It felt like I'd had my right arm torn off.

Two of Maia's team had taken the second truck and were returning it to El Paso. I suspected they also had orders regarding de Socorro, but I couldn't spare a thought for that.

Pia would be on a plane to New Orleans tomorrow. We'd pick her up from the airport and she would take over duty as my Diakon in front of House Labastide.

Rita would be my security team. Since I was down in Louisiana on Were business, Skylur argued it would seem more appropriate to Athanate eyes.

My head was spinning. Things had flipped too quickly. There were too many things happening at once.

My cell beeped.

Gwen.

"Amber, where are you?"

"I-10, short of Houston. What's happening? Did you get through to Gabrielle?"

"No. But this call is about you."

"Why do I feel this is just what I need at the moment?"

"Don't be sarcastic. We're sure about the temple now. It's dedicated to Tezcatlipoca." She spelled it, then sounded the syllables out: "Tess-kat-lih-poka. From Olmec, Maya and finally the Aztec pantheon. God of rulers, of sorcerers, of warriors, and one of the lords of the night. He's depicted in two aspects: the jaguar, and a handsome man with a peculiar breastplate."

Jaguars and sorcerers. It figured.

"Busy god," I said. "I guess the breastplate is significant?"

"Yes. That's where his name comes from. It means 'smoking mirror'. The myths say it's an obsidian mirror with the power to reveal the future and the wishes of the gods."

"Handy."

"The power of divination is complete rubbish, but the breastplate is the focus of his power, and it's what your attention was drawn to."

"You're saying the Aztec god, Tezcatlipoca, lured me into that temple so he could make a better connection with me."

"Probably. Especially if you agree there's also a good chance he's been the mysterious guide leading us to the information we gathered against Matlal. So that leaves us with a couple of questions: What's in it for him, and why it's *you* he seems most interested in."

I shivered. I couldn't find a snappy comeback for that.

One of the Lost Gods—an *Aztec* god, with all the bloodthirsty implications—had gotten inside my head, just when I'd set off on one of the bloodiest missions of my career. It was also a mission to attack Matlal, however indirectly. Matlal, who was drawing some of *his* power from an Aztec god.

The more I learned, the less I liked the implications.

"Anyway," she went on, "I'm sending Flint and Kane down to New Orleans on the same flight as Pia tomorrow. They're up to speed on Tezcatlipoca, and they'll help you create some specific defenses. It goes without saying you should *not* try using any power you're offered."

I described to her the two instances where I'd felt as if I was receiving help. The first to save de Socorro, the second the urge to blast his mansion into smoking rubble.

"Good that you've been able to pick and choose so far," she said. "The advice stands. Don't use this power."

I finished the call and stayed leaning against the Hill Bitch.

The night I'd spent in Mexico had been full of obvious dangers, and I'd accepted them. They were familiar dangers. Now... this was a different battle. A witch queen to find in the swamps, and an Aztec god to defend myself against.

Rita pointed out we were on a schedule—to check on Gabrielle in Lafayette and then get to the airport in New Orleans to pick up the others. She said she'd drive. She also pointed out we no longer had time for the courtesy call on House Broussard.

Fine by me.

No way I was going to sleep. I sat shotgun and listened to the first late night station that came up on the dial.

> *When the road is long*
> *And the heart beats slow*
> *Just stars above*
> *And hell below*

The style was a strange flavor of country, with an uneasy rhythm and a singer that slowed to almost speak the words now and then. The sort of weird music that you could find in the middle of the night on a lonely road. Maybe I'd just close my eyes for a second.

> *The devil's a-dancing*
> *An' when he's good and done*
> *Levee gonna break*
> *And the waters are gonna run*

The words started to seep into my head, like the magic of a centuries-dead Aztec god, and I dreamed the night ahead was full of billowing threats.

Louisiana
Chapter 25

I woke as we crossed the state border and insisted on driving the rest of the way to the witches' house in Lafayette.

Except it wasn't *in* Lafayette. It was beyond. Rita had set up the GPS on her cell and the map was showing me a route into the twisty roads to the east of the city, approaching the Atchafalaya Basin. The ETA was still before dawn, and we'd need to wake the coven if we were going to make the New Orleans airport in time to collect Pia and the Lost Boys.

Rita wrapped her jacket around her and slept until we hit gravel roads a couple of hours later.

She yawned, scratched her head and prodded the radio back to life.

We'd lost the weird music back in Texas, and we'd found a weird preacher instead, slithering up out of the static like a snake.

"You hear tell to repent 'fore it's too late, and *you know*. Yes! You know *right then* they're talking on matters they don't know *nothing* about. It's already too late, people. It's here: these are the end times. You and me, and all of them, we're right here, living in the belly of the beast."

Rita turned it off.

"We nearly there yet?" she said. "I need a coffee and a pee. Not in that order."

"No coffee shops out here," I replied. "But there's lots of trees by the road and it's still dark."

She grinned. "Belly of the beast out there. I'll wait."

"We *are* the beast. But anyway, we're nearly there." I took the last right and had to come to a halt as the road gave up after fifty yards. "I guess we walk. It's only another hundred yards or so ahead."

Without asking, Rita picked our automatics out of the bag near her feet and handed me the HK.

We checked our weapons, clipped them to our belts.

"Better bring a flashlight too," I said. Wolf and cougar eyes could see in this pre-dawn half-light, but the trees were close together here and the path ahead was dark.

We got out of the Hill Bitch and closed the doors quietly.

There was nothing specific to alarm us, but both of us felt cautious. Gwen had told us two things about the Lafayette coven that Gabrielle was visiting: that they were strong and they were eccentric. I didn't want to blunder into anything.

We sniffed the air and took the opportunity to give our eyes time to adjust.

The air was both chilled and sweaty. It smelled of rain and mud. There was a river close by in the darkness, a slow one, meandering, with the sort of smell that said it was rich in life. And where there was life, there was death.

"Cold enough to be irritating, not cold enough to kill the freaking mosquitos," Rita whispered, and waved her hand in front of her face.

We walked up the track that led between thickets of cane grass. Tall pines began to loom over us. After the sounds of the Hill Bitch's engine and tires, we were now surrounded by a chorus of invisible frogs and the cries of birds, which got quieter as we moved along the path.

"The coven must be really serious about this anti-technology thing," I murmured. The path we were on had once been a road, but it had disappeared beneath tall grasses. Now there were scrub oak trees which leaned branches into our way, so that our path weaved back and forth. If the coven even used cars, they would have to park out where we had and carry their supplies in along this track.

A minute later, I could see a house. It was little more than a shadow among shadows, but its bulk gave it away.

We stopped.

The ground surrounding it had been cleared of trees. There were beds of some kind of plants in rows, and closer to us, low heaps I took for compost, but it was a definite clearing. The sort of clearing that a guard with a gun in the house could defend. Or an Adept with a spell.

No lights showed.

My gut began to tense and I stopped Rita.

I flashed finger-talk at her. *Don't like. Wait. Look and listen.*

We crouched down and cleared our pistols from their holsters.

Nothing moved except for the sway of leaves and grasses in the light morning breeze.

It was quieter now, like I'd put cotton in my ears. The animal noises seemed to come from further away, down to the left, where I could see a dull gleam of water. That was the river I'd smelled, at the edge of the property.

This was the Lafayette coven's main house. Twelve of them lived here full time, Gwen had told me, with others scattered through the county. This was where Gabrielle had come to stay.

But the house felt empty.

I let my eukori reach forward carefully. These were powerful Adepts, and I didn't want to piss them off by showing up at this hour and spying on their auras. *Surely* they'd have some kind of warning system.

But I got nothing beyond a sense of strange and unfamiliar workings, magic that seemed to drift like an early morning mist across the ground, unconnected.

My wolfy eyes tried to pick out details.

The old house had been built as a big, plain square, raised off the ground on squat stone pillars to allow floodwater to pass beneath. It was surrounded by a deep porch that wrapped around the house as far as I could see. The roof hung over the porch, at least a yard beyond the railings. A place to catch a cool breeze, or watch the rain fall. I made a bet with myself there were old wooden rockers on that porch.

A set of white painted steps reaching up to the porch was easy to make out, but everything inside was too dark, and the view was screened by plants. The whole porch was choked with flowers from hanging pots, and climbers on the railing. I could make out yellow jessamine, hyacinth and honeysuckle. The rich scents were muted in the cool morning, but I could imagine them like clouds of scent in the afternoon and evening.

I turned my head slowly.

Down on the river, there was another, separate building, which looked to be a boathouse.

All silent.

It was strange. I liked the place. It had a crazy, spontaneous feel to it, but it was empty, as far as I could tell. With no magic wards operating.

Rita flicked fingers beside my face.

Dead dog.

I let the wolf out a little further, took a deep lungful of the air.

She was right. Masked by the scents of flowers and herbs and river mud, there was death. Maybe down near the water.

Guard dog? I finger-talked back, and she shrugged.

Could be. Not good, her fingers said.

I stood slowly. *I go left. You go right. Meet at steps.*

She nodded and moved off with that cougar slink.

I stalked down to the boathouse, moving in the trees, alert to every whisper of sound, every brush of leaves, every hint of scent reaching me.

I had no difficulty finding the dogs.

They were big, a hundred pounds or so, powerfully built. Louisiana hunting dogs. In the uncertain light, their coats seemed shaded in patches. They'd both had their throats torn out. Something with a bite as strong as a bear had killed them and tossed them aside in front of the boathouse.

There were claw marks on the ground, big ones, but it was too dark and confused to say who or what had made them. It looked like whatever it was, it was *much* bigger than the dogs.

I knelt and placed a hand on each dog. I could read the scene; they'd died in a fight they knew they couldn't win, defending their 'pack' of humans in the house.

They'd deserved better.

And they were cold as the ground. They'd died a while ago, yet no scavengers had come. Those drifting Adept workings I could sense were still partly active, keeping creatures out. But the main strength of those workings that had been drained, certainly enough for whatever had come ashore and killed the dogs.

The boathouse had a single small boat in it, an old-style, flat-bottomed jonboat with paddles.

There was enough space for another boat to tie up.

No indication of what had happened.

I met Rita at the steps.

Nothing, she signed.

Two guard dogs killed. Nothing else, I replied.

I tested the steps. White painted wood. Probably designed to creak loudly. I crept up the edges.

The porch was wooden too. It felt unusual. I knelt and touched. The wood was old, smooth. The gaps between planks had tar in them, like an old-time ship. The railings looked strange too.

Oak. Old ship salvage, Rita signed, pointing to the floor, the porch railing and the pillars supporting the roof.

I nodded.

And I'd been right; there *were* rockers on the porch as well. Four of them. Handmade, each slightly different.

The whole place was made of wood that had been recycled, down to the shutters on the windows.

Rita pointed to the door. It was closed, but I could see the lock had been broken. Someone had come from the river, drained the power of the wards, killed the guard dogs, broken the door down...

But I could smell no other deaths in this place.

Abduction?

Was this directed against the coven, and did Gabrielle get caught up in it?

Or was it aimed at Gabrielle, and they took the coven as well?

I tapped my head so Rita would be warned, and then opened up my eukori.

Nothing, apart from the were-cougar beside me. Either no one there, or someone with a shield on their aura so strong I couldn't even detect it.

We eased the door open and slipped inside, one to the left, one to the right.

Living room. Tall ceilings. Wood floors. No electric light. No sign of disruption. Unlit oil lamps. Comfortable, handmade furniture. Books on tables. Unfinished needlework and craft projects, laid down as if someone would walk in and pick them back up at any moment.

Dining room and kitchen. Covered bowls with salad and meat, starting to smell. A door onto the porch where a wood-burning oven sat. No fire, but I could feel the lingering warmth held by the heavy iron oven.

Back inside.

Bathrooms with gravity-fed water. I made another bet with myself there was a tank on the roof that was warmed only by the sun and the excess heat from the stove.

An open passage, like an extension of the porch, led from the back door to a second building, similar to the first but divided into shared bedrooms. Bedcovers thrown back. Day clothes folded over chairs or on hangers. Shoes on the floor.

Still no sign of struggle.

One bedroom with a suitcase of Gabrielle's clothes.

Right up to that point, different scenarios had been spinning in my mind, throwing out reasons why Gabrielle wasn't here. Now the chill settled in my stomach. She'd been here and she'd been taken along with the rest of them. Almost certainly a day ago.

We went back and I gave the living room a second pass. This time I noticed the smaller details: the tired flowers in bowls, the crystals, the small amulets and gris-gris bags at the cardinal points. There were more amulets outside on the porch, hidden among the flowers.

"Give me a moment," I said. "Check the grounds."

I sat on the steps and tried the exercises that Gwen had been teaching me. I generally sucked at magic. I could *channel* workings like some kind of magical six-lane highway, and I could fry someone through a eukori connection, but light a fire? Cool a glass of water? Not so well.

It was driving Tara insane.

What I *could* do reliably well was sense magic.

I closed my eyes and breathed slowly. I visualized the traces of workings as a mist in the cool air, with my nose as a sort of magic sensor. A spirit-wolf sensing spirit-workings. It helped.

What workings had been used here?

Those amulets inside and outside the house had been used to focus the workings, like the running water in the dungeon below Haven was a focus for the shielding spell that protected Kaothos. The amulets were more like anchor points. I could feel the fragments of spells clinging to them more easily than I could sense the texture of workings that hung in the air.

There were amulets on either side of the steps. Eyes closed, I reached out and took one down. Held it in front of me.

Breathed deep.

Pulled all the workings in.

Imagined each had a scent.

Deflections: people out on the road or passing on the river wouldn't want to stop here. There was nothing of interest here.

Under that: guardian wards. A person coming too close would feel a threat. An urgent desire to leave. Then paralyzing fear.

Deeper: alarms. Threads of magic coming together like a spiderweb, so the Adepts in the house would know someone was approaching and the spells were working.

Deepest: attack. Not an active working, but a reservoir of power that could be used by any Adept who'd lived here.

All of them, every working, pulled apart and all the strength sucked out, so that Rita and I had barely registered them when we came in.

And under them all, the traces of something cold that had passed here. Something powerful. Something wild. Something from the east, from the heart of the swamps, where the waters were still, and the roots went deep, deep into the darkness.

Something tall, under a canopy of stars, that stirred as I tasted its scent.

A scent that reminded me of the pit beneath Astilla de Luna.

A real scent. Not a sensation of a working that I was tricking my mind into interpreting as a smell. Something that remained frustratingly out of reach, but closer than before, because this was the time of day I associated with it.

A sun rising with the color of old blood. A wide, wide horizon, the earth an utter blackness, the eastern sky aflame. Cool with the promise of heat. Dust. Strange smells, strange animal noises from the dark.

I blinked.

In Lafayette, Louisiana, today's sun rose unseen behind the trees, and the sky above was becoming the color of violent bruises. My memories faded like dreams.

I'd done one operation with Ops 4-10 in eastern Africa. A rescue in Somalia, extracting through Kenya. What was teasing my mind about that? What connected Africa to Villa Ahumada and Lafayette?

But the elusive memory was gone, along with the sensations of smelling Adept workings.

In place of those I could hear my heart thud, and the flow of my Blood, slow and deliberate as the nearby river. I could hear the creak of wood behind me, as if the house might wake with the dawn. I could hear Rita's steps, quiet as a cat's.

She completed her circuit and came to stand in front of me.

She shook her head.

I took out my cell and called Gwen.

Chapter 26

"Gwen is on the next plane," I said to Pia at New Orleans' Louis Armstrong Airport three hours later. "We could wait for her."

Pia shook her head. "I messaged ahead to House Labastide. They replied that they're expecting us..." she checked her watch, "in an hour and a half. Unless we can provide some vital support for Gwen this morning, I strongly recommend we make the meeting with Labastide."

I stood in thought as the passengers exiting the airport terminal flowed around us like a river.

I *wanted* to be with Gwen, but she didn't need me to show her the way to the old wooden house in Lafayette. She didn't need my help searching out the other Adepts in that community. I *needed* to meet Labastide, and I *needed* that meeting to go as smoothly as possible. Changing the time or date almost as soon as it had been set wasn't a good way to do that.

"I have to be there, with you," Pia said, "and you need someone else in attendance. Since Labastide thinks you're here on pack business, Rita should be the third."

"Leaving you Lost Boys here to wait for Wendy," I said to Flint and Kane. "You have House Farrell credit cards, so you can rent a car."

As one, their eyes lit up.

"Within reason," I hurried on. "Treat them like company credit cards and collect receipts. Get something for rough roads. Rita will message you the GPS location of the coven's house and details of the approach by foot. You'll need the GPS app on your cells."

Flint smiled. Of course they had the app. But Kane tilted his head very slightly to indicate Rita.

Turning, I realized Rita looked intensely thoughtful and not at all happy.

"What's up?"

"I'm not Yelena, but I'm trying to do what she does for you," she started carefully.

I gave her a palms-up, tell-me gesture.

"Imagine I'm someone in Basilikos tasked with attacking strategic Panethus targets in the US," she said. "Let's also imagine my information about Panethus is very good. My objective is to do as much damage as possible, on those specific targets, while others concentrate on secondary targets or assist with distractions. I reject a strike on New York. Skylur is very strong and it's a complex environment. After Skylur himself, the target with the most symbolic and actual value is Haven, in Denver. The trouble is, Haven is even stronger than Skylur. It has Diana, Tullah, Kaothos, Gwen, Bryn, Bian, some Ops 4-10 and some of the Deauville-El Paso packs. Close by are House Farrell and the Denver pack."

I immediately saw where she was going, but it was her analysis, so I let her run with it.

"Let's imagine I have contacts in Carpathia, like House Tucek for instance, contacts with the northern packs in Mexico, alphas like Mauricio Gálvez, and contacts with some Adepts here in Louisiana, maybe this Queen of Diamonds."

Rita was right that House Tucek and her ninja nuns were Carpathian. They answered to Vega Martine, also Carpathian. Unlike Tucek, Vega Martine had been declared an enemy of the Assembly. Hardly surprising, since she'd been the one to mastermind Matlal's attempted murder of the Assembly members when they'd met in Denver. However, as far as I knew, *she* answered to Basilikos. Certainly they'd all cooperated in freeing Matlal, so it was entirely likely they'd all still be working with him.

I didn't like where I could see Rita going.

"So, I make a special deal with Gálvez, the alpha of the Chihuahua pack. I boost his pack and I point him at Juárez, to keep Alex and the bulk of the old El Paso pack tied up in El Paso. I allow Gálvez enough surplus new members that he can even boost the Sonora and Baja packs, until almost the whole super-pack structure that's built up along our side of the border is committed to defending it, tying them in place. Now this boost of pack members comes courtesy of this Queen of Diamonds Adept group in Louisiana, and Louisiana happens to be where Felix and Cameron have been stalled for two months."

The others were starting to look worried.

Rita went on, "Now I get some of my Carpathian contacts to arrive in New York and demand to see Skylur. Whether it's deliberate or not, this results in Yelena and her kin going to New York, and at the same time, Ops 4-10, who have been guarding Haven and Manassah, start being deployed to every major House in the US because Emergence is happening. Meanwhile, more House Farrell have to come to Louisiana to make up for losing Yelena.

"Then Gabrielle is abducted and Gwen is on the next plane from Denver. But even here in Louisiana, we're splitting up. Gwen and the boys are going to Lafayette, while the three of us go meet Labastide, who, let's remember, may well be upset enough at Skylur that she'd contemplate talking to Basilikos.

"Haven's less well protected. Manassah's vulnerable. We're *completely* exposed down here."

"No." Pia raised a hand to stop her. "You've done an excellent Yelena-level paranoid analysis, but you're not Athanate and you're reading some of it wrong.

"Labastide is hardcore, conservative Panethus. She may be breaking away from Skylur, and that would play into Basilikos' hands, but I stake my life on her *not* talking to Basilikos. Others in her House... we'll have to see.

"I take your point that we seem to be driven to splitting up into smaller and smaller groups, but what can we do?"

They were both right. Regardless of whether some tactical genius in Basilikos had planned it, we *were* spread too thinly, like all of Panethus in North America was.

And yet, apart from how exposed House Farrell had become, that wasn't anything new. It was exactly the fear-of-attack kind of thinking that had led me down the path which resulted in our campaign against the Mexican packs.

Which had turned the tables on those packs.

I needed to think like *that*.

"This Basilikos master-plotter may exist, but he's already gotten it wrong," I said. "There's now nothing any outside force can do that will prevent Alex and Zane from replacing the old El Paso pack with White Sands. That means the old El Paso are going to start showing up in Denver this week, and we'd start with them based at Haven. Meanwhile, the Chihuahua pack is badly damaged, and split up without leadership. It'll take months to recreate a working pack structure and in that time, they'll lose a huge part of their territory, including Juárez, to the Coahuila pack."

I squinted and tried to see the whole picture, rather than the details.

"Call Alex," I said to Rita. "Explain your thinking to him and ask him to share with Zane. Bring forward moving people to Denver. Get Scott and Mykayla back home. Ask Zane to loan Denver pack members from Tucson and Santa Fe if we need to. Hell, ask Billie to loan us a few. Wrap it up with training, which is what they're asking for anyway. They can be based at Haven, war-gaming responses to Haven and Manassah being attacked. Training to respond to what might happen. We have enough Ops 4-10 left that they can be the lead on that at least."

I turned to Flint and Kane. "You stay here to wait for Gwen. Explain Rita's analysis to her. Let's meet back up this evening. Meantime, I'll see if Felix can give us back Nick and Olivia, maybe Ursula. Together we can track down where Gabrielle is, and it's my expertise to get people out of those situations. My gut agrees with Rita on one thing: all of this, especially down in Louisiana, is connected somehow. This is huge."

Nods all around.

"I'll call Bian and Felix on the way to House Labastide," I said. "And I'll call Diakon Flavia afterwards and explain our thinking. Skylur will do what he decides to do, but we'll have given him input and warning."

I took a deep breath.

"Whoever it is behind it all, here's the thing: we've hit once already down in Mexico, and that's got to create a distraction. *Now* is the best time to strike again, here in Louisiana. Like I said to the El Paso pack, we're done sitting still, waiting for the next bite and wondering where it's coming from. Now we're going to bite back, and we're going to bite *deep*."

They all liked that.

Hugs all around and we left Flint and Kane heading for the car rental desks while we got the Hill Bitch back from the parking garage.

Rita set the GPS and drove.

Things can't get any worse, Tara said. *It's up from here.*

I didn't agree.

All thoughts of Louisiana being the easy leg of this journey had long gone. I was committed to going in to New Orleans and meeting House Labastide, but Rita's arguments had raised red flags in my mind. All the clues I'd found in Mexico pointed to an intense involvement between Matlal and *someone* in southern Louisiana. Whatever was happening with Were and Adepts, it didn't stack up that there *wouldn't* be an Athanate House included.

Labastide was the biggest.

Granted, the Eastern Seaboard had reluctantly supported Skylur, but only the main Houses had sworn oaths. If Labastide was really calling on the association to think about declaring independence from Altau, against their oaths, didn't that mean they were the most likely point that Matlal, or whoever, would be trying to influence?

And if they had succeeded, were we walking straight into a trap?

I started dialing.

Chapter 27

Calling Bian and Diana was easy. They immediately understood what Rita and I were describing and what they could do about it, if we were right. I had to promise to call again later, but we were finished in fifteen minutes.

Which was only a little less than the time it took to reach the hotel just outside the French Quarter that Pia had booked us into.

"I'm not presenting you to House Labastide unwashed and in your travel clothes," Pia said, and patted her large suitcase ominously.

Forty minutes later I was washed, made up, had my hair woven into a braid and I was dressed in a business suit that looked sharper than I felt.

Rita had taken clothes out of the case, shaken them and put them on. She looked fabulous. So did Pia.

I lost some time discussing whether we needed to take a cab so we wouldn't show up at the Labastide mansion in the Hill Bitch. I won, but it meant that I didn't get to call Felix until we were already getting into the truck for a trip that was only going to take ten minutes, if that.

I explained I had to formally greet House Labastide, and we agreed I'd be in Baton Rouge to meet with him and Cameron later today.

Talking about the reasons that they'd been stuck here in Louisiana for two months would have to wait until I was face to face; as I started to ask, he was distracted by noises I could hear in the background.

At that moment, Rita braked sharply and I looked up, startled, in time to see a showy brunette in an equally showy Porsche convertible pull out of the road ahead of us. A chirp from her tires and she whipped the lipstick-red car around us and away.

"Might finally have some movement here," Felix was saying on the cell. "Call as soon as you're out of your meeting." He ended the call abruptly and Rita turned onto the road where the Labastide mansion was. It was a short loop with only a dozen houses.

Rita pulled up in front of one.

Not what I was expecting.

"This is their town house," Pia said, noticing my look. "I think they usually live outside the city in a place called Talleyrand, their old plantation-style house."

The first thing that struck me with their town house was the lack of security. No fences, no gates. The building itself was brilliant white with two-story, neo-classical columns like a Greek temple. There was a deep porch like the coven's house in Lafayette, but this one had clusters of expensive-looking garden tables and chairs. The front yard was a manicured lawn cut neatly in two by a paved walk pointed at the oversized front door.

The best I could say was it matched all the others on the street.

I hated it, and the hairs on the back of my neck stood up. I could feel eyes watching and waiting.

I took a deep breath and picked up Nekotsume. My wakizashi was covered by a silk wrap because I had no belt to thrust it through. Pia had said an old-fashioned eccentricity such as carrying your sword into a meeting was considered to be on the acceptable side of Athanate manners.

Good.

I felt better that I wasn't going in there completely without weapons, but I couldn't deny I'd have felt even better with my HK Mk23 in my hand.

As I got out of the Hill Bitch, I got a hint of Athanate marques in the open air. A blend of scents, laced with fresh-cut grass and partly obscured by vanilla-scented cleaning agents from the house, but there had been different Athanate here recently. I couldn't tease the marques apart, but I felt my heart rate rise automatically. My Athanate instincts were reminding me that there were dangers here, and they might come from unexpected directions.

Still, it was time to focus on the former Eastern Seaboard association, and this House in particular. If the association were going to revolt, *this* would be where it would start; in the House I'd referred to as the gut of the Eastern Seaboard. The unthinking reactionary part. Possibly already talking to Matlal. Possibly already balanced on the edge of revolt. And equally possibly, so finely balanced, they could be tipped over by a mistake I made in the next hour or so.

And also, a House even more conservative, even more in lockstep with the Agiagraphos than that asshole de Socorro in El Paso.

Look how well I handled that.

Leave that behind and concentrate on today, Tara said.

The door opened to Pia's knock.

A butler, of course. Not a doddering, silver-haired man, but a young woman. She wore a black suit and tie, a white shirt with high-wing collars and a gray vest, with white gloves. Hair was held neatly back in a bun. Her smile was professional but empty, and her eyes coolly assessing as we gave our names. She looked both decorative and functional, and she was accompanied by a waft of Labastide's marque, which made me think of something sharp and cold and ornate.

The mansion's inside was as surprising as the outside, but in completely the opposite way. It was calm and elegant. The entrance hall had a plain tiled floor, two antique French tables on which vases with fresh flowers glowed in light from the windows, and an old oil painting of a pastoral scene on the facing wall. Nothing else. Beautiful and relaxed.

I did not want to relax, and the hint of other marques here had my heart rate up again.

Who had been visiting?

We were ushered through to a spacious living room, where four Athanate in dark gray suits stood up swiftly and bowed to us. I looked them over. If they were a good example of House Labastide's type, she favored them looking young and dressing well. They gave off that hum of politely suppressed violence that marked them as security. Their jackets were loosely cut to allow plenty of space for shoulder holsters.

Ignoring them, the butler led us across the room and opened a double door.

There were two people waiting for us in the room beyond. They sat at a round table, with their backs to an expanse of glass overlooking the garden. It was bright enough outside that their features would be hidden from us until our eyes adjusted, a move that was entirely deliberate.

House Labastide herself hurried in through a side door just as we entered. I hadn't met her at either of the Assemblies I'd attended, but I recognized her easily from Altau's files.

As Pia had instructed, I got to the middle of the room and stopped, flanked by Pia on my left and Rita on my right. I didn't wait for the butler to announce us, nodded rather than bowed, and I spoke in Athanate.

"Amber Farrell, House Farrell, with my Diakons Pia Shirazi and Rita Dawson."

The silence stretched. Then there was the soft scrape of chairs as the two at the table stood while House Labastide moved to stand in front of me.

She was exactly my height. Brown eyes to my green. Skin somewhere between Cameron's Ethiopian black and Billie's rich brown. Black hair brushed till it gleamed, woven into wide braids and pulled back from her face. A face that looked calm and soft, until you took into account the stone-hard eyes.

Clothes formal, expensive and yet subdued.

A powerful presence. Four hundred years old, the Altau files said. I believed them.

"Marguerite Molayo Labastide," she said, her voice lightly French, tightly controlled and even. "House Labastide."

We reached and held each other's arms, slightly awkwardly since I was still holding Nekotsume. We leaned forward into the lamia, the kissing of necks that gave Athanate the opportunity to assess each other's state of mind.

Angry!

However calm her face, her marque was almost eclipsed by the rage that simmered in her.

I jerked back, half expecting her to attack me right there.

Tara forced her way forward and I felt my eyes go wolf-gold as she stared out. I barely held back a growl.

Labastide took a rapid step back and the threat of imminent attack faded.

I stood still, locked in position, heart racing and eyes all wolf.

Had she intentionally provoked me?

I was painfully aware her security team was no more than a few steps behind me, watching through the open doors and certainly armed.

The thought of it made my back muscles tense and raised my heart rate even further.

The moment seemed to hang in the air. Labastide herself seemed shocked at the intensity.

Then...

"Welcome to New Orleans," she said, recovering smoothly and delivering a minimally polite Athanate greeting.

She indicated the man standing on her left, who carefully erased the shock that had appeared on his face as well.

"Gerard Cazenave," he said, stepping forward. He pronounced his name the French way, with a soft G and the stress on the ending. "Diakon Labastide."

He was tall and pale. His hair was chestnut brown to match his eyes, and he wore it long. He had a goatee beard and wore a soft blazer, like a stereotypical professor in an old Hollywood movie.

More kissing of necks. His emotions were being kept under strict control. I learned little, other than confirming that I disgusted him. I wasn't surprised. I knew he was even more conservative than his Mistress;

I'd read his emails to the others in the Eastern Seaboard, where he'd referred to me as the Abomination.

He stepped back, leaving me with the third member of the House Labastide delegation.

"Solange Dupuis, Pelea Labastide," she said.

Pelea. Yes, House Labastide was old, but claiming that ancient title for a bodyguard was a reach.

Dupuis was shorter than me, with sandy hair and gray eyes. The lamia hinted at an edge of aggression beneath her Labastide marque, which she immediately confirmed as we stepped back.

"You're carrying a sword," she said. "That's so delightfully old-fashioned. Is it ornamental?"

I smiled and let the wolf flood back into my eyes again.

"Very ornamental." I let the silk covering slide back to reveal the decoration of the handle and scabbard. "Very sharp, too."

Chapter 28

The meeting had somehow nearly slipped out of anyone's control.

It was as if they hadn't planned what to do, or their plans had changed without discussion.

Dupuis' jaw muscle was twitching as she considered escalating, and yet she held back because she didn't seem sure what her Mistress wanted.

Pia looked worried. We'd agreed she should take the lead in talking, because we knew there was only one diplomat on our side. But I couldn't ignore a comment addressed to me.

Labastide grimaced and shook her head. The tension eased a fraction.

"Let's sit," she said suddenly, gesturing to the chairs. "We favor tea in this House. May I offer you some? Or would you prefer coffee?"

"Tea would be welcome," Pia said with relief, and the two of us took our seats side-on to the window so we weren't being blinded.

Rita stood behind us. The cougar always liked to be looking down on her potential prey. Dupuis matched her by remaining standing, the same distance away, which made me want to snort.

Cazenave made a sign to the butler, who bowed and withdrew, closing the doors behind her.

"Your second Diakon is not Athanate, nor is she... hybrid, I believe. She's Were," Labastide said, her stumble over the word hybrid barely noticeable. "Should we switch to English?"

"Thank you," Pia said, in Athanate, "but that will not be necessary."

"You have a surfeit of Diakons, it would seem," Cazenave said. "Isn't there another called Vylkove? From the Ukraine, I believe. A Carpathian, surely?"

"Attending on House Altau in New York," Pia replied with a smile.

The tea had obviously already been prepared earlier because the butler returned with a trolley. She left it next to Cazenave, bowed and left again.

The Diakon started to pour. The scent was fragrant. No offers of milk or sugar.

All from the same teapot, so hopefully no poison.

With the others distracted I risked a loosening of my eukori, and touched on Pia and Rita.

Tense, alert, but they seemed to agree with me that we'd passed some first hurdle and they weren't going to kill us yet.

I could also sense the security team outside the door. They gave off a quivering alertness, like dogs scenting dinner being prepared.

I reeled my eukori back in when Labastide spoke. "If I understood the nature of your business here in New Orleans, as communicated to me, it was *principally* to do with a meeting of the Southern League of Were, was it not?"

"Principally, yes." Pia's eyes flicked to me. "We've also been asked to make certain inquiries about the Adept communities of southern Louisiana, while we're here."

"Ah, one of those missions. 'While you're here'. The sort of mission that grows inconveniently in unexpected directions. How unfortunate."

We all smiled at each other, and I wondered how long before my face would start to ache.

"Are there more of you arriving to help with these *inquiries*?" Labastide prompted.

A flicker of Cazenave's eyes told me this wasn't the direction he expected the conversation to take either. Had Labastide been on a last-minute call just before we arrived?

Who had she talked to? What had been said?

"Three Adepts from our House are over in Lafayette," Pia answered the question.

Four, said Tara. *If Gabrielle is still there.*

Who was telling me to concentrate on one thing at a time, sis?

"Kin? Adept kin?" Cazenave asked.

"Yes, they're kin," Pia said, as if it were normal for an Athanate House to include Adepts. "We may also be joined by some of our Were, who've been assisting the alphas of the Southern League."

Labastide sipped her tea, her face revealing her dislike of the information. I'd seen what the former Eastern Seaboard Houses said about me, and they'd obviously known my House included Were. Was that distaste directed at the Were? Or the fact that we now had Adepts as well? Or that part of my House had been here in their capacity as Were and I hadn't asked her permission?

Maybe she was finding it was one thing to read the gossip about my House, and something completely different when we were sitting in front of her.

Or does she know something about the local Adepts? Tara said.

I spoke before Pia could take the next step in this verbal dance of protocols and etiquette.

"Something came up recently, with regard to Adepts, that we were going to ask you about," I said. "Your local knowledge might help our inquiries. Then we'd be out of your way that much quicker."

"Adepts have little to do with Athanate, down here in Louisiana," Cazenave said, with a dismissive wave of his hand.

"So you wouldn't happen to know anything about an Adept calling herself the Queen of Diamonds?" I asked.

They were old Athanate. Most of the leaking of disgust so far had been entirely deliberate; it had been their intention to show me what they thought of abominations like me in a way that was allowed in Athanate etiquette. Now they shut themselves off, like a metal shutter had just sliced down.

Ohhh....

Cazenave recovered first. "You'll be telling us you're chasing sightings of Marie Laveau next."

"Nineteenth-century voodoo doesn't interest us unless it gives a clue to a very real, very present day, powerful Adept," I replied. "You obviously know of the Queen of Diamonds. We'd appreciate it if you shared what you know."

Labastide made a small, quieting gesture at her Diakon and spoke. "We don't *know* anything exactly. She's the paranormal community's equivalent of Marie Laveau. The story goes that she was a witch who had to hide in the Atchafalaya Swamp to escape being burned alive, back in the eighteenth century, when this was French Louisiana. She found some source of Voodoo power there and now she enslaves paranormals to do her bidding and enact her revenge on humanity. She lives in the heart of the swamp, in a cabin on tall legs, and is protected by crazed rougarou, a sort of oversized Cajun skinwalker."

"Chicken legs," Cazenave interrupted, and his mouth twisted. "They say the cabin walks around on ten-foot chicken legs, like Baba Yaga's hut, in the Russian forests."

Labastide shrugged. "You'd think that paranormals, who hear humanity garbling myths and legends until they mean nothing, would know not to do the same thing."

"Why the name? Why Queen of Diamonds?"

"Apparently, she owned a Mississippi steamboat called the Queen of Diamonds, which lured gamblers on board," Cazenave dropped his voice to parody the old Hollywood style of ominous narration, "and they were never seen again."

He laughed.

Labastide looked at him, and he shut up abruptly.

She spoke again. "Another story says her magic works best on moonlit nights, deep in the swamp, with nothing overhead but the canopy of stars, like diamonds. That she can reach up and pluck a diamond down to give to those who approach her for favors. But that once her spell is done, the diamond returns to the sky, carrying the person with it, to attend on the Queen of Diamonds forever."

I felt a shiver race across my skin like a scuttling spider, and the feeling I'd had at the coven's house in Lafayette returned.

Something powerful from the heart of the swamps, where the waters were still, and the roots went deep, deep into the darkness. Something tall, under a canopy of stars...

Labastide was watching me.

I cleared my face.

"She's been talked about recently," Labastide said, "though in a very different context."

"All information is welcome," Pia said.

"There's one of those splinter churches. A cult, really. It's called the Church of the Risen Sun. S-U-N."

"I've heard of them." Pia frowned. "They're principally 'anti-vampire'."

"Principally, yes, but they're anti all paranormals. They've always had a strong presence in the delta and the Atchafalaya Basin. They've recently been holding some kind of blessing ceremonies on the upper Atchafalaya, claiming they'll purge the Swamp Witch, as they call her. Pure superstitious rubbish, but an angel told them how, apparently."

It was interesting information, but it certainly wasn't the Church that had attacked the coven in Lafayette. Something much more powerful.

Labastide saw I wasn't going to explain any more, and continued, "Still, even with the three Adepts in Lafayette, that wouldn't be enough human kin for the pair of you if you stay. You've not mentioned other kin." She placed her cup precisely down in the saucer. "Are you here to ask permission to feed on unbound humans in my mantle?"

"We're not expecting to spend time in New Orleans," Pia said. "Or much time in Louisiana as a whole. However, we acknowledge that your territory covers Baton Rouge and Lafayette, so we are formally requesting your permission, should we so need."

I actually enjoyed watching Cazenave pick that apart. Pia had him wrapped up in Athanate etiquette to stop him from even thinking about the possibility that the abomination in front of him was not only a hybrid, but could feed quite happily on Were Blood. Not covered in the Agiagraphos, and therefore more taboo.

But Labastide wasn't tripped up. She looked as if she was about to spring something.

I felt Rita agreed. She eased forward, stopping only when Dupuis's eyes narrowed in suspicion at the movement.

"Naturally, permission is granted under the usual Agiagraphos rules and Athanate manners," Labastide said. "But I understand you *will* be staying in New Orleans. I must insist that you use this house and enjoy our hospitality in the city. I usually spend my time at Talleyrand, my plantation, but Gerard will have to remain here and so I may, too. We have other guests expected, but there are plenty of rooms, so it will be no imposition."

"We're not planning to spend much time in New Orleans," I said. "Unless you know something we don't."

Cazenave was looking confused as well.

"I see that I do." She cocked her head. "It would appear you've been too busy for Diakon Flavia to get through to you. Knowing you were due here, she spoke to me in the minutes before your arrival. It seems our request for assistance with financial restructuring of our businesses that we put in some time ago has quite suddenly been granted."

I frowned.

What on earth did that mean? Why would it have any impact on us?

"More tea? No? Another cup for me please, Gerard." She nudged her cup toward him. "Diakon Flavia had two news items, so I suppose I'd better give them both to you."

She leaned back. Cazenave appeared intent on his task, but the cup and saucer rattled in his hand as he poured.

"We're honored, naturally, to be visited by Altau Holdings' new rising star," Labastide said.

My mouth went dry.

No!

"Jennifer Kingslund kin-Farrell will be arriving tomorrow morning. Naturally, she'll have to stay here to have direct access to our business dealings, which are centered in the city. As I said, that won't be a problem."

My vision darkened.

What the hell is Skylur playing at?

But Labastide could apparently read me well enough that she'd saved the worst for last.

"What *will* be a *huge* inconvenience is that my House is expected to host *another* emissary from the Assembly," she said. "President of the Assembly, House Correia, has decided it's not acceptable to the Hidden Path party that there is only one syndesmon between the Athanate and the Were, because that syndesmon is acknowledged to be Panethus. She has appointed one from her own creed, confirming a most abrupt and unwelcome message we'd just received earlier from that woman herself."

I gripped the armrests of my chair so tightly I felt them creak.

With more time to familiarize myself with the Labastide marque, and the hint from what Labastide had said, I found I could untangle the blend of marques that I smelled in this mansion. I knew who'd come here. She'd changed her appearance since I last saw her, even changed her marque a little. I wouldn't have picked her out across a crowded street, let alone passing in a sports car, but given enough information, my senses zeroed in on that elusive, underlying marque.

Unmistakable.

Unbelievable.

The words forced themselves out of my mouth. "Mirela Tucek."

"Yes."

I came up out of my chair fast enough that Dupuis leaped forward in alarm.

"No," I shouted. "I will *not* stay here with that Basilikos bitch. How can you—"

Labastide came to her feet swiftly, eyes locked on mine.

"You come into my domain, into my very mantle, asking my permission and then tell me what you will and won't do? Tucek claims to be Hidden Path, and until you disprove that, I'm constrained by the impositions of the Assembly. I don't want you here. You're both equally disgusting to me. I've no idea what Altau and Correia think they're doing, but I will *not* have my domain used for some proxy war between Assembly parties. I may have to do the Assembly's bidding, but I will lay down my terms, the same for you as I have given Tucek. You *will* stay here, all of you, under the same roof. You *will* give me your oaths not to harm each other. If you don't like it, then you and *all* your House: Adepts, Weres, humans, whatever, and on whatever business, will *immediately* leave southern Louisiana and not return."

Chapter 29

"Will you just *listen* to me for one minute, you hot-headed fool!"

As soon as we were back in the Hill Bitch and out of earshot of Labastide's mansion, I'd lost no time in calling Diakon Flavia to shout and swear at her.

She was the one doing most of the shouting. "I did *not* order your wife to join you in New Orleans, and neither did Skylur. *She* was the one who requested it."

"I don't care who started it. This is an incredibly dangerous place for her to be, even if it turns out Labastide is *not* thinking of becoming a traitor. We're supposed to be sharing Labastide's house with *Tucek*, of all people. The same evil bitch who masterminded Matlal's rescue from the Hidden Path."

"There are *no* safe spaces, House Farrell, and I've had as much input into Correia's decision to send Tucek as I had in Skylur's decision to send Jennifer. Listen to me. Please."

I was so angry I found it difficult to speak, and Flavia took the opportunity to go on. "Jennifer went directly to Skylur. The work she's done restructuring Altau Holdings is complete, in that her design is in place, and there are others who can carry the detail through. The whole Panethus community in North America is aware she's been responsible for getting such fundamental changes in place, and in such a short time. So Jennifer pointed out that everyone will see it as a huge compliment to the former Eastern Seaboard that she should be appointed to revise their business structures to integrate them into the new Altau Holdings. It will raise no questions that she starts at one end, in New Orleans, and works her way through them, city by city. Jennifer was also quick to point out that everywhere Matlal tried or succeeded in subverting Houses, like the Warders in New York, or Romero in Albuquerque, there's been a financial trail. Who better to find it than Jennifer, backed up by her forensic accounting team in Denver?"

I was about to suggest Jen would be able to work from Denver too, but I knew it wasn't like that. Down here, she could demand access to computers and filing cabinets, and make a point to get it instantaneously.

I went instead for security. "I can't protect her and do everything else that I'm expected to—"

"Skylur understands," Flavia interrupted. "Which is why he's taken steps."

"What steps?"

"House Farrell, there's no point my skating over this, because you will undoubtedly become aware of the truth at some point. I advised *against* all these decisions he's just made. It's not a matter of disliking you at all. My reasoning is that Skylur's actions prematurely elevate your House to such an extent that you will lose the few friends you have in Panethus, and in place of that, you will become a lightning rod for every resentment on your side of the Assembly."

"What are you talking about?"

"Skylur has taken the opportunity to make an open alignment with you. His personal pelea has been assigned to Jennifer."

"Maia? Maia Kiriani?" My mouth hung open.

"Yes, and two of her colleagues. In Maia's place as his pelea, he's appointed your Diakon. On top of that, Yelena's *human* kin, Keith and Julie, have been accepted to return his Athanate security team to full numbers. And on top of *that*, Yelena's other kin, Colonel Laine, has been appointed to a position that's effectively Minister of War."

I was struck dumb.

It was more than an alignment. It was integration, the same way that Bian and I had blurred the lines between our Houses.

And Skylur's personal pelea would be guarding Jen. Whatever treason Labastide might harbor, she wouldn't dare risk anything with Maia around.

That was, unless I'd completely misread her, missed the fanaticism which would think the prize of Jen and Maia might make it worth an attempt.

No.

Labastide hated Basilikos. We had that in common.

"As to Tucek," Flavia went on, "there's nothing we can do about Correia's decision, and on the surface it seems reasonable to have a Hidden Path equivalent to you."

"It doesn't work like that." I managed a short laugh. "If Tucek turns up in Baton Rouge and announces to Felix and Cameron that she's their liaison, she'll be lucky if they don't eat her. She's worked with the Central Mountain Confederation, for heaven's sake. She knows the alphas wouldn't just accept her, even if she hadn't worked for the enemy. Whether Correia realizes it or not, Tucek has some other reason for being here. Something for Matlal, or Vega Martine. But are you telling me there really are people in the Hidden Path so stupid they think Tucek's *not* Basilikos?" I swallowed. "No offense, House Flavia."

Flavia still insisted she was part of the 'real' Basilikos, neither Hidden Path nor Matlal's Basilikos. It was easy to forget that sometimes.

"None taken." Her tone was so dry you could have used it to mop the bathroom floor. "Correia probably knows, but I imagine she finds it's a politically sound decision."

I apologized for shouting at her and we ended our conversation more politely than I'd started it.

Over the next hour we returned to our hotel, changed, checked out, arranged for our luggage to be delivered to Labastide's mansion in Audubon, and got on the road to Baton Rouge.

I spent the majority of the time on my cell, updating with Bian, Diana and Gwen in a four-way conversation.

There were no leads in Lafayette. Other coven members Gwen had found were shocked when they discovered the abduction of their leaders. The coven only met every week or so, and they had no communication between meetings.

Neither did they have any clues to who would do it. Or how. Or why.

Back in Denver, Bian's reactions to Jen coming to New Orleans and then hearing that Maia would be her personal bodyguard matched mine. She still didn't like that we'd actually be staying as guests in Labastide's mansion along with House Tucek.

"Yes, Labastide has made you swear not to kill each other, but I wouldn't trust Tucek's oath," Bian said, and Diana agreed.

Gwen said she would meet us in New Orleans by the time we were back from visiting with Felix and Cameron. That made me feel we would be safer, but we couldn't go on like that. If Tucek intended to try something, she'd just wait until some of us were caught up elsewhere. Or she would simply blow the whole house up.

Tucek had less to lose. If she stayed around, at some stage an Assembly would be called or one of Correia's famous subcommittees would be set up and I would present my evidence. There would be no way for Tucek to lie her way out of that, so she had to know her time pretending to be Hidden Path was coming to an end. If she could kill half a dozen of us before fleeing, she'd take that.

Having given Labastide my oath, I had two options, as I saw it. Break the oath and kill Tucek, which would mean the former members of the

Eastern Seaboard association would go berserk. Or prove beyond doubt that Tucek was Basilikos, because that invalidated the oaths.

Then kill her.

Chapter 30

Felix and Cameron were renting an industrial business property, on the opposite side of the Mississippi from Baton Rouge, tucked away against the bend of the canal that came down from the Port Allen lock. When I'd texted I was on I-10, they'd replied with this address rather than the place they were staying. Something was happening.

The property was at the end of a scratchy road where the telephone poles leaned at drunken angles, and way beyond where the asphalt gave out. Not a place people came out of choice. The site itself was screened by scrub oak, parked rigs and derelict industrial equipment—broken cranes, rusted trucks, even an old pontoon bridge.

We parked by a handful of other trucks at the entrance and got out.

There had been an unsettled murmur in the Call I sensed from a couple of miles away. Nothing specific. An unhappy, frustrated feeling from the pack here. I breathed deep. I could smell the river and the canal, the unpleasant tang of chemicals and gas in the dust... and a lot of pissed-off werewolves: Denver pack. The mix of the New Mexico packs. Tucson. A couple I couldn't recognize.

Everyone was standing around in little clusters, hands in pockets, talking or staring or kicking stones.

Yeah, bored and pissed off.

I caught sight of Felix, in his casual black jeans, surrounded by half a dozen werewolves. He was talking to a couple whose body language told me they were outsiders. Maybe they were some of the Louisiana alphas from the packs that he'd been trying to recruit into the League for the last couple of months.

Why meet out here today?

My gut didn't like this.

Felix raised a hand and pointed at me. One of the outsiders nodded, and walked away to make a call on his cell.

My gut liked that even less.

The group around Felix dispersed and we met halfway.

"Afternoon, Felix. What's going on?"

His eyes swept across Pia and Rita before checking who was nearby. He turned his back to the two outsiders.

"Truth is, I'm not sure," he said quietly. "Something's happened. We've been going around in circles with a bunch of sub-packs. It's been like trying to dig a hole in mud."

Cameron joined us. "And then two days ago: *boom*. There was a day's complete silence where we couldn't get through to anyone, and when they got back, a complete change. Now their top alphas want to meet with us, *right now*, but they want you there as well. They should be here in an hour or so." Her eyes bored into me. "Anything you can think of to explain that?"

"Yes," I replied, stomach sinking. Not how I wanted to talk to them about Mexico. "Gonna have to take it somewhere private. Quickly."

The outsiders were looking over at us. I'd picked up the odd word from their cellphone conversation, so we were too close.

"The site office." Felix nodded at a sagging, singlewide trailer up on blocks.

As we walked across, Cameron asked, "Where's Yelena?"

"New York. Lots of news, but we'd better keep it to what's relevant to today."

I finger-signed Rita and Pia to keep people away from the trailer.

Cameron saw it and her eyes narrowed. I'd gotten the idea of finger-talk from the New Mexico packs, and Cameron could make the same deductions as Zane had about the time that should have been required to make up our own sign language.

Yeah. Lots of news.

As Felix closed the door, I launched straight in.

"I don't trust the packs in Louisiana. I really don't trust what's happening this afternoon. I suspect they may try an attack."

"Really," Cameron drawled. "You tell us why you think that's likely, and we'll tell you how it looks from our side."

"On the way here, I diverted to El Paso, to help fix the situation there, but to do that, I needed to fix things across the border. When I did that, I found links between Basilikos and the Louisiana Were, and an Adept here who goes by the name Queen of Diamonds."

Felix snorted. "We heard about the ambush. We wondered what you got up to afterwards," he said. "We'll talk more later, but give us the bottom line now."

We sat on plastic seats with our heads close together and dropped our voices.

I needed to get the maximum amount of information through to them in the minimum time. There weren't more than twenty of the League out there, and if the Louisiana packs attacked, they would attack in force.

"I'll answer all your questions, and I kept it secret to give you plausible deniability."

Felix and Cameron exchanged glances. They had good poker faces; I really couldn't tell if they were pissed or amused.

"Okay," I went on, "the bottom line is this: all the border problems we've been having, from El Paso all the way down to San Diego, have been orchestrated by Basilikos. I suspect the Queen of Diamonds is a major player in this, and the Louisiana packs have been targeted, partly to stall the League."

"Big claim," Felix said. "Why would Basilikos do this?"

"Targeted? How?" Cameron piled on.

"Why? Because it weakens us," I replied. "Matlal doesn't want Panethus Athanate working with local groups of Were because that strengthens us. I'm guessing he saw a perfect opportunity in El Paso, where the Athanate House didn't want to work with anyone else, and I'm worried he may be several steps ahead of that here in Louisiana. I discovered that the Mexico Were did have a magically-assisted method of creating new Were, as we suspected; that's how the Juárez pack were able to replace their losses and keep coming at El Paso, for instance, and it's almost certainly where the packs here are getting the new members you told me about. But what really concerns me is that it appears that magical assistance came from the Queen of Diamonds, and as I said, she's local to this area."

"You're going to have to go through this step by step," Felix said.

Cameron nodded. "We don't trust the local packs, and we hear rumors, but you're talking a whole lot more than that. From the beginning, the bare bones, please."

That was a direct order, so I went back to the beginning: Matlal's long-term planning with Mirela Tucek and her ninja nuns in Taos, including subverting the Adept community there, then getting the Confederation to attack the New Mexico packs, the destruction of House Romero in Albuquerque. Then I moved on to the border problems with the Chihuahua, Sonora and Baja packs. The ambush in El Paso. The raids on Juárez, Villa Ahumada, Santa Ana, Tijuana and Ensenada. The results from Astilla de Luna. The pit. The comms traffic with Louisiana. The conversation with Díaz, the alpha of the Coahuila pack.

The good thing was they listened without a lot of interruptions, and they were more angry at what had been happening than they were at me for acting on my own. I pointed out that if I'd come to them with my guesses before I'd set out, they probably wouldn't have believed me.

After that I quickly gave them a rundown of what Ops 4-10 would have called 'soft' data. The use of the word rabioso, the name Queen of Diamonds that kept cropping up, the information we'd gotten from the spirit world about the workings that connected Matlal to the Were packs, Labastide's description of the legends, the scent that could be unknown Were at the coven's house in Lafayette, the way it reminded me of the pit and something else.

There was a long pause after I wound down.

"So you think this sudden change in approach here was caused by them realizing what you'd done down in Mexico?" Felix asked.

"I don't believe in coincidences. The timing is right."

"What did they gain before, and what are they looking to do now?"

I shrugged.

"Before... I'd say that their aim was to have the League stalled here and you distracted. I'll speculate and say that achieved three things. You weren't paying full attention to what was happening on the border. Your momentum to gain new packs east of here is gone, and I'll bet that Matlal or the Queen of Diamonds has been to them, offering whatever it was that worked with the Mexican packs."

"Apart from Coahuila."

"Yes."

"You said three things."

"Well, that ties in with what they may be looking to do now. The way I see it, the longer you're delayed here, the better their advantage. You've been sending League people back to their packs, because, hey, everyone has jobs and houses and families and we're supposed to blend in—"

"We've rotated. Sent some back, called some out."

"I'm betting more sent back," I said, and I knew I was right. "Because you reasoned that there's nothing going on here that needs a big pack. It's all just talk-talk. And while you're scaling down, what do you want to bet they've been scaling up? But now they know there's no more new rabioso coming from the pit. And they want payback for that. So now is when they strike."

We'd gotten so intensely into the discussion, Rita's knock on the door was loud and startling.

Chapter 31

Outside, late afternoon had brought gray, scudding clouds and a thin rain.

It had also brought more arrivals from the Louisiana packs. Trucks had blocked the entrance and new arrivals were parking all along the road. Each truck had four or five werewolves.

A few of them were from the League, but two things were immediately obvious: we were outnumbered, and the Louisiana werewolves weren't here to hold a party. Their pack marques were confused and strange, but they were building a Call which showed a straggling unity.

This didn't look good at all.

Felix and Cameron didn't twitch; they called over alphas they knew. Those werewolves came, but the body language was all wrong. Group language was even worse; the League with their backs against the office trailer, the locals in a semicircle at a distance.

No car could have gotten through, but I heard the thumping engines of a couple of Harleys as they threaded their way between the vehicles. Nick and Ursula rode in, coming to a halt on the near side of the League.

The skinwalkers kicked their side stands down and sat looking at the crowd of Louisiana werewolves for a minute.

Then Nick reached into a saddlebag. The front rank of watchers froze and half of them came forward onto the balls of their feet.

He brought out an apple and took a thoughtful and appreciative bite out of it. Grinned at the locals.

I wanted to laugh, but it wasn't really funny.

Ursula slapped him on the shoulder as she walked past.

She came and folded me up into a welcoming hug.

"Good to see you," she said. "Sorry about... this."

Nick was right behind her.

"Hang loose," he muttered. "Not gone to hell yet." He snorted. "The Atchafalaya pack aren't here yet. *Then* it's going to hell."

"They're the top of the pile?"

"Yeah. All these are sub-packs." He ran a hand across his mouth and chin, keeping his voice so low I could barely hear. "They're not real happy about it. Not even real happy with each other, way I see."

"Something we can use?"

He gave a little tilt of his head. *Maybe.*

"You met the Atchafalaya alphas?"

Ursula shook her head and answered for both of them. "The three of them don't come out much."

Three?

It was at that point I felt the Call of the Atchafalaya pack. Not that I recognized it, but it was different from every Call I'd ever heard. Harsher.

And who else would it be?

I guessed they were a few hundred yards away. *Not* on the road.

Others noticed. Heads started to swing around. The Louisiana werewolves' group split in the middle and drew apart, leaving a gap. The gap pointed down the Port Allen waterway, and the steady sound of marine engines drifted along the water to us.

The trees and barrier of industrial junk prevented us from seeing them, but the sounds told us what we needed to know. Five boats, shallow-draft swamp boats like the jonboat I'd seen in Lafayette. One by one, the puttering engines stopped and I could hear them lift the boats out of the water and slide them onto the bank.

They began to emerge from the trees and filter through the screen of industrial scrap in ones and twos. A sense of threat and a taste of violence in the air came with them.

They were big, hulking swamp men and women. Hair long and matted, clothes tattered. Dirty. Faces tattooed with witch symbols. Talking, but I couldn't make out words. Some of them were laughing.

Laughing.

And the smell.

No mistaking it now.

Cold in the Somalian pre-dawn. Break the camp early to cross the border. The sky is all yellow and red. The earth is black. There's noise around us from the dark. The smell—like cheap soap boiled dry.

"Those aren't freaking werewolves," I said.

Nick and Ursula grunted confirmation, frowning as they tried unsuccessfully to process the marque.

"Rougarou," Ursula said. "That's what they call them around here."

Cameron turned back to look at me.

"Hyena," I said. "African spotted hyena. Some mix with wolf."

Over twenty of them. Taking into account the forty-odd other Louisiana werewolves, that made us outnumbered nearly three to one.

And then I saw the alphas.

"That's got to be Bastien and Rochelle Fournier on the left," Nick said. "Brother and sister."

"Which means that's Leandre Quémeneur, on the right," Ursula said.

Rochelle Fournier was even bigger than her brother, and he was at least six-five. Leandre must have been over seven feet. All three of them were solid slabs of muscle and bone. Black hair. Faces sharp and predatory. Eager. Enjoying their entrance.

Felix and Cameron strolled forward to meet them, and that ruined the Atchafalayas' enjoyment. We were supposed to be scared.

Hell, I *was* scared. We were trapped here, and outnumbered, and for sure, they hadn't come to talk about joining the League.

Shit.

But I was an alpha. Time to earn it.

I walked to stand alongside Cameron.

No small talk.

"There only one way that packs join up, Larimer." Quémeneur's voice fitted him. It was harsh and abrupt. "Challenge. Death or submission."

Quémeneur topped him by over a foot. Felix was acting as if he hadn't noticed.

"Actually, challenge for pack leadership is to the death everywhere else I know." Felix grinned.

"We don' waste," Rochelle Fournier said. "'Course we make sure the li'l alphas know they our bitches after they roll." She was looking at Cameron and me. "Never had me an alpha that was real bitch 'fore. Giving me ideas."

Her brother snarled. "We keep 'em 'til they know they our bitches right down in the bones."

There was stirring in the ranks of Louisiana wolves behind him.

"*She* wants this one." Quémeneur pointed at me.

"And you're her bitches, so you do what the Queen says," the little demon in my throat said before I could stop her.

All three snarled at me.

"Damn! Looks like that stung." Felix laughed.

The wall of Louisiana werewolves growled at us. They didn't like the way this was going. The other packs hadn't liked the way the Atchafalaya alphas spoke about them, but that was a long way from doing anything about it.

Nick had said there were differences in their ranks. The main one was obvious: the hyena-wolves of the Atchafalaya, the rougarou, held apart from the other Louisiana packs. But even in the Louisiana packs, there was a tension in their ranks.

I could see clusters within the packs. There would be an alpha, lieutenants, and a close knot of their established wolves. Around them, drifting, another group, part of their pack but not fully engaged, which was a complete contradiction.

New recruits from Villa Ahumada's pit? Rabioso?

I'd bet on that.

I'd also bet, that if it were completely up to the Atchafalaya alphas, they'd have just swarmed over us with their full pack and killed us. But they'd grown their sub-packs so much—basically every Louisiana pack was included—that they had to take account of the way those sub-packs wanted things done. And the sub-packs were still traditional werewolves. They'd agreed Felix and Cameron could come in and talk to them, so they'd only agree to a formal Were contest as a way to backtrack. They could have brought hundreds of wolves, and overwhelmed us, but they hadn't.

Still, sixty of them to twenty of us. Not good odds.

Quémeneur took another pace forward and loomed over Felix, trying to force him to take a step back.

It didn't work.

"You given up talking?" Felix said. "Because I've had enough of your smell."

Quémeneur's mouth opened.

"Challenge!" Cameron shouted so that every wolf-ear in the compound heard it. "I challenge you, Quémeneur, for your pack and all your sub-packs. To the death."

That hit the ranks of the locals like the shock wave of an explosion. I wondered if Quémeneur had had many challenges. Never one from someone so much smaller than him.

But it left the other two Atchafalaya alphas.

It was an official challenge. Traditionally all alphas got involved if there was more than one. Traditionally, it had to be on four legs.

These hyena-wolves looked experienced at four-legged fighting. I didn't have an Adept handy to channel power, so I wouldn't be able to use the tricks I'd used to kill Victoria Oaken when the El Paso alphas had challenged Alex and me.

On the other hand, I'd trained on four legs with Rita since then, and the were-cougar was as lethal as she was unconventional. On top of that, I had Hana and Tara back with me. Hana's instincts would help me.

And I had an issue with Rochelle Fournier after her comments. "I challenge you," I said to her.

"That leaves me with the runt." Felix sighed and shook his head. "The things I do for you girls."

No one outside could see into the compound. Some of the Louisiana Were who'd arrived by truck started their engines and left them running to mask the noise of the challenge. One of them even got out a boom box and we got heavy metal screeching across the muddy patch that had just become an arena of death in the middle of the compound.

Chapter 32

Werewolf challengers spent a lot of time assessing each other before they got going.

So did the rougarou.

The Fourniers and Quémeneur stripped and prowled with the rain running down their skin.

The two guys had obscene erections, and all three of them were wild-eyed and literally frothing at the mouth.

Felix was in no rush. He'd had the plastic chairs brought out of the office so we could drape our clothes over them. They were going to get wet in the rain, but they wouldn't get dirty as well.

Just as long as we were around to appreciate the difference.

"Sure?" Felix muttered to Cameron.

Cameron just nodded. Her eyes had gone all long-focus. She wasn't really *here* any more.

"I think they're pack fighters by preference," she said. "Keep them separate."

At that point Quémeneur changed. Not a straight Were change. I felt the skitter of magic across my skin as he fell onto all fours.

"Oh, shit," I said.

Truly monstrous. He had the sloping back and lower hindquarters of a hyena, but he was bigger than a Kodiak at the shoulder. His head was wolf-like, and the jaws were the length of my forearm. The size of his chest made me wonder if there was anything else in the mix, like freaking lion.

There was a stifled groan from the League behind us.

Dominant alphas increased their size through dominance or the size of their pack, but the only creature I'd seen approaching this size was Theodore Noble, the psycho shapeshifter who'd leeched mass from living victims to increase his size. Like I had when I killed the old El Paso alpha.

Cameron could call on the dominance of being a co-alpha of the largest super-pack ever, but she still couldn't reach that size. Nowhere near. And although there were a lot of factors in a werewolf fight, nothing beat sheer mass when there was *that* much of it. He had to be close to a ton of meat.

My stomach knotted with adrenaline.

Focus.

Details.

Concentrate.

"Those jaws," I said, thinking of the dogs at Lafayette. "I'm betting they're stronger than ours. Probably all of them have bites like bears. I'd advise ripping your skin rather than letting them get a purchase."

Felix nodded, his eyes fixed on our opponents. "Frenzied," he muttered. "Berserker. I'm guessing they'll be immune to pain. Difficult."

"Back of neck looks well protected. But he'll be slow to get all that weight moving or turning," I said.

Cameron put her head back and laughed, the sound carrying across the compound and getting angry snarls back from the watching rougarou.

"Overconfident," she said and changed.

At which point I swore again.

I'd never seen Cameron go to her complete wolf. She was as dark-furred as her skin, as streamlined and long-legged on four legs as she was on two. But she looked like a dainty toy opposite Quémeneur's monster. She hadn't put on *any* mass.

A gasp came from some of the League behind us. They could see she was outmatched.

Hana? What do I do?

Keep the three rougarou separate. Talk to your opponent. Distract her. Hana's voice. *Let Cameron be. She'll be fast. She won't tire. There's advantage there.*

Some hope then.

I held off changing as long as possible. I walked alongside Cameron as she moved to the center, trying to make an angle to push the Fournier sister away from Quémeneur, though it hardly seemed it was going to make a difference.

"It was you at the coven's house in Lafayette, wasn't it?" I said to Rochelle Fournier. "I recognize the stink."

Her eyes were like an animal's, but she understood.

"Me and Bastien." She laughed. "Stupid witch fools, thinking their dogs protect them. That part was good, ripping the throats out. Too quick, though. And can't talk to dog."

"Those dogs knew they were going to die," I said.

Hana's idea was working. I could sense my opponent wanted to join Quémeneur, but she wanted to talk as well. She wanted to taunt me. It excited her to think I was scared. She wanted to enjoy that.

"Yes, but no death for you," she said. "You're going to the swamp. She wants you, and she always gets what she wants. But your choice to turn up whole or broken."

On Cameron's other side, Felix had edged Bastien Fournier away from Quémeneur as well.

Cameron was darting from side to side, whining.

Quémeneur was simply stalking. One foot in front of the other.

What the hell is Cameron doing?

"'Course, when she got you, you want back out," Rochelle said, "'cause what I do nothing on what she do to you. But you all tough like steel 'til it happen. Like the li'l Canadian bitch, an' lookit her now."

The rest of it was noise, but that last sentence got to me, and she noticed.

"Ah. She something special for you." She laughed, a crazy giggling laugh uncannily like a hyena. "This gonna be more fun than I thought."

Out of the corner of my eye, I could see Cameron had run out of room, and I sensed something was about to happen.

I crouched, felt the wolf rising in me, scratching to get out.

Fight. Kill.

Felt Rita's training like a chant echoing in my bones, overlaying the wolf instincts. *Hold. Timing. Speed of attack. Purpose. Relentlessness.*

Quémeneur lunged. It was a feint, to terrify. He was playing with her.

Cameron gave a frightened squeal.

Quémeneur put his head back and howled fit to freeze blood.

And Cameron shot in like an arrow. *Underneath* Quémeneur. Biting. Blood spurt. Out the other side. Yipping like a coyote. Laughing.

Quémeneur had tried to jump back, but there was too much of him to move that quickly.

My focus had narrowed so I barely heard the snatches of shouting...

"... she bit his damn cock off!"

Felix changed and suddenly a second dark wolf was in the arena. He had become *much* more massive than when I last saw him, and he planted himself between Quémeneur and Bastien.

Bastien changed. He wanted to help Quémeneur, but the sight of Felix made him hesitate.

Rochelle wasn't going to hesitate. She changed and didn't even bother to look at me.

She was almost as monstrous as Quémeneur. No way I could miss, but I wanted more than that. I wanted to be accurate. I wanted her throat.

Behind me Quémeneur was screaming with rage, and as Rochelle tensed to spring, I hit her.

Part balance and part surprise, she backed, raising her head instinctively out of the way of my attack. *Mistake.* I went *low*, struck *up*. Jaws closed on her throat.

Kill. Kill.

With all her mass moving backwards, I heaved, pushed. Built on her movement. Forced her back until her back legs stumbled and scrabbled in the dirt.

A roar from the League. Shocked silence from the Louisiana packs.

Screaming snarls behind me. Felix. Bastien. Howls.

I shut it out. Good start for us, but there was a lot of Quémeneur, if Cameron was going to take him a bite at a time. And I was a long way from being able to help her.

I couldn't get any more purchase, and my shock tactic had reached the end of its usefulness. Now it was like a matchup between a sumo wrestler and a ten-year-old kid.

I wasn't going to let go of her throat, but her skin was like armor. My teeth had broken through but even when Rochelle tried shaking me off, her flesh wasn't ripping and my fangs weren't getting any deeper. I wasn't constricting her airways and I hadn't gotten through to her arteries.

Damn, but this was supposed to be her vulnerable side.

She reared up, jerking me off my paws. I took the opportunity to rake her belly.

Blood.

For a moment, I thought it was the beginning of the end for her.

Then she dropped us both to the ground, and landed on me so hard and heavy, I started to black out.

Do not let go.

She rose again, screaming and shaking me. Unable to see how close her last attempt had gotten.

I raked her again.

I needed more power in my bite, or my claws.

No handy Adepts to channel shape-shifting magic. My eukori reached out and felt Rita, Pia, Nick, Ursula.

Nick. Shapeshifter. Magic-user.

Giving up on the shaking, Rochelle slammed me down into the ground again. My vision went dark and there was no way I could reach out and do anything difficult with eukori. Nick was difficult. I'd never worked with him in that way.

I got one foot free and raked Rochelle's belly again. This time I didn't even break skin.

Rita.

At the touch of my eukori, I could feel her willing me on. Shouting advice.

Purpose. Relentlessness.

I had to keep attacking.

Forepaw. Eyes. *Rake her eyes.* Rochelle screamed again as I did.

I was too close in for her paws; they couldn't reach my eyes, or my belly.

But she didn't need to. Her weight came crashing down on me again, and I knew I couldn't last through another body slam like that.

Rita.

Cougar.

Tara reached out to Rita. We used eukori in sparring sessions. Connecting with Rita was easy. But she wasn't a magic user.

Tara insistent. Showing me...

Change.

Nick had told me that all shapeshifters should have any shape they cared to learn. Werewolves went to wolves because that's what they believed they'd go to.

So change.

Not even a full change. Just the claws. The hindquarters.

Rochelle lifted me, pulling herself higher to crush me when she landed on top. This was my last opportunity.

I raked. I raked like Rita would, like a cougar, with a cougar's claws. Violently. Like kicking Rochelle in her belly with daggers on my feet.

She screamed again, and the note changed.

Fear had overtaken anger.

Bite.

A cougar's bite isn't much more powerful than a wolf's, but I renewed my efforts there. Reaching with everything...

Blood.

Huge boost. Like a shocking, second surge of adrenaline, I felt *power*. *Wonderful* power. I felt my jaw muscles swell, fangs sink deeper. Crazy mix of wolf and cat. I clamped down on her neck.

More blood.

Blood all over both of us. Her belly shredding. Her throat starting to tear. Blood pumping, spurting. *Arterial blood*. I'd bitten into her main blood vessels.

I twisted.

Stopped kicking and got my hindquarters under me.

Now she was staggering.

I heaved her backwards and jerked my head, ripping violently to one side. Her throat tore. Her blood sprayed out like a fountain as she fell.

I gagged and coughed out her pungent flesh.

She changed back to human as she hit the ground. Her back arched and her feet drummed for a second as if she were fighting to live, but her body gave one final spasm and collapsed.

I was back to wolf.

Not over yet.

I spun around.

Chapter 33

Bastien Fournier was physically evenly matched against Felix.

Quémeneur was too much for Cameron.

The huge alpha had managed to channel his rage in the way really good fighters can do. He'd started dumb and overconfident, but now he'd reached another level. I could smell it coming off him, something that remained cold inside the heat of the fight.

More magical boosts?

I charged in at his hind legs. Swiped claws on his haunch. Feinted to jump on his back and dodged away instead.

He spun, quick as a snap of fingers. For all his weight and problems with lunging, he could turn in an instant.

Ooohh. Gave that move away, Quémeneur.

He knew it too. His eyes flared and he gave another of those screams that could never have come from a wolf throat.

Cameron yipped laughter again, tongue hanging out, and trotting back outside his reach. As I snarled and threatened his backside, Cameron began to move back and forth in front, always close, always too quick for the potentially crippling paw sweeps and lethal charges he tried.

Quémeneur knew he was in trouble. Even with his frightening size, he didn't want to face two against one, and he could read Bastien was in trouble. If Bastien died, it would be three against one.

There was only one way to go, and I was waiting for it.

The next time Felix's back was turned, Quémeneur charged.

I hit his hindquarters before he'd really got out of his crouch. I wasn't anywhere near his mass, but becoming co-alpha of El Paso had increased my size. Enough that a strike at full speed ruined his aim.

Cameron hit him from the front at the same time. Doing what I had: going low and driving upwards for his throat. But even though we'd deflected his attack, his weight was too much. All three of us crashed into Felix and Bastien.

Everything disappeared into a spray of water and mud.

Bad.

I was half-blinded. Locked into a snapping, snarling, twisting ball of fangs and claws. Tiring. Unable to back off without opening myself to an attack. All momentum lost to the greater weight and strength of the two rougarou alphas.

It got worse.

Another Atchafalaya leaped into the arena and sank his fangs into the back of Felix's neck.

Nothing I could do. Cameron was trapped against Bastien's side and Quémeneur was about to get his jaws on her.

No time. I bit into the only vulnerable part I could reach quickly enough. His belly.

His forward momentum jerked me off my feet.

I rolled up and raked him with my hind claws.

His huge snout whipped around and he bit at the back of my neck. Not enough to get a good grip, but I was caught.

Couldn't let go.

Rake him.

The whole writhing pile shook as someone else hit us.

The newly joined Atchafalaya was lifted, screaming, by a Kodiak bear who broke his back and threw him aside.

I saw Cameron sink fangs into Quémeneur's exposed neck, but most of his weight was on me and the world was going dark again.

I tasted blood.

Felt my body change again. Felt the power. Kicked upwards. Tore.

Got half the weight off me, and saw Cameron was growing, becoming as large as I'd expected her to be at the start. Her jaws were tearing at his neck.

He started to panic. Thrashed. Let me go, but landed back on me like a mountain. I couldn't breathe. I redoubled my efforts, biting, raking, twisting, suffocating, drowning in mud and blood beneath the combined weight of all of them.

Everything began to blur. My lungs burned. Everything hurt.

A long-snouted head slammed into the ground beside me.

Bastien.

Dead.

The weight above me shifted: left, right, back again. Crushing me again. They were fighting on top of me.

I kept biting into Quémeneur's belly, not letting him get up, but it was killing me.

There were screams, spiraling up, rising and rising.

The screams stopped.

I blacked out for a second and lost my grip.

Then the weight was mercifully lifted off.

I lurched to my paws, gasping for breath. Stared into Quémeneur's glazed, dead eyes until understanding finally came.

Done it!

Then I was hit again and again. More rougarou attacked and I was so exhausted I couldn't even evade their bites.

The League rushed to our aid, but I was trapped right in the middle.

Rita, in cougar form, fought her way through to help me, taking all the attacks on one side. It wasn't enough. We were being overwhelmed, so crushed we couldn't bite, couldn't free our claws to fight back.

It didn't really help that the rougarou turned to fight the League werewolves, because we were at the bottom of the pile. We were being suffocated beneath an avalanche of were-hyenas.

As everything darkened, there was a flare of magic. Not a shiver crossing my skin. An explosion of magic, so shocking that everyone stopped to see what had happened.

Rita and I couldn't move, couldn't see.

The next second a wall of water crashed down on the whole compound.

Everyone on top of us, Atchafalaya, Louisiana, League... all stumbled away, trying to suck in air that wasn't full of water.

And right into the space they vacated, something big and bright hurtled down from the sky to land.

I couldn't get up.

Bryn, Gwen's Valkyrie spirit guide, was standing over me. Her sword became a wheel of fire, scything left and right. Atchafalaya heads soared into the air, fell back to earth and rolled in the mud.

Those of the Louisiana packs that had joined the rougarou had had enough.

The rougarou themselves fought on, but the tide had turned. With a flaming sword at their backs and an implacable League along with some Louisiana allies surrounding them, they couldn't even manage a fight to the death.

I was still trying to wipe the muck from my eyes and ears, so I couldn't hear what Bryn was saying clearly. She seemed to be ordering the League and Louisiana Were to capture the Atchafalaya.

When a seven-foot Valkyrie dispensing death by sword and wings demands something, most people comply.

The fight disintegrated into struggling clumps comprising a single rougarou being held by several League wolves.

Bryn strode up to one, reached in and grabbed the Atchafalaya by his hair. She took off, straight upwards.

Seconds later, the were-hyena fell back out of the clouds, screaming until he hit the grid structure of the derelict pontoon bridge at the side of the compound.

Bryn returned.

"You!" She grabbed another Atchafalaya by the hair and shouted into his face. "You can't tell me where the Lafayette coven were taken either, can you?"

"The Church," he stammered. "She gave them to the Church."

"Which one?"

"The Church of the Risen Sun."

"Where?"

"I don't know. I swear. They have a secret church in the delta somewhere. I think there."

Chapter 34

Two hours later in the Hill Bitch and we were 'close' to the church.

We'd acquired a guide. One of the Louisiana alphas, Bill Patout, said he knew the approximate location of the secret church.

His pack had been one of the ones that had come straight across as soon as we'd won the challenge. He'd lost wolves because of it, killed by the Atchafalaya. I trusted him and I was all out of other options.

He'd even wanted to bring his whole pack on this hunt, but the situation back at Baton Rouge was a mess, and Felix couldn't spare any more. He'd called in the rest of Bill's pack, and a couple of others who'd honored the rules, and they were policing the circus.

The Atchafalaya pack had violated the rules of the challenge and would face Were justice.

Some members of the Louisiana packs had joined them. Same outcome.

All the Louisiana pack members who'd joined the Atchafalaya were rabioso, from the pit at Astilla de Luna. I could smell that they were different. I could smell they had something in common with the Atchafalaya, and I was starting to think of that smell as the signature of the Queen of Diamonds.

The trouble was, not *all* rabioso present had joined the Atchafalayas' treachery, and the packs told us that *every* Louisiana pack had received new members as part of the deal imposed on them when they became sub-packs of the Atchafalaya.

I knew those new werewolves weren't to be trusted, but what the hell did you do with all of them?

It was Felix and Cameron's problem for the moment.

I'd hugged my alphas after the battle, all of us exhausted, battered and bruised, filthy with blood and mud.

"We did good," Felix had muttered with a snort, "but that damned Valkyrie is something else."

"Nick and Ursula, too," Cameron had replied. She'd been right. Without those three, we wouldn't have survived.

"And damn, you too, alpha," I said to Cameron. "That trick, changing into such a small wolf. I thought we were dead for sure."

"Oh? Like I should have told you before I went ahead and just did it?"

"Ouch. Yeah, I guess I should apologize for keeping you in the dark."

I tilted my head to offer my throat.

Cameron snarled and bit my neck, but she hadn't changed to wolf. And she ruined it by laughing and spitting to the side. "Eww! You taste like rougarou."

"What you did was needed," Felix said. "But we'd have backed you anyway, and damn the Assembly."

"You have a hostage to find," Cameron said. "Go on. We got this."

So here I was, in the depths of the delta, searching for Gabrielle and the missing coven members.

I'd brought Rita, Nick, Ursula, Pia and Olivia.

Bryn had taken off and disappeared into cloud as soon as we left Port Allen. She'd reunite with Gwen, and then they'd meet us on the way, with Flint and Kane.

That was the plan. Talking them through a dirt-track route that wasn't on any GPS wasn't easy. Bill worked on that over the cellphone while I sat and sorted through our options, which weren't good to start with and got worse the more I examined them.

Not only were we unsure exactly where this church was, we didn't know the coven would be there. We had no idea about the layout of the building. No idea how many members there were, or how they were armed. No idea what they were doing. We only had weapons for three of us.

Once inside, the only person in the group we would recognize would be Gabrielle, and only half of us knew her. The rest of the coven we couldn't tell from members of this Church. This was not a situation we wanted to charge into with guns firing, even if we could; the members of this church were human, and they were in Labastide's territory.

And it was getting dark.

On the positive side, we had two skinwalkers, three if you counted me now, a were-cougar, a top-level Adept with a Valkyrie spirit guide, two cowboy Adepts, a couple of werewolves and an Athanate healer.

The Church of the Risen Sun had a world of hurt heading for them, and thinking that left me wondering: *why* had the Swamp Witch given the Lafayette coven to the Church that wanted her dead? And, seeing as these were powerful Adepts, how were the Church keeping them imprisoned?

"No, the *third* turn across the railroad tracks after the big junction," Bill Patout was saying. "On the left. There's a level crossing. Then once you're past the trees, you can see the levee dead ahead."

There was a reply from Kane, and Bill leaned back and spoke to me.

"That winged nightmare just did a circuit overhead. They're only five minutes away."

"Bryn is a Valkyrie, if you want to keep your head on your shoulders. And how much further to the church?"

"Ten minutes on foot, I guess. Road's not good and we don't want to take the trucks and the Harleys in closer anyway. It's quiet out here and sound travels."

A ten-minute walk. I could manage that. I hoped.

Rita and I got out and hobbled around to get moving again. My whole back had seized and it hurt to move my arms. We'd been in the worst of the fighting at Port Allen and we were both stiff from the drive. Even breathing hurt me. Athanate and Were heal quickly, but not *that* quickly. We had more bite marks and torn flesh than whole skin.

Pia bit us both, topping us up with an Athanate cocktail of aniatropics. It helped, but what we needed was twelve hours of sleep.

Not going to happen soon.

I'd instructed the Lost Boys to get a vehicle 'for rough roads'. I found out their interpretation of that was a top-of-the-line Range Rover as they came to a quiet halt behind Nick and Ursula's Harleys a few minutes later.

I didn't have time to comment to them.

Gwen came out of the Range Rover ready to go. "Bryn says the church is in that direction, about half a mile. There are people inside, and there's evidence of workings. I had to make her promise to wait for you to decide how we do it, and she's not happy."

"What kind of workings?" I asked.

I could see Bryn seething just below the surface in Gwen's clipped answer. "Inhibitory."

Which answered the second of the questions I'd asked myself on the way, about how the coven didn't break free on their own; they'd been bound with spells before being handed over.

"Any indication of alarms or traps?"

"None she could sense flying over. And no indication there are other active Adepts or other paranormals in the building."

"Okay, let's get there." I turned. "Olivia, go to your wolf and run ahead. I want you to get in close. Don't be seen. Circle the building and come back to report."

She stripped and raced off.

Rita frowned.

"Less wounded and smaller than you," I said. "But more important, not threatening. If someone does see her, they'll think it's a dog."

Olivia was back before we were halfway there. I could see her distress even before she changed back.

"Bonfires," she stammered, struggling to get her human voice working quickly enough. "They're having some kind of service inside and then they're going to burn them!"

Chapter 35

"We can't kill them," I said.

I could see from her eyes that Gwen was having trouble holding Bryn back. The Valkyrie wanted to do just that—kill them all, and I had no doubt she could.

"This is another Athanate House's territory," I explained. "I'm constrained in what I do here."

I held up a hand when Gwen started to argue.

"Yes, you're the leader of our coven, and your coven doesn't have any arrangement with the Athanate. But you're also in my House, and I'm bound by Athanate laws."

"Then you can just blur their memories," Olivia said.

"No. Blurring works well when you obscure odd things that happen to one person, but we're not going to be able to blur the whole congregation's memories of us attacking their sick ritual. Even if we could, it would take too long."

"So what do we do?"

"We're going to scare them like they've never been scared before. They're going to find that all these things they believe exist out in the darkness are going to visit them tonight. We are the things that go bump in the night, people. We are terrifying. Let's use it."

Everyone moved into place around the building, and it was up to me to get the ball rolling.

The bonfire wood heaped around stakes was in the back, about fifty yards away. There was no one out there yet. All still inside the church.

It was an old clapboard building that had seen much better days. It leaned to one side. Once it had been painted white, but mosses had colonized the cracks, spread out or leaked down with the rain. There was a steeple of sorts, a square turret with the top leveled off. Instead of a cross above it, there was a glass bowl about a yard across, with a flame inside.

I guessed that was meant to symbolize the Risen Sun.

The bowl cast an eerie, flickering light on the surrounding ancient oaks, all of them draped with Spanish moss, and leaning in toward the church like shrouded wraiths waiting for the light to fail.

I could hear the priest, and although the voice was different from the one I'd heard on the radio, it had the same cadences, the same message to start. Then it got much worse.

"We are here, in the end times, folks. It's too late for living your life right and being full of hope. That's the old way, and the ways have parted. We walk in darkness, and we may not go back 'cross that mighty chasm, save the Lord and His angels give us a path.

"In His mercy, He has given us an angel. He has given us the sign of the Risen Sun in the depths of the swamp, and that angel has guided us to a bridge. Now, that bridge is long and fearful, folks. I make no bones 'bout it. Y'all will need to steel your hearts and fix your eyes upon the path, for terrible things must be done to ascend that bridge and regain the path of light. But y'all can do it, even in darkness, for the angel has showed us a way to light our steps with the souls of the darkness itself."

"We will drive out the darkness with fire. We will not suffer a witch to live, and we will keep those fires lit while there is yet darkness around us, that our steps may be sure upon the bridge of our salvation."

I'd heard enough in the time it had taken me to reach the great wooden door of the church.

I was in no state to force it open, but I didn't need to: Bryn was with me, and she tore the door off its hinges.

I walked in.

I was naked, and the wounds that had been inflicted on me at Port Allen had only just begun to heal. There was no more bleeding—Athanate are good at stopping that—but the flesh was still broken in a dozen places and the bruises... my whole body was a bruise.

I looked like a well-chewed zombie, and members of the congregation screamed at the sight of me.

Warmed my heart.

That was all going according to plan.

Right up to the point where I realized the interior of the building itself had some kind of spell.

As soon as I walked clear of the vestibule, my skin crawled with the intensity of the working. The priest became its focal point.

"*Vampire!*" he screamed. No way he could have sensed me without magic, and it was an accurate spell. Reasonably accurate.

He grabbed a tall rod from beside where he stood, jerked something on the side and pointed the rod at me.

What the hell?

It was a flare he'd set off. The light was blindingly bright.

"Die in the light of the sun, hell-spawn! With me, friends! Die! *Die!*"

"Die!" Half of them screamed the word with him. The other half just screamed.

I would have laughed, but the strangest thing happened. That blinding light seemed to pierce my head like a knife. I became dizzy. My sight faded. I stumbled. The pain in my body soared, wounds opened and all my strength evaporated like morning mist.

No. That's a myth. Sunlight doesn't work, let alone the light of a magnesium flare. What's wrong with me?

Tara and Hana left me, manifested as a wolf in flames.

The screaming redoubled.

Taking the screaming as their cue, Nick and Ursula hit the back of the building. Two massive Kodiaks versus some old wood. No contest. The entire wall disintegrated into dust, moss and splinters.

Shit! Not supposed to happen quite like that.

The whole building groaned.

I was dimly aware of a streak of lightning going past me, and the Valkyrie's wings snapped out to form a protective shield like a cone over the bound and motionless coven at the front. If the lethal bladed wings accidentally happened to pass through the space occupied by the priest, I was in no position to complain.

I was on my hands and knees.

Aware the building was starting to twist and crumple in on itself.

Aware that yard-wide bowl on the steeple would be falling soon. The one with even more flames inside it. The propane supply to the bowl was ruptured. I could smell the stink. The walls were dry-rotten wood, the pews were wood. The air was full of wood dust. There was a magnesium flare on the wooden floor and a wolf breathing flames in the aisle.

Aware that all the rest of my team had followed me in.

And I was trapped, hit by a spell that had robbed me of my supernatural abilities. I couldn't speak. Couldn't hear. All I could see now was a deep blackness with shapes that moved inside.

From the darkness came a word. Not a language I'd ever heard, but I understood it perfectly. Not a word composed of only sound. A word that had shape and weight and power. That made me shiver and moan.

Then the imitation sun was coming down through the collapsing roof and I moved.

I got into the path of the bowl. My team rushed to help me save the damned congregation who, moments before, had somehow been channeling a spell to kill me. We caught the bowl. The fire went out, but now the propane that had been fueling it was mixing in the air with wood dust.

I sucked in what air I could and roared, chasing people out as the building came to pieces. Those that wouldn't run, I picked up and threw as far as I could. Then I joined the others, grabbing the women of the coven and pulling them clear.

We were out. Mostly out, anyway, when the remains ignited. Not an explosion as such, but a soft thump that had us stumbling and ducking.

If any of the congregation were still inside, I left them to it, given what they had planned for the coven. The rest of them were still screaming as they ran into the night. Some of them might end up talking to police, but I could almost smile at the thought of how that report would go...

Then this zombie burst into the church, which the preacher done said was a vampire, and she bin followed by wolves, and one of them wolves was burning, I tell you, but two bears tore the back wall right down when an angel with wings come in and then the whole place blew up.

My burst of supercharged energy was gone. I was back to hurt and tired, but at least I could move and see again. Well enough to see the coven. Well enough to see Gabrielle wasn't there.

Bryn had returned to Gwen and the Hecate was kneeling beside one of the Lafayette Adepts.

I sank gratefully to my knees next to them. I could feel Gwen stripping away the power of the workings that had bound the coven even as she spoke urgently.

"Gabrielle? Where is she?"

"The Witch Queen kept her," the woman said hoarsely. "The witch those idiots in the cult think is an angel in the swamp."

Chapter 36

No one knew where the Queen of Diamonds was, other than somewhere in the swamps of the Atchafalaya.

Everyone was exhausted, and both Rita and I were nearly dead on our feet. There was nothing we could do for the moment.

The group split up, with Flint and Bill taking the coven members back to Lafayette after hotwiring a couple of trucks that had been left in the cult's rush to escape.

The rest of us headed back to New Orleans. Pia was driving the Hill Bitch, with Olivia behind in the boys' Range Rover and Nick and Ursula bringing up the rear on their Harleys.

I wasn't surprised to find myself squeezed between Gwen and Kane in the back of the Hill Bitch. Sort-of good, in that they were keeping me upright.

"It's similar to what you were told by Tullah's mother when she was first explaining workings to you," Gwen was telling me, about the priest's attack. "Everyone accesses the energy at some level, even if it's only in the hindbrain. Humans can access it through learning systems of belief, and triggering mental processes, but the power of that is normally very weak. It can get stronger in groups. What trips it over to the next level is what the League academics call coherence. That's not implying a logical or orderly belief, but describing a lot of people who've been trained to believe the same thing and who reinforce each other's beliefs."

"Like a cult being trained into believing light kills vampires?" Kane asked. "Even though the light is actually only a focus for their working?"

"Yes." Gwen's eyes fixed on me. Even in the night, I could see their pale, icy blue. "We're lucky that most of the congregation was too startled and frightened to contribute to the power of the spell."

"It can be any crazy thing?" I asked.

There was a thought drifting around in my head, too vague to take form, about this. It was wandering between Matlal, the pit at Astilla de Luna, the Queen of Diamonds, rougarou, and the Mexican alpha who referred to werewolves that associated with Basilikos as 'rabioso'.

"To non-paranormal humans, the idea that a human can change shape to a wolf is a crazy thing," Gwen replied. "And *that* transformation is a very complex thing. Far more complex than a working to simply harm someone."

"It was simple, but it was well crafted," Kane said. "Not something I'd expect a random cult to come up with on their own. I got the impression it came in a pre-prepared form, and just needed the priest and congregation to provide the raw boost."

"That's possible." Gwen pursed her lips. "Workings were attached to the building and the priest. One assumes by the Queen of Diamonds. Regardless, it was extremely effective. And yet..."

"I threw off the effects," I said, because I knew that was where she was going.

"Yes..." they said together.

I sighed. "Tezcatlipoca."

"You used his power," Gwen said. It wasn't a question.

"Twice. I think." Talking seemed tiring, so I tried to keep it short. "When I was fighting the rougarou at Port Allen, I was outmatched. I mean, she was close to a ton of muscle. I got a grip on her neck, but I didn't have the power in my bite. I tried tearing her with my hind paws, but they weren't sharp enough."

I leaned my head back and closed my eyes for a couple of seconds to relive it.

"She slammed me down into the ground a few times. Wasn't going to be able to take much more of that. I remembered Nick saying that all werewolves are really skinwalkers and that I could change to anything I wanted so long as I knew it well. How well? Don't know. Okay. I know Rita well. We spar a lot and I use eukori when we do. I guess that gives me some insight. So I tried changing my hindquarters to cougar. It worked. The claws and muscles were enough to tear through the hyena's belly."

Neither of them said anything.

Their faces remained blank of judgement.

It wasn't like the magic I'd used to kill Victoria Oaken. I'd taken Victoria's own strength and used it to kill her. She'd been aware I was doing it. They could argue all day about definitions of dark magic, but I'd *known*. I'd *felt* it. That was dark magic.

This time, it was different. Maybe still dark, but different.

"It got a little blurry then. I remember thinking there wasn't much point changing all the way to a cougar for biting. Cougar's not much stronger than a wolf in the jaw. But then... I don't know, I tasted blood."

I shook my head.

"It felt wonderful. Like I was completely fresh into the fight. Not tired or hurt. I could feel my jaw get stronger and I bit through her neck."

They stayed silent.

"At the time, I put it down to my Athanate taste for Blood or something. But then I felt exactly the same feeling in the church. So now, I think what happened was I part-shifted to jaguar. Much more powerful jaws. And you tell me Tezcatlipoca's signature animal is the jaguar. I think this was his power. Different from shapeshifting. While I was using his power, I wasn't hurting."

"You hated using Kane to channel Ash's power," Gwen said. "Part of the reason I've been somewhat relaxed about your use of channeled magic is you really didn't like it. You don't sound so—"

"Negative about using dark magic any more?" I snorted. "Yeah. This was *so* much better. This was genuine pleasure in using magic. All I've ever had before is pain when I've channeled magic."

"This is dangerous," Kane started to say.

I cut him off. "Because the first few times, there are always good reasons to use bad magic. And then, you're on the slippery slope, because it gets easier and easier to justify it. I remember all the talk."

He frowned. "You don't seem so concerned."

"I'm concerned. I'm just too tired to process it."

Pia was driving us, but she'd been listening. "Think of the alternative," she said.

That made me laugh, which ended up with me coughing and holding my ribs because I hurt so much.

Pia looked back with concern. "I'm not sure I would recommend it at the moment, but normally alcohol actually helps Athanate with this level of damage," she said. "It gives temporary pain relief while the aniatropics do their work."

"Then we'll stop on the way," I gasped. "Rita and I could use a few shots of rum."

A cell started playing Ride of the Valkyries. It could only be Gwen's.

She answered, and a second later she grabbed Pia's shoulder. "Stop!"

Pia pulled over and our convoy skidded to a halt behind us.

Gwen got out in a hurry, agitated.

I realized how much she'd been propping me up when I started to fall.

Kane caught me.

I could hear the odd word from the cell. It sounded like Bian, and one word I caught was 'attack'.

"What?" I croaked.

Gwen got back in, but now the light blazed in her eyes and I knew it was the Valkyrie talking.

"Basilikos have tried to attack Haven. Tullah and Kaothos need me. I have to go. Now."

Oh, shit.

Kane was holding me, and I was holding Gwen because Bryn was gone. Out of the car and up into the sky. Gwen was paralyzed from the chest down; without her spirit guide inhabiting her body, she was nearly helpless.

The others had gathered to see what was happening, and Olivia caught the cell as it dropped from Gwen's hand.

We moved Gwen to the Range Rover, where the seats were more comfortable.

"I'll have to follow her to Denver," she said as we strapped her in. "Jen's being flown down here in her Pilatus tomorrow. The pilot can fly me up to Centennial."

Her words were calm, but she looked haunted, torn between two duties.

"I'll find Gabrielle," I said, but the words weren't strong enough. I was torn as well. I wanted Gwen and Bryn in Louisiana, but all of Emergence was in danger if Basilikos got through to Kaothos. "I swear, on my Blood, I will not rest until find Gabrielle."

"Dangerous," she said. "Near impossible without some kind of spirit quest, and that's even more dangerous."

"Danger comes with the territory," I said. "And I don't think it'll be difficult to find her at all. I have to find the Queen of Diamonds. She has Gabrielle, and she wants me for some reason."

"So she'll find you if you don't find her first?" Gwen huffed. "I'll come back if we're sure Kaothos is safe. But in the meantime, I'm not taking your oath literally tonight. You must rest first, then you can go looking for the Queen of Diamonds and Gabrielle."

Chapter 37

It was 3:30 a.m. before we finally got back to Labastide's mansion.

We'd stopped on the way and I was feeling *fine*.

Who'd have thought a 24-hour store, off an intersection of I-10, in the middle of nowhere, would have such a good choice of rums?

Pia had dosed Rita and me with more pacifics and aniatropics as well.

The result was it looked like we'd been out to party. That was, apart from the wounds and the bruising. A zombie party maybe, with very good makeup.

I was laughing when we staggered up to Labastide's door.

Her staff were going to turn us away, and we would have the perfect excuse to book into a hotel instead. I guess the only drawback was that Rita and I would need to be smuggled in to avoid scaring any guests still up at this hour.

The butler answered the doorbell immediately.

Not the cast-iron butler slash security of earlier. I guessed this was the night butler. The apprentice. A human, in fact. A young woman.

I leered at her.

She looked shaken, but immediately stepped to one side.

"House Farrell, welcome," she blurted out in English. "Please come inside quickly."

We filled the pleasant hall, and she closed the door after glancing out to see if we'd woken the neighbors.

We were a total mess.

Me and Rita, covered in wounds, carrying bottles of rum and being held up by Pia and Olivia, respectively.

Gwen being carried by Ursula.

Kane trying not to laugh.

Nick looming behind us, looking afraid to touch anything in case he broke it.

The butler bowed. "I am Jo Richardson kin-Labastide. Welcome again to the town residence of House Labastide, and your residence while you remain in the city. Before I escort you to your rooms, do you have need of further assistance? We have healers in residence."

"I think we have most need of beds, Jo kin-Labastide," I said. "But thank you."

I liked her. Labastide had good taste. I got a warning squeeze from Pia to behave. Even under the anesthetic of alcohol, that hurt.

Jo took us down a passage and opened doors to three adjoining and interconnecting luxury suites.

"We received your luggage earlier and all the bags are in the first room. Will these be sufficient, House Farrell?"

"The rooms are wonderful," Pia said. "More than sufficient, thank you."

The girl blushed.

"House Labastide wished me to make clear that we should show you every Athanate hospitality."

Ah. Labastide didn't want us biting random people on the street. Her adherence to the most formal of conservative Athanate etiquette meant that she was forced to offer her own kin as an alternative. Despite despising me.

In my state I was finding it funny.

Jo was new to this. I made a guess that the front line butler had only passed the duty over when she was sure we weren't going to turn up tonight.

"Hmm. So, is Jo short for Josephine?"

"No, House Farrell, it's just Jo."

"Call me Amber, please. I like you. Shame about the name. 'Not tonight, Jo' doesn't have the same ring to it, does it?"

"Please excuse House Farrell," Pia said, guiding Jo out. "It's been as difficult a day as it looks from her wounds. Please also convey our thanks to House Labastide. Her kind offer is warmly appreciated."

The door closed.

I stopped being an ass long enough to let them wash me and make sure my wounds were clean. I was barely awake, even in the bathtub.

They discussed security details while Rita and I were laid in the main bed.

"Make sure you wake me in plenty of time to pick up Jen," I mumbled. "Be fine in the morning."

"Of course." Pia pulled the sheets up over us.

And then I was falling into darkness.

Falling to where no amount of rum and Athanate bio-agents could make me forget that Gabrielle was being held in the swamp somewhere and I had to rescue her, whatever it took.

Falling to where *he* waited, patient as a lost god with a long, long view of the world.

Queen of Diamonds

Chapter 38

Such a pleasant dream, after a long nightmare of running through a dark maze, deep mud sucking my feet down at every step.

The jasmine and sea-salt fragrance of my wife. Coffee and breakfast smells.

Not a dream.

My eyes snapped open and I gasped.

"You can't be here, I haven't gone to pick you up," I said, the mouth well ahead of the brain as usual.

Jen laughed. "Pia decided to let you sleep and meet us at the airport. She gave us the Hill Bitch, so I'm here with Maia and friends. Pia stayed with Gwen. The pilot will take them up to Denver and bring Pia straight back. Somehow, honey, the world turns without you pushing it."

I rubbed my eyes. My body was stiff and sore, even if the worst of the wounds had closed overnight. The bruising hadn't magically disappeared however; I knew I still looked like a horror movie extra. Probably a good idea not to go to the airport.

"Speaking of pushing it, why on earth did you volunteer to come down to New Orleans?" I said. "It's not safe."

"Says the woman who fought a hyena the size of an elephant yesterday, and then went straight from that into the swamps to track down a crazy cult."

"She wasn't the size of an elephant," I grumbled. "No more than a buffalo."

"A buffalo with a bite that could take your head off. And I know Livia explained the reason I'm here to you; I'm going to follow the money. It's not glamorous, but if there's a problem in House Labastide, I'll trawl it out in my spreadsheets. No need for you to break down doors waving your pistol around."

Rita came in with a tray of breakfast food and a pot of coffee.

The day was looking up; in bed with coffee, breakfast and wife.

Jen sensed where my thoughts were heading and poured cold water on it.

"I need to get to work and so do you. Felix called Pia and requested you meet them in Baton Rouge."

"Requested? My alphas?"

"Yes. Politely, as Pia told it."

"Need to be on the road soon, Boss," Rita said, with a meaningful look at Jen. "Got to get there and back."

"I was just getting to that," Jen said. "She means that after you get back from meeting Felix, we have a dinner tonight in New Orleans. Labastide has invited us. Pia suggested it wouldn't be wise to refuse."

I groaned. I'd almost managed to forget everything, but now it rushed back.

Gabrielle. Rougarou. Rabioso werewolves. And all of it like a spider web stretching out from the Atchafalaya, where the mysterious Queen of Diamonds sat.

I'd have to leave Jen and her spreadsheets to investigate while I chased this elusive Adept. With interruptions from the alphas and dinner with Labastide.

I drove, so Rita had to dial and hold the cell to my ear. That was what hands-free meant in the Hill Bitch.

"Hi, Round-eye, whose ass are you kicking today?"

I chuckled. "Just calling to hear you're okay."

"We're fine. Gwen's being brought in from the airport now and Bryn came up here last night like the wrath of God. We've got Manassah covered, and your sister, too." She paused. "You know, I'm liking Rita's analysis about how we're spread out more and more. The attacks here feel like they're a diversion. Like Matlal is trying to split us up into smaller and smaller groups until he decides where's most productive to concentrate his effort."

"Is paranoia contagious?" I asked sweetly, even though I agreed with her and she knew I did.

"If it isn't, it should be," she said. "I have to go. I'm working with the team on a few new surprises if they try attacking again."

"Just quickly, I guess you haven't had much time with the kids from Juárez?"

"No, but Diana has. Look, I won't lie, they're going to need a long time to recover, but I think they will, and with those two overprotective wolves as parents, they'll be fine. Now I really gotta go. You, *all* of you, stay safe. Love you."

"I will. You too. Love you."

Rita smirked.

"She meant you too," I said.

"Course she did. And Nick, Ursula and the Lost Boys as well."

I'd sent the four of them to have a closer look at the coven's house in Lafayette. There might be a clue, physical or magical, to where the attack had originated from. Without *something*, we had no place to start looking for the Queen of Diamonds or Gabrielle, and the clock was ticking.

You all tough like steel 'til it happen. Like the li'l Canadian bitch, an' lookit her now, Rochelle Fournier had said.

Where was Gabrielle, and what were they doing to her?

"So tell me about the nightmare last night," Rita said, interrupting my bleak thoughts.

"Did I disturb you?"

"You woke me up. You were sort of half awake. We went back to sleep quickly, but Gwen told me to keep checking on anything that might be related to spirit walks, even dreams."

I blinked and thought hard. I had an impression I'd woken. It was one of those memories where I couldn't quite tell whether it was part of the dream or not. If it was real, then we'd gone back to sleep all tangled around each other.

"I was in a maze," I said. "Underground. Running through mud. I don't think it's significant. Only weird thing was, I was sometimes chasing and sometimes the one being chased."

"Oooh, deep," Rita said. "Probably Freudian or Jungian or something. I'll text Gwen anyway."

She started to enter a message, her thumbs dancing over the face of the cell.

"Thanks," I snorted. "Errr... did we..."

"Cuddle," Rita smirked. "'Bout time you bit me again. Who knows if I'm being tempted to betray you, Boss. You need to make sure of my loyalty, just in case."

My upper jaw throbbed at the points where the fangs would manifest. Nothing to do with her loyalty, everything to do with the enjoyment of my Athanate 'duties'.

I snorted and concentrated on getting us to Baton Rouge.

Chapter 39

Given the late start, it was 2 p.m. before I drove the Hill Bitch into the driveway of the mansion where the alphas were staying, on the shores of University Lake in south Baton Rouge.

I parked beneath a magnolia tree heavy with ivory blossoms.

"Nice place," Rita said. "I guess we don't need guns this afternoon. At least not in plain sight."

She lifted her pant leg to show her cute little Ruger pistol in an ankle holster.

I nodded. "Not ideal, but probably okay today."

Which set me wondering what kind of ammunition we'd need to take down rougarou when we located where the Queen of Diamonds was holding Gabrielle. I wanted my old Ops 4-10 Tactical Assault Weapon, the brutal cannon we called the BFG, but when the government had disbanded the Ops 4 group, the only company that manufactured the ammo closed the line. Without the option of the BFG, I really didn't want anything less than 50 cal and I couldn't exactly carry Ma Deuce strapped to my back. Maybe I could get hold of an AX 50, or a Barrett for distance work. Maybe my Mk23 would be okay for close up.

We got out and I waited while Rita came around to stand close by my shoulder.

She wasn't Yelena, but I was already comfortable with Rita having my back. Louisiana was all about compromises. Yelena would have had the edge when we went in to get Gabrielle back, but Rita had been more effective in the fight yesterday. Yelena's presence at my shoulder was a threat that only fools took lightly. Rita commanded respect in Were society—she was a threat too, but a respected one. She'd earned that blend of fear and respect as a lieutenant in the Albuquerque pack, and she'd earned it all over again here in Louisiana. I could see it in the guards' eyes as we walked up the steps to the front door.

Me... they weren't getting over the idea I might want to siphon a little Blood from their throats. I got an alpha's respect, but I could taste it was still tainted with a Were's distrust of Athanate. Maybe I'd never get rid of that.

Once inside, I found the Southern League were running this place more like an Athanate House than a pack HQ. People scurried around, intent on their business. We were met by one of the lieutenants from the Santa Fe pack and ushered into a huge living room.

The doors closed behind us, leaving us with the Southern League alphas and a couple of strangers I didn't know. They were sitting on casual chairs on one side of the room. The other side had a computer and screen, as if there had been a presentation.

I bit my cheek. *Really* not like the Were normally.

Everyone stood as we approached; Felix and Cameron rose stiffly.

"Hell, we're all so bright and beautiful today," I said to them, laughing. "Good afternoon, alphas."

Felix snorted. The alphas looked as beat-up as Rita and I did. It had been rough in the middle when the rougarou piled on. At least Rita and I had had Athanate healing help from Pia.

I turned to the other two Were and got carefully neutral stares back.

Cameron introduced them: "Clay McGowan, alpha of the De Soto pack, from Hattiesburg, Mississippi. Alan Sanders, alpha of the Mobile pack, Alabama. Gentlemen, Amber Farrell, co-alpha of Deauville pack in Denver and one of three alphas running New Mexico and Colorado for us. Rita Dawson, her lieutenant."

McGowan and Sanders exchanged handshakes and murmured greetings with Rita and me. The two alphas were keeping it under control, but I could see they didn't like the Athanate scent they got off us.

I managed to stop my eyes from rolling.

"Bill Patout will be joining us in a couple of minutes," Felix said, indicating we should sit.

I sat. Rita remained standing, taking a position behind and to the side of me where she could watch most of the room. Got a small smile from Cameron, who knew her habits well.

So... Patout, McGowan and Sanders—I guessed Felix and Cameron were looking to set up some kind of hierarchy for the coastal states. They'd certainly wasted no time after breaking the lock in Louisiana.

"We hear you had a mostly successful night down in the bayou," Cameron said.

"Yeah, mostly," I said. "But Gabrielle is still missing, and I think we're going to need to get her back from way deeper into the swamps than we went last night."

"From the Witch Queen of the Atchafalaya," Felix said, his eyes narrowed.

I nodded to Felix, seeing McGowan twitch out of the corner of my eye. That set me wondering whether he was running scared of the witch, or he'd been negotiating some deal with her. Entirely possible. I doubted her ambitions or threats stopped at the state boundary, and De Soto wasn't even an hour away from the Louisiana border.

"What's your priority?" Sanders' voice was all soft Alabama, but his question was sharp. "This missing girl, or this ritual which we heard so much about?"

"This missing 'girl' is a member of my House," I snapped. "What would your priority be if a member of your pack was kidnapped?"

"So, Athanate before Were," McGowan said.

"My pack, my House, my oaths, associations and allies, hell, even my favorite barista in the coffee shop before a couple of snarky jerks that I owe nothing to."

They'd caught me off guard, and the demon in my throat was speaking before I engaged my brain.

The doors opened and Bill Patout strode in, laughing as he caught the last bit. "Damn! What did I miss?"

Everyone remained seated—which was probably a good thing, with tempers up.

"You all know Bill Patout, alpha of the Alexandria pack," Felix said. "What you missed, Bill, was we started talking about running a halfies' ritual down here, but I guess we set off from the wrong point."

I breathed out slowly. Willed the eyes to go back to green. Athanate-black and Were-gold weren't a good mix for a peaceful meeting. Neither was what I had to say, really, but it had to be said.

"Maybe the point we should have started from," I said, "is that it's my obligation to run the rituals wherever they're needed, regardless of association. My alphas use them as an opportunity to talk with packs about joining the Southern League. Joining has a lot of benefits, especially now. Being in the League gets you a voice at the Assembly, and it's the Assembly that the government will talk to about the paranormal community. Emergence is coming, alphas. And it's real close."

Felix frowned. I'd pissed everybody off now.

Apart from Bill. "What she says. And it's gonna take time to get halfies to a ritual. If'n she takes out the Swamp Witch in the meantime, I won't be shedding no tears."

"I agree," Cameron said. "It's all very well talking about the League, and we're fine with witches in general, but this witch is poison."

"Why?" McGowan asked. "Yes, she's talked to me. Why is what she's talking about so different from what you're selling?"

"You're kidding me," Bill said.

"Amber," Cameron fixed me with her keenest stare. "I don't doubt your team has put together evidence from your expedition to Mexico into some kind of a presentation for the Assembly when it's asked for. Give us a preview."

I laughed. My alphas, for all their distrust of politics and Athanate machinations, had maneuvered me into giving their sales pitch to the Were of the Gulf Coast states with a step worthy of Skylur.

"Give me five," I said.

Someone brought coffee as I checked the presentation system's computer and screen. Matt and David had given me a memorable link that I logged into for a secure connection. A couple of clicks and I was through to the servers at Haven. My team had been too busy to set up anything polished, but Cameron was right, the outline was there and its rough implementation would actually make it more believable somehow.

Of course it wasn't complete either. All the evidence to tie the pieces together was missing.

It'd taken me ten minutes to set up and I'd missed the coffee, but Rita and I needed to get this done and get back to New Orleans, so I launched into it as soon as they'd rearranged their chairs.

I hurried through the preliminaries, all the signs we'd picked up about the way Matlal had dealt with Mauricio Gálvez, alpha of the Chihuahua pack, how Astilla de Luna had become the center of a Were association from Baja to Juárez. That part was well laid out. McGowan and Sanders understood it easily enough, but I could see I hadn't really caught them.

That was okay.

"So what did we do? Welcome to my vacation scrapbook," I said, and launched the next section. It was assembled from a jumble of body cam clips and stills, mixed with eye-in-the-sky drone shots to put the clips into the context of the overall assaults.

Felix and Cameron knew approximately what was coming. Patout, McGowan and Sanders didn't. They went wide-eyed at the violence that had been unleashed on the Juárez and Chihuahua packs. Flamethrowers, a 76mm naval gun and four Ma Deuces chewing their way through the opposition had a way of making a point.

Then I showed them the pit at Astilla de Luna.

Which was when a small box opened on the side of the screen: 'David wants to talk. Open two-way link for videoconference?'

I clicked on 'Yes', and got his face in the top right corner.

He had shadows under his eyes. I wondered if he'd slept at all since we'd parted in El Paso.

"Just got some info we hadn't had time to add, if you want me to talk about it."

I glanced at Felix, who nodded.

"Go ahead."

"Yelena retrieved a couple of bodies from the pit, and they were brought up here." David rubbed his face. "Savannah's been working on them. I mentioned to her the stuff about Díaz from the Coahuila pack calling them 'rabioso'. Gave her an idea. As it turns out, Díaz may mean it literally, in a sense."

"Rabies? They have rabies?"

"Not exactly. The standard rabies virus hacks into the neurons to attack the brain, and that infection leads to various bizarre physical and cognitive problems and then death. Post-mortem analysis will show changes in brain structure for rabies victims. Okay? Now, Savannah's seeing brain structure changes, but clearly not ones leading to death."

Something from that Ops 4-10 mission in Somalia came back to me, and linked with yesterday's fight.

"Am I right, hyenas are immune to rabies?"

"Yes. That's the connection Savannah made. It's pure speculation, but she thinks the Queen of Diamonds has found some way to use the biology of were-hyenas to create a tamer version of the rabies virus that delivers the prions, the protein strings, that are the bio-agents of Were infusion."

"Is she a witch or a biochemist?"

"Does it matter?" David answered. "However she did it, she's found a way to make becoming a werewolf quick and sure, but only for those that get past the initial reaction, which is so severe they have to be confined. That's why there's that pit at Astilla de Luna."

"And the resulting werewolves?" Felix had come up to join the conversation.

"If you're asking me how they behave in comparison to traditional werewolves, I can't answer you definitively from Savannah's analysis of two brains. Both showed unusual developments to the prefrontal cortex." David ran tired fingers through his hair. "How did Savannah put it? 'All paranormals have a higher requirement of impulse control. If there's damage to the prefrontal cortex, it's possible that might fail. There may be a tendency for these werewolves to go rogue, or behave in unpredictable ways.'"

The rest of them clustered around the screen.

Bill Patout spoke: "Damn near every pack in Louisiana has some of these new werewolves from the witch. They're odd wolves, I grant you, but they haven't said squat about any pit. None of them have gone rogue either."

David shrugged. "Yes, and I bet they all have strangely vague stories of how they actually became werewolves. Look, there's nothing in the physical evidence that would tell us, but if Basilikos are involved, we've seen all sorts of long-term compulsions and memory suppression they use. Frankly, even if you can't prove they came from Astilla de Luna, I wouldn't trust any of them, whatever they say."

"With a rabid dog, there's something sets them off, usually," Sanders said. "Like being startled or whatever. You think it might be like that?"

David shook his head. "There were rabioso at Port Allen yesterday. If the trigger was just a stressful external stimulus or a jolt of adrenaline, you'd say some of them would have gone off when the fight started. No, if I were designing a way to undermine the packs in Louisiana with rabioso, I'd make sure that trigger that sets them off would be under my control. A hidden compulsion. I think you just got lucky that the Queen of Diamonds wasn't close enough when the fight kicked off yesterday."

Both Patout and McGowan had turned pale. On the other hand, it looked as if Sanders hadn't accepted any rabioso, and he looked mighty relieved about it.

"Gentlemen, I see you might have pressing business to attend to," Felix said. "Maybe we should reschedule this meeting in a couple of days' time? Why don't we schedule a ritual as well?"

Patout shrugged. "No need to persuade me, I'm in on all counts. The way we've been tricked in Louisiana, there's no doubt in my mind we need the League, and I've got dozens of halfies."

McGowan looked at his feet and shifted his weight. "Reckon so," he said.

Sanders kept silent, other than to mutter farewells as they headed for the door.

"Excellent little presentation," Cameron whispered in my ear when we heard the front door close.

"Yeah." I looked her up and down. She was still moving stiffly. "You two want a bit of a boost with some Athanate healing?"

She snorted.

"Don't have to bite you in the neck, if you're worried about evidence. There are... other places." I tried channeling a bit of Bian's outrageousness.

"Stop it, Amber." Felix was trying to keep a straight face at Cameron's reaction. "We'll be fine."

"You've given the League plenty to think about," Cameron said. "We'll recover as we sit and think. What about the Athanate?"

I raised an eyebrow, Skylur style.

"From what I understand, the basic mechanics of infusion are the same for Were and Athanate. What's to say the Swamp Witch isn't trying to create instant Athanate as well?" Cameron sat back down. "Or, if she's gotten hold of the sort of strong compulsion spells your colleague was talking about, what about living zombies?"

"She's at the top of my list until the ritual," I said. "To get Gabrielle back really, but two birds with one stone."

"You have Bill's contact information. If you need his help..."

"He has his hands full," I said. "But I may anyway."

Chapter 40

We left the League's HQ at Baton Rouge with an agreement that we had two clear days until the next ritual. On the other hand, we had no clue where the Queen of Diamonds hid, and a search area of 150 miles long and 20 wide. Nearly 1.5 million acres. About the same size as the state of Delaware.

Rita was driving us back.

"Head for Port Allen first," I said. "Where we fought yesterday."

"Okay. What are we looking for?"

"Any clue as to where the Queen of Diamonds hides out in the swamp." I wrinkled my nose. "It's a long shot. If they'd come in cars, I'd hack their GPS systems. Maybe they have something on those boats they came in."

"The rougarou didn't look like GPS type people to me, Boss."

"Yeah, but we haven't got much else to go on."

Bill was going to text me the name of a guy in New Orleans. It was another long shot, but Bill had heard this guy was a recruiter for 'special' hunting trips in the Atchafalaya. Not the normal kind of hunt; 'monsters' was the word on the street. Hugely expensive.

Maybe it was a scam. It was about as tenuous a lead as I'd ever heard, but I had no option but to chase it. Which was why I was also willing to check if there was a clue in the rougarou's boats as to where they'd come from.

It was only fifteen minutes away. From the approach road alongside the canal we could see all the trucks that had been parked outside were gone, and the gate was open.

Inside the compound, all signs of its use were also gone. There were no bodies, no sign of the fight. The ground itself had been bulldozed and re-flattened by the League's cleanup crew. The old pontoon bridge had been scraped clean. The door to the trailer hung open, waving in the breeze.

The place was deserted.

We parked nearest to the point where the rougarou had emerged through the scrub oaks.

Deserted or not, no way was Rita relying on her ankle holster here. She grabbed our weapons duffle and pulled out a Benelli M4 semi-auto shotgun.

Not that I expected to need it, but I retrieved my Mk23 and checked it. Full magazine. One in the chamber. Safety on.

I clipped the holster on my belt and got out.

The place had been cleared of evidence, but I could still smell rougarou. It was the kind of pungent smell that would hang around for days.

"The stink makes me edgy," I said.

"Yeah. After yesterday, not surprised."

The rain of the previous day had given way to scudding clouds and low temperatures, which made me shiver. The forecast had said there were storms coming in off the Gulf. I hoped not; heavy rains would make searching the Atchafalaya a pure joy.

Rita was still in the car, feeding shells into the Benelli.

"Got a hatchet in the duffle?" I asked. "Or a machete? That scrub looks thick."

She pulled Nekotsume, my wakizashi, out of the duffle.

"Very funny. I'll tell Bian."

She laughed. "Oh, please, no. Anything but that. I'd never hear the end of it."

I really didn't want to use a samurai sword to clear brush out of my way, but it was better than nothing. I slipped it through my belt as she joined me. We walked past the derelict cranes, into the scrub.

As it turned out, having rougarou walk through undergrowth was a good way to clear a path. It stank even worse, but the going was easy, all the way down to the sloping mud bank of the canal where they'd pulled the five flat-bottomed boats up out of the water when they'd arrived yesterday.

Five boats. I remembered the sounds of five boats.

"Why are there six boats?" Rita said, swiveling around and raising the shotgun.

I pulled my pistol free and slipped the safety off.

Good thing; for all their size, the rougarou were light on their feet and halfway to us from their hiding place in the scrub as we turned. Three of them. They'd gone to half forms: head and chest changed to the terrifying hyena-wolf mix, but with human arms and legs.

Huge.

Not as big as yesterday though. And I had a gun.

Rita and I fired at the same time. My three to her one.

Tap, tap. Tap. Body, body, head. A human would go down with three rounds from the Mk23. Not a rougarou.

He hit me, the best part of a ton traveling at 25 miles per hour. I'd been standing upright in a brace position and it felt like being hit by a car. We went down into the mud, and I tried to ball up and use the momentum to kick him over me.

The momentum part worked better than the kicking.

Where's the third one?

Rita hadn't tried getting off three shots. After one, she'd danced to one side and let the rougarou try unsuccessfully to stop in the deep, slippery mud.

The third had been coming for me but had swerved to attack Rita.

Rita and I both fired at him. We hit. And then I was back to worrying about the one that had attacked me first.

I'd blown half his face off and hit him twice in the middle of his chest and he was *still* coming.

I copied Rita. Fired once and threw myself to one side, out of the way of his charge.

Then I blew both his knees out from the back.

Rita fired again, shots blurring together.

I rolled and started to rise, turning, looking... just in time for the other rougarou to backhand me. And knock the Mk23 out of my hands into the mud.

No time to pick it up, and the barrel would need to be cleaned before I could fire it again. I was out of options. I rolled again, flipped up and pulled Nekotsume out of the scabbard.

Just twelve inches of steel. I could see the rougarou laugh as he charged.

Let them underestimate the short sword. Bian's training voice seemed to sing in my ears. *There is no artery deeper than the blade's reach. No neck you cannot cut. No heart you cannot reach. No muscle you cannot slice.*

With a full katana, I'd have tried to cut him in two. With the wakizashi, I slipped to one side and sliced at his abdominal muscles as he passed.

He screamed with rage, ignored the pain and managed to swivel on one foot.

Shit, but these rougarou were *tough* and *fast*.

No space to swing. No time.

His arms spread out to grab me and I used the only move I had left. I thrust upwards with the sword—into the belly, aiming for the heart.

He was too quick and he was prepared to take a blade in the belly. It went straight through and out his back, but then his rib cage prevented me from jamming the blade upwards. His arms closed and the force of his attack knocked me back. We went down together in a tangle.

I had one hand twisting Nekotsume in his belly, the other gripping his throat so he couldn't get those jaws down near my head. Another couple of inches and he'd rip my face off. And he was crushing me so I couldn't breathe.

We writhed in the mud and blood, but I couldn't get out from under him. Even if he was dying, he'd clearly made it his last task to take me with him.

Somewhere seemingly far away the Benelli fired again, but for me, there was nothing but the snarling monster on top of me. I was seeing spots in front of my eyes. Slowly but inexorably, my arm was bending and his jaws were getting closer.

Tara manifested and I could smell his flesh burning on the back of his neck. He ignored it.

Something hit us hard enough to rock him.

Rita. Changed to cougar and sinking fangs into the back of his neck, joining Tara.

Not enough. I knew how tough it was to make that bite work quickly. One way or another, severed spine from bites or bleeding out through the stomach wound, this rougarou was going to die, but he'd kill me first.

I couldn't change. I had to keep a hold on his throat. Couldn't part change. My legs were wrapped up in jeans and boots. I'd never get them free in time to do any damage.

Couldn't breathe. Being forced deeper into the mud. Blackness spreading across my vision.

I didn't have the skills to sap his strength to feed mine. I'd need to channel power or hijack an Adept like Kane to do that.

You can, but there's another way.

Shapes moved in the blackness.

Blood all over me. Mud creeping up my body, my face.

Reach.

I let go the sword and reached with hand and eukori, both fading fast.

Show her.

Nick Gray said you could change to anything if you knew the form.

Rita didn't. She knew how to change to a cougar. But I knew how to change to a jaguar, and a jaguar would be strong enough.

I tried to feed the image to her, how it felt, the steps that blurred together.

It all seemed so difficult, so far away.

There was no strength in my arm. I couldn't keep his jaws away.

Tara left the back of his neck and bit down on his muzzle, wrenching his head to the side and dripping fire into his eyes.

Still he wouldn't let go.

So much blood.

A worthy sacrifice.

There was a crunch and the rougarou spasmed.

Tara wrenched again, and tore his upper jaw off.

Rita had gone to jaguar, moving like a shadow from the darkness, all strength and sinew. She pulled, tearing his spine. Tara pushed. The weight lifted from me.

Gasping. Sucking in air. Struggling out of the mud's grip. Mouth filled with blood. Heaving him off.

Rolling to my feet. Like a dream-vision. Spirit-walking beneath a sky the color of drying blood. The whole riverbank is dark with mist and legions of tattered ghosts slide like eels above the shining waters of the canal. Trees lean in with leaves swaying like feathered headdresses, and they reach down with shrouds of mossy fingers. Every hole in the mud beneath my feet is a mouth from hell.

I hear chanting. I feel the hilt of an ancient, named sword in my hand.

Strike hard. To the left of the breastbone. Crack the ribs wide. Plunge in a hand and rip the living heart from his chest.

The ground shook with a voice so deep I felt it in my bones.

A worthy sacrifice for a returning god.

Welcome, my priestess.

Chapter 41

My ears were still ringing. My arms and legs felt sluggish.

I staggered through the mud over to the surviving rougarou, the one I'd shot in the knees.

Unfortunately, because I'd blown half his face off, he wasn't going to be able to tell me why they were here, or where to find the Queen of Diamonds. He finished bleeding out as I rolled him over.

Rita had her cell out and was talking to Cameron, explaining that we needed a cleanup crew here quickly.

Gotta talk to Gwen. Tara nudged me.

"Yeah."

There wasn't an inch of me that wasn't covered in either mud or blood, or both, including in my jeans pockets and all over my cell. It'd have to wait until Rita was finished and I could borrow hers.

I picked my HK up. That too: I'd need to strip and clean it before using it again.

Later.

I went to check the boats; the rougarou had risked coming here for a reason. Maybe something on or in the boats that could lead me back to them?

All six jonboats looked the same. Aluminum. Dirty green. Flat-bottomed. Square-nosed. Transom at the back holding a small outboard. Couple of unpadded seats across the width. Jerry can with more fuel.

No map of the basin with a big X marking the spot.

No papers of any kind.

But there were serial numbers for the engines. I got Rita to photograph them while I checked the bodies for ID.

Nothing.

They'd stripped off jackets and shirts in the trees before attacking us. There were wallets with cash. Nothing else.

"There's this," Rita called out, taking a photograph of some kind of emblem that had once been painted on the sides of a couple of the boats. It looked like a cartoon gator body-surfing. "Maybe they bought the boats from a tourist place close to home."

It was better than nothing.

I couldn't stand the muck anymore; I left my pistol and cell on the back of the nearest boat and walked into the canal to wash off. Rita joined me.

Ten minutes later, soaked through and shivering, but feeling much better, we met the cleanup crew at the compound.

Once they arrived, it was their site.

We got into the Hill Bitch. Rita drove. I cursed the lack of warm air from the fans.

I called Labastide's Diakon, Cazenave, to explain that we were going to be unavoidably late, due to being ambushed by rougarou. That got a frosty reception. I couldn't help pointing out that he'd all but said they didn't exist, and promised to describe them and the problem they caused, in *great* detail, to House Labastide.

Then I called Gwen and told her I'd just channeled Tezcatlipoca again, but worse.

"What's changed?" Gwen said. "You were a lot calmer about this yesterday."

"Yesterday, I was too exhausted to be worried. I could also argue I was doing it for others. Today, the only person who benefited from my using dark magic was me. And I get the feeling I'm using blood as part of, you know, whatever it is that makes this stuff work. If that's not a definition of blood magic, I don't know what is."

Rita scowled. She hadn't said anything, but she didn't agree there was a problem.

"Yes. What else?" Gwen asked.

"If that's not enough, then there was this really freaky thing at the end where I did a sort of Aztec-style sacrifice on one of the rougarou. And Tezcatlipoca spoke to me. He called me his frigging *priestess*. If that's not going to freak me out, then nothing ever will."

"How is Rita?"

She was on speaker. I held the cell up for Rita to answer for herself.

"Rita is fine," she said. "I got to be a jaguar. *Yee-ha!* I got to save my boss, helped by her awesome spirit guide. Then, unfortunately, I got to listen to her bitching about it. I am relaxed about everything except the last part."

I took the cell back. "Can't get good Diakons these days."

"Probably because your Health & Safety procedures suck," Rita said.

Gwen heard that and laughed. "I'm sorry, Amber. I *am* taking it more seriously than it sounds. I'll talk to Nick and the Lost Boys, and we should have a conference call with them as soon as possible. Please try not to use the power again, if you can possibly avoid it. The fact that you're freaked out by it and called me immediately means you're not under the thrall of this god as of yet. Rita's reaction is a good sign. My concerns are that this is happening more frequently, it's getting easier to use, and you're finding using this magic pleasurable while it happens."

"So there's nothing we can do until then?"

"You're already doing it. You question why, and don't accept simple answers. Neither do your team: your House, your pack, your coven. If you find you're doubting yourself, you could do worse than trust your team. If we sense you're not okay, we'll tell you."

I could tell Tara had chilled out and Rita was more concerned about getting back to New Orleans in a hurry.

I was still uneasy, but I tried to put it aside and figure out what I was going to say to Labastide.

Chapter 42

We were even later than I'd suggested.

I knew I looked like hell before I got back to Labastide's mansion in Audubon, but it was the reaction of the butler when she opened the door that alerted me to how bad it was.

It was the daytime butler. The woman in the suit with the cool eyes and the movements that told me she was part of the security team.

Those eyes blinked in astonishment when I walked in, still damp and dirty.

She cleared her throat. "I'll call ahead and warn House Labastide you may be a bit later than anticipated," was all she said. "She's been out and she'll be meeting you at the restaurant."

Jen was more forthcoming. "What the hell? Strip, shower. Now."

The mirrors in the bathroom showed me what they were talking about. The dirt and tangled hair I knew about, but the rougarou's backhand to my face was just starting to swell up and bruise. I hadn't gotten rid of yesterday's bruises, so now my bruises had bruises and I was going to have two black eyes.

The repairs all blurred together. Jen did some clever concealing makeup while Pia braided my hair. I had clothes that Jen had brought with her laid out on the bed. Pale tan pants, deep brown jacket. I got a silk scarf around my neck which looked like part of the outfit, but was in fact to cover the neck bruises. There was nothing that could be done about my eyes, so to top it off, I got a pair of huge sunglasses.

I had to laugh. "Good thing I have wolf eyes, or I'd be blind wearing these inside."

In addition to Rita, Jen and me, our party included Maia and one of her team to escort Jen.

A cab dropped us off outside the restaurant at the junction of Higgins and Tchoupitoulas, where House Labastide was waiting.

I'd expected something chokingly elegant with starched napkins and dim lighting. I was pleased to see an airy, open restaurant with plain wooden tables and chairs. Neat. Welcoming. Classy without being stuffy. And the kitchen smells made my stomach rumble.

House Labastide had taken over one end of the room. I was at a table in the corner, alone with Marguerite Labastide herself. The others were guided to a table next to us with Cazenave and Dupuis. Another group of tables held Labastide's security and other House members. They formed a sort of barrier between us and the rest of the room.

I didn't appreciate being separated from my House, but this was her mantle, her invitation, and Pia had stressed I should be a good little guest.

"Sorry I'm late—"

"Doubly late," she interrupted. She chose to speak English.

I got the feeling House Labastide had been working up a head of steam to complain about my behavior. Given everything that had happened over the last few days, my patience was wearing thin, but I knew it was really important not to blow my top.

Be calm.

I bit my lip and kept quiet.

"House Farrell, you are intelligent and well aware of the diverse nature of the Athanate community. It's obvious we both know that you and I are at opposite ends of the spectrum when it comes to the interpretation of the Panethus creed. Thus, we start from a position of some difficulty."

Under stress, her French-speaking heritage became more apparent and her voice developed a growl. I would have enjoyed it, but for what she had to say.

"I'm sure you're also aware of the negative speculation in the community, not merely about your behavior and opinions, but even the level of your unorthodoxy."

Now I understood why she was speaking English. What she'd just said, translated to Athanate, would have been too close to saying I should be executed as a rogue.

"You will understand it was not a pleasure to hear you would be disturbing the calm and orderly conduct of my territory. You have visited the mantle of Lafayette, and twice Baton Rouge, and yet failed to acknowledge the resident Houses in any degree. I grant that the rumors would have suggested that you'd turn up tonight in military fatigues, so I'm pleased that you have made an effort in your appearance, late though it made you."

I couldn't help reacting. I felt the Athanate crisis hormone elethesine kick in. If I hadn't been wearing the sunglasses, she'd have seen my eyes go Athanate black. I wasn't going to be able to prevent myself from responding, nor was it sensible in Athanate society to allow another Athanate to behave like this.

Why is she doing it?

Is she deliberately trying to provoke me?

I kept still. She'd smell the elethesine soon enough. I needed to understand what she thought she was achieving.

"You say you're here primarily on business for the Were League," she waved a hand, "with some Adept matters added, but rumors just reaching me of the outcome from your visit to El Paso indicate you may have other objectives. I would be negligent if I did not make clear to you that I do not appreciate this subterfuge—"

I stopped her by taking my sunglasses off.

Easy, tiger. Tara was holding me back from speaking my mind. I guess there had to be a first for everything.

I spoke quietly. "My business here is both for the Assembly as a whole and the Panethus party in particular. I'm often present where changes need to be made, House Labastide. Not my intention, just unfortunately the way things are at the moment. I'll apologize to House Broussard in Lafayette and House Leandre in Baton Rouge for being impolite when the time and opportunity are available."

We'd locked eyes and I wasn't going to blink. My veins felt like they were filled with dry ice—cold, but it *burned*.

"Since you raise the issue of your 'calm and orderly' territory, I'll point out that I wasn't late tonight because I was spending too much time making myself presentable. I was ambushed by rougarou in Baton Rouge this afternoon. Now *that's* what I call impolite: it's the second time they've attacked us in two days. They're the same rougarou that you and your Diakon were willing to dismiss as figments of the paranormal community's imaginations only yesterday morning. It turns out they're real. They're a pack of were-hyenas based in the Atchafalaya and they're trying to undermine the Were community in your territory. It also turns out that the Queen of Diamonds, another figment of the imagination according to you, is their leader. She's the one you described as the 'angel' of inspiration for the local Church of the Risen Sun. And we only managed to prevent those fanatics from burning Adepts at the stake last night by being too impolite to waste time calling on the Houses whose domains we passed through. One last thing about the Queen of Diamonds: she has links with Basilikos, and her ambitions are almost certainly not going to be restricted to the Were and Adept communities. All of this is happening in your 'calm and orderly' territory."

Labastide was no freshly-infused Athanate; she didn't flinch, but the very fact that she didn't try to interrupt told me she was shocked by the extent of what I was telling her. She was also perfectly capable of assessing whether or not I was lying.

I went on, "Yes, I know about the diverse nature of attitudes in Panethus that you mentioned. For instance, I know at the ultra-orthodox end of the spectrum, like the former Eastern Seaboard association, they think the Athanate belong at the top of the paranormal pile. That Athanate get to decide what happens in the paranormal community. I always thought that meant they also had an obligation to *protect* the rest of the paranormal community. Possibly I got that part wrong. What I'm sure I didn't get wrong was the directive by Altau last year that Houses in his territory should form bonds with the Were and Adepts. Even de Socorro in El Paso, who failed in other ways, attempted that."

"Enough," Labastide said.

I sat back and put my sunglasses on again. I was beyond angry, but I was getting better at this diplomacy shit: I hadn't leaped over the table and strangled her.

The tables around us were tense. They hadn't missed the anger on either side, but they'd kept to their seats and let us settle it in words.

Maia, Rita and Dupuis were watching us, and each other, like cats. If they'd had tails they would have been thrashing from side to side.

Labastide nodded at Cazenave at the next table, who immediately spoke into a cell.

She turned back to me.

"Good," she said. "We understand each other better and I have some confidence that this evening will not end in a deadly knife fight at a restaurant in my mantle."

"What?" I frowned.

"I do not expect people necessarily to be polite," she said and sniffed. "House Tucek will be joining us shortly. And we will sit with our enemy, House Farrell, and eat and drink. And *talk*."

Chapter 43

After indulging in a brief fantasy about 'accidentally' omitting to warn Maia, resulting in her killing Tucek on sight, I finger-signed Rita that Tucek would be arriving, and she passed the news on.

"Your own sign language. Fascinating," Labastide said, and invited Jen to join us. She also invited one of her kin, a young guy, outrageously handsome in the style of her House. He introduced himself as Xavier and shook hands.

Jen was better for this than Pia. My Athanate Diakon knew every nuance of every rule in the Agiagraphos as well as the accumulated customs of Panethus Houses, and Jen didn't. But Labastide would forgive any small mistakes Jen made; Jen would quickly spot that she had and fix it. Jen was also able to talk easily to anyone about anything.

Still, Labastide had an agenda. She chose to talk business.

"I'll tell you more in a couple of days," Jen said, after a lightning summary of her work that left me dizzy. "Your business model is sophisticated, but there are a lot of high-risk investments and too much fluidity. It's overcomplicated, but the main problem is that it has aspects that we don't support."

"The offshore accounts?"

Jen nodded. "That's the big one."

I could see Labastide preparing to argue that, but Tucek's arrival interrupted us.

The woman had balls, or ovaries, of steel. She was alone, in the middle of enemies, and apparently unconcerned. I watched her approach.

She wore black: leather pants, silk shirt, well-cut cotton jacket, boots. Her dark chestnut hair was pulled back in a ponytail. Glossy lipstick the color of Spanish terracotta set off her brown eyes. Gold earrings and a small gold clutch purse provided contrast.

She looked fabulous.

Sitting just across from me, Xavier caught his breath as Tucek arrived at the table.

"House Tucek, welcome." Labastide's greeting in Athanate was minimal and cool. She gestured to a chair. "Please join us."

"House Labastide, House Farrell." Tucek nodded formally as she sat. "I'm afraid I haven't had the pleasure of meeting your companions before."

"Jennifer Kingslund kin-Farrell," Jen said.

"Xavier Carré kin-Labastide." Xavier looked as if he might stand to reach across and shake hands, but he controlled himself.

"I love the old French names like Carré, and Labastide of course," Tucek said. "Very Acadian. And Ms. Kingslund; I know you by reputation in business circles, naturally. I am delighted to meet you."

Her voice was like satin, and I had to remind myself of the things she'd said in that same seductive tone. She'd even tried a compulsion on me when we'd met at the fake convent down in New Mexico. She'd never try that here, among so many, but I needed to remember her voice was a weapon.

"I like even numbers," Labastide said and waved at one of the other tables.

Jo, the butler from last night, came and sat with us. If I'd been rude then, she'd apparently forgiven me; I got a small but genuine smile. She sat beside Tucek and introduced herself—a mouse saying hello to the cat.

"To keep it simple, I have taken the liberty of ordering food and wine for all," Labastide announced as one of the waiters brought us bottles of wine in a bucket of ice.

Labastide made a show of asking Jen to taste the wine first, and we had an interlude of polite exchanges about the wine and the restaurant while more waitstaff brought plates and covered our table, tapas-style, with dishes that were a fusion of French modern and traditional Louisiana cooking.

When they were done, we began eating.

Tucek said, "You can take off the sunglasses, House Farrell. Your bruises might frighten the staff, but they aren't going to upset me."

"What would you know about my bruises?" I took the sunglasses off anyway.

"Come now, you aren't the only House that uses aerial drones with cameras."

"You're spying on me?"

"No. At least not deliberately. I'm gathering intelligence about the Southern League in preparation for offering my services as consultant between the League and the Hidden Path. It's been interesting watching the events in that compound they rented at Port Allen."

I kept my face blank. Had she been spying for the rougarou? Given that the Queen of Diamonds had some of her own brand of werewolf among the Louisiana packs that had been present, it seemed unlikely they'd need any more sources of information.

"You realize they'll kill you when you walk through the door?" I said.

"Hardly. I'm here as an official of the Assembly."

"Which they're still not full members of, and which they're not convinced is in their best interests. They'd kill me too, if I were plotting against them with the Confederation."

Tucek sighed and made a dismissive wave with her hand. "I admit I was in New Mexico. At that time, the Were League didn't even exist. I had exchanges with the Confederation but I wasn't their ally and didn't materially support them. My House certainly wasn't with them when they fought the Denver pack in Carson."

"No, you were too busy making good your 'rescue' of Matlal."

Labastide cleared her throat pointedly.

Tucek took a sip of wine. "One simple question for House Farrell, then. My sources tell me you're willing to perform one of your rituals for the Confederation. How well does that go down with the League?"

"Badly. But they haven't killed me yet."

"Neither have they allowed you to do one."

Labastide stopped us again. "House Tucek, did your covert presence in New Mexico indicate a policy by the Hidden Path party?"

I bit my lip. A neat flanking attack.

"I freely admit I'm not entirely within the Hidden Path party, although I *am* here at their request and on behalf of the Assembly, as I've explained. Personally, I prefer to think of myself as Basilikos."

The rest of the table tensed, and Tucek laughed.

"Come on! Diakon Altau calls herself Basilikos. Even if it's a blatant political move by Altau himself, it's clearly allowed."

Tucek was good. She'd not only dodged Labastide's question, she'd distracted her by accurately pressing her Eastern Seaboard buttons.

"So you admit it was a Basilikos plan to have your House disguised as ninja nuns and hiding out for years in Taos?" I said. "More wine?"

She held up her glass, her hand as steady as a rock, and I poured.

"I'll answer, so long as you'll listen to the full reply."

"We're listening," Labastide said.

"Yes," Tucek said. "A Basilikos plan. Not a Matlal plan, not a plan produced by the Assembly party, but still a plan by Athanate, labeled by the Assembly as Basilikos. Altau created that division, that anything not Panethus is by definition Basilikos, and it threatens to break the Assembly. It's worse outside of the Assembly. It casts Carpathia and the Empire of

Heaven as enemies. No Carpathian can be trusted inside Panethus, whatever the appearances."

The table was silent. Xavier and Jo were looking hypnotized by Tucek. Labastide was unreadable. Jen was immune. She knew what Tucek had done, and nothing she heard was going to change her mind about the woman.

As for untrustworthy Carpathians, Skylur had appointed Yelena as his pelea. That was trust.

Tucek went on, "What Altau calls Basilikos is a mixture of beliefs and systems that has no absolute reality. The Theokos party crossed the floor in the Denver Assembly meeting, leaving Basilikos to join Panethus. Did they change one single thing they did? Even one minor item of their creed? No. But suddenly they're Panethus. It's all political smoke and mirrors. The vast majority of 'Basilikos' are closer in creed to the late, lamented Eastern Seaboard cohort of Panethus than they are to the wild extremism of Matlal."

"Then all those moderate Basilikos should apply to join Panethus," Jen said. "If all we're talking is a preference for a little fear with their Blood, there will be enough humans for whom that's an acceptable exchange."

I loved my wife and I could hardly tell her to take a back seat, but it chilled me that Tucek became focused on her. I didn't want Jen on any list that Tucek kept. I didn't want Tucek even thinking about her.

Tucek had other ideas.

"Everyone has a little fear, Ms. Kingslund. Even between humans in their most intimate relationships, there is a little fear. It adds piquancy, like this excellent sauce." She speared a small cube of meat and took it delicately in her teeth before chewing appreciatively.

"Mmmm." She swallowed and licked her lips, eyes fixed on Jen. "So good."

"A little fear is not enough then?" Jen said, ignoring everything but the words.

"No. *Absolutely* not enough. Ask anyone who has ever enjoyed extreme sports, for instance. There's the moment before..." She switched to English. "When your heart is in your mouth, you feel weak, you're trembling with every thud of your heart, every pulse of blood through your veins, knowing in that perfect, endless moment of revelation the most certain possibility of death and pain is so close. Truly fear brings you to the point at which you can reach out and touch and *feel* that which is sacred: life itself. Then, afterwards, there's the rush that follows surviving a brush with death. Nothing is more life-affirming."

She was looking at Jen's throat, her eyes darkening. I was tensing, ready to defend Jen, but then Tucek blinked and looked away, resuming in Athanate, "My toru experience this, over and over. Through my powers, I enable it and experience it with them. I cannot lie and say I will tire of this. I also cannot lie and say that human and Athanate are equal, not even in this sharing." She picked an oyster and tilted the shell so it slipped into her mouth.

Xavier had stopped eating. He was watching her. Any more and he'd be drooling.

"To the first part of the point you made, that there will be sufficient people to willingly feed our Rahaimon, you are correct. That's already the case," Tucek said. "But to join Panethus? Any political system needs checks and balances. Panethus needs an opposition. No leader is without blind spots. Certainly not Altau."

"We agree on something," Labastide said and clapped her hands. "But enough of business for the moment. Is your visit to Louisiana going to be nothing else but your official duties with the Southern League? Have you planned enough time to see the sights?"

The thought of Tucek on the tourist trail almost made me smile. Almost.

Talk drifted to the best way to see the French Quarter, upcoming jazz festivals and plantation visits.

I rested a hand on Jen's thigh and let the rest of the table carry the majority of the conversation until they got around to discussing swamp trips and alligator spotting.

"You've been to the Atchafalaya, House Tucek?" I asked.

"Not personally, no."

"But some of your House?"

"Associates." She shrugged.

"To meet with the Queen of Diamonds?"

Tucek looked hard at me. "People don't casually meet with the swamp witch. Subordinates emerge from the deep swamps and talk for her. She's intriguing, House Farrell, but even more than that, she's dangerous. I'd advise avoiding her."

"Unfortunately, I can't. She has a member of my House. I have something of a reputation in rescue missions and if you have a means of communication with the Queen of Diamonds, you might give her a warning. It will not go well for her if I have to enter the swamp. Tell her to ask the rougarou. Or her friends in the south."

Tucek's face was closed but she *knew* what had happened at Astilla de Luna, and she knew who'd been responsible.

In her silence, I sensed an inner conflict, but even as I watched, she came to a decision.

"Very well. Make time for me tomorrow night," she said. "I have things to show you."

From her purse she extracted a cell and tapped it. My cell, being held by Rita, pinged.

So much for security, Tara said.

My number isn't that deeply hidden, I replied. *I hope my calls are secure.*

"I'll call you from this number," Tucek said, returning her cell to her purse. She dabbed her lips with her napkin before laying it down. "Now, I must say good night. This has been stimulating."

"Leaving so early, House Tucek?" Labastide asked.

"Yes. Thank you for the invitation and introduction to a good restaurant. One hunger has been very well satisfied. But it remains that I am of the Basilikos creed." She looked around the table with heavy-lidded eyes, lingering on Xavier, Jo and Jen. "Even were you to offer me the freedom of your House, you would find it rude if I exercised my unrestrained desires on your hospitality, and restraining myself would impair the experience. I will need to satisfy myself elsewhere."

"In a manner approved by the Agiagraphos," Labastide said. She meant Tucek would need to ensure she was discreet, didn't kill anyone and blurred the memories of anyone she fed on.

"Naturally. Some of us still do follow the Agiagraphos," she said, her gaze passing over me, slowly enough for me to notice it, quick enough that I couldn't call it an insult. She was right anyway; I hated the book of rules more with each day.

Xavier rose politely as Tucek got up, and she rewarded him with a smile that was designed to reach deep inside him and *squeeze*.

Everyone watched her walk away. She had that effect.

"Well, that was interesting," Labastide said. "An... impressive woman. How strange to be sitting down to dinner with Basilikos, outside of a formal Assembly meeting."

"Strange times indeed." I laughed and shook my head. "For example, I gave a bunch of werewolves a slideshow presentation this afternoon like we were in an office."

"Presumably before you were ambushed by rougarou?" Labastide said.

"Yes."

We turned to a discussion of the Atchafalaya, the difficulties of the terrain and the impossibility of searching the entire swamp.

An hour later, I called it a day.

As we rose from the table, Labastide said, "To be clear: we're allies, House Farrell, but we're not friends. In a way, what Tucek was implying is right; we're only associates because of the presence of another—her. You should keep that in mind as you go about your business with the Were, and your 'inquiries' about the Adept communities. You may not regard this territory as well run, but I would *not* appreciate a paranormal war breaking out in the Atchafalaya basin. I remind you that Tucek is currently under my protection, and I have both your oaths."

"Then she's safe from me, unless she abuses your hospitality or breaks her oath," I countered, and got a frosty smile in return. I bowed my head. I'd keep her warnings in mind, but if it came to it, I'd do whatever was necessary to get Gabrielle back safely.

"Also, my offer of hospitality to your House stands," Labastide said, and nodded at Jo and Xavier.

They got up.

Pia was at my shoulder in the blink of an eye. "Our warmest thanks for your ongoing generosity, House Labastide," she said formally. "We accept and welcome it."

Chapter 44

There were enough of us to need two cabs, and I made sure Pia was with me.

"We've just accepted Jo and Xavier..."

"To spend the night with us," Pia confirmed. "To satisfy any of the needs of our party. A level below 'freedom of the House', but a significant honor."

I snorted and exchanged a little smile with Jen that sparked a warmth in my belly. Not an honor *I* would be needing.

But in the back of the cab, business. I had retrieved my cell from Rita. I called Yelena in New York.

She was off duty and had time to listen to me quickly update her in Athanate on what had happened.

"So, good progress with Labastide," she said. "Not getting in Jen's way, offering you hospitality—"

"To keep an eye on us," I cut her off.

"Yes. Paranoia is good. Seeing things that aren't there is better than not seeing things that are there. But Labastide is not your problem at the moment. Tucek and the Queen of Diamonds and Gabrielle... they are your problem. I don't like Tucek offering to help. The devil gives gifts, but he expects them back."

"I knew you'd have some Ukrainian sayings for me."

She laughed. "We are so wise, it is our burden to share our wisdom with the rest of the world." She paused, and went on more seriously, "I can hear, you are not happy."

"Yeah. Tucek. It's like fighting with someone, and getting in some good hits, but none of them slow her down."

Like the rougarou, muttered Tara in my head. *But we got in the last punch there.*

"Yes, but you're not fighting, you're talking," Yelena said. "She's clever. It doesn't mean she's right."

"What about this offer to show me something about Gabrielle, then?"

Yelena laughed again, this time a bitter sound. "If you have no other leads, maybe you need to see. Don't go alone, whatever she says."

"And this thing about Carpathians not being trusted... what do you think she meant?"

"She's heard the rumors and she's using it to, how do you say, get inside your head." I could hear some background noise. Yelena was off duty and she wouldn't be alone—she had all four of her kin there.

Yelena went on, "The rumor is true. Skylur has split Maia's old job while she's on duty with Jen. I am still Skylur's pelea. But the other role, the Head of Security, he's made a temporary placement for an Athanate from House Elicott in DC."

Clever political move. House Elicott was a respected senior figure in the Eastern Seaboard association, *and* he had been upset by Naryn temporarily establishing himself in DC while Emergence needed to make its way through the levels of bureaucracy.

"So nothing to do with trust," I said. "Everything to do with politics."

"Yes, exactly. Not a problem for me. I get time off this way."

"Mmm. I can hear someone in the background. I guess it's not Skylur, is it?"

"No, it's not Skylur." It was Vera, Colonel Laine's wife, I could hear speaking. Her voice had taken that husky, lazy quality that told me she'd been having a very enjoyable time before I'd called.

"Hi, Vera. Sorry to interrupt."

"Not to worry, Amber. Your calls are always important."

"How are you?"

With Colonel Laine working to make sure the Athanate in America were ready for any outcome from Emergence, and Yelena on bodyguard duty for Skylur most of the time, I wondered how she was filling her time. Not that she would ever complain.

"Life is good," she said. "The Athanate here in New York have a quite different outlook, and that's good, too. It helps me see things from other points of view. I feel I'm approaching the center of where we should all be. We're the sum of what we've done, but we always spiral in, and yesterday weighs more than last year."

Vera had been shot when I rescued her and the Colonel from the rogue Ops 4 group that Matlal had infiltrated. Bian had healed her, but it was a matter of pulling her back from the brink, and the tsunami of bio-agents that had been necessary to do that had produced some repeated, rather strange episodes where she spoke like an obscure visionary.

Yelena loved it and talked to Vera whenever she could, and I guessed that was helping in the healing process. To me, their conversation always sounded as if they were *almost* making sense.

We'd arrived back at Labastide's mansion.

I said goodbye and let the pair of them get back to whatever distraction they chose for the rest of their evening.

There was a third butler on duty. Another handsome, human guy, who welcomed us and waved us straight in.

It made me wonder how many butlers Labastide had. I guessed three would give them each eight-hour shifts on duty. I could tell from seeing butler number 1 at the dinner this evening, that she was definitely a senior part of the security team.

Butler number 3 looked the part as well.

Which left Jo, and my growing suspicion she was more than she seemed.

We all crowded into the living room of the middle of the three suites that had been allocated to us. Nick, Ursula and the Lost Boys were back from their recon down in the Atchafalaya, and were sitting drinking beer. They had no new information on the Queen of Diamonds, but Kane now told me he was sick of saying Atchafalaya. It was now to be called the 'Hatch'.

I introduced Xavier, and reintroduced Jo.

How to word this?

Pia came to my aid: "Think of it that they're temporary members of our House," she announced to everyone.

Flint and Kane both looked at Jo with renewed interest.

"Give us the room for a couple of minutes," I said to my House, indicating Jo and Xavier should stay.

Pia looked worried, but she obeyed and led the way for the rest of them.

Maia gave me an unreadable glance as she left, but I suspected, of all of them, she knew exactly what I was doing and why.

"Sit."

I pointed at the sofa. Jo and Xavier sat. Obedient, fresh-faced. No trace of guile between them.

"Closer together."

They looked puzzled, but shuffled until they were hip to hip.

I sat, straddling their legs, facing them. Up close. Resting a hand on each of their chests.

"So. Here we are: an evil, predatory, near-outcast House and a couple of sweet innocents adrift on the sea of politics."

They blinked in confusion and glanced at each other, their faces mirroring their uncertainty.

"Oh, you're *good*, you two. Butter wouldn't melt and so on."

I ran fingers along Xavier's fine jawline. "Poor boy, so fascinated by the beautiful, sexy House Tucek he nearly made a fool of himself in the restaurant."

I stroked Jo's cheek. "And sweet Jo, all flustered and blushing and clearly out of her depth greeting important guests in the small hours of the morning. Well done, both of you, but you're busted. You can drop the act now."

There was a long moment of silence before Xavier cleared his throat. "It wasn't really an act for your benefit anyway."

"And I *was* flustered," Jo added, looking embarrassed.

I grinned.

"As if House Labastide has made *any* choices over the last couple of days that she didn't weigh three times. Including who she invited to eat at the table with us tonight. The pair of you could probably fool a genius and tempt a saint, but if Labastide doesn't already know it, Tucek was on to you. That stuff about needing to find her own prey was just to give her an out."

I cocked my head as I looked at them. "Your House put you in a position that she shouldn't have. Tucek wouldn't have made a mistake with you that Labastide could use, but she might have taken up an offer. She *could* have gotten into your heads. Trust me on this, you don't want that. And I hope you don't believe her talk about how much fun her toru have."

Jo bit her lip. "Okay. But like Xav says, it's not the same deal with you."

I laughed. They weren't making any attempt to deny they'd been prepared to spy on Tucek, but I wouldn't get them to admit they were also expected to spy on my House.

Better this than sweeping for bugs and cameras, Tara said.

"Anyway," I got up. "You are genuinely welcome. The rest of the House will return. I'm going to try for some beauty sleep I'm desperately in need of. But one thing I should make clear."

They looked up expectantly.

"It doesn't matter if you're here following Labastide's orders. These rooms are temporarily House Farrell, and we don't expect anyone to offer body or Blood under threat or compulsion, whether that's the mundane type or paranormal. If you want to enjoy yourselves with my House, it'd make me happy. If you don't, or even if there's one person you don't want to be with, then there is no obligation, no breach in manners to say 'no'. You can leave at any time if you want."

They didn't. My House streamed back in and I headed for the shower where my wife was all hot and wet and soapy, if I was lucky.

Chapter 45

Jen *was* hot and wet and soapy. She lost no time in getting me into the same state when I joined her in the shower.

"I was starting to think you had other duties again, honey," she murmured. "Poor you, so much to do, it'd be no surprise if you left some part of your responsibilities... unsatisfied."

I chuckled as my hands enjoyed the smooth sweep of her back. I imitated her drawl: "Why, Mrs. Farrell, I do believe you are flirtin' with me."

"Oh, heavens, no, Mrs. Kingslund. Flirtin' is promises you may not keep. I tell you straight, I have every intention of keeping my promises."

Teasing each other with our pet names gave way to a kiss: a deep, unhurried kiss that lit fires in our bodies. Our passion would always be like a banked fire; all it needed was the stir of our bodies against each other, a breath, a sigh, and it burst into flames again.

Wary of all my wounds, my wife had me turn around and pressed against me from behind. She had one arm wrapped around my ribs, one hand cupping my breast and teasing the nipple, the other hand free to wind like a serpent across my belly, testing, seeking. My heart threatened to break out through my ribs and it was all I could do to clutch her arms and keep myself standing.

She didn't take the usual route with our eukori linked, which would have slowed us down and stretched out the pleasure. She wanted to make me come hard and fast. She whispered it in my ear, along with husky, breathy suggestions about what I'd have to do for her later.

"Yes. Yes. All of that," I gasped. "I promise."

The way I surrendered my body completely to her touch excited her. At the last moment, she allowed my eukori in, and we shared the perfect, primal pleasure as it exploded through our bodies.

At that exact point, with the shocks still echoing through me and my legs threatening to fold, I sensed one of my House approach.

Rita came in the bathroom, holding my cell and tapping hesitantly on the shower door.

"Sorry, Boss. I think you want this."

I guess I did. Not as much as I wanted to stay in the shower or move to the bed, but life had a way of being unfair.

It was David, with urgent news.

I staggered out to the bedroom, leaving a muttering wife behind.

The alpha of the Alexandria pack, Bill Patout, had promised me the name of a guy who organized 'special' hunting trips in the Atchafalaya basin. I hadn't believed it, but there was no harm in getting a contact, and a complete lack of clues about where the swamp witch might hide meant I would look at anything.

Bill had sent that contact, but Rita checked and found a dead end. So she'd sent it to Matt and David to see if their technical wizardry could provide up-to-date information.

David was calling with the result.

"The guy exists all right," he said. "But he's working hard at becoming invisible. I found an old copy of his website on the Dark Web. He turned it off, but these things bounce around until the echoes die down. I haven't got an address for him, but watching a couple of the videos, I think you need to find him. This is the real thing. He's hunted rougarou and he knows stuff about the Atchafalaya."

"I guess somewhere in that bad news about *not* finding him, you still have a reason for me to *not* get into the shower and then go to bed."

"Yes. When I hit the blank wall, I went sideways. Your friend Captain Morales..."

"As in Denver PD? He's not going to be much use in Louisiana."

"Maybe, but he has a friend on the New Orleans force who owes him."

"And this is a reason I have to go out, leaving my wife here?"

"Yes, I'm afraid. He's scheduled for a week's vacation, starting tomorrow. Morales called him and set up a meet tonight. In... about half an hour."

"Okay. Thanks to the Captain, and the pair of you, too."

I didn't want to waste time unpacking, so I started putting the clothes I'd just taken off back on.

"Nice thong," Rita said. "We have to take Flint. Gwen's new orders: one of them any time you step outside now."

"Okay. Better extract him from the party before he gets in too deep. If you know what I mean." I could already sense it was going to be a *good* party next door.

"It'll break Jo's heart."

My wife snarked from the bathroom, "I'm crying here."

Rita snickered and left me to finish dressing.

"And warn Maia she has security until we get back," I called after her.

"Yes, Boss." Slightly exasperated.

I was still fine-tuning working with Rita. I'd never have said that to Yelena because I'd have known she would do it. I was getting there with Rita.

Scarf to hide neck bruises. Shoulder holster with Mk23. Brown jacket. The pistol interfered with the cut of the jacket, so I'd have to leave the buttons undone. Fine.

Sunglasses to hide the black eyes and facial bruises. Spare pair for Rita—she wasn't as badly bruised as me, but I didn't want our contact to think we were battered wives or something.

I was ready. Now I just had to go into the bathroom and explain to my hot, wet wife why I was going out again, but that I remembered I had promises to keep.

Just over half an hour later, we were at the Bon Temps bar in Tulane-Gravier.

"Crappy-looking bar," Flint said.

"Probably not Lieutenant DiMarco's favorite bar. Just a place he meets strange people introduced to him over the phone by an old friend."

I checked my cell for the photo I'd been sent of the lieutenant.

It showed him as a slab of a man in a hard-wearing gray suit, and I saw him the moment we walked in. It was probably the same suit.

He was sitting on a stool, resting his elbows on the bar and reading the Times-Picayune, neatly folded in half. There was a glass by his hand.

As we'd planned earlier, Flint took a seat while Rita and I went on to the bar.

"Lieutenant DiMarco?"

He flipped his paper, folding it one more time, and then turned.

"I'm guessing you two... three," he amended as his eyes found Flint, "are my mystery guests. I wasn't sure. I could never tell when Morry was pulling my leg."

"He wasn't pulling it this time."

DiMarco's face was red and puffy, seeming to squeeze his eyes until they were little more than slits, but the look was sharp. The man didn't miss much.

He grunted.

The bartender came up and gave me a smile that went on and off in one continuous move. "What'll you have?"

I spotted the Old New Orleans rum I'd enjoyed the night before and asked for three. "And whatever he's having."

DiMarco nodded thanks for the drink, watched all of us and said nothing while Rita took Flint his rum.

"So, Lieutenant," I started, "we're looking for someone, and you come recommended."

"Yeah. Look, I'm sure Morry owes you big time for him to call me, but you're gonna have to tell him his check didn't cash. Tomorrow I get on a boat and I go spend a week doing nothing but fish and drink beer."

"What bait do you use to catch beer?" Rita asked.

"Hey, funny girl. Wait, that was a movie, wasn't it? Funny Girl?"

"It was," Rita said. "Barbra Streisand and Omar Sharif. You probably remember it for Barbra." Her voice dropped. "I get to remember it for Omar."

Rita was doing a good job of loosening him up, so I sipped my rum and waited.

"That's sad," he said and wrinkled his nose. "You seen a recent picture? Omar's gotten old."

"Not in the film."

He smiled thinly. "You're good. Morry tells me you're some bad asses up in the Rockies, but you come in here looking like California fashion victims. And you know what? I don't like talking to people wearing sunglasses. Makes me think they're hiding something."

I took mine off and laid them on the bar. Rita followed suit.

His eyes widened. "Jesus, Mary and Joseph! Since you're standing here, I'm guessing I should be looking for the other guys' bodies?"

A difficult question, when asked by a police officer.

"No," I said. "They're... out of your jurisdiction."

DiMarco took a slug of his drink and thought about it, his glittering eyes back to their narrowest. Then he laughed.

"I like that," he said. "'Out of my jurisdiction'."

He drained his drink. "So what ya got?"

Rita handed over a printout with a picture.

"Frederico 'Freddy' Walker," she recited. "Louisiana native. Thirty-eight. Six-two. Ex-Ranger. Boat mechanic sometimes. Other times—"

"Con artist." DiMarco tossed the printout on the bar. "Yeah, I know of Freddy. Not been around for a while. What'd he do to get your attention, all the way up in Colorado? I hope you haven't come all this way to collect some old debt."

I smiled. "Nope. Need to talk to him about illegal hunting trips into the basin."

DiMarco didn't look convinced. "If it wasn't Morry asking..." He shook his head.

He stood up abruptly and handed Rita back her printout.

"Now?" I asked.

He nodded. "I got a date with a boat tomorrow. Middle of the night will be the best time to catch someone like Freddy. If he's around. This type of guy ends up as fish food, no one ever knows."

Chapter 46

The first five places DiMarco took us to were a bust; his informants weren't there, or they hadn't seen Freddy. No one had heard any news about him.

We didn't crowd him, but we were close enough to hear DiMarco wasn't just going through the motions.

It didn't look good to me, but he shrugged off my pessimism. "Not how it works. Just rattling cages so far."

Stop number six wasn't a bar. It was the mouth of an alleyway between two bars on the outskirts of the French Quarter.

It smelled of piss-damp bricks and garbage. Street lights gleamed on puddles oozing out of dumpsters and sagging pyramids of trash bags. Music screeched from a portable player, blending with bass thumps from the bars.

"Hears yas looking for Freddy," one of the hoodies said. He had old wounds to his throat and his voice came out as a harsh whisper.

"You seen him?"

"Maybe."

I took a couple of steps closer.

"Whys ya looking?" I could see his gaze drop to my belly, and it made me smile.

"Want to talk to him about hunting trips," I said. "Heard he used to do that a lot."

They all laughed, a sort of snuffling sound.

"Yeah, he did that. He did. Big game."

They thought it was a con, and I was falling for it. I didn't care.

I took some bills out of my pocket and rustled them. "You know where we can find him?"

"He don't come here. Sometime he down the river park, near the pier, sometime he stay Desire someplace."

"Need an address," I said. "Need to know where."

They formed a huddle. There was a lot of headshaking, and 'no, man'.

"Know who know," the guy with the whispery voice said when they broke up.

"That's worth half, because I still got to pay the person who knows."

"Don't pay, you know jack shit."

"And you got jack shit in your pocket."

He settled. We got the 'business' address of a guy called Cordell they said Freddy was working for, they got fifty.

DiMarco grimaced as we walked away.

"This is no good," he grunted. "This guy, Cordell Jarvis, he's a gang dealer. And this place... CP3? The old Calliope Projects? Not where we want to go without backup."

"Trust us."

He shook his head, but we got back into the Hill Bitch and he directed me across the city to the other side of the tangled junction where the Superdome sat.

DiMarco gave me a brief rundown of how Jarvis worked.

We passed the big interstate junction and arrived in a very different area.

"Bordered by railroad shunting yards and the interstate," I said. "Hey, I would never have guessed that the Calliope Projects would turn out bad."

"It's cheap," DiMarco replied. He wasn't happy here.

"Not a good idea to park and leave the truck," Rita said, head swiveling to watch all sides. "Not if we want to drive back."

"I only need to know where Freddy is now," I said. "It won't take me long, but it's probably better for you to stay with the car, Lieutenant. Drive it around the block a couple of times."

"Uh, no. No." DiMarco had been getting more on edge as we'd driven here. "Look, I thought you'd be smart enough to bail when you saw the place. I can't let you go in, not even with the big guy." He indicated Flint in the back. "You won't come out in one piece."

"It's okay, really," I said. I reached with eukori and used it to lean a little on him. Not a compulsion. Just a nudge.

I still felt bad about it.

Rita stretched over the back of his seat. "Come on, Lieutenant," she said in his ear. "It's what we came out to do. Morales vouches for us. We'll be in and out too quickly for things to go wrong. It's the only way. You know you can't come in with us. You'd see criminal activity and then you'd have to make an arrest. Which would mean you'd be tied up with paperwork and that boat would leave tomorrow without you."

It was exactly what was needed. She used my eukori to divert his decision processes from thinking about us going in, to not wanting to get involved himself.

A little blurring of his thoughts. Later, he'd justify it by putting it down to the drinks he'd had.

Meanwhile, we were getting out of the truck and he hurriedly moved across to the driver's seat.

"Couple of circuits of the block," I said, and walked off to the apartment building. Then: "Flint, I really need the lights to go out when I say."

"Yeah. Thought you might want something like that. Slow down a little and give me a hand."

He was still walking, but his eyes were closed and we had to guide him through the trash piles, up the path to the broken front door. I could feel the skin-tingling ripple of a working coming off him.

Our target operated out of the corner apartment on the ground floor.

DiMarco had said he wouldn't have drugs in this apartment. His whole operation was a demonstration of just-in-time business practice that legitimate executives would envy. He had street corner guys all over his territory in the city. They had the minimum amount of product in their pockets, and called on cellphones for more. Runners would bring them the supplies from stashes that were kept in cruising cars which never ran a light or failed to indicate a turn. Other runners would collect the money. Those runners would stop outside a bar and talk with a guy on a motorcycle, shake hands, stroll away. Then the motorcycle and the money would come back here, nice and regular, or Jarvis got 'anxious', and when he got anxious, someone often died.

It was all a matter of whether he was here, or out on one of his 'patrols'.

"Located the fuse boxes," Flint said. "Ready when you are."

I pulled the door open, and a guy sitting on a plastic chair in the lobby snarled at me, "You lost? What you want, you stupid bitch?"

"Good evening," I said, smiling. "I'm going to talk to Cordell. He is in, isn't he?"

He was. I could read it in the reaction I got. The guy surged up off his chair and I punched him in the jaw.

Turned out he had what boxers used to call a glass jaw.

I caught him and shoved him out of the way. I checked the handle of the door he'd been guarding. It wasn't locked. Cordell thought a guard on the door was enough.

Maybe it was, for the people he'd been expecting to come here.

"Lights please, Flint."

The lights snapped out in the lobby and I threw the door open.

Small apartment. Pitch black.

Rita and I went forward like a pair of cops—Rita to the right, me to the left. The darkness wasn't as much of a problem for our shifter eyes as it was for the people inside.

"What the fuck—"

A solid crack of a blow and the thump of a falling body on my right told me another of Cordell's guards was getting some shut-eye.

A third shuffled blindly toward me, one hand stretched out, the other waving a pistol uncertainly.

I kicked him in the stomach and took the pistol away.

On the theory that Cordell was the smartest person who'd been in the room, I guessed he was the guy on the floor, crawling away.

I grabbed him by the back of his shirt and lifted him up.

He swung at me.

Knife. Block. Trap arm. Twist.

When he'd dropped the knife and was screaming in pain, I threw him backward into an easy chair. Hard.

And then I put his own knife against his throat.

"I can give you money," he croaked. "But it's not here. You need me alive."

He was lying. He probably had a few thousand dollars of the night's takings somewhere in this apartment.

"Not interested in your dirty money, but you need to know this: I know you're lying."

He thought about that. "What you want?"

"Information."

"I ain't no snitch. Who are you?"

I laughed.

"Away from the lights, people are afraid of the dark, Cordell Jarvis. We're the reason they are. And here you are, in the dark with us."

"You fucking crazies."

But I'd read his reaction. He *was* afraid. He couldn't see, and being helpless around women with knives seemed to be a phobia of his. I couldn't help feeding off that fear a little.

"Maybe we *are* crazy," I said. "If you tell me what I want to know, I let you keep all your bits connected to your body. I guess that makes me crazy."

I scraped the knife up and down his throat to emphasize my point.

"What... what you need?"

"I want to know *exactly* where I can find Freddy Walker. If you tell me a lie, I'll know. If you get it wrong, I'll come back, and not all the electric light in the world will be enough to keep the dark away."

He giggled hysterically.

"You want that crazy sumbitch? You *is* crazy, too."

"Why?"

"Cos he's crazy. Flat *gone*. Can't use him for nothing. Last I heard, got Jesus with them Risen Sun people to get rid of the devils and now he got twice as many. If he ain't drunk, he's high."

"So he doesn't work for you?"

"Used to. Like I say, can't use him no more."

He gave me an address in the area of New Orleans called Desire.

Truth.

But hidden beneath the fear was a taste of satisfaction. He thought he was tricking me.

I pressed the knife so that his skin broke and blood trickled down his throat. His heart rate leaped again and his breathing came short.

"And what is it that you're not telling me?"

"He got guns. And dogs."

"There. That wasn't so difficult. Now, you sit there for a few minutes and think about your life choices," I whispered to him. "Think *hard*. Because I'm not going to be that far away. Think especially hard because half the day is night, and the night belongs to us."

Outside, Rita and Flint took up a position looking both ways while I wiped the knife and tossed it into one of the bigger piles of refuse.

"Came close to telling him we're paranormal," Flint said.

I snorted. "He's not going to say two women claiming to be monsters scared him. If he says anything, he'll make up some shit about being jumped by SWAT and escaping out the window."

The Hill Bitch drew up. DiMarco hurried to make way for Rita to drive, looking at the dark apartment blocks nervously.

As we drove off, he could see the broken skin on Rita's knuckles. He caught me checking mine as he looked into the back.

Flint just smiled at him.

"What use are you, big guy?" DiMarco said, trying to get some control back.

"Me? I'm her spiritual advisor," he replied, deadpan, and we laughed.

Chapter 47

We dropped off a bemused Lieutenant DiMarco with our thanks and best wishes for his fishing vacation. I promised I would explain what had happened tonight when I was allowed to.

Using the GPS in Flint's phone, we made our way to the address in Desire. It was another dead-end neighborhood, cramped by freight railroad lines, the interstate and a working canal.

Freddy Walker had his own derelict clapboard house, hidden behind an overgrown yard complete with broken furniture, rusting cars and a tottering pile of used tires. At one stage there had been a chain-link fence around the property, but it had rusted away.

The dogs I'd been warned about stirred inside. I could feel them, sniffing, searching the air, growls building.

I reached out with eukori and touched them.

I am alpha.

Dogs weren't wolves, let alone werewolves, but they got the message.

From them, I sensed they were bored, frustrated and hungry; it was a good thing we'd stopped at an all-night store and bought meat at the same time we'd dropped off DiMarco.

Which left us a crazy man with guns to worry about. An ex-Ranger.

We walked quietly up to the porch, spread out.

With my eukori probing, I could feel him inside the house, so I knocked on the door and stood to one side.

"Hi, Freddy. I'm Amber. We're not here for trouble. We want to find out what you know about the Atchafalaya."

"Go away."

Not friendly, but at least he hadn't fired through the door.

"Can't do that. See, I need information and I hear you're the person to ask."

There were more noises as he moved around.

"What have you done to my dogs?"

It didn't sound like he was steeling himself to try shooting me. In fact, he sounded drunk.

"Your dogs like me, Freddy. I've brought them some food."

"I don't know you. I don't trust you."

"You ever known your dogs to be wrong about a person?"

He didn't answer. I could hear him still moving uncertainly, his weight shifting on bare wooden boards that creaked.

"Dogs need to eat," I said. "I've got enough food for them for a couple of days."

"Leave it on the porch and go."

"Not going to happen."

I heard bolts slide, and the door opened a crack.

If he was expecting his dogs to go wild and scare me off by barking and snarling, he was disappointed.

There were three noses stuck through the gap. Big hunting dogs, I reckoned. Tails wagging in the shadows, heads lowered, little whines of excitement coming from them.

"Let them out," I said. "I won't hurt them."

The door opened a little wider and the three of them pushed it open in a rush.

Walker had two local Louisiana hunting dogs, the breed they call Catahoula Leopard Dogs, and an Irish wolfhound. They came and said hello enthusiastically, tails lashing, no more than a bark or two each, bouncing, pawing gently at me, dabbing me with cold, wet noses.

"Happy to meet you too." I made a fuss of them. Not too much. I didn't want them more excited than they were already.

They were sleek, muscled and well cared for. I got the impression they'd exaggerated their hunger just a little. Still...

Food? Alpha has food?

Rita passed me the bag with the meat. The dogs weren't so sure about her, and I could see her nose wrinkling with a silent snarl in response.

I waved her back and fed the dogs what I judged to be a meal each.

When they were happily occupied with that, I stood up.

Walker was watching me from the doorway.

I held out the rest of the bag of meat and after a long pause, he took it.

"Never seen anything like that," he said, his wording careful with too many drinks. "Get you burned a couple of hundred years ago."

"Get me burned now, if people knew. If they knew things like you know things."

He swayed as he watched. "You a witch?"

"Yeah. And a vampire, and a werewolf."

His eyes narrowed in concentration. "You're the enemy. Church says so."

"Your dogs don't think so," I said. "Tell you what I think: you don't know who your friends are anymore. It's not Cordell Jarvis. It's not the Church of the Risen Sun. It's not the swamp witch."

"Not that bitch, for sure."

He moved away from the door, leaving it open, and I cautiously stepped inside.

I hadn't seen a gun, but that didn't mean anything. On the other hand, the man probably couldn't hit the other side of the room in his state.

It was dark inside. I could see, more or less. Walker, even drunk, knew his home well. He didn't bump into things. Not that there was much in the way of furniture. He made his way unsteadily into the living room and sat down with his back to the wall.

I sat in the middle of the floor, facing him.

"Beer?" he said. "Whiskey? Weed?"

"I'm good, thanks."

"Stay outta the Hatch," he said.

"Atchafalaya? Can't. Got a job to do. Extraction. That's why I need to know what you know about it."

"An extraction? You got military experience?"

"Some."

He laughed quietly. There was no humor in it.

"Won't do any good. Look, I'll save you time. Save your life. Whoever you've lost is gone. She doesn't let go."

"You mean the Queen of Diamonds."

"That's the one."

"Tell me how a Ranger comes to this."

It was the wrong way to put it. He was embarrassed, which made him angry, and I tensed. But his dogs returned from their dinner on the porch and slumped down contentedly between us. They calmed him.

He ignored the sound of Rita patrolling the rest of the house. He ignored Flint standing in the hall. He took a swig from a bottle and started to talk erratically. The dogs liked the sound of his voice. He could sense that and it helped him.

"Last deployment out there..." He stopped. "You were there, right?"

"Some," I said.

"Yeah. 'Some'. You were one of those spooks, weren't you? Always fucking passing through in the middle of the night, like you were made of sand and shadows. Scared the hell out of everyone. Especially them. The stories you heard..."

He shook his head. "Anyway, my last deployment, it was bad at the end. We got chewed up and then we found we got screwed. That last patrol... no one out there knew who authorized it. Shouldn't have been there at all. No support. Because we weren't on the list, they wouldn't believe we were out there. They didn't move until half of us were dead."

His dogs sensed the anger and sorrow. They pressed against him.

"Got back. Got out. Drifted. Ended up down here. These boys saved my life."

He scratched necks and got tails thumping the floor.

"Worked. Did some fishing. Hunting. Then one night in a bar, this woman sits down and talks to me. Craziest shit you ever heard. Magic and stuff. Got me talking." He stopped. "Like you."

"I'm not the Queen of Diamonds," I said, "and I don't think I'm much like her. All I need to know is how to find where she is in the basin."

He shook his head again. "Can't tell you in any way that makes sense."

"Tell me however you can."

"Yeah. Okay. Got me talking, even about what happened on that last deployment." He took another drink. "Then she says the craziest thing. Says she can find them. Says she can get them down in the Hatch, and what would I like to do about it?"

"So she did, and you killed them?"

It took a long time before he answered. "There were three. Some scam on military supplies I couldn't even figure out, but they were getting rich. Our lieutenant had gotten suspicious. Was going to report it. So they got him and half the patrol killed to stop it from getting out. Would have gotten us all killed if that was what it took. Witch was as good as her word. Got them to boast about what they'd done. How much they'd made. Yes, I killed them. Hunted them down one at a time, so they knew I was coming for them. Not sorry about it."

My eukori was very carefully easing into his mind. He wasn't lying.

"No judgment on that," I said, "but it's a long way from there to running monster hunting parties for rich men in the Hatch."

"Yeah." His head bobbed and I could feel the tension returning to his arms. "Once she got her hooks in me, she didn't let up. There were other people like me, she said, who'd been wronged, who needed what I needed. All I had to do was lead the hunt. She said I couldn't refuse them."

I heard Rita finish checking the rest of the house, and take up a position at the back so she and Flint could look out both ways.

"The first few were like that," Walker went on. He sounded like he'd forgotten I was there, even when I spoke. I was just a voice in the darkness he needed to answer.

"Then it changed slowly," he said. "Always small steps. Reasonable. Always people who deserved it. But it ended with her choosing people to die because she said they had let her down. Even her own people."

"And the hunters?"

"Just part of the way she gets her hooks in any group. She has a playbook. Doesn't go after number one. She goes looking for a person in the highest position with the biggest secret want. Then she promises them that. She delivers. Then they're either addicted or she's got proof they don't want getting out. Then she works from there."

"And there were 'monsters' as prey?"

"Rougarou. Werewolves. Anyone who'd pissed her off. It was different every time."

"And you stopped because?"

"Someone I'd taken on a hunting expedition ended up on the other end. Figured out it was a matter of time before it was me."

We fell silent for a while as I processed all that.

"You must have needed interaction with her. You know where to contact her."

"No. Calls on my cell. Emails with instructions. Meet the people, take them out into the Hatch. We wouldn't see anyone else. We'd go to sleep in a cabin in the swamp, and we'd wake somewhere... different."

He shuddered.

"Different place?"

"Not exactly. Looked the same." He ran a hand over his face, suddenly less certain. "No one else noticed. But it wasn't the same place. It had a feel. Maybe you'd notice. You ever feel something in Afghanistan? When a place that had been rocks and sand suddenly became something else? Even if it looked the same. Made your skin crawl. Like that."

A substantiation? An Adept version of the Atchafalaya?

"What are you going to do now, Freddy?"

He just slumped back.

"Waiting. She'll come for me. Tried to get away. Can't. I mean I can walk to the bus station and then suddenly I'm walking away and I can't remember why. I thought she'd put a curse on me or something."

He was reliving it as he spoke. I was no expert, but it felt like a compulsion to me.

The Queen of Diamonds had trapped him in New Orleans and left him to wait until she came for him.

"That was when you went to the Church of the Risen Sun?"

He laughed then.

"Yeah. Some of that. Some idea I could make amends. Then they told me they had an angel in the swamp that was telling them what to do. She got to them like she gets to any other group."

He put his face in his hands, his voice broken and muffled. "She's coming for me. That bell will start tolling one night, and I know I'll just go to her. She'll come for you too, if you try to get to her. Get out while you can. Take my dogs. Please. They like you."

The dogs whined and pushed their muzzles against him.

"I'll do better, Freddy. Give me your cell with all the calls and emails you had with her. Show me on a map where this cabin was. Tell me anything else you think might help me find her. In return, I'll get you and your dogs to Colorado. I'll put you in contact with some people there who can genuinely help you."

It took an hour before I judged we'd wrung him dry and made the arrangements.

Flint could negate the compulsion enough to get the pair of them on Jen's plane, which was still at the airport. There was a pilot on standby 24/7 who'd fly them up to Denver. Flint could hand Walker over to Gwen and get flown back down in time for a late lunch.

As we were about to leave the house, Walker stopped.

"You going after her, you need these," he said.

He knelt by the front door and levered up the floorboards. Underneath were four large-caliber rifles and a box of ammunition.

Not just large—50 caliber. The sort of rifle that snipers used to hit people from over a mile away. One of them had the stock removed and the barrel shortened, so it was technically a pistol.

"She's surrounded by rougarou," Walker said, and shrugged. "But these take them out okay."

We dropped Flint and Walker at the airport. Jen's 24/7 pilot was there to greet them, and didn't turn a hair at having to get up in the small hours to fly a couple of scruffy people and three dogs to Denver.

It wasn't just their appearance; Flint was blocking Walker's compulsion, so the ex-Ranger was stumbling around like a zombie, having to be guided. The obvious smell of alcohol coming off him was a good excuse.

"Lot of running around tonight for not much," Rita said as we headed back out.

"It's more than we had before," I replied, trying to be positive. "We have the location of a cabin that belongs to her. We have cell phone records and email addresses, and serial numbers from the engines on those jonboats that David and Matt can chase. We can probably say she's going to be away from other people and places where swamp tours go. When Flint gets back, I want him and Kane to hire a helicopter. They can survey the basin. Fly over with infra-red scanners and their Adept senses to check for things that shouldn't be there. No one can completely hide in the basin."

Rita nodded. "And there's that company logo we saw on one of the jonboats as well: the surfing gator. Maybe someone will remember it and give us another data point. Still a lot of swamp to cover, Boss."

"Meanwhile, so much for our much-needed beauty sleep," I said and got my cell out again.

Something that Walker had said had been niggling at me. The way the Queen of Diamonds targeted people in groups, not going for the most obvious person at the top, but someone high up that she could seduce with promises.

"Just for argument's sake," I said to Rita, "let's say the Queen of Diamonds wants to get her hooks into the local Athanate House. Who does she go after?"

Rita hummed. "Not Labastide herself. It's either one of the top people in her House, or one of her sub-Houses: House Broussard in Lafayette or House Leandre in Baton Rouge."

"Yeah, I'm betting it's closer than the sub-Houses. Someone very close to Labastide."

I dialed Jen and prepared myself to apologize for waking her, but she was obviously up, despite the hour. She answered immediately.

"Amber, honey? Are you okay?"

"Yes. Sorry it's taken all night, but we've just had an interesting conversation about how the Queen of Diamonds operates. It's just a gut feeling, but I think you should broaden the financial search to the people closest to Labastide herself. I'm guessing that's Dupuis and Cazenave. Of the two, I'd go for Cazenave."

"Oh, you just felt challenged when I said I'd do it with spreadsheets, honey. Anyway, I have done that very thing, and the reason I'm up so early is my investigation spooked him. Cazenave and his kin caught flights to Mexico City last night. House Labastide requests our presence at a breakfast meeting as soon as possible."

Chapter 48

Dawn was breaking as we walked into Labastide's mansion through the hallway. That side of the house flooded with golden light.

But the person who let us in wasn't House Labastide. He was one of Skylur's security team. One of the ones who had been sent to El Paso after we'd met Skylur on I-10.

"They're waiting for you in the room in the back," he said, and took up a position watching the street.

Crap.

Trouble seemed to follow me around.

There was no Labastide security team sitting in the main living room, and I could feel a prickly silence over the house. People all around, sitting and keeping quiet, like the place was holding its breath.

Labastide and Jen were waiting for us in the room overlooking the garden, which was gloomy and cold. House Labastide herself was sitting silently, ramrod straight, absolutely still and utterly furious.

Jen gave every appearance of being relaxed, apart from a tightness around the corners of her eyes. She stretched up to kiss me.

"Morning, honey."

There was only one other person in the room and it wasn't Labastide's pelea, Dupuis, whose place would normally be at her side for meetings like this. It was Maia Kiriani, Jen's pelea... the woman whose other role was head of security for Skylur. She stood to one side, arms folded, face expressionless. She wore a pistol openly.

"Okay if Rita joins us?" I asked Labastide. "It's been a long night."

Labastide's head inclined fractionally. "I'm not sure the question should be addressed to me," she said, but she reached for a tiny gold bell on the table and rang it.

It was Olivia who responded rather than one of House Labastide's butlers. She gave me a small, quick smile and then concentrated on Labastide.

"One more for breakfast, please," Labastide said, and Olivia went back out.

I poured the coffee and waited for someone to tell me what the hell was going on.

"So, you're not really here for the Were rituals," Labastide said. "Any more than you were on your visit to El Paso. You're one of Altau's security team. You came here under false pretenses."

"You're wrong," I replied. "I'm not on Skylur's security team. And Skylur wasn't even aware I was in El Paso until afterwards."

I ducked the one about being in New Orleans under false pretenses.

"And yet, Skylur's security team follows you around."

"Coincidence. There was an Athanate problem in El Paso I came up against while I was there to work out some issues with rival werewolf groups across the border. If it had been up to me, I wouldn't have even met de Socorro, or his late Diakon. But Athanate politeness meant I had to say hello, and it all blew up from that."

"And now they're both 'late'," Labastide said. "And Altau is installing an old friend of his from the Caucasus in El Paso. House Herazade Sevaneli."

I shrugged. "We're thinly spread in the US. I've no idea how he went about choosing a replacement for de Socorro. And while we're on it, I have no regrets that he's dead. He killed his Diakon to cover for his own mistake."

"She took her own life."

"Argue it whichever way you want. His mistake. Her life."

"And now his life as well. We're spread thinly in the Caucasus. Moving Sevaneli from Georgia is weakening Panethus in that region at the expense of his domain in North America."

"*Way* above my pay grade, House Labastide. Not sure it's relevant either. Someone tell me what's happening. Please?"

I'd thought my appetite would be spoiled, but Olivia re-entered the room with a trolley of food that had me salivating. She served us while Jen brought me up to date.

"I didn't feel I was getting the real picture with the standard financial reports, so I set up an extraction to run last night. It must have triggered an alarm for Cazenave, and he was at the airport in an hour. That triggered one of *our* alarms and Maia woke me."

I could tell Labastide did *not* like the idea we had surveillance on her House at airports.

"He was right to run," Jen went on while I ate. "From the standard financial reports, he just looked as if he was running too many risky investments and cycling too much through cash reserves offshore. Truth is, he was not only skimming for himself, he was using House Labastide's funds to build up a portfolio that we can see is ultimately owned by someone in Mexico."

"Matlal?"

Jen shrugged.

"Okay, so are we assuming the worst?"

Jen's glance strayed hesitantly to Maia. "Yes. Which brings us to a problem. Maia put House Labastide in lockdown while we investigate..."

Maia interrupted. "My primary task here is to keep you safe, Jen. I can't do that *and* secure this House *and* investigate their loyalty. With the two returned from El Paso, I have a team of five in New Orleans. Even with the assistance of Amber's House, there's not enough to secure even this building for any length of time, let alone the plantation or the sub-Houses in Lafayette and Baton Rouge. I tried calling on Felix for help, but the Southern League is in turmoil following Amber's revelations about the Queen of Diamonds and her rougarou. I have no contacts in the local covens and no trust in them at this point."

It was the most I'd ever heard her say. I could hear the frustration in her voice, and it wasn't just the size of the task.

"Okay, we definitely have a problem," I said. "What am I missing?"

"House Labastide exercised her right to call Skylur."

"But he's busy with... oh." I stopped. "You didn't get through to him. You got through to Diakon Flavia."

"Yes," Jen confirmed.

Shit.

Labastide looked defiant.

Maia said, "My advice was that we should *not* speak to her until we had completed an investigation."

"What was her reaction?"

"She's arriving this afternoon at the airport," Maia said.

"I acknowledge I was hasty in calling her, and undiplomatic during our conversation," Labastide said. "But her response has not been reasonable."

"Her intention is to resolve the situation by the shortest path," Jen said. "Even if that means bringing in a complete replacement House from somewhere else we're overstretched."

'Complete replacement' would mean House Labastide would be executed. It was entirely in alignment with Agiagraphos rules, which stated the Master or Mistress of a House bore the responsibility for the actions of those in the House.

I became aware that Maia and Jen were looking at me.

"Huh?"

"No. This is a deliberate affront," Labastide said.

I blinked slowly and caught up.

"You want *me* to use eukori to tell if any of House Labastide is part of the betrayal by Cazenave? And you want me to do it before Flavia arrives?"

"You are a House in good standing with Altau," Maia said. "From what I've heard, I judge you capable, and no offense is implied to House Labastide."

"A *hybrid*," Labastide muttered. "Granted the status of a House by Altau last year while unable even to speak Athanate. Not even a year into being Athanate. You would put *her* in a position to rule on me?"

"And yet, last night we'd gotten as far as being allies," I said.

She glared at me. "You might be freakishly strong, House Farrell, but I have *centuries* on you. You couldn't possibly be capable of determining any guilt on my part, and relying on what you say would be as good as tossing a coin. I doubt you'd be able to do much better with any of my House. My former colleagues in the Eastern Seaboard association have the appropriate seniority and are sworn to Altau. They should have been called."

I was irritated from a long night with no sleep, and frustrated that there was yet another obstacle in the way of going out and finding Gabrielle.

You need Flint to come back and help Kane with the searches before you can do any more. Solving this could help integrate the Eastern Seaboard into Altau, Tara said. *And sleep is overrated.*

I got it all wrong in El Paso, I replied.

Then do it right here. Do it for Isabel Cuarón.

To Labastide I said: "I might agree with you if you'd asked for someone in the old Eastern Seaboard right away instead of demanding a call to Altau. Now, they couldn't get here in time. I'll try. But I'll do it my way."

Chapter 49

It was all the members of the House that needed to be checked, not just Labastide. There were more of them, out at Labastide's plantation, but I needed to start with the twenty in New Orleans first. They were the heart of House Labastide.

There was no way to disguise what I could do. My House knew that my Carpathian inheritance was a stronger eukori. Maia obviously knew. It was going to be a surprise to House Labastide, and I guessed it would be common knowledge in the Athanate community soon afterwards. That couldn't be helped.

Labastide's main argument might be right, that making a judgment on her was beyond my capabilities for now. But if I passed everyone else, then only Labastide would need to face House Flavia.

So...

I got all twenty in the mansion brought into the room overlooking the garden. The tables and chairs had been moved out and I told them all to sit cross-legged on the floor facing me. None of them had bolted when they had the opportunity, which was a good start.

Jen and Olivia were beside me. Maia stood and watched. One of her team had been left with Labastide in the living room; another was sitting between Jen and Olivia. Flint was still on his way to deliver Freddy Walker to Denver, but the rest of my House spread themselves out though the room and waited.

It was a difficult job. One of the Adept's top truth sensors like Alice Emerson could simply ask a question like 'are you loyal to Altau' and tell if you lied. She could probably tell how disloyal you were and whether you were going to do anything about it. But Alice wasn't here, and as Labastide had argued, even before we'd started, it was fine to be loyal to *her* rather than Altau. Yes, fine, so long as *she* was loyal, or at least loyal enough not to start a rebellion.

I wanted to get deeper than that. I wanted to know if Cazenave, the Queen of Diamonds or even Matlal had started to influence them. I wanted to know how. I wanted to know if there was any way to track back and find the swamp witch.

There wasn't just one question I could ask and expect a useful answer from. It was all going to take time. Bian had run investigations for Skylur and she'd described them to me: *like running a lie detector test, using only Braille.*

Great. I'd made the wrong choices in El Paso. I didn't want to have to live with more in New Orleans, but I was faced with a wall of guarded faces and hostile looks. No matter how powerful my eukori might be with my own House, this wasn't a receptive audience. I needed a way in. I needed a channel to them. Someone they trusted.

Jo might have been the easiest, or even Xavier, but they were human kin. I needed an Athanate, and I needed one of the more senior ones.

The butler that had greeted us the first day—she was senior. Probably the head of Labastide's security team. I glanced at her. She was one of the guarded faces.

Or Solange Dupuis, Labastide's pelea. One of the hostile faces.

Dupuis had been aggressive with me when we'd arrived, but I sensed that was more complex than it seemed. She was older than the others, and her eukori probably stronger, but somehow I felt she was the one to try. It was as if any genuine interaction, hostile or otherwise, had created the beginning of a eukori bridge between us.

Interesting thought. And I have to start with someone.

"Solange, please come and sit with me."

She looked as if she might refuse, but a glance at Maia persuaded her that wasn't a good idea.

I was sitting on the floor with my back to the wall, and got her to sit in front of me, between my thighs and facing away from me. I pulled her gently back until she was leaning on me, tense as a wild cat.

"Just relax, please." I wrapped my arms around her.

"Have you ever done one of these investigations before, House Farrell?" she asked pointedly.

"No. Have you ever been investigated before?"

Her jaw worked before she managed to say, "No."

"Then this is the first time for both of us. Relax. And call me Amber, please."

She sighed, and some of the tension reluctantly left her muscles.

I spoke very softly into her ear.

"You were really upset when I first arrived, weren't you?"

She snorted.

Her eukori was prickly as a cactus. My Carpathian heritage meant I might be stronger, but I didn't want to force my way in.

"I got the feeling you weren't just following the official Agiagraphos line."

She still didn't reply, but I could tell by the returning tension in her body that I was on to something. And I could tell she knew it. She forced her muscles to relax again. Her breathing and heartrate evened out.

"Good. That's much better," I said. "Well done."

The compliment pissed her off, as it was supposed to, but she managed to keep from reacting physically.

"Now, I don't expect you to tell me what it was that made you so aggressive when I showed up, but let's take some guesses and see where we get. Ease into it, if you like."

She snorted again.

Strictly speaking, I could order her to open up her eukori, but I wanted her active help with the others and I didn't think I'd get that without the eukori equivalent of a seduction.

Of course, she chose that moment to ask, "Are you trying to seduce me?"

"Would you like me to?"

Ah.

She'd almost laughed at that. Progress.

"I don't want you to feel uncomfortable, and I want you to remember I'm doing this for the good of your House," I said.

"Why? What do you care?"

"I have lots of reasons. It's partly because I got things wrong in El Paso, and I liked Isabel Cuarón."

That caught her attention.

"So... all that aggression when I first arrived here," I went on. "I get some of it was that you're part of a conservative House. Was some of it because you were angry at yourself?"

"Why would I be?"

My lips touched her ear as I breathed my question: "Because you found the idea of breaking the Agiagraphos rules exciting."

I couldn't tell whether I'd hit on the exact right reason, or if it was just because we were interacting, but her prickly, defensive eukori thawed.

Our hearts began to sync.

"Ridiculous," she said, but with no heat.

"Okay. Let's put all that aside. Just work with me to make sure I get it right. Please."

"I'm a hundred years older than you, so stop patronizing me."

"If Cazenave was on his own, looking out for nothing but his own benefit, then help me clear the rest of you."

Our breathing was in sync now. The weight of her leaning against me felt comfortable. The tension she'd been controlling was gone.

"I will," she said finally, after a minute of silence.

"Thank you, Solange."

"Don't mention it, *Amber*."

Her tone was still sharp as a wasp, but I could live with that.

Our eukori touched, recoiled, touched again. *Warmed* somehow.

Her hands, which had been clenched when she sat, relaxed. One came to rest lightly on top of my arm.

She sighed and our eukoris merged.

I could feel her sensation of my arms, the heat of my body, my breath against her neck. Just as she could feel the sensation of her weight resting against me, the coolness of her ear against my warmer lips. We shared the shiver that ran through her when she realized that my eukori was stronger than hers.

To distract her from that, and because I suspected she was intrigued by the forbidden thought of being a hybrid, I let her dive into my wolfy memories: the exhilaration of running through the pine trees of the Bitter Hooks forest, the rich spectrum of scents that my wolfy nose could distinguish. And while that overwhelmed her attention, I used her eukori to wrap around mine and pulled Jo and Xavier, then the other butlers and the rest of the Labastide security team into what we shared. Each one accepted the contact because it came with the flavor of Dupuis' eukori.

"This is what the Carpathians call communion," I whispered in Athanate as she gasped.

Although they were all familiar with eukori, such a wide sharing of it was disorienting. It could quickly end in panic, so I let them settle, let them sort out the feeds of sensation into their awareness. Then, several minutes later, I began to pull in their kin, one by one.

Then Jen, Rita and Olivia.

And finally, Maia's lieutenant, leaving Maia to watch in case anything went wrong.

Chapter 50

It took the bulk of the day. No time for food or drink. A couple of minutes for comfort breaks. In the late afternoon, I was sitting in exactly the same place and the room was still full of House Labastide members.

I was numb. My butt from sitting, my head from keeping the eukori communion open so long. Despite everything, Solange had stuck with me, and she was in as bad a state as I was.

But we'd processed nearly every member of House Labastide, apart from Cazenave and Labastide herself. Most of the ones who'd been staying out on the plantation had been brought in around midday.

I felt dazed. I'd never used eukori for such a long stretch of time, and anyway, it was usually with my House and friends. A Carpathian communion, over the course of hours, using the combined power of the many to question each individual... it was disturbing.

On top of that, most of them didn't like me. Some of that was because of Labastide's opinion about me and the conservative nature of the House. Some of it was because they resented I held this power over them. And some because they were scared.

Jo and Xavier were okay with me, but they were 'only' human, so they didn't count for much.

Solange had made great progress, but hadn't even made it to feeling neutral toward me.

For me, weirdly, it didn't matter. They weren't my House, but it felt like I'd adopted them, and as we brought the communion to an end, I found I couldn't completely disengage.

And at that point, I felt a stir in the air, a different marque. A disturbance in the eukori.

Diakon Flavia had arrived.

I'd seen her on the conference call, but the effect of her actual presence was very different. There was the same dark hair, the same sharp, strong features like an old Roman statue, but the woman in person was clothed with a sense of power and threat.

She stood at the doors and looked at the members of House Labastide like a wolf looks at a flock of sheep.

As awareness of her presence spread through the room, they turned, like flowers facing the sun. And then they backed away.

"What's wrong with them?" Flavia asked.

"Disoriented," I said. "They'll be fine."

Pia and Olivia helped me off the floor.

"Maia tells me you've questioned them on their loyalty," she said, her voice clipped.

She was radiating displeasure at everyone. She stalked into the room, glaring at the people there. I got a kick of adrenaline in my stomach and I tried to clear my mind. I needed to be sharp. Death had entered this room.

"Yes. I've tested them," I answered. "Cazenave was the point of weakness. I believe only nine of the House have been approached by him. Three of those were at the plantation, and bolted rather than face any questions. We didn't have enough people to catch them."

"And the other six?"

"Two turned Cazenave's approach down flat. They were told it had been a test and they weren't allowed to mention it to anyone else. They believed their Diakon. Four of them didn't turn him down, but neither did they progress. They didn't understand what it was, nor where it was heading. One of Maia's team is holding those four in a room upstairs."

"You've achieved this using a Carpathian trick with your eukori?"

"It's no trick, Diakon, but yes, a Carpathian technique. It involves bringing them all into a shared eukori. It's possible to lie to one person, but not to your whole House while you're connected to them through eukori."

Better for her to be thinking it was just a technique that could be learned, rather than part of a suite of Carpathian abilities which might just set off the Agiagraphos crowd into another chorus of 'abomination'.

However, whichever way she took it, Diakon Flavia's attitude to the members of House Labastide didn't seem to soften.

After studying a few more faces, she wheeled toward me. "How sure are you about the results?"

Maia's lieutenant came to my rescue. "I was involved in the shared eukori, Diakon. I can't prove I wasn't deceived, but I'm convinced."

Was it my imagination, or had Flavia relaxed just a fraction? I could feel a few relieved breaths quietly taken in the room.

It didn't last.

"And House Labastide herself?" she asked.

"In my opinion—"

"I wasn't asking your opinion, House Farrell."

I gripped onto the surge of anger in my belly. This wasn't about getting upset at being interrupted or having my opinion discarded. It was about keeping the people in the room from being treated as traitors.

I cleared my throat. "I haven't tested her yet, Diakon. She's much older and more powerful than the rest of the House. But with everyone else tested, I'm sure I can question her now with the same technique. She's waiting in another room."

She stared at me for several moments.

"I wonder about Carpathians," she said. "They seem to be like one of those enigmatic Chinese symbols. Opportunity wrapped in risk and danger." She shook her head, as if dismissing the thought as irrelevant. "With Cazenave gone, who's senior here after Labastide?"

The casual words covered their potentially chilling meaning.

Is she asking who's left in charge if she executes Labastide?

"I believe it would be Pelea Dupuis," I said. "But there should be no need. I could use this as an opportunity to demonstrate the same technique to you. I'd advise—"

She made me pause with a raised hand and stony expression. It seemed my advice went into the same trash container as my opinions and recommendations.

I swallowed my anger again, but I was going to speak whether she wanted to hear it or not.

"My opinion is that House Labastide is not a traitor, even though her Diakon is. If she were, I'd have found more evidence in the other members of her House. I didn't, and I think the rest of the House shouldn't suffer for the weakness of their Diakon."

"And yet," she came back immediately, as if she'd known I would raise that point, "that's *exactly* what the Agiagraphos rules say. She bears ultimate and absolute responsibility, regardless of the guilt of her House members."

She returned to stand in front of me. Tall. Hard as iron. Visibly not happy with me.

"Putting the case of Marguerite Labastide aside for a moment, what about the four members who didn't immediately turn Cazenave down?"

I couldn't tell whether I'd gotten a concession that Labastide was not to be executed out of hand. But presumably, if she was asking about the four, she regarded them differently from the remainder.

Should I just stop defending them? It was clear the longer I argued, the worse my standing with Diakon Flavia became.

Most of this House regarded me as an abomination anyway. Nothing I did was going to change that. Those four were potential traitors that Panethus couldn't afford...

And yet I'd formed the beginning of a bond with them. I'd touched them all with eukori. Not just them, but their friends and lovers within House Labastide as well. Like the roots of a plant, to touch one in shared eukori was to become entangled with them all.

They weren't like members of my House, but neither were they strangers anymore, and I found I couldn't just stand aside. They *hadn't* actually become disloyal, unlike Cazenave.

I squared my shoulders.

"Not even them," I said. "The Diakon wields the authority of the House. Even the strictest interpretation of the Agiagraphos wouldn't say it was a fault to trust him as far as they did."

Flavia snorted. "There are differing opinions on what constitutes a 'strict' interpretation. What interpretation would you think de Socorro would have had?"

"That's not a valid comparison. House de Socorro was sick. He demonstrated appalling judgment. He'd have taken whatever seemed most in line with his thoughts at the time, but he's irrelevant to New Orleans."

"Really? Maybe you're right about that. He's no longer relevant to anything. So then, let's look at it another way. What interpretation do you think House Labastide would use, if the situation were reversed? If it were four members of your House and I asked Labastide what to do?"

Caught in her basilisk stare, I felt the sweat cooling on my forehead, the uncomfortable thudding of my heart, the pounding of my pulse. I also felt Dupuis, still in sync with me, still slightly connected through eukori—heart dropping as she realized the inevitable.

No!

"I can't answer for House Labastide," I said, trying to buy time.

"You mean you *won't*. You know she'd have you executed, probably even without the excuse of treason."

"I don't think she would," I said. I knew that sounded lame and I licked my dry lips. "I think you should ask *her* about that, and about the issue of seniority."

The rest of the room seemed far away. Outside of Skylur and Diana, I'd never felt such power in an Athanate, and yet I was aware she was controlling it, revealing no more than a hint.

Skylur's new Diakon scared me, and it looked as if I'd crossed a boundary.

Without looking away from me, she spoke.

But not to me directly.

"Pelea Dupuis."

Dupuis took a step forward, a tremble quickly dispelled, steeling herself.

"Yes, Diakon?"

"You are temporarily in charge of the mantle of New Orleans and the domain of Southern Louisiana, in place of Marguerite Labastide. Do you know and understand the charter of the House?"

Dupuis' mouth moved silently before she managed, "Yes."

"And do you accept the authority of House Altau, and the terms of this commission, on your Blood oath?"

Dupuis swallowed.

I knew, as she obviously did, that to accept it was to also accept that the next command from Flavia's mouth could be to execute members of her House.

"I do." Her voice was low and hesitant.

"Good." Livia sniffed. "Inform the sub-Houses, House Broussard in Lafayette and House Leandre in Baton Rouge, to present themselves to me in New York within the day. Prepare House Labastide and the four members of your House to travel with me."

Dupuis bowed; there was nothing else she could do.

"Yes, Diakon."

Flavia wasn't finished. Her eyes seemed to grow until I could barely see anything else. "Jennifer," she said, "I understand your aircraft will be available again shortly."

"Yes, Diakon." Jen's voice seemed thin.

"We will return to New York in it. We leave as soon as possible, and you will accompany us."

It was as deliberate as a slap in the face. A challenge. Using my kin. I couldn't stop the surge of anger, the rush of power into my eukori like a dam had broken...

Chapter 51

The glare of Diakon Flavia's eyes was broken abruptly, and I was looking at the back of someone's head.

Maia and Jen stood between us as I struggled to control the urge to attack Flavia.

I barely registered Maia's hand on my arm, the door to the garden opening, the sudden release from the claustrophobic room.

"Feeling better?"

Maia was peering into my face.

I ignored that. "She did that—"

"Stop." Maia gripped my arms. "You're exhausted. You're not thinking clearly."

"What?"

She didn't answer until we were at the end of the garden, out of sight and hearing of the people back in the mansion.

"This is not some playground dispute, Amber," she said. "This is Athanate politics. Livia has just done you a favor."

"By taking my kin? Trying to provoke me into a fight?"

Maia smiled crookedly.

"Yes. Although I understand it doesn't look that way. Especially to the other people in the room."

I frowned.

What did she mean?

"She did it for them to see?" I said.

"Yes. At least some of it. Jen's a different matter, but she only has herself to blame. She's made herself a valuable strategic weapon that Skylur has to redeploy, now that she's achieved her task here."

There was a convenient bench. I couldn't sit, but I leaned on the back.

"As you say, Maia, I'm tired. Please explain it."

"Flavia will have us flown first to the Caymans. House Labastide and Jen will empty those offshore accounts, legitimate and hidden. Then we'll return to New York. As soon as we're there, I imagine Skylur will send Jen and my team down to Washington DC, to do the same job she started here: looking for financial evidence of Matlal interference and merging the accounts into Altau Holdings."

"The same job she hasn't finished here."

Maia shrugged. "It's at a point where the rest can be handed over to someone else. And after DC, or after Philadelphia or Atlanta, maybe the role she's been doing can be handed over as well. She's not being stolen forever, though I suspect she'll have to spend as much time in New York as Denver for a while yet."

Split between two cities. I could handle that if I had to. My heart rate was coming down.

"And the rest of it?"

"Labastide has to go back to New York to be questioned."

"Why?"

"Ignoring the fact that you're exhausted and it would be Flavia who would question her here... because the person who *will* question her in New York will be the person who temporarily has my role as Skylur's Head of Security."

I started to see some of the pattern of Athanate politics emerge.

"It's the guy from Washington, isn't it?"

"Yes. Jacob Tosun from House Elicott, the same House that was the leader of the former Eastern Seaboard association. Tosun has to be involved so there's no possibility of a complaint from the old association that we have some kind of grudge against them. Labastide even requested that someone from the association question her, so we're doing what she asked. Tosun will have to tell the rest of the association that yes, Labastide's Diakon was involved with Matlal, and Labastide wasn't. At which point, Labastide returns to New Orleans and takes up her position again."

I nodded. "I get it. The Eastern Seaboard's feeling of being separate is lingering, and DC is a specific weak point at the moment. That's why it's someone from House Elicott in your position as head of security."

"Yes. Apart from House Elicott standing with the former association, he's also in a position to make things extremely difficult for Naryn, who's patiently working his way from one level to the next in the government hierarchy. We're on the clock. We can't afford to lose control of Emergence, and Naryn is the tip of that spear."

"Okay."

"The rest of it was for the members of House Labastide."

"You mean insulting me?"

"Not quite. Forcing you into a position where you, the *abomination*, were all that stood between them and summary justice according to the rules that *they* hold sacred and inflexible. In accordance with the Agiagraphos, either Labastide or her whole House are accountable for the defection of her Diakon, and death should have been the outcome. You may not quite be the good guy to them yet, but you're on the way."

I had recovered enough that I managed a snort at that.

"And while doing that," I said, "Skylur has undermined support of the Agiagraphos. Because he's never doing one thing at a time."

"Yes. Like I said, Athanate politics. Livia is doing exactly what Skylur would have done. She's really good at it, too."

I took a deep breath. "And you're not the killing machine that you're made out to be, either."

She smiled. "I am that, and I'm good at it. I suspect you can be too. But neither of us is *only* that. Come on, we better get back inside. You'll want to wish Jen farewell."

The room was empty but for Flavia, who exchanged glances with Maia before the latter disappeared into the rest of the mansion, from where sounds of hurried movement came.

Flavia stood, arms stretched to the sides, demanding the lamia, the Athanate greeting.

We kissed necks.

The greeting is supposed to allow each side to gauge the other. Flavia's marque was all cold iron, like the woman herself. What she got about me, I wasn't sure. Probably that I was still pissed at her.

"You played your part perfectly," she said. "That there was a lingering connection in eukori was an unexpected benefit."

"I'm still angry," I said, and she nodded.

I went on, "I apologize that I nearly lost my temper and attacked you. I guess I should also thank you for not responding."

"You're far stronger than you've any right to be, and stronger than you believe you are."

"But not as strong as you."

She shrugged. "No. But half of the difference is your expectation."

She gave that shake of the head that she did, as if physically dismissing something that was not relevant. "There's one more obstacle for you to negotiate before we leave."

I was instantly back on my guard.

"What's that?"

"Labastide will say farewell. I don't know her, so I can't guess what her parting words will be, but I'd very much like to be in the position that she has no complaint about her treatment at our hands."

I frowned.

"You think she'll tell me to get out of Louisiana? That would be difficult. I have a Were ritual coming up in a couple of days."

"No, she can't do that," Flavia said. "She's been temporarily relieved of authority for the area, and I don't think Dupuis will ask you to leave."

I could hear them approaching. There was no time for anything, so I fell back onto a phrase my mother used about making nice with people. "Well, I'll meet courtesy with courtesy, and I won't react if she's unpleasant."

What could she do?

As it turned out, Jen came in first. She was a little teary, but I could tell she'd been given the same reasoning I had for ripping us apart again.

We hugged and ignored everyone else for a few moments. I took simple enjoyment from her presence, her warmth, the way her body fitted so perfectly against mine.

"Don't know about you, but I had a lousy time in New Orleans," she whispered, "apart from being with my wife."

"Definitely not enough of that."

House Labastide came in, accompanied by Solange. The effect this long day had had on Labastide was dramatic. Her face was drawn painfully tight, with the lines of tension still clear. Yet her back remained as straight as the day I'd arrived, and her eyes were no less fierce.

I gritted my teeth and prepared for an all-thanks-to-you type of bitter farewell.

But she reached out and took my hands, struggling to speak.

"Thank you, Amber," she said finally. "I have told Solange I wish you to have the freedom of the House."

My mouth fell open.

Labastide's previous reluctant offer of 'hospitality' had only been her way of telling me to keep my nasty fangs off her nice, clean streets, but 'freedom of the House' was so far beyond that, it wasn't in the same universe. You might offer it to visiting Athanate dignitaries that greatly outranked you, for political purposes. You might offer it believing the fusion of Athanate Blood would benefit your House. Or you might offer it as a first, tentative step toward association of Houses. It was a long, *long* way from her words at the last dinner: 'we're allies, but we're not friends'.

I had to say something.

And I could see from the lines in between Flavia's eyebrows that I was expected to reciprocate.

I had to clear my throat. "Marguerite. Thank you. I am honored. I..." I could see Pia at the back of the room trying to urge me on.

It is all theoretical, isn't it?

My House is here, and in Denver.

House Labastide... Marguerite... is going to be in New York, then back here.

"Of course, I also offer you the freedom of my House in return."

Flavia favored me with a chilly smile and urged everyone out to where a row of cars waited.

Including Jen, who would be in New York with Marguerite, briefly.

I swallowed painfully and said my muted goodbyes.

Too late to take it back.

Chapter 52

At Pia's insistence, Rita and I ate and showered and prepared for bed, even though it was early.

"Your bodies are healing, but they do that best with sleep," she said.

She had a point. I'd pulled plenty of long hours in Ops 4-10 and afterwards, but never when I was quite so extensively physically damaged. The extra energy my Athanate put into healing, on top of mental exhaustion from the eukori, meant I was ready to pass out.

Nick took over security.

"Tucek's still out there," he said. "And what better time to try something, than when House Labastide is disrupted, like today."

"She gave her oath," I said, but I didn't argue it any more.

Nick arranged it so Rita and I would share the room at the end of the corridor, so we'd be undisturbed.

Apart from one last visit that Nick allowed.

Jo and Xavier. Freshly scrubbed, looking horribly full of life in comparison to me, and apparently dressed in nothing but bathrobes, which was one more garment than Rita and I were wearing.

Xavier began. "Solange said—"

"What I told you yesterday applies," I interrupted rudely. "In this House you offer what *you* want, not what you're ordered to."

Their faces dropped, and I relented. "At the moment, I'm exhausted and I look like a gargoyle with all these bruises, so I think I'll pass. Maybe another time."

Jo's face took on a stubborn look. "We could give you a massage." She held up a little basket of scented oils.

"It's what my coach used to recommend for muscle injuries and bruises," Xavier added. "I have training."

"And I want to," Jo finished.

I grinned. "In principle, naturally, I refuse this out of hand. In real life, however, I'm just going to roll over now."

I got Xavier, and Rita submitted to Jo.

They were *good*. I may have groaned several times as Xavier's thumbs alternately teased and dug into my back and butt. As he worked, he murmured the Latin names of the muscle sets like longissimus and trapezius, sounding like he was trying to summon demons.

I was desperately trying to stay awake to enjoy the sensations, but I must have floated away sometime after he rolled me on my back and began a much gentler massage of my face and neck, arms and hands, taking his time to travel down to my legs and, *oh, bliss,* my feet.

I half woke when they turned off the lights on their way out. It must have been more than a couple of hours after they'd started. I felt fantastic, like I was floating. Rita rolled up against me, nuzzling my neck, mainlining the feel-good pheromones my Athanate glands were putting out.

I stroked her hair, which was still loosely twisted in a quick braid, and my fingers began to work out the tangles.

Like a puzzle. A message. A meaning that eluded me as I sank into the darkness of sleep.

It's the sort of darkness you get below ground. Heavy. Claustrophobic.

I move forward slowly, my only guide a knotted string in my hands. I have to keep going. The message hidden in the knots of the string will only make sense when I have it all. I need to know it all.

Was it like my roll call string? I kept a knotted string with one knot for every person I knew who'd died in a way that directly led to my staying alive, starting with Handsome Joe in Ops 4-10.

No! I needed to go back and do it again, because it wasn't Joe first. It was Tara. The sequence was all wrong now.

Or was it like the necklace Chatima had given me in Albuquerque, with three messages layered, one on top of the other? Patterns, Chatima had called them.

> *I will choose my path.*
> *I will master my way.*
> *I will exult in my being.*

It didn't have that same feeling of being almost understood, and yet just out of reach.

Or it was something new.

Or maybe something older. Something dark...

I moved from a tunnel to an open space. There was still no light, but I could feel the walls stretch away on either side, and the roof was far above.

And there was someone here, who'd been waiting for me to fumble my way down to him.

"Welcome, my priestess."

His voice was deep, echoing. It filled the space without being loud.

And he was speaking Athanate.

"I'm not your priestess, and I'd appreciate some light."

"There's a brazier in the middle of the room. My priestess can light it herself. She has the power to do that, and more."

Irritating bastard. Still, it was only a dream. I could do whatever I wanted. I built a picture of the room in my mind's eye and found the center. There was a wide stone brazier there, a bowl on a tripod, filled with wood soaked in oils.

Of course there was.

How to light it?

The air split with the blue-white flash of lightning, ripping through the air above the brazier and touching it like a dragon's tongue. The wood exploded in a shower of sparks, but what was left caught fire.

So much easier in a dream.

The fire showed Tezcatlipoca in the same shade of red as I'd seen him first, in the City of Lost Gods. It lit the walls and made the paintings on them move as if in a dance.

"The Lost Boys call you T-cat," I said. "Less of a mouthful."

"The little sorcerers in your House? They should be more respectful of the god of sorcerers."

"Sorcerers, the night, jaguars, winds and wars," I said.

"And kings, the sun and the sky, the earth, obsidian, beauty, temptation and divination."

"Busy."

"A god must be, my priestess."

He walked closer to the fire. He was beautiful, even with what looked like thick, straight bands of blood painted across his face. He wore the cloak, the jaguar tunic, the feathered headdress and that obsidian breastplate. Everything else took a glow from the fire, but the breastplate didn't. It remained black, and looking too closely at it made it seem as if there was movement inside it.

"I'm not your priestess," I repeated.

He laughed and gestured at me to look at myself.

I was dressed in feathers, and my skin had been blackened as if I'd been rubbed down with soot.

"Well, it's only a dream," I said.

"Is it? You are more like you are here than you are in your waking world. But no matter, that knowledge will come to you. We have more important things to discuss."

"Ah, this is the part of the dream where you explain it to me."

"Or you work it out for yourself, following the messages in the knotted string."

He held up the end of the string I'd been following.

"It leads to you."

I walked toward the brazier, pulling the string through my fingers, feeling the knots, feeling the meaning. Was it like a Chinese pictogram, with elements made from the size and spacing of the knots? A sort of physical mnemonic for something I already knew? Or just letters?

Simple. Not complex at all.

Athanate letters.

Chi, rho, upsilon...

A chill seized my chest. I knew where it was going.

"We have no time left for puzzles, my priestess. It's a puzzle because you make it so. No time left. You are in danger, and you need to come into your powers. I promise, they will come easier as you use them."

The flames danced between us, and the whole cavernous room seemed to move with them.

Something stirred in the obsidian depths of the breastplate. A reflection of me appeared on the surface. And a shape *within* that I knew was me, but not me. Me... reversed. Then behind them, something huge, threatening, whose breath came like clouds, with eyes of red and a shrill cry like a kettle screaming.

T-cat spins on his heel. His cloak flares out to cover the brazier.

The hem brushes my face.

Darkness falls.

I was struggling to disentangle myself from Rita and the sheet that had been thrown over us.

Nick loomed above.

"Sorry," he said. "You need to decide what to do with this."

He handed me my cellphone. There was a message from Tucek on it. I'd completely forgotten, she'd said to keep this night free to meet her.

I said I'd have something to show you. Your missing witch.

Meet me at the riverfront, the Moonwalk, before midnight.

We had half an hour.

Chapter 53

We made it to the riverfront with ten minutes to spare.

The Moonwalk was a brick lane running along the riverside in front of the French Quarter. It made its way through a couple of parks with statues, and allowed you to feel the bustle of the city's nightlife while being slightly apart from it. It gave great views of the river itself, the barges, the lights on the Crescent City bridge, and the far shore.

At this time of night, it wasn't busy, but there were lovers strolling and drunks singing.

All good possibilities for a disguised ambush, Tara pointed out.

"Too visible," I murmured.

Rita turned to see if I was talking to her.

Every member of my House in Louisiana was with me, spread out in front and behind. They were not happy about me coming to this meeting, and that was the only way they'd agreed to me being here at all.

Nick, Flint and Kane. Tucek wouldn't have the Adept firepower that I was bringing to the party.

Rita, Olivia and Tara. A cat shifter, a werewolf and a fire wolf.

Pia. Athanate.

And me. I was all of the above and I was ready for a fight, if that's what was coming.

We also had five of House Labastide's security team on loan, all packing some serious firepower and intent on using it to defend their domain, should Tucek try anything.

I couldn't see how she would. She was Basilikos, yes, but she was also a supporter of the Agiagraphos, and keeping out of sight of humanity.

At least until Basilikos feels they have the upper hand over humanity, Tara snarked. *Then they'll decide it's time to update the Agiagraphos.*

I huffed in amusement. Better safe than sorry, so even as bone-tired as I still was, my Carpathian eukori, boosted through my House, reached out and searched for threats in the shadows.

Tucek was here. I couldn't tell where exactly, but I couldn't feel any sense of an ambush. There was... worry. Almost fear.

"Straight ahead, sixty yards," Rita said.

Tucek had gotten off a bench and begun a slow stroll to meet me.

She was alone on the path, but I caught the faintest traces of other Athanate fading away into the night. She'd been here with her House, and she'd sent them away.

Interesting. Not an ambush then.

Her dark hair was braided. She wore all black again: an athletic bodysuit which showed off every sculptured muscle of her perfect legs, and a man's short leather jacket, several sizes too big. Boots.

The jacket was probably hiding a pistol of some kind.

Fair enough—I had my HK as well.

She walked like a panther, giving off confidence and power, and completely obscuring the hint of nerves I could still feel, even though her eukori was shielded.

"That outfit suits you better than your old mother superior robes," I said as we closed.

"Thank you, Amber."

"Just to be clear, we're not friends." It took a while for my sleepy brain to remember her first name, but I got it finally: "Mirela."

"Very clear." She looked around, her gaze taking in my little army.

Was she nervous because she had put herself in my power? In truth, the only thing stopping me from capturing and killing her was that I'd given my word to House Labastide about keeping the peace. Would I trust Tucek in the reverse situation?

Probably not.

"It doesn't make any difference," she said. "Anyway, you're not here to make friends, you're here to see Gabrielle, and you have my oath you will."

"The swamp witch has given her to you? Where is she? Is she all right?"

"First question: no. Second: close." She frowned. "Third: all right? Yes and no. I realize that's confusing. Bear with me. Let's walk as we talk."

She turned and started walking.

I caught up with her. "If you've hurt—"

She stopped me. "I don't have her, and I haven't hurt her. I'm only warning you because when the Queen of Diamonds gets hold of someone, they're never quite the same."

Even in the warmth of the night, that chilled me.

Never quite the same. Like Freddy Walker, slumped in the darkness of his house, held in New Orleans, all hope leeched away, resigned to his fate and unable to walk away.

We'll repair him. We'll repair Gabrielle if it's needed.

Sounds of faraway laughter from Jackson Square drifted through the air.

"We're meeting the queen?" I asked.

"No," Tucek said, and a shiver passed through her. "We're not meeting her. I told you to stay away from her, and I follow my own advice."

"Then I don't understand. Who are we seeing? And why are you here?"

"Gabrielle's being brought here by some of the queen's subjects. And I'm here because my Lady wants me to be."

"Your Lady? You mean Vega Martine? You know, I was beginning to suspect she was the swamp witch herself."

Tucek shook her head.

"Much more complicated. Even though my Lady wanted the two of us to meet in New Orleans, she would not have kidnapped Gabrielle to force it. She wants me to reach an understanding with you, and that hasn't been helped by the queen taking Gabrielle. In fact, it's probably harmed our chances, so she's angry about it."

I was reeling.

The Queen of Diamonds and Vega Martine *were* working together, but it wasn't going well for them. And Vega Martine wanted me to be on her side, or for her to join mine?

There was something strange here. I needed to dig deeper. "To be clear, this is Vega Martine and *not* Matlal?"

"Just as Panethus has its factions, so does Basilikos. Matlal is powerful, but he's... extreme."

"And now Vega Martine wants to join Panethus."

She laughed. "No. She wants *you* to join *us*, to give all Athanate an alternative to the extremes of Matlal and Altau."

I swore.

Tucek held her hands up. "Not my idea. And it's not some kind of prerequisite for seeing Gabrielle. I just wanted it out in the open."

"How does she think..." I wasn't sure how to voice the craziness that was bound up in what Tucek was saying.

"Because we're more alike than we are different," Tucek said. "And we both start from the obvious reality that Athanate are superior to humans."

I shook my head angrily and then looked away from her, out into the expanse of darkness that was the Mississippi. Despite the sticky Louisiana heat of the day, the midnight breeze coming off the river was cold enough to make me shiver.

The Mississippi here bent more than ninety degrees to get around the hook of Algiers Point, visible only as a low, dark mass with strings of lights twinkling in the night. It had to be closer than half a mile, but it looked so far away.

In one of those strange acoustic tricks, a sound carried across that wide stretch of water. A bell.

A church bell? In Algiers Point? What was it tolling for at this hour?

"Where's Gabrielle?" I said.

"Close," Tucek said. "Almost here. So, you don't agree that we're alike?"

Something is wrong, Tara said.

I shivered again. My skin was prickling, goosebumps running up and down my body. I looked around, but there was nothing to see. Tucek was relaxed, strolling, hands in her jacket pockets, looking at the ground. My House was spread around me, looking outward, alert but not alarmed. There was a fog rolling upriver, but apart from that, the night was clear. People still walked by. Cars drove only a dozen yards away. The city murmured quietly behind us, but everything seemed distant to me.

"I can sense a working," I said. I touched the butt of the Mk23 inside my jacket.

Tucek let out a long, slow breath that plumed in the air.

Surely it wasn't *that* cold.

Rita was just behind me, along with Flint and Kane and Nick. I could stretch an arm out and touch her if I wanted. We had plenty of power to face down whatever showed itself.

Nick had felt something too. He was preparing himself, head down, a sort of haze of aura gathering about him.

"Okay, Boss?" Rita moved up.

"Yeah," I said. "I was wondering what kind of weather conditions make for a river fog on a night like tonight."

"Huh?"

It seemed to be getting darker. Rita passed me to look up and down the river.

The prickling intensified.

"What fog?" Her voice sounded thin.

I looked. The fog was impossible to miss; it covered the river now. The lights of Algiers Point were fading out.

The bell rang out again.

"Shit," I said. "Suckered! Trap!"

The lights along the river were gone, leaving a depthless emptiness. Something stirred in that starless void. A huge shape, threatening, churning at the waters, and breathing out the fog that chilled and silenced the land.

It screamed at me with a voice of iron and steam.

I felt the ground beneath my feet slip away, like sand on the seashore when the waves came in.

There were other sounds, voices, far away, calling me.

"Amber? AMBER!"

My team reached for me with hands and their workings, but the pull of the substantiation in front of me was stronger. I couldn't see anyone in the fog except Tucek, standing at my side, looking out onto the river.

I started to back away and reach for my pistol. She grabbed my arm. For the first time since I'd met her, she opened her well-guarded eukori to me. It pulled me in, so hard and fast it felt like a slap across my face.

"On my Blood oath, I mean you no harm, Amber."

I nodded that I'd heard, unable to speak for a moment.

"I won't lie. This is dangerous, but you're in no more danger than I am," she said, and her eukori told me she was telling the truth. "If you run now, you might escape, but if you want to see Gabrielle, you have to stay. Choose."

Chapter 54

I'd given my Blood oath to get Gabrielle back—I stayed.

There was no sign of my team in the fog that surrounded us. It cut us off from everywhere else. There was barely a hint of the New Orleans I'd been strolling through a minute ago.

Right above me, the fog couldn't obscure the measureless stars glimmering in a moonless sky, but at the horizon, that great bowl of lights merged into the night, so that there was no way to tell where the sky ended and the earth began. I could make out a scatter of gleaming points that might be city lights, I could hear a murmur of muted city sounds, but it wasn't the city I'd been in: there were no cars, no traffic sounds, no skyscrapers, no glare of electricity.

The fog swirled and sank, and rose again with the tattered spirits of the ancient, peaceful dead in its cold embrace—a multitude, whispering a million secrets I couldn't hear. Passing time had rendered these spirits no more substantial than the fog itself, but in contrast to them, here and there in the night, the body of the fog curled and thickened, and became solid with the shapes of living people walking toward me.

"My advice is to ignore them all," Tucek said as I twitched. "The spirits can't harm you unless you let them, and the people, well, they're not here for you. They're only human. Potentially dangerous, but only if you engage with them. Usually."

"What?"

It grew lighter and the bell sounded again over the water. Loud and close. I swung around.

Now we were standing on an old wooden pier that reached out into the Mississippi. All along the pier's edge were gas-burning lamps, hissing quietly and shedding soft light into the misty air.

A tall African-American man stood on the pier with hurricane lamps in his hands. He was dressed in black: an old-fashioned, long-tailed suit with a top hat. He lifted the lamps high, and the river monster screamed again, closer, the sound less distorted by the fog.

This time I recognized the sound from old movies. It was a riverboat.

The huge Mississippi sternwheeler emerged from the fog. That scream was coming from an array of steel whistles, blown by steam vented from the engine. The boat was taller and wider than any riverboat I'd ever seen. Its crowded, three-tiered superstructure looked like it was pressing the boat down into the water, yet it was graceful, each level surrounded by a covered walkway with the sort of arched, Spanish-lace ornamentation that gave the French Quarter its iconic galleries. It seemed to glow in the fog. It seemed more real than the fog.

I could feel the boat drawing me, as it seemed to be drawing the spirits from the ground. I *wanted* to get on board.

The substantiation pulled. It had started like the gentle tug of the current near the riverbank. Now, I was deep in its grip, and all around was the casual power of a billion tons of water sweeping me away to wherever it chose: down, down to the sea.

Panic kills people before they drown.

Stay afloat.

A woman in a flowing dress stood on the prow of the boat and struck a bell mounted there. The sound shivered all the way into my bones and I remembered something Freddy Walker had said: *that bell will start tolling one night, and I know I'll just go to her.*

The steamer slowed, angling close enough that the pier lights picked out a name on its low bow.

Queen of Diamonds.

"They're on the boat?" I asked. "Gabrielle? And the Queen of Diamonds?"

"Gabrielle, yes. I've been assured the queen won't be on board. This steamer is just one of the ways she uses to... meet with people."

I was shivering. Cold. Fear. Reaction to the sheer force of the magic in full flood.

I clenched my fists and spoke, forcing the words to be casual. "A full-blown substantiation. Involving the whole river."

Tucek snorted. "The lower part of the Mississippi, up to about Natchez, and the entire Atchafalaya."

"That's some power. How come no one else can run a substantiation without getting chewed up by the City of Lost Gods, but the queen gets a free pass?"

"It isn't separate; this is part of the wider City," Tucek said. "She's tapped into the powers of the ancestral gods that lie behind what we now call voodoo. And yes, she's *strong.*"

As we stood there, spirits flowed off the pier, summoned across the water, where they were absorbed into the light of the boat, making it glow brighter.

Greater substantiations consumed lesser ones in the spirit world. Even strong spirit walkers could be consumed by the City of Lost Gods. These tattered spirits called from their resting places stood no chance.

Both Tucek and I were shivering. So were the living people, from the mist gathered on the pier around us.

They were dressed in riverboat-era clothes: spreading dresses and long coat suits. They stood silently, in groups or alone, their eyes fixed on the riverboat. A face here and there seemed familiar, but I couldn't place anyone.

And, studying them, I saw there was something about their eyes—they shone with a mixture of fear and fascination.

"This was *not* my idea," Tucek went on. "But the Lady wanted you to understand what powers are in play here. And this might be the only way you ever get to see Gabrielle."

Her eukori was still half-open. She was telling me the truth, or some part of it. Or what *she* thought was the truth.

At least eukori worked here in this substantiation.

My gun? I reached up to reassure myself, but there wasn't a holster hiding under a jacket. In fact, no jacket. I was wearing one of the era's dresses, a sort of purple satin creation that I immediately hated. Tucek was dressed the same way. She saw me looking and shook her head.

"Everything in keeping with her style," she said. "At least approximately."

"Nineteenth century? So there are guns? We just don't have them any more."

"No guns for passengers. Crew wouldn't need them."

My eyes followed where she indicated with a tilt of her head, and my blood froze. On the top and bottom deck were the hulking shapes of Rougarou in half-changed form, hyena heads on human bodies. Some seemed to sense I was looking and turned from their tasks. Their eyes glowed red.

"We're just going to get on, take the opportunity to see Gabrielle, and get off," Tucek said. "The crew won't bother you if you stick to that."

The boat nudged the pier and everyone stumbled.

I caught Tucek and held her up.

"Thank you. Damned dresses and heels," she muttered.

A gangplank went down and there was movement on the ship's deck. There were people to get off first.

And among the ones stepping down, there was a figure I recognized.

This is impossible.

A portly little man. Round-faced, yet sharp-eyed. Black hair oiled and combed down flat. A peculiar short-paced walk, as if his hamstring muscles refused to stretch. He looked completely at home in his black-tailed dinner jacket, starched white shirt and muted bow tie.

Judicator Phillipe Remy had died last year.

"*Mesdames*, welcome, *bienvenue.*"

"You aren't Remy," I said.

"And yet, Madame, can one ever be sure, here?" He gestured to the night around us. "Am I not as alive as you, here in the spirit world?"

Dead is dead.

"What do you want, Remy?" Tucek asked.

"Why, to welcome you aboard the *Queen of Diamonds*, naturally. Also to present you with your tickets and the key to your cabin." He held up a packet in both hands. "Finally, to wish you *bon voyage*. One must observe the niceties, *n'est-ce pas?*"

"A cabin? How long is this supposed to take?" I said.

"We're not here for a cruise." Tucek snatched the packet and opened it to inspect the contents. "My Lady got permission for us to board and see Gabrielle while you're docked. In and out."

"Well, one must say, we are not docked for long, and *my* Lady says it takes as long as it takes."

"This is shit," Tucek snarled.

"I do urge you to take it up with the management," Remy replied with an oily smile, and bowed.

The air seemed to freeze around us, and a second snarl got caught in Tucek's throat.

Still part-tangled with her through eukori, I felt the blossom of fear like a pale, night-blooming flower.

The people waiting to board shuffled back and bowed their heads.

A small figure descended the gangway from the deck to the pier.

She wore a pale dress of an even earlier era, with a high waist, which gathered under her breasts. The neckline was wide and square, the sleeves ending at her elbows. A dark silk shawl with lace trim covered her shoulders. Her black hair was piled on her head, caught up in a glittering diamond tiara, with escaping ringlets hanging beside her face.

A singular scent wafted over the pier. Sweet pine and camphor. Eucalyptus and moss.

"House Tucek. House Farrell." Her voice was level, formal, old South: plantation with a shadow of French beneath. "I see Remy has given you your packet. Welcome to my floating palace."

"Madame." Tucek's stiff neck almost bent. "There seems to be a misunderstanding. My Lady assured me that this would need only a short visit while your ship was in dock. She was quite clear that we should not disturb you any further with an unimportant matter."

"I'm not disturbed, but a steamboat moored is not a steamboat. It is only what it can be on the river it was born for. As for me, it happens I have business ashore tonight. If I complete that before you complete yours, I shall return and why then, it will be my pleasure to be your hostess."

"We should not be long. It's not important," Tucek said.

"I'll be the one to decide what's important."

She looked at me.

I couldn't see her eyes clearly in the lights of the pier. They might have been gray or blue. Something pale and hard in contrast to the soft features of her face.

"House Farrell doesn't think the matter is unimportant, does she?"

"Madame," I said, following Tucek's lead. "All members of my House are important to me. Gabrielle is a member of my House."

The politeness cost me nothing, while I worked out how bad my situation was. This was the Queen of Diamonds' substantiation, but I wasn't powerless. Eukori worked here.

I dug deep into my reserves. A thousand bloodied hands held against me, a thousand oaths, sharp-thorned hate growing through a framework of vows, feeding the anger. I'd taken the power of the Threefold Spiral Coven, the power of their curse, and if the Queen of Diamonds opened a channel to me, I would burn her with it.

But there was no opening.

"A member of your House," she said. "Now also a member of my coven. Who's to say which is the greater claim?"

Tucek sensed my anger and broke in before I spoke. "As my Lady stated, we're simply here to see Gabrielle and depart, under the terms of our partnership."

"Our *partnership*, House Tucek? Oh, yes, I have invested considerable effort into our *partnership*, and I am wondering whether my decision on partners was badly misguided. So many plans, so many assurances of success. Plans to overturn the whole Athanate Assembly by mass assassination, plans to capture the Panethus dragon spirit guide, plans to unify Mexican and Southern US werewolf packs under Mauricio Gálvez. All plans that required elements of my powers to be used by the *partnership* in ways your Lady and her allies dictated. All such powers of mine freely shared." Her voice began to rise, sentence by sentence. "And all those plans have come to nothing. In the latest debacle, the alliance of Mexican packs has been torn apart, Gálvez is dead, and the impregnable fortress of Astilla de Luna is no more than a smoking ruin in the desert. Plans built up over *years*. Destroyed in the course of a single night by a single person."

She turned to me again.

"It occurs to me that maybe I have the wrong partners," she said.

I would rather kiss a rattlesnake, but whatever it took to destroy the obviously fragile bonds between Matlal's allies.

"Over my pay grade," I said. "But you should definitely talk to House Altau."

She laughed at that. "Oh, I don't think the world is wide enough for me and Altau, any more than it is for me and Matlal. Neither really wants me."

Tucek was going to protest, but the Queen of Diamonds cut her off. "Have you worked out why Vega Martine wanted you two together on my riverboat?"

"To see Gabrielle," Tucek said.

"That's simply an excuse that worked to bring House Farrell here. It's not the real reason. Vega Martine understands the power of connections made in the spirit world. The girl? Beyond irritation that I took her, House Tucek, your *Lady* doesn't care one way or the other about little Gabrielle."

She whirled, making her dress float out around her, and strode over to the people waiting to board the riverboat.

Some bowed, some knelt. Some reached to touch the fabric of her dress. The eyes that had held fear and fascination now gleamed with reverent awe.

"Spirit connections, my Athanate friends," the queen called to us as she walked. "Connections like your Houses. Like packs. Like covens. Magic works best in connections between people. All my subjects connect to me, and my magic flows down to them. I am the river of their lives."

She completed her circuit and stood in front of us again.

"Vega Martine wanted a connection of auras between the two of you. Put the pair of you in shared danger, she thought, and let magic find its course. Surely not, you say, but it does, here in the spirit world, whether you want it to or not. Love or hate, attraction or repulsion; every little discovery, every word exchanged, every emotion elicited, forms a strand, and every strand spirals around another, and another, until it forms a cable."

She threw her head back and laughed. "It would have been worth it, if only to see how that worked out. You are alike, you two. You will connect. But which way will the connection flow, eh? Every moment tonight will be like a drop of rain in the headwaters of two rivers, seeking its path to the sea. Who has the greater pull? Which of you has the foundation to resist the pull of the other? Who would have benefited? Vega Martine or Altau?"

She turned away, but continued to speak over her shoulder.

"And all the while, *my* connection to you grows stronger. My foundation is as broad and wide as the river. *I* will benefit. So enjoy your night. Meet your challenges. Win your rewards. Prepare yourselves for my blessings to flow down to you."

Blessings? More chills flowed through me.

She started to walk away and stopped to look down at herself. "Ah! I have been so distracted. This won't work, will it?"

One hand pulled the tiara from her hair, loosening it. In the time it took for her hand to fall back to her side, she changed. She was suddenly a six-foot-tall, African-American man, dressed in an elegant charcoal gray suit with a silk tie. She now looked to be in her forties; laughter lines edging her bright eyes showed humor, but were balanced by a hint of gray in her hair. A man who'd seen life and gathered wisdom. A man you'd trust with the key to your safe deposit box.

"That's better," she said. Her voice was now deep and warm, giving off measured tones, and full of the sounds of an expensive East Coast education.

In her right hand she held a mahogany walking stick—a fashion accessory, because she moved like a dancer. She tapped Tucek on the breastbone.

"You, House Tucek, you're a gambler, aren't you? As brash and tasteful as Vegas."

Tucek's dress disappeared, to be replaced by the skintight black pants I'd seen earlier, along with a frilled white shirt under a shiny gold vest, topped off by a long black jacket with a yellow carnation in the buttonhole. The vest squeezed and pressed her breasts up.

A riverboat gambler as dreamed up by some Vegas show designer.

"And you, House Farrell." The cane remained poised for a moment before descending to touch my collarbone gently. "Yes. That works. You're a principled, capable person who finds yourself on the losing side."

She whirled and strode away, disappearing into the fog as I looked down at a heavy, double-breasted jacket in gray. Gold buttons. Yellow cuffs with ornate, loopy insignia on the forearms. A yellow sash belt. I reached up and checked the upright collar. A star.

She'd made me a major in the Confederate cavalry.

"Very funny," I said, but my voice sounded odd.

I felt odd, too. When I'd been reclothed in the Hecate's substantiation, the clothes fitted me and felt familiar. These didn't. The way the cloth seemed to stretch and press. The sensation...

Tucek laughed with a hint of hysterics, and then cut it off.

"I'm sorry," she said. "In our situation, a woman in an outfit like mine shouldn't find amusement in such an elegantly dressed companion."

I looked down as the truth of it broke over me. I wasn't over-endowed in the breast department, but I wasn't *that* flat. And my hips weren't *that* narrow. And I *really* didn't have *that* in my pants.

Chapter 55

"Aboard! All aboard!"

The tall man in the top hat who'd held the signal lamps on the pier was ushering people up the gangplank.

The Queen of Diamonds was messing with my head again; the man had Top's face and voice. How had she done that? Had she invaded my mind? Researched my history?

All it achieved was to make me angrier.

What made me angry, made Tara angry, but she had the advantage that her physical body hadn't just been switched, so her thinking was cooler.

She's doing it to unsettle you, weaken your defenses. There will be more of that before this is finished. Stay strong. For all her power, you can probably stop her from invading your mind if you keep cool.

Concentrating on Tara, I could share her perceptions of the effects of the queen's magic. How much she could do, and maybe what she couldn't. Tara couldn't manifest. I couldn't shapeshift. There was no pulse in my jaw at the thought of Blood, so I doubted my fangs would manifest. My Athanate healing was probably similarly blocked. My Athanate senses seemed undimmed—I saw and heard beyond a human ability. Despite being poured into a different body, I felt my Athanate strength and speed were unchanged. Strangely, my eukori seemed to slide past any barriers, but my aura that I'd use for spirit walking was caught; not erased but stunted.

Tucek looked rattled rather than angry, after the exchange with the queen. She was frowning, and I sensed she was catching some trailing sensations of my thoughts through eukori.

She tried to hide her own reaction. "Baron Samedi upsetting you?" she said, indicating the man in the top hat.

"The queen is using the appearance of people I know," I said.

"Let it go. As she said, any emotion in this substantiation is an opportunity to get her hooks into us. We don't want that."

"*We. Us.* So, we're both in this together, are we?"

"Yes."

"Or is that another kind of hook for a connection? Between the two of us, like Vega Martine wanted?"

"Yes," she said again, taking a deep breath. "Again, like she said, if we're united in defense of each other, here in the spirit world, we'll form a connection, a pathway of auras, between us."

Which might favor Tucek.

As if it were the most natural thing in the world, she slipped a hand through my arm. My body automatically responded, bending at the elbow.

She stepped closer to me, almost touching, and whispered so low I could barely make it out.

"We have to talk privately. Working together is our best chance of getting out of here. And as for spirit connections, who would you prefer, me or the queen?"

The touch of her hand on my arm was disconcerting. So was the closeness of her body and the intimacy of whispering.

Was that exactly as distracting as she meant it to be, or was she right? Did I need to use her as an ally to help me rescue Gabrielle and get out of this substantiation?

The thought of staying and being subjected to the queen's 'blessings' was paralyzing.

I was thinking about the queen's words and what they meant. Her 'gifts freely given'. I started to connect things. The appearance of Remy on the pier. The discussions we'd had in Denver about the strange and powerful compulsions that had killed the real Remy and forced the Denver coven to obey Weaver. The pit in Astilla de Luna. The rougarou. The strange werewolves joining the Louisiana packs.

What if all of those were the queen's gifts?

What if I ended up like Remy?

What if I ended up sent back to my House and friends with the seed of destruction inside me?

By now, the others who'd assembled on the pier had walked up the gangplank onto the steamer. Only Tucek and I remained.

Baron Samedi with Top's face loomed over us, a leer twisting those otherwise familiar features. "Welcome," he boomed. "Welcome to the unforgettable steamer, the riverboat of dreams, the *Queen of Diamonds*. Please, step aboard, Major, my lady."

I hesitated, something making me not want to set foot on the gangplank. "Where are we going?" I asked.

He laughed. Whatever the queen had used to mold her servant into Top's likeness, she got the laugh wrong. Top laughed from the belly up. Baron Samedi's laugh was like a stone rattling down a long tin gutter in comparison.

"That very much depends on where you want to be," he said.

"*Tout dépend*. Nowhere. Everywhere." Remy was behind us, waving us on. "*Where* doesn't really matter as much as *here*, when the good times are rolling."

I moved, if only to get away from them.

My booted foot was an inch above the wooden gangplank when I noticed a stirring in the riverboat. An awareness.

My foot landed.

I could *feel* the river flow beneath the hull, like I could feel Tucek's hand pressing on my arm, like I could feel my stranger's masculine body, familiar and unfamiliar, moving, reacting. I could feel the wind press the tall sides of the riverboat. The tug of hawsers holding against the pier.

All of it mingled with my own senses, becoming a torrent. The scents of coal fire and kerosene and waxed wooden floors and brass polish drifted over me, blending with ladies' perfumes and rich river mud. Murmurs of voices came from all over the riverboat.

I gasped. Hid it behind a cough.

We walked up the gangplank slowly.

Something of what I was feeling communicated itself to Tucek.

"Don't say anything here," she said quietly and urgently. "We can talk in the cabin." She looked at the packet we'd been given. "Top floor. *Shit.* Next to the queen's suite."

There were steps to the next level on our right, and we moved up them without speaking.

My body handled itself well. It just felt odd, especially overlaid with the sensations from the boat itself.

Most of the passengers had reached their cabins already. As the walkways became emptier, I could see the red eyes of rougarou watching us as we moved up the steps to the top level. There weren't any more passengers up here.

"Stop," I said.

As we halted, I felt the sway of the riverboat coming away from the pier. I sensed the change from being partly attached to the land to being entirely a creature of the river. I felt the churn of the paddle and the swiftness of the water, the way the wind veered.

I anticipated the movement of the boat, swayed with it. Tucek stumbled against me.

She wasn't feeling the boat the way I did. Or maybe she did, but she was using exactly the sort of technique I would have used if our positions were reversed. Distract with flirting and misdirection. The way I'd distracted Zane at the poker game in Albuquerque, and cleaned him out with a cool hand.

Having stumbled against me, she hadn't moved away. In the same disturbing way I felt the riverboat, I was acutely aware of the weight and warmth of her body. And the reaction my body was having.

"Cabin," Tucek whispered. "Now. We have a problem."

The cabin would be a good place. I could sense rougarou all over the ship, and I wanted to get out of their sight, but I needed to understand what I was also sensing about the ship itself.

I shook my head and reached out a hand to the walkway's ornamentation. From the pier, I'd assumed it was ironwork, the same as the decoration on the galleries of the French Quarter.

I touched it.

"This is wood," I said.

"How fascinating."

She didn't get it.

"No. *Living* wood. The entire riverboat is made of wood that's alive. Floor, walls, ceilings. It's formed of living trees magically trained into shape, it's..."

"Weird, but not important. The cabin..."

I let it go, and we walked toward the bow.

There were three cabins on their own at the front. The queen's in the middle, and one to either side. The walkway cut in behind them, so these cabins would have uninterrupted views of the river in daylight.

A large brass key from the packet we'd been given opened the door, and we slipped inside the cabin with relief.

It was quiet in here, sealed off from the rest of the boat in the embrace of a luxurious cabin.

The shutters were closed and locked. There were three gently hissing hurricane lamps, making everything gleam with a buttery light. A stick of mild incense burned in a vase, sitting in a niche by the door. It had a strange scent, familiar, but I couldn't place it, though the scent stirred something deep my body.

The cabin was split into day and night. A bed took up most of the width of the night cabin to my right, separated from the day cabin by an arch of rosewood. I walked over and touched the arch. It was living wood—all one with the floor, walls and ceiling—almost the whole boat. The tables and chairs in the day cabin were rattan, with soft cushions for the chairs, and glass for the tabletops. At least the rattan furniture wasn't alive.

I trailed my fingers over the wall of the cabin, where it blended seamlessly with the rosewood arch. I could feel the boat, and touching the wooden structure made that sensation a hundred times more vivid.

Back in Denver at Christmastime, the Lost Boys and I had spirit-walked in trees. I'd shared minds with the soultree of the Threefold Spiral Coven. Did this mean I had some affinity for trees?

Or was this all a trick in the queen's substantiation?

Why make a boat this way? To show that she could bend things to her will?

The tickle of incense intensified. I felt restless, seeking an outlet I couldn't name yet. My clothes felt too tight. It was too warm in the cabin.

My body, moving of its own accord, shed my jacket.

Tucek did as well. She opened her vest.

And I had bigger problems than thinking about how or why the *Queen of Diamonds* was constructed the way it was.

Chapter 56

We were in each other's arms without any conscious thought on either side. Her lips softened beneath my urgent kiss.

What?

Nothing else mattered. *Nothing.*

She was a monster. I'd seen this woman casually kill an innocent bystander: Frank, a teenage store clerk in Taos who'd had the bad luck to work in a shop I'd visited. Tucek had killed him in front of me, grunting with pleasure as she drained his blood.

But this balls-for-brains body the queen had given me decided all that didn't matter. I was being swept along, and so was Tucek.

My mind filled with a kind of muscle memory I didn't have. I gripped her butt as she wound powerful arms around my shoulders. She broke the kiss to lift her body up and offer me her breasts while her legs climbed me and fastened around my hips.

The steamer slipped across a deep eddy, seeking the central channel of the river to thrust against the current there.

We swayed with the boat.

I shoved her against the door.

Touched the rosewood.

Felt the shock of that tree awareness all the way down my body. Leaked some of it into Tucek.

Just enough to break the headlong rush for both of us.

"Fucking magically enhanced Athanate pheromones," Tucek hissed. "It's a trap. You can make them. You can counter them. Concentrate."

She pinched out the incense stick with her fingers, even though her body was still pressing and grinding against me in ways that threatened to short-circuit all thought.

I let go of her butt and placed both my hands against the door; leaned past her and rested my forehead there as well. Skin contact seemed to work better. It let me borrow some of the stillness of the living wood.

The queen's magic was working to stop me from projecting my aura, so I couldn't spirit jump away, but I could just about spirit walk into the trees that made up the boat. Trying that gave me something to concentrate on instead of that brain-stunning, overwhelming lust. Gave me enough breathing space that my Athanate responses could start working, suppressing the pheromones.

The sensation the boat returned wasn't exactly calming. It wasn't like spirit jumping into the trees in Denver. I didn't get the feel of roots and branches, of reaching down and up, of soil and air. Instead, I got a feeling of bands tight around me, of being imprisoned and squeezed and crushed. Not a good feeling for trees, but maybe exactly what I needed at that moment. I needed to crush these sensations and desires that were threatening to derail me.

And seeing how the queen had forced her will on the trees gave me some insight into how she'd done the same to me.

"Okay?" Tucek's breath on my ear threatened to undo the restraints all over again. At least she'd stopped moving against me and the incense stick wasn't releasing any more aphrodisiac pheromone scents into the air.

"Sort of," I said. "She played us from the first, didn't she? We were being compelled as soon as the fog came up the river."

"Not exactly, but you're on the right track."

I suddenly had a thought. "Can she hear us?"

"I don't think she eavesdrops. Not her style. Still could be someone in the crew listening. Keep it down."

So we're going to keep whispering in each other's ears. Wonderful.

She had quit climbing up me like an ivy plant, but my body was still crushing hers against the door.

The thought of how close I'd come to having sex with her was sickening, and yet my body remained unconvinced of my change of mind.

That made me angry. Anger was good. Anger was strong.

I forced my muscles to relax and my mind to think about the situation.

Anger might give the queen's magic a small opportunity to hook into my mind, but it was nothing compared to the opportunity that would have been available for the queen to invade our auras while we were having sex. I could still remember Alice Emerson, speaking primly and warning me about physical intimacy opening pathways into my aura. Whatever the dangers had been back then, they were made a hundred times worse in the spirit world.

In the damn City of Lost Gods.

If anger helped me, I should make Tucek angry as well, but I didn't trust my eukori, not with the pressure of her body still against me, so I tried words.

"Should I trust what the queen said? For instance, that Vega Martine didn't actually tell you what your true mission was tonight?"

Tucek huffed. "Altau explains everything he's planning to you? In which parallel universe?"

I managed a smirk. "You're right, he doesn't, but just now and then, I get to tell him what I've done after I've done it."

That felt better. I eased my body back, although it was reluctant to let those sensations go. The hot pressure of her body against mine was replaced by cool air and a regretful ache.

Think of Frank dying. Think of the pit at Astilla de Luna. Think about Rosa, the kidnapped girl thrown into that pit.

It helped.

I moved a step away, keeping one hand on the wooden door.

"You suggested it was urgent to get to the cabin," I prompted her. "That we need to talk."

Tucek also took a step away and I could see her focusing on her breathing.

Her shirt was undone. I couldn't even remember undoing it. She was naked beneath the flimsy material. It was insanely distracting, and I wanted her to button it back up, but I didn't at the same time.

Focus!

"From the way she spoke," Tucek was saying, "the queen has broken the alliance with my Lady. That leaves us in a dangerous position. We're prisoners here in her substantiation unless she lets us go."

She was right. Both of us were supposed to be under Vega Martine's protection. Without that...

"Broken with Matlal as well?"

"She didn't say that, and she's not as powerful as him. Not a smart move."

"You're telling me the Queen of Diamonds has her own substantiation working inside the City of Lost Gods, and yet she's not as powerful as Matlal?"

"Yes."

Shit.

She clearly didn't want to explain how that could be. I could practically see the thoughts crossing her face. Her loyalty was to Vega Martine, but if Vega Martine was still allied with Matlal, and the queen was allied with Matlal, then maybe that alliance would keep the queen from doing whatever she wanted to us.

In which case, she didn't want to be giving away Matlal's secrets to me.

My problem was that being handed over to Matlal would be as bleak an outcome for me as being kept by the queen.

Tucek spoke formally, concentrating on every word, as if her mouth might run away and say something different. "My only course of action is to carry out my Lady's wishes and make the connection with you, so we can help each other prevent the connection with the queen, while I continue hoping my Lady will get Matlal to intervene."

"Not exactly giving me a warm feeling, being saved by Matlal or held by the queen. How do we go about preventing the queen from getting her hooks into our heads?"

Tucek frowned. "I'm not an expert. What the queen is calling a connection, Adepts call pathways for aura. A channel. Like the queen said, the theory is that every interaction creates a strand of connection between people. Enough strands and you have a way to magically reach someone that can't really be cut off. The more it gets used the easier it is to use, and the more potential it has."

I remembered Alice and Gwen talking about it in Denver, but more in the context of how Weaver and the Denver coven had been affected.

"But then, everyone is connected to every person they've met."

"Potentially, yes, but if we're talking about connections in the human world, they form slowly and you need a lot of power to use the pathway."

"But here in the spirit world, everything to do with aura is boosted."

"Yes."

"And when you talk about using it, you're talking about compulsion, right?" I said. "That's the queen's 'gift' she's talking about?"

"One of them. Influence is what they tend to call it, but yes, compulsion is the end point of that spectrum. We weren't under a compulsion on the pier. We weren't *forced* to get on board against our wills."

"Yeah. Instead, every step felt like it was the right one and a decision I'd made. Risks seemed reasonable. Sort of compulsion lite."

A compulsion I convinced myself was my own wish. Very, *very* scary.

I thought for a few moments more. "There's the beginning of this aura pathway between us there already," I said, "and it would have gotten stronger if we'd kept going just now."

"Much stronger."

And more in her favor as well, Tara said. *Sex is only a tool for her.*

But she resisted too.

"But while we were busy making our *connection*," Tucek couldn't prevent her mouth stressing the word and making it full of sexual overtones, "we would have been completely vulnerable to her."

"Even though she's not on the boat?"

Tucek nodded. "This is her substantiation. The whole thing is part of her. She knows everything that happens, if it involves magic. She'll have left a working which will just keep on probing at us."

"Back to my question. If I agree for us to act together, how does that stop her from getting her hooks into us?"

"If we have a strong connection in auras, that's a defense in itself. And we need to hold each other back, calm each other down. Keep each other focused."

"While waiting for the cavalry to rescue us, in the shape of Matlal."

"Or my Lady, with Matlal's backing."

Or I found a way out of here, rather than either of those unappealing options.

"If it's my Lady, I will take your side and argue for you to be let go," Tucek said. "I've given you my word."

Which Vega Martine would ignore.

What Tucek proposed made sense for her—that I agreed to form exactly the connection with her that Vega Martine wanted, because it was my only hope to not become one of the queen's compelled zombie slaves...

Or did she just 'influence' me to make me think this was a good idea?

I tried to clear my head. I was a *long* way from trusting Tucek, but what she'd said really seemed like a sensible way to proceed in the short term.

Which is exactly what it would do if she were influencing me.

Stop! Think!

However evil Tucek and Vega Martine were, my gut was telling me the queen was far worse, and much more danger to me right now. I needed an alliance, a *temporary* alliance, with Tucek.

As long as it was genuinely me making that decision.

I had to stop that. I could feel madness creeping down that train of thought.

But regardless of the supposed difference between Matlal, the queen and Vega Martine, the outcome for me was unpleasant whoever won in this faction fight. All three of them would find some way to use me against Panethus.

And there was one other issue...

"There's Gabrielle to think about," I said.

"She may not be the same person. I warned you that people change when the queen has them for any length of time. That's worse here, in the spirit world."

"What are you saying?"

"She may be too damaged. She may not *want* to leave."

I hadn't abandoned the children that Matlal twisted. I wouldn't abandon Gabrielle. The Threefold Spiral coven would heal her if Diana couldn't.

"At least wait until we've seen her to decide whether we can help her," Tucek said.

"No. I'll agree to a connection with you," I said. "But not for us to wait around for rescue while fending off the queen, and not to leave Gabrielle behind. We work together to rescue Gabrielle and escape, whatever it takes."

"How? How are we going to escape?"

"I don't know. *We* will find something."

She thought about it. There wasn't much to think about. It wasn't any worse for her and had the potential for escape.

"Okay. Truce."

"Temporary truce. It's just to escape the queen's substantiation. You're still an evil bitch."

"And you're the most appallingly naive boy scout, way out of your depth. But I agree. Temporary truce. Any escape plans must be to get both of us out."

"All *three* of us."

"Yes. Fine. Three. But I'll say it once more. The queen's had Gabrielle for a while. Everything you're scared about becoming... she may be there already."

I shuddered, remembering fighting with the rougarou, Rochelle, at Port Allen. What had she said about the queen getting to Gabrielle? *You all tough like steel 'til it happen. Like the li'l Canadian bitch, an' lookit her now.*

"Rescuing Gabrielle is not negotiable," I said.

Tucek nodded reluctantly. "Okay, so the first step is we've got to see Gabrielle and assess how difficult it might be to escape with her. That means we'd have to go along with whatever crazy scheme the queen has tonight just to get to see her, and then we still wouldn't be sure how we'd be able to rescue her."

"And how do we make this connection without..." My eyes flicked to the bed and back. Bad idea. My body had one urgent suggestion, pulsing with need.

"Eukori?" Tucek said.

Eukori was good. I probably had more power than Tucek suspected. But what if she had some similar power? Eukori felt too intimate.

This connection was a pathway for aura, and that was something I had that Tucek didn't, as far as I could tell.

My thoughts were interrupted by a knock on the door. Through the boat itself, I sensed one of the boat's ordinary crew, rather than a rougarou. Had he been out there listening to us?

With adrenaline coursing through my system, I didn't stop to think.

I shoved Tucek out of the way and yanked the door open abruptly.

There was a man in the walkway. Crew uniform. Dark blue pants, pale blue shirt, dark blue tie and white gloves. His head was bowed over a bucket on a stand which contained a bottle of champagne. He held a large printed card.

His head came up.

"Compliments of the captain. The evening's entertainment in the ballroom begins in half an hour," he said, offering the card with both hands.

His face. His voice. It was Frank, the teenage store clerk that Tucek had murdered in Taos.

No.

He wasn't really Frank any more than the servant on the pier had been Remy, or Baron Samedi was Top. The queen had picked his image to try and mess with my head.

I took the card, willing my face to remain neutral. I wasn't going to let the queen's tricks get to me.

He lifted the champagne stand.

I was aware that Tucek and I were both standing there with our shirts open. I took a hold of the champagne bucket.

"I'll take that. Thank you."

I closed the door in his face.

"Another one from your past?" Tucek said. She was doing up her buttons. I had to look away in case my lust caught fire again.

"Frank. The kid you murdered in Taos."

"Oh."

"Yeah, 'oh'." I put the champagne in its stand beside the table, where glasses had been left out, and my doubts flooded back. "Are you really going to help me? Or is this all a trick the queen agreed on with Vega Martine, for me to lower my guard with you?"

"Like I said, we could try opening eukori. That might convince you, and we could form a connection at the same time."

"Which is exactly what I'd expect you to say if this was all to get me to lower my defenses."

"It *is* a problem, isn't it? Treat me with suspicion, then, but be even more suspicious of the queen. We have a task, and at the moment neither of us can begin to see how we'll achieve it. What are you thinking? That maybe we time our escape so the ship comes alongside a pier and we run for it? That we bet the queen's substantiation doesn't spread far from the river?"

But from what I knew of substantiations, the Queen of Diamonds controlled everything as far as her boundaries. Surely she could stop us?

Tucek knew exactly what was going through my head.

"Not eukori. This connection is a pathway for aura," I said. "Let's try aura to open it."

Tucek grimaced. "Not one of my skills."

"It shouldn't matter; you still have aura whether you use it or not."

"It's one way. You to me."

"Aura's not like that. It's like eukori. You can't get a one-way aura connection any more than you get a one-way eukori connection."

She turned away angrily, wrapping her arms around herself. Scared of being vulnerable to me, but even more scared of remaining vulnerable to the queen.

"I give you my oath, I will not use the aura to gain an advantage over you," I said.

I reached out with my hand, held it above her shoulder for a moment. She didn't move away. I touched the bare skin of her neck.

We hadn't completely purged our systems of the pheromones. She started to turn into my touch, catlike, then caught herself.

I pulled her closer.

Had to stop and squeeze my eyes closed.

I wanted to hold her against me. Kiss her neck. Open that shirt again. Feel her body respond to mine.

I froze. I couldn't move forward.

Can't do this. Have to control myself. Think of Jen. Alex. Bian.

I tried to think myself into a feeling of distance with aura. Of not being so closely bound. But Tucek and I had already touched each other with eukori, back on the pier. It lingered. I could feel Tucek. I could tell she felt me. We felt the blood pounding in our hearts. Felt each other's labored breaths, lungs heaving again, mouths dry, our skin alight with anticipation. We were one careless caress away from ripping off our clothes and lunging onto the bed.

Concentrate on aura. Less about each other's physical sensation. More about the intangibles.

Tara's advice. Easier said than done.

But slowly, by not succumbing, by working together, the fire of eukori diminished. My aura moved to take its place: cooler, carefully sensing the equivalent for Tucek.

There was a moment when I felt our auras use each other as a boost. Like our Carpathian eukori combining, our auras working together were stronger.

We could feel the riverboat move beneath us, slow and seductive.

We could feel the living wood that formed the boat, bound and bound again, so tight, so desperate to be free. So very different from trees I had spirit jumped into before.

And there were workings, the queen's workings: slithering along the walkways, creeping up walls, dripping from ceilings, searching out openings—soulless, relentless, evil.

Our auras stopped reaching out. They retreated back to the cabin, forced together by the threats all around us. They touched, aura to aura. Probed and slipped and tested like lovers' tongues. And then, like two drops of water on glass, they suddenly merged.

We stumbled, gripping the cabin's chairs for support.

It was *disturbing*. A swirling confusion of currents. Colors leaking from one side to another and back again. A hint of knowledge. We sensed the good and evil we could do. The power. The pleasures calling us. The light and dark twisting around each other like the yin-yang symbol, each containing some part of the other.

But one thing was clear now. There was *us* and there was *not us*. Our unsettled auras had a clear boundary between our turmoil and the seething mix of everything else on the riverboat, which comprised the crew, the passengers, the queen's workings and even the boat itself.

And given that ability to make a distinction, they did what auras wanted to: they reached out, sweeping in the darkness above the river, falling into the temple of night, mixing with eukori, finding a knotted string between our fingers, making letters of fire in the obsidian air: *chi, rho, upsilon...*

There was a presence looming above the storm of winds. Laughter.

Hello, my priestess. Now you have need, now is the time to come into your powers.

And flying back, back, down into the riverboat, down into our own bodies, snapping back because I *knew*, I knew what that knotted string said, and I knew what T-cat meant when he said *come into my powers.*

"What the fuck was that?" Tucek gasped. She tried to stand, rocked back against me.

The crazy edge to the lust had weakened, but it was far from gone. I pushed her away. "A reminder that there's more in the City of Lost Gods than the Queen of Diamonds' little river domain, Tucek."

She turned and stared at me for a long moment before speaking. "I may be an evil bitch, but I think you could manage to call me Mirela after that."

"Okay... Mirela." I occupied my shaking hands by pulling the cork out of the champagne bottle and pouring it into the two glasses. "Against all odds, I think that worked."

"Better than I expected... Amber. Well done." She accepted a glass and tapped it against mine. "I doubt it's enough to face down the queen herself, but we have breathing space to make a plan."

"First things first. Talk to Gabrielle, then make plans to rescue her." I sipped the champagne. "But the queen is not going to just send Gabrielle to talk to us, is she? Especially when she realizes we're working together."

"No." Tucek picked up the card that Frank had brought. "It seems Gabrielle's the star of the entertainment tonight, and it looks as if you're going to have to win a chance to meet her."

Chapter 57

We'd boarded after midnight, but time flowed differently in the substantiation. Half an hour later, when we went down to the ballroom, it was 8 p.m., riverboat time.

I stopped at the entrance.

The saloon took up the whole length and width of the superstructure on the main deck. Light came from glittering oil-lamp chandeliers suspended from the ceiling. The floor was a couple of steps down from the entrance. The stern end was cleared as a dance floor, and the bow end as a stage. In the middle, there were tables set for a formal dinner, with brilliant white cloths. There were twenty tables, and I estimated from the chairs that there were about fifty passengers. There were gaming tables in the space between the dining area and the dance floor: roulette, blackjack, craps.

More interesting to me, at each corner of the room and halfway down both sides, there were massive wooden pillars reaching from floor to ceiling. They were kingposts, the sort of internal bracing needed for wooden ships. This room was the unbeating heart of the riverboat.

Mirela followed me in silence as I strolled from the entrance to the nearest pillar and leaned against it, pretending to watch the gathering guests.

The pillars in the middle were swamp cypress; the ones in the corners alternated between ebony and mahogany. They were all part of a colony of trees that made the riverboat, and they were alive and aware. Not like a person, and not in any way that I could see would help me tonight, but the trees had been sculpted by magic to form this riverboat, and as much as trees could, they hated the queen.

"Every time you connect with the queen's riverboat, you're increasing our aural connection with them, and the queen is going to know about it," Mirela said.

She took my arm, both our bodies moving as if on muscle memory. It felt as natural as offering my arm to Jen. It wasn't as bad as what nearly happened earlier, but even this made me feel guilty all over again.

"There's a pathway for aura between us and the trees," I said. "Maybe we can use it, maybe the queen can, but I'll tell you this: the boat hates the queen."

Still, I stepped down onto the main floor with Mirela at my side.

"We're at the captain's table," she said.

"Is that a bad thing?"

"She's scary in her own right. And here she comes."

A tall woman detached herself from a group and came toward us. The dark blue pants and pale blue shirt with dark blue tie seemed to represent the standard crew uniform, even the officers. Over that, she wore a double-breasted white jacket with gold stripes on the cuffs. Very naval and masculine, but tailored to ensure there was no doubt of her femininity.

She was beautiful—exquisitely made up and with hair the color of burnished copper, wound up into an elaborate chignon.

"Welcome, Houses Farrell and Tucek." Her voice was low. She had the trick of making it sound intimate, as if she were talking to no one else but me. "I'm Donatienne Gaudreau, your hostess in the temporary absence of the queen."

She wore a perfume that made me think of hothouse honeysuckle. It was good, but not so good I didn't get a hint of her scent beneath.

She was rougarou. A hyena-wolf hybrid shifter.

"Captain Gaudreau," I replied, and Mirela echoed me.

"We're sitting together for dinner, so I'm sure we'll have plenty of opportunity to get to know each other better, but at the moment I'm begging a favor, Major."

I had a momentary brain fade figuring out who the Major was, and then an instinctive wariness. Nothing like psych 101 'ask for help' to make me suspicious, but I tried out what Jen called my neutral, inquisitive smile.

"We like to start with a couple of dances before dinner. It helps break the ice. Inevitably, everyone waits for me to lead the way, and I can't think of someone I'd rather start with."

"My companion—"

"My first mate, Raymond, is hoping to accompany House Tucek." She gestured at a man in the same uniform making his way over. Her voice oozed sincerity as she added, "Please."

Mirela and I exchanged glances. We'd be separated, but in sight of each other. She nodded warily.

"Of course," I said, and my body, working on automatic pilot again, offered my arm to the captain.

I reminded myself that this woman shifted into a creature who'd enjoy tearing that arm off. The rest of my body noted that she was graceful and attractive in a feral sort of way.

She was about six feet. As a woman, I was five-ten. From where she came up to, walking next to me, I worked out that, as a major of the Confederate cavalry, I was six-one or six-two.

We walked together onto the area kept clear for dancing, and a small orchestra over by the stage began playing a gentle waltz.

I took the lead and, as I expected, Gaudreau was a gifted dancer, so we didn't scare the other guests off. Mirela and the first mate joined us, and within a minute, half the guests were dancing. It was quickly apparent that one of the benefits of a cruise on the *Queen of Diamonds* was a magically applied knowledge of classical dances.

"I suppose you aren't allowed to tell me," I said, "but I wonder who these other guests are."

"I normally don't give out any details, but you are a very special guest," Gaudreau replied. "They're a mix. You mustn't believe the queen is only interested in powerful people, or that we invite only those with vices for us to exploit."

We turned to the music.

"In confidence," she went on, "see the gentleman now behind me with the red handkerchief in his jacket pocket? He's dancing with his wife, who's been dead for five years. They're both in their twenties again."

I looked at them.

"He knows it's not really his wife?"

"He did at first. Deep down, I think he still does." She looked toward the tables, where some guests were gambling. "In contrast, look at the young lady playing craps with three gentlemen friends."

'Gentlemen' was a polite term. Even in dinner jackets, those three didn't qualify. I knew Gaudreau wanted me to ask about the woman. Given my own transformation, I could well imagine her trying to shock me with the story that she was really a middle-aged man with a wife and children, who went to church on Sundays.

"Athanate know better than to judge people on their domestic situation or sexual preferences," I said.

"Oh, good. Hold that thought," she said quickly, and I realized I'd stepped into a discussion trap. "The queen represents power, and power is no more good or evil than the purpose it's used for. Hold your judgement. Listen to what we say tonight with an open mind, and think about the good you could use that power for."

In another minute, the waltz came to an end.

"Thank you, Major," Gaudreau said, a smile playing on her lips as she used my bogus rank. "I'm required to mingle. I'm sure your companion would enjoy a dance and no doubt will be full of advice for you. Remember what I said. Above all, remember where you are."

I bowed, which seemed to be in keeping.

Mirela was at my side a moment later. She wanted to dance, and I found she was very good at it.

"How was the beautiful captain?" she asked.

"I've never been so politely threatened in my life," I said.

"I'm glad you see it. They'll keep being polite for the moment, but we're both in danger here and... shit! *Shit!* It's just gotten worse."

"How?"

She was as light as air in my arms, and yet she turned us so I was looking where she'd just been looking.

"Cazenave!"

"Yes! This is bad, Amber."

My brain had to reset. Cazenave was a traitor to my side. Why would it matter to Mirela if he showed up on the riverboat?

She could see I was puzzled. "He was going to Mexico City," she said.

"Yeah, I know that. Easier to get a flight there than direct to Yucatán."

"You don't understand. Cazenave is in Matlal's faction, not the queen's. And Mexico City is my Lady's domain. One of two things has happened. My Lady has decided to send him to the queen as some kind of offering—"

"She'd be crazy to ally herself with the weaker faction," I said. "Which means the queen had him kidnapped from under Vega Martine's nose."

"Yes. We can't expect a rescue. We have to escape as soon as we can."

Our auras were still connected enough for me to tell how much this had affected her.

"We have an agreement. Not without Gabrielle, Mirela."

Distantly I heard the bell at the bow start tolling. We were coming to another pier. There was a response in the boat itself, a drawing back.

"What do you bet that's the queen about to get back on," I muttered.

No one else paid it much attention. Inside the ballroom, a gong sounded and the music hushed.

The fake Remy stood on the stage.

"Ladies and gentlemen, dinner is served. *À table, mesdames, messieurs.*"

Chapter 58

The captain's table was the nearest to the stage. It was set for five places, a sort of throne with its back to the stage and two normal places on either side.

The stations of the pentagram, Tara noted. *Maybe the swamp witch doesn't rely on just voodoo.*

"The queen will be joining us presently," Gaudreau said, taking her position at the seat to the right of the throne.

Cazenave was with her, angry and sullen.

A waiter and waitresses appeared at our elbows, all wearing the likeness of members of House Labastide. A fake Jo guided me to the seat on the left of the throne. Xavier took Mirela to sit between me and Cazenave, whose waitress was Solange Dupuis, former Pelea, now Diakon Labastide.

Cazenave was glaring at Dupuis, unable to be absolutely sure whether she was the real one or not.

I ignored the staff. I'd noticed there was something about their faces that I couldn't put my finger on, but which warned me they were fakes.

And if Dupuis were real, I suspect Cazenave would have been dead.

"The queen has decided to provide House Farrell with a different body tonight," Gaudreau said, "but actually we have all been introduced to each other. I hope we can dispense with formalities. Please call me Donatienne. Are you happy with Amber, Mirela and Gerard?"

Mirela and I nodded. It cost us nothing.

Cazenave sneered. "I prefer Cazenave."

"Then I should formally reintroduce you, as Cazenave of House Matlal," Gaudreau replied. "I believe that's correct now."

The sneer turned into a half-snarl, but what could he do, captive here in the heart of the queen's substantiation?

It was the same question Mirela and I faced. Where was the queen's weakness, if there was one? How were we going to get out?

"What do you hope to gain by this?" Cazenave asked Gaudreau. "Do you really believe House Matlal will tolerate this?"

Gaudreau smiled easily. "Matlal currently suspects Vega Martine has kidnapped you. Even if he knew the truth, what would he do?"

Waiters placed bowls of soup in front of us, and hot rolls on our side plates. Another poured a white wine into glasses.

"Kidnapping Cazenave has created a division," Mirela said. "A division that will require you to keep him here."

Cazenave paled.

"Possibly," Gaudreau admitted, with a thoughtful tilt of her head. "Though we would hardly need representatives from Vega Martine and Altau at the same time to achieve that. There's much more to the queen's planning, which she will explain to you, and there are ways all of you can return to your lives with very little disruption."

She gestured at the soup. "Please, enjoy your food. Our cooks are excellent."

It was a shrimp soup and I could smell the spices.

With the spoon already hovering above the bowl, I remembered the myths about never eating food offered to you in fairyland. When I'd spirit walked into the City of Lost Gods, the Hecate had warned me not to take *anything*. Surely that included food?

Bring back nothing but knowledge, the Hecate had said. *And even then...*

Just looking at the statue of T-cat seemed to have made some kind of connection, some aural pathway, between him and me. Was I making connections to the Queen of Diamonds' substantiation by eating her food?

I glanced at Mirela, and she gave me a twitch of her shoulders and took a spoonful. I was starting to be able to read her, and I guessed she was saying something along the lines of: *yes, but a minor connection. Might as well eat.*

I took a sip, looking up to see Gaudreau watching me, smiling as if she knew exactly what was going through my mind.

"I think the purpose of a soup course is to make you anticipate what's coming later," she murmured, "but this one seems to stand all on its own, don't you agree, Amber? I find it delicious."

Her eyes fluttered in pleasure.

I could hear the suppressed snort from Mirela, and I knew I was getting played, but my damned male body didn't seem to care.

I had to clear my thoughts. I tasted the wine.

"It's very good," I replied to Gaudreau. "Back to this planning. A simple meeting between Matlal and Vega Martine would get rid of any misunderstanding between them. They'd combine against the queen."

"Despite working together for so long, Matlal and Vega Martine don't trust each other, so they'll never meet, never open their eukori to each other. Unlike you and Mirela clearly have."

Cazenave looked up at that, face full of calculation. He had to be asking himself which of us was in control of our arrangement, and how he could use that to his advantage.

But that wasn't what he asked.

"What's Farrell doing here? You can't imagine Altau is going to trust her after this."

"Maybe, but Amber could also be here entirely on her own merit," Gaudreau said. "She's demonstrated an ability to strike deep into enemy territory and wreak havoc. You'll have to wait for the queen for more insight, but I'm sure we could use those abilities of hers."

"She won't turn against Altau unless you compel her, and that damages the ability—"

"Did I suggest we would use her against Altau?"

Cazenave shut up.

Hearing Matlal and his allies were attacking each other was great news. However, I didn't see how I could use that to escape, and I had no wish to stay and be the queen's weapon against Matlal. Compelled or otherwise.

The gong sounded again. Gaudreau immediately stood, and all the crew who were seated at tables joined her. Everyone else joined them in a ragged wave. The wait staff all stopped where they were and turned to face the front. Silence fell. Even the boat itself, which I could sense around me, grew still.

It wasn't the woman in the historical French dress, or the elegant African-American man who emerged and glided toward our table. The queen wore a riverboat-era dress, more formal than the others tonight, narrow to the point of severity on top but wide and complicated below her hips, with folds and frills spreading out in the shape of half-opened theater curtains. Other people might have described the dress as a dark red, fall color. I thought of it as resembling drying blood.

Her facial appearance was now Chinese, though the black hair was arranged in European style, with ringlets hanging down again.

She sat, and gestured for everyone to sit back down.

"Good evening, everyone." She smiled. "What have I missed, Donatienne?"

Gaudreau summarized the conversation so far as the queen ate her soup.

"I see," the queen said when Gaudreau finished. "I'm going to enjoy the irony of explaining the reality of the situation to my guests in the dining saloon of my riverboat."

She took a sip of wine.

"I will not waste time. Let's start with the most fundamental truth: you are all entirely dependent on my will. No one is coming to rescue you. No one can find you. You are mine. I am your everything, and I will be in every part of your life from now on. Let that sink in for a moment and reconsider your positions."

"You should understand you have a new chance. Going forward, where you have come from and what you have done will not matter to me. I am only interested in what works for me, and works efficiently. This will now become the basis of all your actions, whether that's what you currently want or not. Your personal decisions tonight will dictate how pleasant or difficult this will be for you."

"If you accept me, if you commit yourselves to be in complete alignment with me, life will be very good for you. If you don't, it won't. I will speak to each of you in more depth, but you have only tonight to make your decisions."

She paused to let that sink in, and Cazenave took the opportunity to speak. "You're talking like the Emperor of Heaven, who also thinks he's the summit of all power. You're both wrong. Matlal is stronger than you. Altau is stronger than you. You're sitting here picking a fight with Matlal and drawing Altau's attention to yourself, making yourself a target, and you want us to join you?"

Gaudreau began to rise, but the queen raised her hand.

"I'll allow it this evening, and it's a fair question for someone who does not yet see the bigger picture."

She signaled the waitstaff to remove the first course.

"Matlal certainly has great potential, if you accept his claim that he is deriving his power from his link with Quetzalcoatl. Certainly, the Nahuatl gods are very strong in the City of Lost Gods. And yet, Cazenave, here we are, untouched in my riverboat. My powers derive from ancestral African gods so lost in time that they have become nameless and formless, yet Quetzalcoatl has no purchase here, on my river of dreams. I'm sure that if Matlal could direct Quetzalcoatl to find me, he would have. Instead, he continues to concentrate all his energy on reviving the worship of Quetzalcoatl in the physical world. Matlal believes it will channel Quetzalcoatl's power there for him to use. It won't work like that. It's a way for Quetzalcoatl to pull more power from the physical world, until he's strong enough to return in his true physical form, using Matlal as nothing more than a channel, a stepping stone. Matlal is doing

Quetzalcoatl's bidding, not the other way around, and even if he became aware, it's still a fight Matlal will lose, one way or the other.

"It's not just Matlal's strategy that's flawed, it's his followers. You can see the proof of my words in the insanity that infects them. Take his grand project to subvert the southern states of America with werewolves that would answer his call—"

"A project you worked on," Cazenave interrupted.

"I gave him the tools. The means to create wolves quickly, discarding those that are unstable. The means to instill deep but subtle compulsions that will control them when you call. Those were my gifts to our joint enterprise. The fault was in how Matlal used them, ignoring my advice. He chose Mauricio Gálvez, who was unstable to start with, and the power Gálvez was granted made that worse. He was completely out of control. His pack had no need to be involved in trafficking and drugs. He had no need to use the pit at Astilla de Luna as he did. He did all that to feed his lusts and his pleasure in causing pain. It was wasteful and inefficient. I abhor waste and inefficiency. I enjoyed hearing the project was terminated."

She smiled at me, but I wasn't getting a good feeling from her expression.

"*We* understood. We spoke out against Gálvez's behavior," Mirela said.

"Spoke out but couldn't stop it." The queen drank more wine. "As for Altau being stronger than me, Cazenave, you base that assessment on the dragon. But the dragon doesn't belong to Altau. I have plans for both Quetzalcoatl and Kaothos, but not to share with you, not yet. How can I get you to focus better? Maybe start with talking about matters closer to you. Your kin, for instance."

Cazenave's fists clenched and his voice became hoarse. "What have you done to them?"

"Nothing at all. They boarded their plane for Yucatán. The one you booked for them. By now they'll be safe in Matlal's hands, where you sent them. Unless you think that isn't a safe place to be."

"Of course it's not! I was supposed to be there."

"And you would make such a difference standing between them and Matlal? What would it be that makes you so valuable to Matlal?"

Cazenave couldn't answer.

"Good," the queen said. "Now you're thinking in useful ways about how you could become invaluable to Matlal, and how you could persuade me to allow you to go and do that. That should keep you occupied for a while, and some good may come it. This evening is more about how we will get the dragon to ally with us. However, I don't want to hurry into that."

She stood.

"Which leaves Mirela, the representative of Vega Martine, as the odd one out tonight. Don't be concerned; I have plans for you, too. Come with me."

I stood, my body reacting before I had time to think.

Mirela shook her head. There was nothing I could do at that point.

"What a dashing gentleman you make, Amber," the queen said. "All of you, excuse me for a short while. Entertain yourselves." She turned to the orchestra. "A dance, please."

They began to play, and I found Gaudreau at my side, slipping her hand through my arm while the queen and Mirela left the saloon.

Chapter 59

Gaudreau and I made our way to the dance floor, and I let my body lead her in another waltz.

In the strange way of the spirit world, it felt as if I'd danced with Gaudreau a hundred times instead of just once. Comfortable and familiar.

"I have a suggestion for you to consider, if you'd like to hear it," she said.

"I'm listening."

"This evening, the queen is going to make you the sort of offer you can't refuse. Of course, I advise accepting, because you can't get away and you will work for her one way or another."

"You mean if I refuse, she compels me?"

"Yes, and because a compelled person is less capable generally, the compulsion will limit what you are allowed to do and how you achieve it. I'm sorry, it's not pleasant, but the queen will do anything to ensure her plans."

"That's your suggestion? Give in?"

"Not exactly. That's my starting advice. Look, all factions on both sides accept Emergence is coming. We're just arguing over the details of how we manage it. Matlal wants complete control and the subjugation of humanity. Altau wants humanity to welcome us, against all sensible expectations. The queen wants the greatest good for the greatest number of people, human and paranormal. To achieve that goal efficiently, we acknowledge a limited amount of targeted violence will be necessary. Believe me, if it could be done without that, the queen would change her tactics."

I opened my mouth to argue about the violence, but I knew Gaudreau was just waiting for the opportunity to point out that my trip to Mexico had been all about applying a lot of violence to a very specific target.

She obviously saw I was thinking that through and smiled.

"You've no idea what a pleasure it is for me to talk to someone who thinks about what they're saying and is able to accept arguments," she said.

I didn't think I was being influenced by some subtle manipulation of aura, but carefully offered praise certainly seemed to have more effect on this body than they would have on my own body. There was obviously a skill to being male. Just as there was to being female. In the meantime, I was going to hold off on agreeing that I accepted her arguments.

"I'll leave the queen to persuade you, but I think what she's going to offer you is excellent — that you continue what you're doing against Matlal, with her help, and you act as the liaison with Altau so we don't get in each other's way."

"Why kidnap me to make that suggestion?"

"Would you have listened unless you had to?"

"I might have, and at least I wouldn't have a threat hanging over me if I didn't agree."

"A fair point, and I won't argue with you over that, other than to say she does what she does to ensure the right outcome. It's too important not to. I think you'd agree that Altau does the same."

"Hmm. All of which I understand isn't your actual suggestion..."

"You're right. Assuming you can work with us freely, my suggestion is simple. Work directly for me. Bring your House to live on the river, and enjoy the safety here, whatever happens in the physical world when Emergence hits. It's not just the safety aspect. The queen can be... difficult to work for. You're inclined to speak your mind, and she doesn't always appreciate that. I'm used to her and she's used to me. I can act as a buffer."

"That's very kind," I said. *Go me! Diplomatic or what?*

"Think about it. I'll be honest with you; this would be for my benefit as well. It would make me clearly the senior person in the queen's service. The same sort of position as a Diakon in Athanate society. I will be fair, and like the oaths you Athanate make, I will return loyalty for loyalty, trust for trust."

Her body swayed a little closer. "It doesn't have to be limited to a professional relationship either. Given my position, I don't have many options that have interested me. Certainly no one that has attracted me as much as you have in the short time we've known each other. If that arrangement worked, you'd find me flexible, energetic and enthusiastic, whichever body you chose to wear."

"You make a strong case," I said. It was the hard truth as far as parts of my body were concerned, but inside, I wasn't at all convinced.

Mirela chose that point to return. I was startled at how pale and wide-eyed she looked. I stopped dancing immediately.

"Donatienne, I believe Amber is my partner this evening," Mirela said. Her voice sounded forced.

"Of course." Gaudreau dipped her head and moved back smoothly to allow Mirela in. "We'll be resuming the dinner shortly. Enjoy the rest of the dance and think about what I said, Amber. My offer would include any... extended House or associates, in the Athanate sense."

Her eyes passed over Mirela meaningfully. Gaudreau clearly thought there was more here than there actually was.

But I *was* worried about Mirela.

"Are you okay?" I asked. I could feel the tension in her body as we began to dance.

"She has Salar," she whispered.

"What? Who?"

"I'm sorry. My Diakon, Salar Lazarescu. Kidnapping her was one of the 'tasks' she had when she went ashore."

"Is Salar all right?"

"So far, but it's clear that will only continue if I agree to do what the queen has asked."

"What has she told you to do?"

"Mainly, to persuade you to accept the queen's offer tonight."

I started to speak, but Mirela overrode me.

"And not just persuade with words. She wants me to use the connection we have in our auras. To prove to her that I'm stronger. Then she'd accept me as an ally and I would be responsible for keeping you in line."

We danced in silence for a few moments. I wasn't sure I knew every way I could be persuaded or influenced through aura; it seemed much more subtle than eukori. Regardless, I didn't feel as if Mirela was trying to force me to do anything through that route. Our auras had unconsciously reconnected, and there was nothing changed in her that I could sense.

"Why are you warning me?" I asked.

"I'm not warning you, I'm telling you because we're in this together. I gave you my word. I don't know if we've got any chance of getting out of here, but it's got to be better than my chances of getting off this boat with my mind intact."

Interesting.

"What would Vega Martine think of what you just said?"

"I'm going to deal with one problem at a time. I could equally ask what Altau would think about you making a truce with me."

I snorted. "We both have some explaining to do."

"The current problem is that we have another person to rescue. I can't leave without Salar."

I was going to argue and stopped myself. Yes, we had an agreement that didn't include Salar, but it was clear that if I thought working with Mirela was better than working alone, we had to make a new agreement.

"Okay," I conceded. "Gabrielle *and* Salar."

"Thank you."

"Still not sure how we're going to do it. I mean, do you even know where she's being held?"

"She's chained in our cabin, to remind me."

"Well, that's good. One less unknown."

The music ended, and people returned to their tables as waiters started bringing out the main course.

"You looked a bit shaken when you got back," I said as we walked to the table. "Feeling better?"

"I am," she replied and frowned. "Are you saying you actually care?"

I grimaced, surprised to find I did. "It seems you're my favorite evil bitch."

"Your bitch?" she murmured. "After we get off this goddamn boat, perhaps we should extend the truce. Just for a while. To take care of business between us."

"Don't push it."

"I wasn't thinking of pushing at all, handsome."

I wanted to laugh. Other parts of my body chose to react in different ways. It continued to be disturbing that I was being torn in two directions. I *knew* she was still an evil bitch, and yet I was starting to regard her as an ally. And I *had* been concerned for her when the queen had taken her out of the saloon.

Was this just the effect of the spirit world? One of the queen's subtle workings? Auras working together?

Or was it only my loaned body leading me astray by pumping me full of hormones?

The queen was absent from the table. Cazenave glared at us for seeming to be in better spirits than him, and Gaudreau just smiled.

The main course was a jambalaya with boudin and andouille on saffron rice. It gave off a rich paprika aroma. There was a salad with sharp dressing, and we got a smooth California red wine to replace the white.

The queen returned and entertained us with interesting and amusing stories of New Orleans from the times of the Louisiana purchase. Then, when the course was cleared and the orchestra changed to dance music again, she waved the rest of the table away.

"Leave us. It's time to talk with Amber."

Chapter 60

"How are you enjoying your cruise on my riverboat?"

Gaudreau had sort of warned me that the queen might lose her temper if I spoke my mind, but it would be better to know that, so I went for honest.

"I can't say I'm enjoying it, but it's been a better reception than I imagined I would get after killing so many of your rougarou."

If that irritated her, she didn't show it.

"The rougarou were always an experiment. Useful, but even if I produced them on an industrial scale, it would take far too long to make a difference. In any event, Emergence is coming sooner than that, and I would not want an army of rougarou. Apart from a very few, like Donatienne, their only ability is violence. It's extremely difficult to do delicate work with such a blunt tool."

"Yet you tried to take over the local packs with them."

"And failed, although I still have enough of my influenced werewolves out in the packs that it will be very difficult for the shifters to move against me."

I didn't point out that the packs knew the werewolves who'd come from her were suspect.

"I don't think of the overarching law as survival of the strongest," she said. "It's survival of the plans and people best fitted for the purpose. Rougarou will continue to provide my loyal guards, but I'm not going to unleash a horde of them on people."

Her eyes narrowed.

"I assume Donatienne has given you the basic outline of what I'm going to achieve?"

"Hmm. She said that your guiding principle was the greatest good for the greatest number."

"Yes, but everyone claims that. No one truly agrees on what's good, any more than they agree what the right balance of benefit would be between the elite and the rest. Do you know, Matlal's original concept was peace and prosperity for humanity in exchange for acknowledgment of the superiority of Basilikos." She shook her head. "Sadly, he's become so infected with Quetzalcoatl's bloodthirsty visions, humanity has sunk to the status of prey. Now, Altau's vision is much more humane. He wants the paranormals to live side by side with humanity in an open, symbiotic relationship. Laudable, but unrealistic and likely to produce even more deaths than Matlal's path."

"And you're the happy medium," I said.

"I was closer to Matlal's original ideas, until he became jealous of my powers from the spirit world and unwisely chose to deal with Quetzalcoatl. Now, it would be easier to adapt Altau's vision to mine."

Or hers to Altau's, but I didn't say that out loud.

The queen signaled a waiter for more wine.

"To achieve that," she said, "I need the very best tools for the job. I think one of those is you."

"You're very kind."

Damn, I was *really* getting the hang of this diplomacy stuff. Say anything that might mean something or nothing. Box checked.

"But where Altau tends to think the appropriate method is to make the case for the best solution and let people sign up to it," the queen went on, "*I* think we've run out of time. That means I have to work with both promises and threats."

On another occasion, I might argue that with her. Altau certainly made it clear to me what might happen if I didn't choose what he thought was the best course. And yet he remained flexible. He was able to accept actions on my part that he hadn't agreed to, and integrate them into his plans.

I got the feeling that the queen wasn't that type of person.

The dessert course came out. Light pastries I didn't recognize. The wine changed again. The rest of the table saw we were still talking and sat elsewhere to eat. A show started on the stage. Can-can dancers or something.

The queen ignored it all, and so I did as well.

"You've proved yourself beyond doubt in the physical world, in combat, with victories against the Juárez pack, and taking on and defeating Mauricio Gálvez in his impregnable fortress of Astilla de Luna. As a shifter, you more than did your part in the defeat of the rougarou at Port Allen. You're well regarded and integrated into the Were community. They've started to think your role as the witch that leads their halfies' ritual makes up for the fact that you're also Athanate."

Her lips twitched and she sampled the wine.

"You've shown that you're not simply a soldier. You've led changes in Were and Athanate communities. Helped them work together.

"Yet you're not so deep into paranormal society that you have forgotten what it is to be human. All of which is good, because the job I have planned for you is to be the visible glue that holds *all* the communities together: Athanate, Were, Adept and human. And for that, there remains one area where you still need to convince me you're the best tool for the task. Not purely for my benefit, but also for your own." She paused before continuing. "The spirit world. That's what this evening is about."

I let the list of achievements roll over me. I did what needed to be done when it presented itself to me, and they were far from a glorious roll call of wins. But this conversation was about to go downhill quickly. If she thought I was some hotshot witch, I was going to fail her test. I could channel other people's workings with the best of them, but I was the lousiest witch in the west, as far as I could see.

"So how do I do that?" I said. "How do I prove my abilities in the spirit world?"

"Nothing so spectacular as creating a substantiation," the queen replied. "You're new to it, and the actual manipulation of the spirit world and energies is second in importance to your ability to focus aura for your own purposes. So instead of something spectacular, I arranged for you to have two tasks which would demonstrate you have the capability to influence and overcome compulsion in another's aura."

Skills where I was an absolute newbie.

"I have no clear idea what you mean by that."

"You will have to understand the theory in due course. I have no doubts you can manage that. There's no time tonight, but I'll give you a basic description."

She settled herself back on her throne-like chair.

"When I talk about influencing through aura, it means changing that person's mind with direct aura-to-aura contact, but not in a damaging way. It's like convincing someone to change their mind and then letting them go off and do what you want them to do, but they're acting on their own decisions."

"Like on the pier, when I decided to get on board."

"Yes. It was barely any effort on my part because I understood you had a commitment to Gabrielle. I made sure that was strong enough to override your legitimate concerns."

I didn't let any of the reactions I had cross my face, and had no time to dwell on it as the queen went on. "Compulsion is at the far end of that same ability. Where no amount of influencing will make a person do what you want them to do, you have to compel them."

I got goosebumps and hid a shiver by drinking some more wine.

"If you can influence using your aura, you can compel, though there is a certain amount of training you would need, so I'm not expecting that from you tonight."

Small mercies. "But back to influence. You say I'm supposed to be able to influence with my aura," I said. "Without having any training, that's also impossible."

The queen found that amusing.

"The greatest lesson you will learn tonight is how much you limit yourself. Outside of what's familiar to you, you regularly persuade yourself you can't possibly do things. But here's the thing: the first of the two tasks I set for you tonight was for you to use your aura to influence Mirela to join forces with you."

"You're not saying—"

"I am. Come on, Amber, think it through. I took her back to your cabin to realistically threaten the life of her Diakon unless she did what I told her I wanted, which was for *her* to use her aura to overcome *you*. But as soon as she came back into the saloon, she made a beeline for you, and it wasn't to attack you. She told you everything, didn't she? You've already influenced her to be on your side. You've exceeded my expectations on the first test."

I couldn't deny that Mirela hadn't behaved the way I'd expected. And we had deliberately made a connection between us. But then *I* wasn't behaving as I would have expected either. So had Mirela influenced me in return?

"I'm convinced you will pass my second test too, so I need to talk to you about what will come afterwards. I take no pleasure in threats, but in the same way I offer incentives for people to work with me, I must threaten those who don't. And I must follow through with those incentives and threats so that they remain potent forces of persuasion."

"Decide to work with me, swear your Athanate oath to do it, and I'll let you go untouched. I'll even let you take Mirela with you, if she swears as well, and you undertake that she will comply. On the other hand, if you refuse to work with me, I will compel you."

"The compulsion will ruin my effectiveness."

"You couldn't perform the task I want you to, but I will find a task you could do under compulsion. It will not be pleasant, so why not work with me? It's work you're already doing, work you want to continue doing. Fighting against Matlal, coordinating between paranormal races and humanity—"

"Persuading Altau to change his course," I interrupted.

"A little, and for sound reasons, which you and Altau would all come to realize were correct."

That felt wrong, and yet I couldn't put my finger on where the problem was in the progression of her logic. I was sure it was there, and yet the more I looked, the more it slipped away from me.

"Wait," I said. "You said I could take Mirela with me. What about Gabrielle?"

"Ah. Well, Gabrielle is part of your second test tonight. I have placed a compulsion on Gabrielle. You need to overcome it. You won't be able to remove the compulsion, but you must show me you can override it. Do that, agree to work with me, and I'll see about removing Gabrielle's compulsion."

She stood.

"As I said, I regret what I have to do sometimes, but I will not flinch. You have great potential, Amber. In fact, you have a potential to achieve more than me, but I know you won't be able to grasp that opportunity, and so it falls to me to carry the burden.

"You're about to see Gabrielle and attempt your second test. I am sure you will succeed. However, I don't see that you need the rest of the night to make your decision. You have until midnight, two hours from now, to decide to work with me. Use your time wisely. I am called away, but be sure I will return in time to hear your decision."

She turned and left the saloon, crew and passengers bowing and scuttling to get out of her way.

Chapter 61

I sat at the table, still feeling confused at the way the conversation with the queen had gone.

I couldn't see why I shouldn't work with her, and yet I was still certain it was wrong at some fundamental level. But surely, with time running out and one test remaining, I had to put aside doubts?

There was a lot of movement in the saloon. Apparently, not everyone had been invited to see the part of the show with Gabrielle, and some of the passengers were leaving. I tried to ignore the distraction, but I couldn't. The ones that were left included more people with Adept abilities. I could feel a tension ratcheting up in the room, hairs standing up on my arms.

Then Mirela sat down abruptly beside me.

"You've been screwing with my head!"

I blinked.

"That's what the queen just told me I did," I said. "If it's true, I apologize."

She wasn't expecting an apology, but it set her back no more than a moment. "I thought we were going to try and work together."

"That's what it felt like we were doing. I didn't do anything consciously. What did—"

"After the queen threatened Salar I came to you to..."

She stopped, looking puzzled, as if she'd just realized what she was about to say wasn't what she had expected to come out of her mouth.

"You came to me to try and influence me?" I guessed.

"Yes, but... then you asked if I was okay... shit, this has all just been us being set against each other, hasn't it?"

"Maybe. It seems to work until we talk to each other."

"Until we re-connect auras," Mirela said. "It's not the words. I think it's the distance. We have to stick close together. Even in the same room, our connection seems to be weak when we're more than a few yards apart."

"It'll get stronger—"

"And? A pair of untrained newbies against the queen?" she interrupted me. "I don't think it'll get that strong that quickly."

"Well, she'll be gone for a couple of hours." Mirela looked skeptical so I added, "I can feel it in the boat."

"Anyway, two hours, two days; it won't make a difference against her. She's the damned Queen of Diamonds. She's been working magic for over two centuries, and she's strong enough to maintain her own personal space in the City of Lost Gods."

"Point. So why does she need us, then?"

"Is she running scared of Kaothos?" she said.

"That might account for an interest in me. You? Maybe she's running scared of Matlal, too. If he has a connection to Quetzalcoatl, and that threatens her—"

"And she thinks having the two of us provides her with some kind of point of attack on those two targets," Mirela interrupted me.

"An attack which will be stronger if we're not compelled. So she doesn't want to compel us, but for some reason she needs our auras connected."

"Not too connected, because she sets us against each other."

"Double bluff?" I suggested.

"What do you mean?"

"If she *doesn't* want us to do something, maybe the best way is to tell us not to do it."

"You think remarkably like an evil bitch for someone who calls other people evil bitches."

We laughed. One part humor and one part surprise at finding humor together.

"What else does she get from this?" I asked.

"If she has control over you," Mirela said slowly, "that might mean she had control over the one person who can provably deliver reduced infusion times for Athanate."

"Assuming that none of my ehvasi have inherited the ability."

"That's why Matlal is attacking Denver. He thought you'd be too well protected, so he wants those ehvasi. I warned him that House Trang would chew him up and spit out the pieces."

We stopped.

Both of us had been talking freely with each other, in a way we would never have done, just a day ago.

What if that was the real plan? Distract me with theories of what the queen wanted. Let me form a bond with Mirela and spill a bunch of secrets.

Or was the queen out to trap me by getting me to let my guard down with Mirela? Would a stronger aura connection give Mirela or the queen more power over me?

Was there even really a falling out among the Matlal factions?

But with nothing else I could depend on, I wanted to go with my gut reaction, and that was in favor of trusting Mirela over the queen.

"We seem to have come down to my way of doing things," I said.

Mirela snorted. "Nonsense. It was *our* decision on how to proceed. But, if someone has screwed with my head through aura, all I can say is rather you than her."

She was mirroring my thought processes.

"Is that some kind of backhanded compliment?" I asked.

"I don't know. It's probably just what an evil bitch would say." She inched closer. "Gaudreau's heading this way. If we're going to try strengthening our aura connection, we better do it before she reaches here."

The second time was easier than the first.

Neither of us really knew what we were doing. There was a reaching feeling, like I had with eukori. Then that *pop* as our auras reconnected. The light and dark of the yin-yang, each containing some part of the other. Stronger than before. Much stronger.

And yet, not strong enough to close out everything else.

Because out in the huge darkness beyond the riverboat's lights, came the looming presence of an ancient, bloody god. A hint of movement like a jaguar passing in the night. The scent of flowers. The sound of many voices, far away.

An ancient god. Waiting.

Waiting for me.

Back.

We came back with a jolt into our separate bodies, with nothing but a lingering sense that our aura connection was stronger than before. The pressure from other magic in the saloon remained there, but it felt more distant somehow.

Mirela was staring at me with narrowed eyes. "You have a lost god on speed dial or something? What's going on? Who *is* that out there?"

"*That* out there is an unpalatable option," I said. "Trust me. One step at a time. Let's get Gabrielle first."

As Gaudreau reached our table, the fake Remy mounted the stage to stand in front of theater curtains.

"You realize this is a competition—" Mirela was interrupted by Remy.

"*Mesdames, messieurs,*" he called out as conversations died out. "The grand finale of tonight's entertainment. A new show. An amazing challenge. We present for your delight a beautiful young Adept from

Canada. Gabrielle, a favorite of the Hecate of the Northern Leagues, and a powerful witch in her own right. All her skills remain intact, ladies and gentlemen, but the Queen of Diamonds has worked her cleverest magic. The prize? The young lady's charms and her skills will be yours and yours alone to command. She will do entirely as you wish. She will cast at your requirement and live for your slightest demand. Above all, she will satisfy you, because the queen has commanded that she must. But first... first, you must win the challenge against all others present."

He made a sweeping gesture over the crowd.

I looked at some of them and understood that the queen had raised the stakes for me. Failing at this task was not just failing for me, it was failing Gabrielle. It was leaving her a slave for the winner.

"How to win? Indeed. The strength of your aura, ladies and gentlemen. Gabrielle will submit to the strongest individual aura. The winner will be the person she bestows her favor on. One word of warning. She may touch you, but you would be well advised not to touch her until you have won the lady."

He laughed and raised his arms.

"On! On with the Dance of Medusa."

Chapter 62

The lights flickered and went down.

Clever with the hurricane lamps, Tara snarked. *But still a cheap trick.*

It worked: I came up in goosebumps. It wasn't just the lighting. Magic wound its way around the saloon, and the air itself prickled with an electric charge, like before a storm. There was the feel of a breath in my ear, a word someone was about to say. A memory that shimmered and slipped away.

A player in the darkness where the orchestra sat picked out a few quiet, plaintive notes on a Spanish guitar. Another sketched out an outline of a rhythm on the drums, as if practicing.

Every eye was fixed on the stage.

We were all caught by surprise—lightning flared through the saloon's open windows and doors, blinding me. There was a sharp clap of thunder, and a sudden wind which blew through the saloon, rich with the scent of rain on the river.

I blinked. I hadn't seen the stage curtains open, but they were now, and a stubby, flat-topped pyramid shape filled the gap. On top of the pyramid, indistinct in the light, a writhing darkness moved and twisted to the sound of an oboe now rising above the guitar and drums.

"What?"

The darkness was shifting, swaying above like a tall crop in the breeze, flaring out below.

A Hindu goddess?

A headdress? A cloak?

I couldn't see clearly, but there seemed to be too many limbs. Maybe there were two people dancing close together. More.

Small lamp flames spurted from the lowest level of the pyramid, revealing its stepped Aztec style.

On the top, a figure turned and turned, seemed to spin faster and faster. A cloak flowed out, obscuring the details. But then something went wrong. The cloak became unclipped. It fell in a waterfall of silk, right into the row of flames, and caught fire in a rush, like a distress flare.

There were shouts. The threat of fire on a wooden ship. Chairs banged backward as people leaped up and onto the stage.

But there was no fire. No cloak. No figure.

Just the empty pyramid, with a curl of smoke above it that seemed to move in time to the only sound on the ship, the music from the guitar, oboe and drum. Spiraling, around and around. Driven by a pulse that throbbed in every dry throat.

The chandelier above the roulette table guttered, making us all turn.

The dancer was there, in the shadows, every now and then some part of her skin catching and reflecting the warm glow of the lights.

Gabrielle, dressed in a sort of harness of black leather straps, with a necklace of beads, a feathered headdress... and two rattlesnakes, each over twelve feet long.

Her head and feet were still. Her arms and hips moved sinuously, like the music, around and around. The snakes were draped over her shoulders, heads and tails weaving shapes like extra arms, tongues testing the air, eyes glittering, rattles shaking.

Were the snakes following the hands, or the other way around?

She stepped onto a chair, then down onto the floor, each movement slow and timed to the beat of the music.

People fell back as she paced forward, each of her steps deliberate as a stalking cat. Everyone knew rattlesnakes didn't grow as big as anacondas, but they *looked* like rattlesnakes, and they *sounded* like rattlesnakes, so maybe they *bit* like rattlesnakes.

She used an abandoned chair to step up onto one of the dining tables.

She whirled and weaved. Reached down smoothly to pick up a brandy bottle from the table. Beckoned to the man standing closest.

It was one of the passengers. Someone nudged him forward, and he ended up pressed against the table, looking up with his mouth slack, hypnotized by the dance.

Gabrielle poured a little brandy over her fingers and wiped them over his lips.

One of the snakes hissed and he stumbled backwards.

She stepped down via another chair.

A man half reached out to her with one hand.

The nearest snake head shot at him and stopped, mouth wide, ready to strike.

He fell over.

There was nervous laughter, people shuffling out of her way as she headed for another table.

"She's moving away. Do something," Mirela hissed.

My first mistake had been to try and combine Mirela's aura with mine. If it was like eukori, then our auras would be stronger working together.

But reaching out to Gabrielle... there was nothing there to connect with. It was like trying to grab smoke.

Remy had said the strongest *individual* aura.

I disentangled myself from Mirela, ignoring the whisper of the riverboat all around me, the odd music, and leaned back in my chair, arms resting on the table.

Comfortable and in control.

Gabrielle had said that was the way to prepare for projecting my aura.

What had worked that time when she'd directed me in a spirit walk to Weaver's house?

The feel of the halfy ritual. The pulse of Native American beats. The thought that I would get up and dance, any second now, and when I did, there would be smoke all around, with figures dancing through it, spirit and flesh.

My boots twitched and I tapped out a rhythm with my fingers on the tabletop. HEY-ya, hey-ya, hey-ya, HEY-ya, hey-ya, hey-ya.

Warmth. Eyes shut. Calm. Floating.

Now I see the riverboat whole again. Old gods. Gods so ancient they have forgotten their names, and they manifest as trees and have their forms bent and locked together. They hold us up in the shape the queen has forced them to.

This will end, they sigh. Bonds and shapes and desires are fleeting. Such things pass and we will remain.

The saloon is full of ghosts. They flicker and stir like restless dreamers, half aware, pursuing the unattainable.

Cease and join with us, whisper the gods. Let the heart cease to beat. Let the lungs cease to strive. Simply be.

I breathe in, long and slow, filling myself with the dream of life.

And exhale. My breath becomes a thread, a tendril, a serpent of aura. It moves to the beat I have given it, overcoming the music of ghosts, brushing aside the dreamers.

Their dream of music falters and becomes one with mine.

And across the room, the dancer hesitates.

My eyes snapped open as Gabrielle's head turned and she looked over her shoulder, directly at me.

It was Gabrielle, and it wasn't. She wasn't some servant of the queen wearing Gabrielle's face. Gabrielle was *there*, somewhere beneath the compulsion, unable to rise.

Her head was tilted back and her mouth open in pleasure.

There was no recognition of me in her eyes, only of the call of my aura.

Heartbeats stretched out.

The lights flickered, fell to pitch blackness, and when they returned, Gabrielle was kneeling on my table, looking at me with an utter concentration mirrored by the snakes.

There were cries and a babble of words from the other people in the saloon. It was just noise to me.

Other auras tried to make a connection with Gabrielle. I brushed them away like cobwebs.

Gabrielle's body continued to move, though it was my music it moved to now, while her snakes wove their patterns around me, their tongues tasting the air, and their rattles shaking in my ears.

I stayed absolutely still, apart from my hands keeping the beat going on the table.

Our eyes were locked.

Gabrielle?

A shadow seemed to pass behind her eyes, but then they closed. The snake heads turned from me and began to slide up her body and against her face. Hands moved, tracking upwards. She groaned and I got a sudden insight. The queen's compulsion rewarded her for following the queen's orders. She was in ecstasy.

Her hands went behind her neck and when they returned, her necklace was swinging in front of my eyes like a hypnotist's watch.

I raised my hand slowly.

The beads of the necklace collected in my palm, circling, growing.

A heartbeat where it stopped.

A flash of lightning, followed by darkness.

I felt the fall of the rest of the necklace into my hand.

When the lights returned, there was no Gabrielle on the table.

Chapter 63

I wound the necklace around my fist like a rosary, and worked the beads through my fingers.

"It seems Gabrielle has favored you," Gaudreau said. "The queen was sure she would, but congratulations anyway."

One bead, two, three and on. They were slightly slippery, warm from Gabrielle's body.

Her body. Was Gabrielle really still inside? Or was she a sort of living zombie?

If she was there, had she tried to pass me a sign in the necklace? A message, like Chatima had once left for me in a necklace?

Beads passed through my fingers, but if there was a message, I wasn't reading it yet.

I'd lost that place of calmness I'd needed to spirit walk. But my aura was still wide open, registering the people in the crowd.

There was anger and jealousy, but one stood out from the others like a dark rock on the seashore.

Cazenave.

"I challenge," he said, leaning over the table.

"The contest has ended. What exactly are you challenging?" Gaudreau said.

"This..." Cazenave gestured angrily at the whole saloon. "This was just a show. There was no contest. That girl did what the queen wanted her to do."

Gaudreau shrugged. "If you think she did, then you'd need to take it up with the queen."

"No! The queen said to me that I would have an opportunity to win my freedom. Even if the contest wasn't rigged, I couldn't do that. I have no skills with aura. So my opportunity is now with a challenge to House Farrell."

"What would you hope to achieve?"

"If I win, I take Farrell, Tucek and the girl back to Matlal. This will repair the damage that the queen has done by kidnapping me. If not... You all think you're safe here, on the queen's riverboat in the queen's little corner of the City of Lost Gods, but you aren't. Matlal is more powerful."

"Putting your threats of Matlal's power aside, what does the queen get from this?"

"She becomes Matlal's second in command. Matlal will give Vega Martine to her."

"That's a bold suggestion. What makes you think you can deliver it?"

I could see Cazenave thought he knew something about Matlal's plans. He thought that what he was suggesting was something he could deliver.

Gaudreau saw it too, but she wasn't going to take all the responsibility.

"The queen said you would have the opportunity to earn your freedom, without specifying how, but that didn't include the right to make side deals." She shrugged. "I'll split the difference. If you succeed in your challenge against Farrell, you win your right to freedom and I'll throw in Gabrielle as well. If you want more, then you can petition the queen on her return."

"What challenge did you have in mind, Cazenave?" I said. "I'm guessing you're not talking auras."

Laughter from the crowd.

Cazenave's face went pale, but he kept himself under control.

He pointed to the far wall, above the dance floor, where some military-style decorations hung.

"Sabers. You've taken the appearance of a cavalry officer. Either admit it's just a sham, or accept the choice of weapon. Surely nothing could be more appropriate."

"Trick," Mirela hissed in my ear. "Don't do that."

I smiled.

With what he had to work with, Cazenave had set this up well. If I refused his choice, he'd make out that I was refusing his challenge and he'd won. I didn't know if Gaudreau would back me against that, but I couldn't risk it. Not with Gabrielle as the prize. I'd have to take his choice and beat him.

With a damned cavalry saber.

"Okay. Let's do it. I assume they're not just display weapons?" I asked Gaudreau.

"They're working weapons and kept razor sharp." She made a sign and some crew hurried to fetch the sabers.

Mirela was whispering in my ear. "He's a championship fencer, Amber. He wins competitions against other Athanate, and the saber is his favored weapon."

"I'll take care never to face him in a competition." I grinned at her. "I've had an excellent instructor. Think on who that might be."

Mirela eyes widened. "House Trang?" Then she frowned. "But it would take years to learn her skills."

"Not necessarily. Help me get my boots off, please."

Her eyebrow twitched, but she didn't argue.

The boots had been good for dancing, but I wanted to feel the floor when I fought.

My bare feet touched the floor and I felt a little shock as the awareness of the old gods returned. I'd need to ignore them for the moment.

I stood and took my jacket off.

"Kill him for me," Mirela muttered.

I thought for a moment she was going to lean in and kiss me, but she stopped the movement short, and just took my jacket instead.

"No. I'm not going to kill him, and I'm not doing it for you," I said. "I'm doing it for Gabrielle."

"I understand about Gabrielle, but why get squeamish about killing him? Unless Gaudreau stops him, that's what he'll do to you."

I stretched my neck and started to loosen my muscles up. "I'm not sure. Working with aura has a lot to do with the symbolism you use to manipulate it. My gut says killing someone tonight is a bad idea." I shrugged. "Or maybe I'm afraid that there are workings here in the spirit world that would use something like that to sneak into my head."

She nodded.

I walked to the dance floor, and one of the boat's crewmen stepped up and handed me a saber.

It was a cavalry saber. The old style that they'd called wristbreakers. It was heavy, formed by a yard of slightly curved steel, sharpened on both edges, with a leather-wrapped hilt and a three-bar guard that gave protection to the fist. Bian had given me a session with this style of sword. We'd had blunt weapons and enough padding that I was only badly bruised by the end of the session.

I was no expert, but one thing Bian and I had agreed on before we'd even started training was that being an expert in a weapon wasn't always a guarantee of success.

I felt the weight of it, tried a couple of diagonal slashes, a thrust. I had an odd double memory. This loaned body had muscle memory of using the saber, as if the queen had taken someone's memories and passed them to me with the loaned body. And I had memories from Bian's training.

I could almost hear Bian's voice: *Stop holding the sword. There is no sword. It's part of you.*

Long, painful sessions, with Bian's bokken like a living thing, made of air when I tried to strike it, made of lead when it struck me.

I rolled my wrist. This body had powerful, flexible wrists. The muscles were strong and quick. If the queen's substantiation had handicapped Cazenave as much as me, we were both going to be fighting at Athanate levels of speed and power, but our ability to heal from injuries was at a more human level.

I quickly found the loaned muscle memories weren't much use. Whoever the queen had taken them from, he'd actually been a cavalryman. His use of the sword had been slashing from horseback.

Cazenave was testing out his saber by running through a series of lunges and fencing poses. They all looked very good. Something you'd see in a manual.

I swapped hands a couple of times.

I was ready. I began to weave a figure eight with the saber tip.

"Messieurs," Remy called out.

The crowd had formed a ring around the dance floor.

"A contest of skill with the blade," Remy said. "No rounds, no rests, no points. You may concede or be unable to continue, at which point the contest is over. Are these understood and agreed?"

We nodded.

I kept my saber moving in its figure eight path. I could tell it was irritating Cazenave.

I swapped hands again. Saber on my left. Swapped back. It wasn't a clever move because the guard getting in the way made the change uncertain, but Cazenave's eyes narrowed. He started thinking about what he would need to do to combat a left-handed attack.

He took up the classic fencer's pose, side on, starting with his saber held toward me, the tip level with his eyes. Then he went through the fencing formalities: heels together, feet making a right angle, saber lowered and held slightly away from me. Moved gracefully back into the basic en garde and saluted me with the saber.

I stood in a neutral stance, good for almost any martial art: legs bent, weight evenly distributed, slightly angled to lead with my right hand. I made no acknowledgment of his salute. The tip of my saber continued its dance.

"You would be thrown out of any competition for refusing the salute," Cazenave sneered.

"This is not a fencing competition," I replied. "There are no competition judges watching. And that thing in your hand is a real blade. A cavalry saber."

"*En garde!*" Remy called out.

I ignored him. I had no intention of playing by any rules other the ones he'd announced.

"*Allez!*"

Cazenave feinted a thrust. I ignored it, continuing my pattern. I had no interest in extending this bout any longer than necessary, but neither did I want to rush in.

Anger. He didn't like what he perceived as a lack of respect.

He launched a genuine attack, his weight forward, committed. I let his blade sing against the outer edge of mine and moved to the right.

He was back in, quick as a snake. High then low.

This time I pushed his blade to the right and stepped back to where I'd started from.

Then as he stepped back, I swapped hands.

Dangerous, but I wanted this done. I wanted him second-guessing and third-guessing.

The problem was, he was better than that.

He launched a flurry of blows, each seeming quicker and harder to stop. My left side was weaker. Not a problem against a lesser opponent, but I'd underestimated Cazenave.

A slashing blow came, low to high, intended to gut me.

I sprang back, feeling the ice-cold shock. The passage of the tip, through the shirt and across the skin of my chest, opening it. The heat of my blood. The shout of the crowd.

I landed with my saber back in my right hand and I nearly caught him as he overbalanced to return his blade. He was too quick for my thrust at his belly, but I nicked his forearm.

Now we were both bleeding.

As Athanates in the physical world, the cuts were nothing.

I didn't know how slowly my body might heal in the spirit world.

We'd shocked each other. Both of us had underestimated our opponent, but I now knew how good he was.

He was far better than me as a fencer. It was time to change to my style.

First... make it quicker and force him out of his style. I charged him. In a competition, the game must stay on the mat. A few steps back and he could stop everything.

Not this time.

I slashed up and kept the saber high, the tip threatening his face, but leaving my body open.

Hearing the crowd parting behind him, with the wall looming to prevent any further retreat, he switched to attack.

Both my hands were high. My chest and stomach were targets. He lunged. I could see him sensing a trap, and holding himself well balanced, ready to back away.

Bian in my head: *Movement is commitment. Absence of movement is commitment.*

I kept charging wildly, knowing that his blade would find a target. Not what an opponent would do in a competition, and surely not what an opponent would do in a battle—wound himself.

Bian again, every sentence accompanying a painful strike. *There is no game. There is no judge. There is no time. There is no pain. There is one purpose. There is one rule. There is one outcome. Win.*

My hands were raised, out of position. My saber pointing down. Fatally weak position. I had abandoned my defense.

My blade turned his from stabbing me through the heart, but it was too weak to block entirely. I felt the shock of his blade's point against my ribs, no pain yet, the saber passing through shirt and skin as if they were a dream in a world of steel. But my bones were not dreams and his blade was upright. It couldn't pass between my ribs. There was a rasp, metal on bone, once felt, never forgotten.

And my left arm was descending, my body was still pushing forward.

There is no pain. There is one purpose.

Too late he understood that he couldn't swing or thrust with a sword if his opponent was inside the reach of his blade. And that my left arm now trapped both blades in the bloody mess between us.

A competition would stop if the blades were caught. Reset. Return to your places, gentlemen. *En garde.*

Not here.

I hit him with the guard of my saber. I hit his nose, my whole strength and momentum behind it. Instant disqualification in a competition.

A saber has edges for slashing cuts, the point for thrusts. Everyone forgets the hilt and the guard.

A blow to the nose is painful, stunning, massively distracting. The brain freezes. Martial arts experts claim they can kill with it.

I didn't care about any of that except the part about stunning.

Pain was flaring in my chest. Skin tearing. Muscle.

I hit him again. And again.

Because my right arm was raised, elbow high, out of position for fencing, he couldn't hit me back except to the body, even if he'd been aware enough to do it.

By the third blow, he was scarcely aware enough to realize his only option was to drop the saber and retreat. Or concede.

I wasn't interested in his surrender.

There is one outcome.

I hit him again. Blood exploded from his facial injuries.

My knee came up into his groin. His legs started to buckle and I stamped sideways into his knee.

He collapsed. His saber cut free of me and clattered onto the floor.

Blood everywhere.

I followed him down, hit him with the guard again.

Again.

Someone was gripping my wrist.

"Stop!"

Mirela.

"Stop, Amber. No need. You've won. You said you didn't want to kill him. You won't want to remember this later if you do."

There really was blood everywhere.

I stood, with my feet in it, with my hands red with it, my chest sliced open and bleeding. I stood in the unbeating heart of the riverboat. Panting. Drinking in the sheer size of the queen's power in this place.

And forced to look inside me. To judge and find myself wanting.

I couldn't defeat the queen.

We were of the same nature, the two of us. Dark magic, blood magic, but she was far more powerful than me here, in her own long-prepared substantiation.

She was not omnipotent. There were ways she could be tricked. Ways to get around her. The old African gods that were the bones and blood and body of this ship could see that. But the same dispassionate gaze they turned on her works was turned on me. They knew me. They recognized me.

I couldn't defeat the queen here.

But I had a path, a way. It had a price.

It always does.

Chapter 64

"If there are no more challenges?" Mirela called out to the crowd.

A woman stepped forward with a glint in her eye.

Smart move. I was weakened and tired from fighting Cazenave.

Also stupid, apparently.

"I chall—"

The woman got no further.

Mirela lashed out. Being in pants rather than a dress helped with her kicking technique, which was too showy for my tastes, but exceptionally effective. The challenger was launched over the craps table to land in a shuddering heap, where she lay twitching.

"Any more challenges?"

A silence had descended in the saloon, broken only by the sounds of the last challenger sucking air, struggling to breathe.

Gaudreau stood to one side, watching. She raised her hands in an 'all yours' gesture.

"We'd like Gabrielle in our cabin," I said.

"She's there now," Gaudreau said.

I nodded and turned my attention to the journey. A couple of sets of stairs. A few feet and I could sit down in the cabin. Until then, I'd have to concentrate on not falling over.

Mirela and I started walking, and Gaudreau fell in alongside us.

The remaining passengers and crew moved away from us. You could understand it. One of us was still holding a sword, and the other had just kicked a woman right over a table.

"You make an impressive team," Gaudreau said. "I extend the offer I made to Amber to both of you. It will be much better for you to work through me. The queen knows me. I can get concessions from her that you won't be able to."

"We'll think about it," I said.

We reached the bottom of the steps up to the middle walkway, and Gaudreau stopped.

"I understand. The queen will be returning in half an hour. She'll want your answer by then."

"She'll get it," I said.

"One other thing."

We paused on the steps, even though I was feeling unsteady.

"The compulsion on Gabrielle... First of all, do *not* try and remove it. I can sense that you've been gathering strength the entire time you've been here in the spirit world, but you are not up to this level. Any attempt will have a disastrous consequence for Gabrielle. Wait for the queen to reverse it."

"Which she may or may not do, and will choose her time," I said.

"Which she *will* do, when she feels the lesson about her power has been completely understood." Gaudreau shifted her weight. "I'm sorry for Gabrielle. It was her resistance and the lack of time available that resulted in such an unsubtle compulsion."

"What do you mean?" Mirela said. "Unsubtle?"

"There was no time to create a compulsion that worked on her higher motivations so that she could feel like a normal person following her own decisions, even though she wasn't. The queen was forced to tap into very basic controlling options. While this compulsion is operating, even though she currently has her skills and abilities, she's child-like. She needs simple instructions that she can perform, and reassurance when she does. She has an intense desire to please you."

"That is sick," I said. So much for diplomacy.

"I understand," Gaudreau said. "Look, I don't like it. Try not to bring it up in those words with the queen. I promise, I'll ask her to remove it. She'll listen to me more than to you."

"Thank you," Mirela said, while I struggled to say something that wouldn't be insulting.

We left Gaudreau standing there. Mirela guided me up the stairs.

"Is Gaudreau on your shit list now?" Mirela whispered as we began the second flight up to our level.

I felt lightheaded. "I think you're jealous. The queen is on my *real* shit list, which is a list of one. Gaudreau is on the next list. And you're still on that one as well, after we get off the riverboat."

"Looking forward to getting off with you," Mirela said, opening the cabin door. "Interested to know how."

A woman staggered up from where she'd been crouching in the middle of the room, chained with a huge bolt set into the floor.

"Mirela!" I could see her sense my marque. "*Farrell?*"

Salar, I assumed. Diakon Tucek.

Gabrielle was sitting on the bed, still dressed in the peculiar straps she'd danced in. As soon as she saw me, a huge smile broke across her face.

For one glorious moment I thought the compulsion was gone, and Gabrielle was back as I knew her.

"You're here. What can I do?" She knelt at my feet and looked up. I couldn't decide which was worse, the look in the saloon when she'd danced, or the look she gave me now. The eyes saw me, but not as Amber.

Child-like.

The room seemed darker. I wanted to kill the queen. I wanted to scream and I couldn't, for Gabrielle's sake.

"That's very good, Gabrielle. All I need at the moment is for you to sit quietly." I put down the saber and pulled out one of the rattan chairs for her. "Here."

She sat down, hands in her lap, and watched me.

I sank into another chair.

Mirela had brought Salar up do date with a succinct summary.

They were trying to see how far the chains allowed her to move.

"Here." I knelt beside them and put my bloody hands onto the floor. "Let me."

The room spun, but I reached down, down into the unbeating heart of the riverboat, where it was still and quiet and as dark as my soul.

I took hold of the bolt in the floor and lifted it. The wood parted, and flowed back when the bolt was gone.

"Neat trick!" Salar said. There was no way she was any friend of mine, but she was taking her cue from Mirela.

"Not my trick. I find friends in strange places," I muttered. It seemed a very long way up, so I just lay down and listened to the old gods speaking in many voices.

Wake from your dream. Join us in the forest of night. Let striving cease. Be immutable. Here, with us, nothing changes, nothing matters. We do not live or die. We endure. There is no pain. No decay. No future or past. An eternal present. Hear the song the stars sing to us.

Mirela and Salar tore off what was left of my shirt.

And then they started licking my wounds.

Chapter 65

I wanted to say something clever, but as soon as I opened my mouth, Mirela told me to shut up.

In changing my body, the queen seemed to have put some blocks on my Athanate abilities. Bad as my wounds were, they would have stopped bleeding quickly back in the physical world, in my own body. Not here.

But Mirela and Salar hadn't been changed or blocked. Their Athanate healing abilities were fine. The bleeding stopped. I could feel the flesh start its process of repair.

And with great timing, the rest of my body decided that blood would be better diverted to other areas, which made Salar snicker.

"You're going to have to feed, Amber."

Nothing was making much sense. Least of all Mirela's words and her wrist pressed against my lips. She was offering me Blood?

"Don't think I can," I mumbled. "Blocked. Part of the working that changed my body."

"Don't give me that shit. If you're going to be able to get us out of here, you're going to have to do better against a simple block."

After a few seconds, she swore again, and I felt her move. There was a weight across me.

"Can't help Gabrielle if you can't help yourself," she said softly into my ear.

"You mean help *you*," I shot back.

"Naturally. As well."

Her throat pressed against my lips. I could feel her pulse calling to me. My tongue stretched out and touched. There were responses from all over my body, but the one that really surprised me was the familiar, urgent ache in my jaw.

It turned out my body's fang-memory was stronger than the queen's suppression.

Good to know.

Not so good was that the sudden need erased any caution about opening eukori with Mirela.

No more joking and evasions.

Eukori and aura were the same phenomenon, but different aspects. Not like two sides of a coin. More like two sides of a face.

Eukori shared sensation and emotion. It allowed me to invoke physical changes in another person—to slow their heart or speed their healing. Aura worked on the mind and spirit.

I could influence someone using eukori. There was some truth in what Basilikos and others said, that my Athanate abilities to invoke pleasure in another person could have the overall effect of changing that person's view of me. But aura could work more directly. It could be used, as the queen had used it, to influence and persuade. Subtly used, the person wouldn't even be aware of their mental states changing.

A pair of newbies like Mirela and me had effectively slammed our auras together and hoped for a good result.

In the searing glow of pleasure as my fangs pierced her neck, I saw my visualization of our auras combining as yin-yang was surprisingly accurate. Light and dark twisted around each other. Each took some part of the other. Became a little more like the other.

My aura was more trained. It was stronger. Mirela's aura was older. More layered.

We both moved. Changed. Became capable of doing things differently.

We were both compromised. More so now that we'd used eukori as well.

And we both understood this entanglement wasn't temporary. Against all common sense, we had the beginning of a binding between us. The ramifications of that spread out like ripples in a perfect pond, echoing off the shores and returning to collide with the next set.

The image of this disaster hypnotized us.

Luckily Salar was Carpathian too, and her eukori was strong enough to break into our stunned contemplation.

"Running out of time," she hissed at us when we had enough attention to spare.

We made it worse. Boosted by Salar, our joint eukori slipped out of control and flowed out over the ship.

In the saloon, Gaudreau looked up and got to her feet.

"She's on her way," Salar said, as my fangs disappeared.

I licked Mirela's neck quickly where it was bleeding. Having broken through the queen's block on parts of my Athanate capabilities, my healing abilities had returned. The bleeding stopped.

We disentangled from each other and stood. I could have done with a lot more rest and recovery, but there wasn't time. The boat told me that Gaudreau was already climbing the second set of stairs.

"She's alone," I said. "Let her in, Mirela. Gabrielle, go stand by the doorway to the bathroom, please. Open the door a little and keep looking inside until I tell you otherwise."

I picked up the saber and hid behind the door.

"Are you sure?" Salar didn't trust me. She looked to Mirela.

"She can force her way in, or get reinforcements," Mirela said. "We need to get her inside, alone. Pretend your chain is still bolted to the floor."

That was what Gaudreau saw when the door opened—nothing suspicious. I was obviously cleaning up my wounds in the bathroom, watched by Gabrielle. Salar was glaring from the floor.

Mirela had opened the door to her knock and stepped aside.

Gaudreau came in and sensibly stopped when she felt the steel of the saber at her throat.

"One move," I said, kicking the door closed. "One call for help." The blade pressed enough to dimple the skin of her neck.

Salar stood up.

"What do you think you're doing?" Gaudreau's voice was hoarse. "The queen will be back in ten minutes."

"In ten minutes, the rest of us won't be here. You have a choice, *Donatienne*. You can stay and face the queen, or come with us."

Mirela and Salar looked as if they'd been slapped.

"Wha—" Salar shut up before she even finished the question. Mirela trusted me. Salar trusted Mirela. I would have to work with that for now.

Gaudreau kept very still.

"*If* you were gone, and I was still here, I wouldn't survive," she said. "If you're still here, and I've obviously been captured, it would be a little better. Please."

"You understand. Good." To the others: "Rip up some bedsheets and tie her up. Gag her."

They were quick and efficient.

I brought Gabrielle back and sat her down again.

"Seven minutes left. Can you do it?" Mirela said. "What if the queen comes back early and finds Gaudreau missing?"

I tapped the wooden floor with my foot, still bare after the fight. "I'll know as soon as she's back, but it won't happen like that. Trust me when I say this is all going to hell in a couple of minutes."

I sat in one of the chairs and ran my hands tiredly over my familiar/unfamiliar face.

"In fact, just trust me," I said.

"You have that god or whatever lurking outside. Call him," Mirela said. "Him. It. Whatever."

"I can call him and we can *talk*. Basic spirit walk, but we need to get ourselves *physically* out of this riverboat and not just dumped into the City of Lost Gods with no way home. He can't come in and pluck us out of the queen's substantiation unless we open a portal and move ourselves outside of her barriers. That's what I think I've worked out."

"You *think*—" Salar started.

"So how do we do that?" Mirela interrupted. "I know you have an idea."

"It's a fine balance and a short timescale. I need your help to make this portal, but I also need to bargain with the god to protect you."

Gaudreau had gone pale. She would have said something if she hadn't been gagged.

Mirela noticed. "Who is this god?"

"His name is Tezcatlipoca. Thanks to what passes for humor in my House, I call him T-cat."

Gaudreau moaned and started to struggle.

I put a hand on her. "I am not presenting you as sacrifices, Donatienne. None of you. That's why I have to bargain."

"Tezcatlipoca. The enemy of Quetzalcoatl," Mirela said.

"And also the *brother* of Quetzalcoatl. He shares his vices." Salar shuddered. "This is an improvement on our situation?"

"It will be."

"You sure? What are you bargaining with?" Mirela asked.

"Myself. T-cat wants me as his priestess."

"Seriously? With all that entails?"

"No! I'm not doing what Matlal is doing. I'm not going to build pyramids and tear the hearts out of people on the altar to feed him. I have to persuade T-cat that the defeat of his brother is more important to him."

They had questions, but I overrode them.

"I need your help to open the portal. We have to do it quickly. As soon as we start, the queen will know we're punching holes in her substantiation. I have to get through and reach a deal in seconds so you'll be protected while I'm gone."

"Wait! You're not coming with us?"

"No," I said. "Gabrielle needs help that T-cat can't provide. I have to get back to New Orleans or Denver to take her to the Hecate. And I have to rush, because then, I need to come back and finish the queen as a threat."

"You and whose army? You can't match her."

"Well, I have ideas about that, but it has to be done soon. Her power will never be this low again. She's lost her rougarou, her prisoners and her captain, all in the space of a couple of days. Her own self-doubt is what will make her weak until she recovers."

"Why not take us with you, then? We can help."

"Because if I take you back to New Orleans, either it would be as captives, or everyone would be suspicious of me. I can't spend time arguing when I need to be gathering my army."

"You make a deal with a Lost God, and they're going to be more than suspicious."

"It's necessary. If for nothing else, they need this to balance Matlal's advantage."

They'd understand. Yes, I needed to do a deal to save my own skin, but with the City of Lost Gods anchored over the physical world by Matlal's connection to Quetzalcoatl, Skylur and his allies needed a counter.

Despite my confident words, this was a Hail Mary pass in overtime.

I had been gathering myself for this effort as I spoke. I wasn't recovered from the fight, hadn't had a decent night's sleep in days, and I wasn't trained in the powers I was trying to use...

I pulled Mirela and Salar into my eukori. That felt almost familiar.

Should I use Gaudreau as well?

She might know a way to project through the queen's substantiation.

No. I couldn't risk it.

I spoke carefully so as not to lose concentration. "Gabrielle, I need to use your aura to focus us."

The queen had left her skills intact, but she was in no state to understand and implement what we needed, so I went on: "You'll need to pass control of the focus to me. But I'll need you to tell me what to do."

"Yes," she answered.

I felt the addition of her aura to our mix. It was an odd mixture of power and knowledge with no focus.

"That's good. Come sit on the ground in front of me."

When she'd directed my first spirit walk, she'd stood behind me and braided my hair. I tried to pass my memory of that sensation of simple pleasure through my eukori.

For all their doubts about what was happening, Mirela and Salar helped.

It began to work; Gabrielle relaxed against me. The tension left her shoulders.

I eased my aura deeper. I could sense the queen's compulsion, locked like an animal around Gabrielle's mind, shimmering dangerously if I got close.

I needed more time to learn how to work with aura, but that wasn't possible now.

"We need to be ready to spirit walk, Gabrielle. You remember how to do that?"

"Oh, yes."

I could feel the movement in her aura, the way it felt as if we were about to leap out of our bodies.

"Very good. Now we're going to need to prepare two portals at the same time. Can you do that?"

I remembered her saying she could, in a conversation back in Denver. It all seemed so long ago.

I felt our aura shift, and split.

"Good. This is going to be the difficult part, because we have to push through the barrier holding us. When I say 'go', I'll push forward and you push backward. We use all the strength that we have together. Both of us have to get through. Okay?"

"Yes," she said.

"When you get out, I want you to think of..." I stopped. She didn't even remember me. "I want you to look for some friends who are looking for us. Maybe they'll be in New Orleans, or Denver. Look for friends. And whatever you do looking that way, I'll be doing the same thing, looking for someone who wants to reach me on my side."

"I understand. Friends. Looking for us."

Every simple, robotic answer made me angrier.

I felt the riverboat stir beneath us, start shrinking into itself again; the queen was coming back. We were all out of time.

"Go!"

Chapter 66

I couldn't spare much attention to her once we started.

I felt what she was doing, the strange sensation of leaping forward, like her aura lunging forward in a fencer's thrust. I copied it.

There was a numbing, deadening resistance. We failed.

"Again! Go!"

The boat shivered and groaned. The queen knew what we were doing; she was hurrying back, and we were well short of getting out.

You are strong enough. Tara. *You just have to convince your...*

No time.

I grabbed Gaudreau. Lifted her arm. Fangs manifested. Bit down on her wrist.

She was screaming. Mirela held her. Salar helped.

I *pulled.* Gaudreau's Blood raced through my taryma, lighting them up. Pleasure exploded through my body, and it felt like nothing could stop me.

We were all wrapped together, physically and in eukori. I lifted Gaudreau with us into our bonded auras. There was no need for me to speak again. Everyone felt my aura tense. I grabbed Gabrielle. Everyone joined in and we leaped together.

Into the vast temple of night. Into the presence of a waiting god.

I'd left Gabrielle's necklace wound around my wrist. It slipped and I caught the beads. Began to work them through my fingers.

I had reached the end of the road on this denial.

Each bead passed, and I wrote in letters of fire in the obsidian air: *chi, rho, upsilon.*

My heart thundered in my chest. No breath seemed enough for my lungs. I felt the others around me, terrified, wondering. All of us crushed beneath the weight of unseen eyes.

The beads moved again, and the remaining letters blazed.

Sigma... omicron... sigma.

"*Chrysos,*" whispered Mirela. "You acknowledge it, then. You are the Golden House of Carpathia."

"And all that it entails, here, in the temple of night." I raised my voice. "I am here, Tezcatlipoca, as you knew I would be."

A gale of laughter.

"Welcome. You bring me offerings."

"No. I bring friends for safekeeping."

"Friends?"

There were braziers in the darkness, but I knew better than to ask him to light them.

I'd done it in a dream before, but this was no dream. I was here, physically, in T-cat's temple within the City of the Lost Gods.

I raised my hands, felt the heat in them, and *tasted* the path down from the night sky, where the power brooded. Lightning crashed down and wood exploded into flame in two braziers.

Now we could see him.

He was unchanged from my dream visit. Beautiful, marked with bands across his face, cloaked, adorned with feathers and furs, and that breastplate that reflected no light.

"Friends," I repeated.

"To be protected from the upstart swamp witch. You seek favors. Yet you deny me." He moved, jaguar-like, stalking forward to stand between the braziers.

"I don't now. I am your priestess."

"You always were. But we are so much more... my daughter, ancestor, inheritor of House Chrysos. We are bound together like the roots are bound to the tree, and the tree is bound to the flower. If the roots bring no nourishment, the trees and flowers must die."

He paced closer, a crooked path like a ship tacking into wind.

"Amber?" Mirela was getting nervous.

I ignored her.

"We came here. We can choose other places. I am bound to you, but you are bound to me, and I regard it more like a graft, if we're going to continue your image of a tree."

"You can't deny you are House Chrysos."

"I am the ehvasi of the last, mad survivor of that House. I killed him. I cut down the tree. I won't deny it was his infusion and that I inherit from his Blood, but I won't behave like him, I won't descend into madness. Or evil."

"Bold words." He turned on his heel. "Why would I nurture this *graft*?"

"Because the one thing you want, above all, is to overcome your brother."

He paused, between one step and the next, becoming a statue.

"You're talking of the conflict between gods. Of mighty galaxies colliding in the night sky. Not of some petty dispute between humans."

"It's those petty humans who fuel the gods. And Quetzalcoatl is far ahead of you on this."

T-cat turned again, stood between the braziers and looked down his long nose at me.

"If Matlal can reopen the path for my brother, why can't you do the same for me, and make my path broader and more glorious?"

I could almost hear what I knew he meant: *a great road, bordered by the skulls of my enemies and washed with their blood.*

I shook my head. "What I'm offering is to close that link between your brother and the physical world. To erase everything that Matlal has started, before it can spread. Those battles will be more than enough to feed you."

"And then leave us both..."

"As you were before."

"It's not enough," he said. My heart thundered in my throat. Time seemed to stop. "But it's enough to start with. You'll need to return and bargain more with me. What do you want in the meantime?" He began to step backwards into the darkness.

"A substantiation of my own, where my friends can stay safe and where I can come and go. One that has your protection from the rest of the City. One that collects the other members of House Tucek for her, at her direction."

Another step back. I could barely see him.

"As long as you keep returning, and our bargaining makes progress. My offers are subtle and powerful, daughter. You will come to appreciate their strength."

I shivered.

"Think on this substantiation, priestess," he said. "How should it appear?"

Back when I'd been in Ops 4-10, Keith and I had taken some R&R on the way back from an operation. We'd ended up in Hawaii. We thought we'd found heaven on earth in a little bay on one of the small islands.

The darkness swallowed T-cat, and in the next moment, we were standing on a hill above the ocean. He'd pulled the place I'd been thinking of out of my head. He'd recreated it, down to the color of the sea.

"There are huts down there." I pointed. "I'll return as soon as I can."

"Clothes?" Mirela raised an eyebrow.

I laughed. We were all stark naked. Salar's chains were gone. Donatienne was untied. "He has a sense of humor, obviously. Maybe there will be some in the huts."

"Amber, we need to talk—" Mirela said.

"Later."

I put my arms around Gabrielle and spirit-leaped backwards to the other waiting portal...

...in a flicker, passed through a riverboat that was screaming with the anger of the queen...

...and fell down toward the connection that Gabrielle had sensed.

This didn't feel the same as the last leap.

The Northern League Adepts had called it 'projection', and that was a good name for it. You projected your aura. Especially when you took your physical body along, it felt like it took effort.

This didn't. This felt like I was on a slide going downhill, faster and faster. Backwards.

There was no sense of the auras I had expected. No Gwen, no Nick, no Lost Boys. Instead I half-recognized workings. A style of magic I had seen before. Where?

We were out of the queen's substantiation—I had to take that as a positive. We weren't going back to where I had hoped.

Too late to do anything about it.

Chapter 67

We were *not* in the spirit world.

I'd gotten so used to the feel of the place that it had dropped below the level of my awareness. Now that we'd left it, the absence of that eerie, brushing-against-the-skin sensation was shocking.

Fine by me. Out of the spirit world was a huge step.

And I was back in my own body. In my own clothes. I was holding Gabrielle tight against me, and she was pressing the reassuring bulk of my holstered Mk 23 against my chest.

Gabrielle was in her everyday clothes. Coveralls and bulky boots.

We were sitting on a floor. Hard. Concrete. A ghost building, a looming empty space, warehouse-style, emerged as I looked around.

There were shapes of witch-fire on the floor. In the air. Witch-smoke drifting. Chanting.

A pentagram? A circle?

What the hell?

A shadow of the pentagram on the floor, like an afterimage on the back of our eyeballs, tumbled around us in three dimensions, trailing spirit smoke. It traced out a sullen sphere, extending into the floor beneath us. All of it centered around the space where I hugged a trembling Gabrielle.

Tara manifested, her spirit-wolf aflame, her nose seeking out the familiar, seeing the amulets at the anchor points on the pentagram, tasting the tethers of workings interacting all around us. All elements I'd sensed before.

The workings of the Lafayette coven.

But we weren't at their house in the Atchafalaya Basin. We were in New Orleans. In a warehouse. In the center of the sort of symbolism that crackpot Adepts or pseudo-witches tried to use to summon demons.

They'd *summoned* us.

Five of them sat in line with the pentagram's points. Another five slightly behind them, in the spaces between, supporting their sisters. Even more sat behind them, rippling out. Chanting, waving smoking herb-sticks.

All of those elders that I'd saved from being burned by the Church of the Risen Sun, and the rest of their coven.

We can break this, Tara said.

Wait a moment, I replied. *Something strange.*

A door, oddly tiny against the size of the furthest wall, opened. Sunlight poured in, momentarily obscured as a figure hurried through.

"Hold her!" she yelled, running across.

This woman I didn't know.

She wasn't from the Lafayette coven, with their hippy style.

She was a slight woman, and at first glance, she looked completely out of place here. Jen would have skewered her type with a description: a woman you'd see on Fifth Avenue, emerging from a ritzy shop with that new handbag that she simply *had to* buy, trailing a silken scarf and fragrant Chanel, hairdo by Ferretti and makeup by Saks. Off to lunch with friends at the latest insanely-priced restaurant.

Incongruous, but not totally out of place here. Not with the power I could sense coming off her, flowing through the haze of workings and smoke from the Lafayette coven.

She came to a halt behind the Adept elder that I was facing at the apex of the working's symbols. Whispered in her ear.

"Who are you?" the Adept intoned.

I almost laughed. She sounded like she was right out of an old Hollywood movie about witches. *How to communicate with a demon 101.*

"You know very well who I am," I said. "I saved your ass from the cult. And you can just talk to me."

They conferred in whispers. I caught the word *evasive.*

"Oh, hell. Okay. I'm Amber Farrell, House Farrell. You've helped rescue us from the Queen of Diamonds' substantiation, so a big thank you for that. Makes us even. Now, please let me go. There are things I have to be doing."

The woman who'd just come in stood straight and puffed herself up.

"My name is Faith Hinton," she said. "I'm the Hecate of the Northern League based in New York. I want to impress on you how much importance has been placed on your rescue, by so many of the paranormal community. We're so pleased, and a little surprised at the success here, I have to admit."

"It's the connection," I said, taking a wild guess. "The spirit world connection that Gabrielle felt for the Lafayette coven, having stayed with them recently. She was looking for a path back and this just seemed right, so we came. Now, if you don't mind..."

"Is she all right?"

"No. That's one reason I need to be out of here—"

"As soon as we can," she interrupted me. "You understand, of course, that we're both pleased, and naturally cautious."

Tara growled, which just about mirrored my impatience and growing anger, but probably wasn't a great idea.

I understood how Athanate and Were societies worked. I really didn't understand the power structures in the Adept world. Would breaking out of this coven's magical cell without Hinton's approval cause Gwen problems?

"May I call you Amber?" Hinton said.

"Yes."

"What's precisely wrong with Gabrielle, Amber? Why isn't she speaking for herself?"

"The queen put a compulsion on her." As the words left my mouth, I realized that this was a hole that was getting deeper with every word I said.

"Yes. I understand. But you said she was the one searching for a path..."

"She was." It was getting even worse, but I couldn't *not* answer Hinton. "Part of the compulsion is that she has to do what I tell her. That's one reason I have to go. I need to get her back to Gwen. To Gwendolyn Enkeliekki, the Hecate of the North."

"I completely understand, but I hope you can see, we have to go through some little tests. After all, if one's under a compulsion, might the other be too? Or might the compulsion have many layers that aren't evident to the casual inspection?"

"I really don't have time for this. It's not just Gabrielle—"

"We really need to check first. You've been gone a couple of days—"

"A couple?"

"Yes."

Two days! That meant...

"I really, really need to go. The werewolves have a ritual today—"

"They're well aware of what is happening and why. Even before we get into the possibility of compulsions and so on, I need to be sure that you are *you*, if you see what I mean."

She cleared her throat. "Let's start with something easy. Please tell me the significance of frogs to a childhood friend."

I got up slowly, lifting Gabrielle up with me. She didn't understand what was going on. She was trembling, staring at my face, worried that my growing anger was directed at her.

"You did very well, Gabrielle." I kissed her forehead. "This is not your fault. I'm not angry at you."

Hinton was waiting. The good sign I took from her question was that she would have had to talk to someone from my House who knew the story. They would know what was going on.

"I had a disagreement with my friend, Cassie," I said. "One of many. So, I climbed up the side of her home one evening, got in through her window, and put frogs in her bed."

We can break out, Tara growled.

Only if we absolutely have to. It could get messy. Don't want them knowing I can do it. Not just yet.

"I can't stay here answering your questions," I said. "I need to get Gabrielle to Gwen, and then I need to run that halfy ritual."

Hinton was going on regardless. *"I* am the one who's been put in charge of ensuring that the real Amber Farrell, unchanged and under no compulsion, is returned to her valuable roles. Which I will do when *I* am convinced."

I wasn't going to have any stranger poking around inside my head.

Tara showed me the weakness in the Lafayette coven's prison, and I started to prepare.

The door Hinton had come through banged open and Rita stalked through, followed by the Lost Boys and House Labastide's security team.

The Lost Boys were holding some kind of potentially lethal working between them. The security team were all armed. Rita had that dead-eyed look she got when she was in the killing zone.

Oh, shit.

Chapter 68

"Drop the barriers," Rita said. "We're taking Amber out now."

"You can't," Hinton said. "This is an official operation—"

"Of an association of Adepts who have no rights against the Athanate. You're not part of the Assembly yet, so your *official* means nothing to us. Take the barriers down."

Hinton pointed at Gabrielle and me. "They're part of a coven affiliated with the Northern League, and subject to—"

Rita laughed. "If you're going to start talking about the new Denver coven, let me warn you: you don't want to be holding Amber and Gabrielle in that working when Gwen gets here."

Her Sig appeared in her hand like magic.

One of the Lafayette coven who wasn't in the front line keeping me imprisoned tried something witchy.

Kane *pushed*. All the way across the room. I didn't see anything, but the Adept slumped as if he'd punched her jaw.

I could see Hinton's power coalesce into a shield.

"Stop!" I yelled. "Everyone stand down."

Rita took a step back, trying to keep one eye on Hinton and one on me.

Gwen burst in and saw us. "Gabrielle? Amber?"

The working around us cracked like an eggshell. A silent part of me noted how she'd done it and filed that away.

"Gabrielle?" Gwen had come to a halt in the ruins of the summoning. She reached her hand toward us, then stopped. Gabrielle hadn't turned. Her face was pressed against me and she was crying.

"Compulsion," I said. "The Queen of Diamonds put her under a compulsion. I don't have time to explain, but she obeys what I say. You and the coven know about undoing these compulsions. Everything we've been seeing—Weaver and the old Denver coven, the working Weaver tried on me, Remy, Pruitt, the Taos coven—they're all the queen's work or variants of it."

"You can't take them," Hinton said. "I demand you hand them over to me to assure they're who they say they are and not under any influence. The Northern League has appointed me. You know you're in no position to be impartial on this, Gwendolyn."

Gwen's face took on that terrible starkness that signaled danger. Her eyes turned to blue ice, as they did when Bryn was ready to use her power.

I was out of time. I spoke directly to Hinton.

"We're done here. I'm going to hand Gabrielle to Gwen, as the best expert to look after her. You're going to agree to that."

She chewed on that for a second before she reluctantly nodded.

"Gabrielle, honey," I said, "I'm going to give you to Gwen here to look after. She's very good. I'll be busy for a while, but I'll come back soon, okay?"

She was clutching at my jacket as if she didn't want to let go, but she whispered an agreement because she had to.

"Gwen is going to take you somewhere else that's quiet and peaceful. She's going to take you right now. And I want you to listen carefully to her, Gabrielle. You have to do what she says as if it was me speaking to you. Do you understand?"

Gabrielle nodded once, quickly. Very unhappy.

It tore my heart. I wanted to be with her, but I needed to stop the queen *now*, for everyone's sake.

Gwen and I worked together, as gently as we could, to untangle Gabrielle from me. Gwen had immediately picked up on how to talk to Gabrielle, and her voice was sweeter than I'd heard from her before.

Her eyes had lost none of their anger.

"Go," I said to her when she had Gabrielle. "I've got this."

Gwen sent one piercing look Hinton's way and then left. I finger-talked at the Lost Boys to go with her. They knew Gabrielle, and they were very good at workings, despite being somewhat 'unregulated', to use Hinton's description.

Which left me with Nick, Rita and the Labastide security team to confront Hinton.

"I've conceded to your reasonable demands," Hinton said. "I expect reasonableness back from you."

"And you'll get it, but we may not be able to agree on timing. I have an urgent task that cannot wait on your investigation."

"So you say. What is so urgent?"

I would rather talk to her about this than reveal anything else that had happened. I could barely imagine her reaction if I told her I'd saved the lives of three enemies, and made a pact with an evil, bloodthirsty god.

"The queen has been damaged. I need to use the halfy ritual to put an end to her. The ritual generates a huge amount of power, and I intend to take that into the queen's substantiation and use it against her."

She couldn't hide her reaction. This was as bad as telling her I was pals with T-cat.

But I didn't have time to think up any other arguments.

There was someone else coming to the warehouse. Someone whose presence was heavily shielded. Someone I wouldn't have been able to sense if I hadn't made deals in the spirit world. Someone who shouldn't be here. Really, *really* shouldn't be here.

Chapter 69

The figures that entered next had none of the obvious drama of Rita's entrance, or Gwen's.

Two nearly identical young women—slim, straight black hair, somber faces, dwarfed by the immensity of the warehouse. Up close one of them would probably have the faintest trace across her skin, like a net, outlining the shape of her scales from her true form.

Tullah and Kaothos.

Kaothos let a little of her shielding slip. Her power hissed and crackled through the gloomy air, making it difficult to breathe.

They were supposed to be sheltering in the shielded dungeon below Haven. The whole structure of the Assembly was built around the barefaced lie that Kaothos and Diana were dead. Diakon Huang suspected we were lying, but as long as it was only a suspicion, he could maintain the illusion of belief which allowed the Emperor of Heaven and Skylur to run the Assembly from the shadows.

If it became common knowledge that Kaothos was alive, all bets were off.

The only thing worse than Kaothos being out where she could be discovered, would be if Diana were here as well.

She was.

She followed them in, frowning until she caught sight of me.

Everyone in the warehouse had just become a potential security leak. Or they would have, if they'd all been awake. The Lafayette coven and Hinton had collapsed to the floor.

"Amber!" Tullah and Kaothos ran across and hugged me.

I folded myself in their embrace, swiftly joined by Diana and Rita, and had to stifle a cry of pain from the saber wound.

"Thank you." I managed a shaky laugh. "But I may have trouble explaining this to Hecate Hinton later. Not to mention the Lafayette coven."

Tullah snorted. "They're just going to have to deal with it. Kaothos knew it was you as soon as their summoning picked you up."

Kaothos said nothing. She knew it was me, but I guessed she also knew that my aura had changed in the spirit world.

"Let's leave quickly," Diana said.

"You really shouldn't be here, any of you."

Kaothos had clearly been casting some kind of shield over them, but if I could sense through it at close quarters, what might the Empire's Adepts be able to do?

We all trotted toward the door.

"Staying away was not an option," Tullah replied. "We came straight here. Rita gave us enough clues about where you were, and we were trying to figure out how to project into the Queen of Diamonds' substantiation when the Lafayette coven tried summoning. Crazy that worked."

"It didn't really. Gabrielle did most of it. She was just reaching out for some kind of direction. If Gwen had been projecting, that's where we would have gone."

I looked around. The Labastide security was right behind us.

"Thank you all, and I don't want to be rude—"

"We've given our oaths, House Farrell. We see nothing, we say nothing. Diakon Dupuis has put us in your service for as long as you need."

Freedom of the House, Marguerite Labastide had said. We were linked together by far more than the right to share kin and Blood.

"We're based at the town house, at the moment," Diana said. "Everyone that can come has come. Jen and Alex should be there by now. Bian sends her apologies, but she's worried that there are too many of Matlal's forces in Colorado. Yelena has been specifically refused permission to leave New York. It seems the Carpathian issue is at a critical point."

I shook my head.

"We can't react like this just because I'm in danger. Of course Bian and Yelena can't come. For that matter, you should be at Haven in case Matlal attacks."

"His forces already have. They found it was a very bad idea."

We were outside, in an empty business park with half a dozen warehouses. There were cars waiting for us and we got in hurriedly, even though Kaothos had made a haze in the air around us that would have hidden our identities from anyone more than a few feet away.

"How urgently do you need the halfy ritual to run?" Rita said as we drove off. "Felix and Cameron have been seething. They understand, naturally, but there are hundreds of werewolves milling around. It's starting to become obvious."

"We need to go tonight." I looked out the window. I normally didn't need a watch, but the spirit world had screwed up my sense of time again.

It looked to be about midafternoon. "But we need to be at the right location."

"Nick picked a place," Rita said. "It met the criteria you laid down."

"Mission's changed."

Diana and Rita looked at me.

I slumped back and tried to catch a few moments' rest. There weren't going to be many chances for that in the next few hours.

"We're going on a hunt," I said. "The rituals I've run so far just skimmed the surface of the spirit world. Spirit walking, basically. That's not going to be enough tonight. This time, I've got to harness the power of the packs and punch through into the City of Lost Gods."

"But we can do that anyway," Diana said.

I shook my head.

"All that recon was spirit walking." I snorted. "I was told I needed an army to take on the queen, and I do. So I've got to take one there."

"Hold on. You're saying the queen is in the City of Lost Gods?"

"Not that simple either. The City is a massive, self-sustaining substantiation in the spirit world that eats other less powerful substantiations. But the City itself is not a monolith. I guess you'd say it has suburbs."

They all looked confused.

"I'm sorry," I said. "I'm trying to explain this all in a hurry because I don't really know all the details and because we're on a countdown here. The Queen of Diamonds was a powerful Adept in her own right, probably from a voodoo background, a century or so ago. Somehow she tapped into the power behind voodoo, all the way back to its African roots. She's trapped those old gods, and they're the real source of her power. I've got to break that connection while we still have the chance."

"Then you need Gwen to help you."

"Gwen has to heal Gabrielle first. Every moment that Gabrielle remains compelled, her aura weakens. And my gut says I can't wait until Gwen's finished. I have the opportunity to take the queen down tonight, or she'll erect new defenses and we'll have even more of a problem with her."

"So you've got to get into her substantiation *inside* the City of Lost Gods. And then what?"

"Then I trap her riverboat."

"Riverboat?"

"A genuine, old-time paddle steamer called the *Queen of Diamonds*. Look, I need to talk to the alphas. I need to review the maps of the

Atchafalaya we were working on. And I'm also going to need explosives. A *lot* of explosives."

Chapter 70

Other than being held in the middle of the night, this wasn't going to be like the rituals I'd run before.

For starters, the packs were working hard just to get here, deep in the wilds along the real-world Atchafalaya. But it was more than that. Although this *was* a ritual, and I hoped to get every single halfy to change, the other purpose, the hunt, was more important and we were running late. Very late.

Rituals usually started with Ben and his crew of 'graduates' working their way through the crowd of halfies, boosting their confidence. Because that's what the biggest part of the problem was—confidence. It seemed crazy that werewolves would lack that confidence, but there was a huge gap between believing in yourself, and believing you could turn into a wolf. Ben had been doing his best tonight, but the roiling mass of people in the darkness, half of them still arriving from every direction, made everything impossible.

There were no roads in this section of the Hatch, and no good parking options, so a lot of them had been trucked in to the nearest point, given a compass and told to walk.

To make it more challenging, the latest tropical storm to hit the Gulf Coast had begun to push up through Louisiana. Landfall had taken the edge off it, but the winds were still gusting to over seventy miles an hour and several inches of rain had fallen since nightfall. Power had gone down in half a dozen counties. Trees had fallen. Roads had been flooded and bridges closed. A quarter of the trucks delivering werewolves had to divert.

For those that were here, once they'd fought their way through the wetlands, there were no welcoming fires set up, no barbeques and beer.

There was no anxious, cohesive mass ready to listen to my words in the flickering firelight. Instead I had sullen, wet groups snarling at each other as they flowed in, gathering beneath the hulking darkness that was the levee I stood on.

Even among the halfies, a lot of snarling was directed at me.

That was okay, as long as I could harvest it.

For me, an exercise like this was kinda nostalgic. It was like one of the easier night marches, back in Ops 4-10. Better to *not* make that comparison to anyone else.

The general location had been picked from the work that Nick and the Lost Boys had been doing. They had made a huge map of the Atchafalaya Basin, with roads and buildings marked. Overlaying that had been a web of tour guides' routes, recommended hunting and fishing areas, places people visited, the location of the shack that Freddy Walker had used.

And in the middle of all that data, right next to Freddy's shack, a large blank area had emerged. A place people generally didn't go.

That's where we were.

I'd reached it hours ago, in the fading light of the afternoon. They had been hours spent on a satellite phone persuading Felix and Cameron to go ahead with the ritual, mixed with walking the levees with Nick, skimming the spirit world and searching, sensing and estimating.

Finding just the spot I needed.

Here. This was where I'd take on the Queen of Diamonds, and these angry wolves would be my army.

It had felt right at the time, but it was starting to look as if this spot was too far upriver.

The paddle steamer was coming. Its pace was steady, but it was riding the surging waters that were already swelling with storm runoff. The river was running faster, and the way the queen had set up her substantiation, just touching the real world, her Atchafalaya was running faster too.

I wasn't ready.

There were supposed to be a thousand werewolves here already. Not just the halfies and some pals from their packs. It was supposed to be every loner wolf that had joined a local pack, every 'gift' wolf from the Queen of Diamonds. Down to every wolf in any Gulf State pack that the alpha thought wasn't totally, one hundred percent, a pack wolf.

It wasn't anything like that number.

There were no lights out here. Heavy cloud. No moon, no stars. My wolfy eyes could see individuals and the shapes of groups, but there was no way to count. I had no more than three hundred so far, and time was slipping away. The *Queen of Diamonds* kept churning downstream through the flooding river, faster with every passing second, which meant the night was running against me.

I wanted more, but it wasn't going to happen.

There was a peak of emotions I would need to use. If I waited too long, then the three hundred I had here would begin to act as an anchor to any more who joined. I sensed that Felix and Cameron were close, and I had promised to wait for them, but I couldn't let the riverboat slip past. I also couldn't let the mood of the packs sour.

Time.

There was also a very obvious problem I hadn't thought of. With the trees shaking and the wind roaring, those in the back were hardly going to be able to hear me.

My first hurdle was to get a critical mass of them on my side. If it went my way, I could hope for a snowball effect which would spread through this group, and any others that joined us.

Where to start...

"Ten years ago I was in the army," I started yelling.

"Can't hear!" someone shouted from the back.

"Then shut up and listen. You either got wolf ears, or you shouldn't be here. Come closer."

There was a reluctant shuffling, squelching movement, and it achieved a slightly greater concentration of steaming misery just below where I stood. Pack pressed against pack in the falling rain. The closer they came to each other, the more the inter-pack rivalry amped up.

I could see the heat of their bodies, hundreds of faces turned to me. I could taste their anger.

Then, just as I was about to start again, a stir at the back turned heads.

Felix, Cameron and a bunch of local alphas. And Alex, with Rita and the Labastide security team, all carrying heavy packs of all the explosives they could lay their hands on.

The mass of wolves parted, and they made their way through. Climbed up onto the levee beside me.

Oooh.

The grunts were angry. The alphas were furious.

A soaked Cameron brushed close to me. "This had better be good, Amber."

I snorted. "Don't you worry about that. I promised you something spectacular."

More arrivals followed the alphas and started filling in the space in the back. Maybe we'd get four hundred. Maybe it'd be enough. I didn't know, and I was out of time. I needed to get them warmed up before I could tap into their power.

I started yelling again. "Ten years ago I was in the army. This kind of night exercise was something we used to do all the time. Apparently, it was good for moral fiber or something."

Some halfhearted snorts. At least they were listening.

"After a while, we complained to the sergeant. We said the night marches didn't have any purpose to them. He nodded and said we had a very fair point. We were stupid enough to think that was a good thing."

One or two chuckles. There were some out in the mass of wolves in front of me that had done their time in the service.

"The sergeant said we were right, and that once we finished training, a march at night would have a purpose. It would get us somewhere to do something. Blow up a bridge, ambush a convoy, something like that. But given that we were only training at that point, and blowing up bridges in the Carolinas was unacceptable for some reason, there wasn't much we could do. After all, it wasn't so bad, having nothing to do at the end of a march. And some idiot said: yeah, imagine we got somewhere in the middle of the night—cold, wet, pissed off—and had to dig."

Some genuine laughs. The anger hadn't gone away, but it wasn't so focused on me.

"Yeah. So that's what we did every time we were on a night march from then on. We went somewhere, we dug, we filled it back in, we marched back."

"You want us to *dig* tonight?" someone near the front called out.

"Digging? What about the ritual?" A newcomer at the back.

Felix answered before I could. "You'll dig, but you're right, that's not what you're here for."

All my time coaxing him on the phone this afternoon had apparently paid off. As pissed as he was about being here, I had his full support. Until I didn't.

In the meantime, his words had taken the mood up a notch or three.

It was up to me to run with that.

"This is different from the other rituals," I said. "You haven't come here to have dinner and dance in the firelight while some of you get comfortable with the fact that you're shapeshifters. Tonight, we have a purpose, and it's not a training exercise—or a meaningless task like digging a hole and then filling it in."

Now I had their attention, and more people came out of the tree line and hurried to join the back of the group.

"Tonight, we learn about being a super-pack. You halfies will change because you will *need* to. You already know how to do it, deep down. And tonight, there will not be a way you *can't* change, because you *need* to be one with the super-pack. You other newcomers to your packs, you'll understand what it is to be fully part of those packs, because there is no way you cannot be."

I hadn't quite caught them yet. I had to step it up.

"There *is* a purpose in being here. The Southern League has been under attack. You've heard it, if you've listened to what's come out of the border packs like El Paso and Tucson. But you've been under attack as well. A slower attack. Even more deadly, because it was almost impossible to see. You've heard about the challenge at Port Allen. You've heard about the rougarou. A pack of hybrid were-hyenas sitting right in the middle of your territory."

A subliminal growl passed through the group.

"A pack that grows quicker, the longer it's left. A pack that wants all of you to bow down."

The packs were stirring. Their anger was becoming a thing. No longer pointed at me. It was a monster waking in the darkness. One I had to ride into battle.

"The rougarou aren't even a pack in the way we know packs. They have hierarchy and they have alphas, but it's not the alphas who run the rougarou. They're run by a witch. Some of you know her as the Swamp Witch. Some of you think she's helpful, and she can be, so long as she gets what she wants. And what she wants is all of you to bow down to her, to the evil she brings with her. To turn you into her slaves. The sort of slaves who behave like the Mexican packs, running drugs and trafficking people."

Growls.

"You gonna do that?"

This wasn't like me with the El Paso group, where I had the authority as co-alpha, but they could see their alphas behind me, and that was as much authority as they needed.

Their anger was taking a shape, rising from them like a blood-red monster in the boundless night.

I'd miscalculated. The Hatch was a sacred ground, where the spirit world brushed the physical world. Actions that might harness magical energy in the physical world took on a different dimension when the spirit world came into play. This monster I'd called was far more powerful than I'd anticipated. It was growing too quickly. It needed a target, otherwise this group of packs was going to explode in fights.

I gave up on building it. I had to get on with using it, before it got out of control.

"Tonight, the queen comes. Tonight, we *hunt*," I yelled. "Tonight, we *fight*."

I opened up everything and just followed where my instincts led me.

"Tonight we are *one pack*." I pumped my fist at them. "We are the *Southern League*, and we have an *enemy*, and she is close."

The monster surged through me. It set my body alight with power.

I felt the alphas at my back; they were unhappy, as they always were when I talked about being one pack. Tough. Explaining how we were one pack and yet many packs wasn't going to get me the gut level response I needed.

With the power of the packs crackling through me, I reached into the spirit world the way Gabrielle had taught me. I felt the City of Lost Gods hanging over me, swollen with threats. I sank into it and I found the queen's substantiation. I felt the *Queen of Diamonds* on the river. *So close*. I had a spirit connection with the queen herself, but it was nothing in comparison to the connection I felt with the trees that made her paddle steamer.

She could sense me. She could feel the pack at my back. There was a knowledge that we were a danger, even in the fortress of her own substantiation. There was anger that we dared threaten her. And contempt for us. Pack or not, she thought she was safe on her boat in the middle of the river, surrounded by deep running water and guarded by her rougarou. Many more rougarou than had been on board when I was.

I channeled all that in both directions. She could see the pack, and the pack could see her.

Back in the physical world, the pack howled at the sight of their enemy.

HUNT!

A pack Call screamed out, every pack mixed together, and it started to flow outward like fire in the veins. All those still lost and staggering through the dark woods felt it, turned their steps to where it came from, and ran.

I didn't have the opportunity for the usual ritual buildup about buddies and everyone looking out for each other, because that was built into their sense of pack now. Baton Rouge would help Alexandria, just as Alexandria would help Biloxi.

One super-pack. The Southern League. One monster linked by their Call.

More joined us every second, wide-eyed faces emerging out of the rain, panting and eager. Some of them started to strip and change to their wolves.

I felt the weight of the Call, the way it flowed and stretched. I pulled it with me, visualizing it forming the same way Gabrielle had formed her aura when she'd prepared portals to escape the *Queen of Diamonds*.

This was what I needed all the power for.

I tensed, visualized the power gathering itself like a horse coming to a jump.

I leaped into the queen's substantiation, using the pack's power to tear a portal from the physical world into the spirit world.

And on, right into the queen's substantiation.

Not all the way to her riverboat. I could smell traps there.

I wanted the portal between worlds, but without moving from the place I'd chosen—the top of the old levee that held the Atchafalaya on its course in the queen's substantiation.

Like the rest of the queen's corner of the spirit world, it was based in the 19th century. It had been built by hand. By convicts. Some of them were buried under it, and I could feel them as they started to seep up through the earth toward the power that had come into being in this place.

The pack knew we'd gone somewhere strange. There was no difference they could see, but wolves' noses could tell they were in a completely different place. A little bit of old Louisiana that had been copied out of the physical world and placed here to remain unchanged.

The shock of the change dampened the monster.

"We're gonna need that riverboat to come to us," I called out. "And the first step to make that happen is you need to change. And then you need to dig."

More of them were rushing through the portal. There was no time to get any better control of the situation. All of them started changing. It was a headlong rush, and it was all taking place in the spirit world. Part of what held halfies back in the physical world was that there were billions of people there who didn't believe in the paranormal. They didn't believe a person could change into a wolf. And as the doubt spread, it was unintentionally amplified and focused by the pack on the newbies.

None of that applied here.

The spirit world *felt* different. This was where the energy that powered the paranormal flowed close to the surface. And there were *no* doubters in this substantiation.

They changed. Some of the newbies forgot to get clear of their clothes first. Thanks to previous experiences, Ben had made sure everyone knew to come in simple clothes they didn't mind losing, but there were still some running around furry with pants or shirts half on.

Before it could descend into laughter, Felix started organizing them into teams.

The alpha had to use all his willpower to *not* change, and all his dominance to get the wolves working when they were hot to fight.

But they dug. They dug down into the soft back of the old levee, down and down until they came up against the hard rock and rubble that formed the bulwark against the river.

That was where we buried the explosives.

More and more flooded in through the portal, their link with the rest of the super-pack holding it open without effort on my part.

HUNT! KILL!

Chapter 71

"Get them clear!"

No time for careful placement. No time for backfilling. No time for anything more. Packs of explosives were flung down and wolves sent scrabbling up along the levee by alphas who were now changed, snarling and nipping to get the point across.

In the darkness, I felt the *Queen of Diamonds* come around the bend, and the river was racing now.

Time for my part.

I was running along the levee, following the pack away from the explosives. I'd estimated I needed a hundred yards' clearance. I didn't have time to get it.

I stopped at fifty.

Alex came to a four-footed halt and loped back toward me. Nick and Rita were shedding clothes, changing. Jaguar-cougar, Kodiak bear. Ursula's Kodiak emerged at the back of the pack, snarling to keep the rest of them moving.

My House. Idiots! Get further away. Further.

No time to argue.

It was time to find out if I could ride the monster I'd created.

I raised both hands. My wounds from the saber fight tore open and started bleeding again, but I felt the heat of power flood through my body. I wasn't in control of it. It felt more like riding the back of a whale.

Witch fire tangled around me, leaped up from my fingers. In the sky above me, fintyne twisted—the white fire, the witch equivalent of napalm.

But the lowering clouds thundered at me.

This is not how my priestess summons fire. These are the toys of humans and witches. You are in the spirit world, daughter. Use your strength. Glory in it.

He was right. I could not deny him now. I let the fintyne go. The levee plunged back into darkness and I felt the queen's laughter, like a wind rushing across the broad expanse of river, like a gale that wrapped itself around me.

I let it.

My hands were still outstretched. The winds rose and rose, until they shrieked in my ears and shook me and spun me around, and then the winds twisted upward, to where the clouds reached down, like the whole night sky was made of rippling, spinning screams.

I tasted the path. I traced the fractures in the night sky with my fingertips, caressed the weakness in the air, touched the power that would break the earth.

The sky split open and lightning crashed down.

Not one bolt. Not two.

The sky opened and a host of lightnings danced upon the levee.

> The devil's a-dancing
> An' when he's good and done
> Levee gonna break
> And the waters are gonna run

The explosives themselves were lost in the mayhem. A hundred yards of levee downriver from where the explosives had been set just disappeared, launched into the sky as a fiery wave, falling like tracers back into the floodplains.

Given a new path, the great serpent of the river turned, carrying everything with it, including the riverboat.

Again! Call the lightning!

T-cat wanted to blast the riverboat out of the water.

No.

The riverboat was turning against the flow, trying to return upriver.

I reached out across the water, hunting for traps, but the queen was distracted. I broke through the wards and connected to the boat itself, the ancient gods that formed it. Gods too old to speak, and yet too strong to simply fall beneath the powers of others. Gods that had grown tired of the demands that the queen made.

To feel the soil beneath us again. To sink roots deep, deep into the earth. To reach with arms for the sky above. To grow. To feel the pulse of life from the sun. To sleep and waken with the seasons.

None of that was allowed by the queen.

She knew I was there. She still ruled this substantiation, and it gave her power over the channels that ran through it. She sent her response and it burned through me.

For all her power, she could not make magic hurt me more than it already had. I was used to this. I would not let go.

And while she was fighting me, the boat was drifting toward the huge breech in the levee.

With a snap, she changed tactics. She poured power back into her wards, and the boat began to turn downriver. She was going to try and outrun the effect of the breach.

She looked as if she would make it, too. Then another fifty yards of levee gave up the struggle and let the river find its new course. The breach was widening even as the boat struggled to clear it, inching closer, the paddle churning the water.

The river ran deep in this stretch, and the boat was built for shallow waters, but with the river suddenly draining into a million acres of wetland, it was only a matter of time before something grounded. Being dragged backwards meant it was the paddle.

I heard the crack of the paddle splitting over the roaring of wind and water. The riverboat started to sway and swing around, so the stern now aimed to the wetlands.

With nothing to fight the current, it began to match the pace of the water, and shot through the gap.

It grounded just beyond the remains of the levee, but it was at the other end of the breach and we were separated by a lot of fast flowing water.

Only in the spirit world. In the physical world, the levee would be there, but the boat wouldn't. If I could persuade the old gods that made up the riverboat to come back into the physical world, their powers would be much less, but...

I spoke through the wards that the queen had put up. I used the power of the packs and I spoke to the ancient gods.

Soil, water, sunlight, and your own sacred space. Peace.

I could feel them stir in response. I fed them the anger of the packs, and they threw off the queen's bindings. I could see the way the riverboat began to sag as they lost the form that had been forced on them.

"Alex! Quickly. Take the packs back through the portal. The boat's going to end up in our world."

I felt the movement of the werewolves behind me, and the power they'd been giving me began to ebb.

The queen redoubled her efforts, tearing back control over the riverboat.

I had to stop her, but I couldn't leave the spirit world and I couldn't call lightning on the riverboat.

I ran along the top of the levee, toward the breach, desperately holding onto my fading connection to the riverboat.

The old gods responded again. I was running in two places.

The breach on the old levee stretched out in front of me, but every time my foot hit the ground, I found the physical world's levee, dark and solid beneath it. I kept my eyes fixed on the boat, *willing* the old gods to fight the queen and move all of us into the physical world.

The riverboat began to pulse with strange lights. There was a sound that dwarfed the roar of the river. A note, deep as a chasm, a note so deep I felt it in my breastbone, shaking my body, shaking the ground itself.

And we ripped through, out of the queen's substantiation, into the physical world.

I was sprinting along the levee in the dark, legs pumping, left side slick with blood from the re-opened wounds. The packs were howling behind me. By the witch lights around it, I could see the back of the boat turn and twist. There was another enormous explosion as something hit the water, and everything disappeared in steam.

The riverboat had jettisoned its boiler.

As the steam cleared I could see the structure of the boat collapse, and figures fell out of it and began to race toward us. Huge, shaggy shapes with distinctive low hindquarters.

The queen's rougarou. Hundreds of them.

I'd planned ahead for *some* rougarou. I'd left Labastide's security on this side with Freddy Walker's outsized half-inch guns and IR scopes. They fired, but they weren't going to make enough of a difference, and once the two sides started close-in fighting, they wouldn't have clear targets.

I had no way of knowing how many there were on either side. Maybe five hundred werewolves against four hundred rougarou.

The levee was about thirty yards wide. The rougarou were bunched up on the top. Cameron was leading the opposing charge along the top and she overtook me, sparing a snarl as she went by. Felix was leading a second group along the bottom of the levee. I could see them only as a flood that seemed to have boiled out of the ground itself.

The werewolves ran much faster than I did on two legs, but I didn't want to change. I didn't want to get completely caught up in the Call. Two legs it was, and two arms. And two swords.

Bian had sent her apology for not coming down to Louisiana in the form of a gift. Onibi was the name of the companion katana to the wakizashi called Nekotsume. I had them both strapped to my back, and I unsheathed them as I ran. Even though there were no lights and no moon, the long blade of Onibi seemed to glow with a reflection.

Cameron and the wolves with her met the rougarou fifty yards in front of me. Both were running at full speed, and I could see the shock of contact shudder through the ranks on either side.

The rougarou were bigger, but in the confined space on the top of the levee, there were more wolves. Another thing: Cameron was clearly leading the wolves, whereas the rougarou hadn't replaced the alphas we'd killed at Port Allen.

There were wolves and rougarou thrown into the air by the force of the crash. Some landed in the river. Others fell down the bank.

The two sides compressed, and I couldn't get through.

Rougarou were dying, each swarmed by two or three wolves, but the sheer weight of the rougarou was driving the wolves back. They were gathering momentum, and momentum was everything in this kind of battle.

Which was when Felix led his group up the slope of the levee and hit them from their unprotected side.

HUNT! KILL!

Whatever the rougarou had as an equivalent to the Call, it barely registered in comparison to the Southern League.

Felix's group had cut the rougarou in half. Their front line was surrounded and there was no way through on the top of the levee for those in the back. A good alpha would have led them down the side to circle around and hit Felix the same way he'd hit them.

If they'd come, that's where they would have found me, scrambling up the side of the levee, whirling two blades.

The rougarou fell back at this second attack, not expecting swords. I didn't concentrate on any one individual. I wasn't trying to kill with one blow. The sweep of my katana was aimed to cripple, to get the rougarou to back up, to interfere with each other, to distract those who were trying to reach Felix.

It worked for a while. There was confusion in the darkness. The rows of rougarou wavered.

I didn't know what changed that.

Maybe I pushed too far forward. Maybe one of them smelled the blood from the unhealed saber wound that soaked my left side, and that triggered an automatic response. One of the larger rougarou with a little space around him leaped at me. I couldn't slash at him and move on. I had to concentrate on three hundred pounds of muscle and fangs flying through the air.

He died with Onibi piercing his neck, but in the time it took me to free the blade, another two had leaped at me, and there were more behind them.

Tara manifested, snarling and biting, but there were too many.

Jaws on my leg. I slashed with Nekotsume, felt blood spraying. There was no space or time to swing Onibi. I smashed one snarling rougarou between the eyes with the hilt of the longer sword. I was enveloped in a twisting clump of fur and fangs. The clump shook as another rougarou hit.

One right in front, going for my throat.

I drove Nekotsume upwards. There was blood on my face. My arm was seized, fangs piercing flesh.

Dropped Onibi. Drew my Mk23. Slammed the barrel against a chest. Fired twice. Twisted away, trying to get clear.

Another set of jaws. My thigh. Too close to arteries. Staggering. Fired right into his head.

Falling. Mustn't fall. To lie down here would be to die.

Jaws on my wrist. Dragging me down. Every second there was more weight on top.

The whole staggering structure toppled through the sheer weight of rougarou. More jumped on even as we fell. My lungs were crushed.

And then a different impact, one that shook the whole pile. Followed by a roar to freeze blood and muscles, stomach and lungs. The weight lifted off. Rougarou screams suddenly snapped off like light switches being thrown. Two huge shapes stood above me, hurling broken-backed rougarou away in every direction.

Nick and Ursula in their Kodiak forms.

Rita was there, as I lurched back onto my feet, leading Bill Patout and the Alexandria pack in like an arrow aimed at the backs of the rougarou.

I felt the queen then, reaching out to every member of every pack that had passed through her hands, one way or another, from outright rabioso to those she'd only influenced. She had her own version of the Call, intended to make them turn on their fellows.

But it was lost in the great shout of the Southern League's Call, which doubled as more packs raced out of the night.

The rougarou lines broke.

Most of them leaped into the water, which carried them swiftly away. A few had gone so berserk they didn't notice the odds had changed. They stayed to fight, and each of them disappeared under half a dozen wolves.

Despite the urgings from T-cat, I had no interest in that.

Flanked by Ursula and Nick, I limped to where the riverboat had grounded.

There was no shape left to the proud steamer. The ground was littered with brass fittings, glass, rope, bits of metal, chairs and tables that hadn't been part of the structure.

Instead of a boat there was a forest of strange, moving trees. They didn't walk, but they sank roots into the ground on one side and lifted others out on the other. Trunks groaned. Branches rubbed against each other. Leaves sprouted and shook in the winds.

The gods brought their own trees, and they welcomed those already there.

Swamp cypress and willows made their slow way to the outside of the spreading forest.

The inner trees were ebony, rosewood and a dozen species from around the world. The outer trees were the cypress, willow and scrub oak of the wetlands.

Every one of them housed some ancient, nameless African god. Every one of them murmured a wordless satisfaction as I walked through, placing my hand against their tall trunks in thanks.

There was no sign of the queen, no trace of her magic, no lingering connection to her.

Chapter 72

I stood up to my thighs in the wetland creek and listened.

The battle against the queen's rougarou seemed far away and long ago. As soon as it had ended, Felix and Cameron had turned the packs back and had them disperse under the cover of the dying storm. Even if we were spread out over miles of the Atchafalaya Basin, several hundred werewolves and the bodies of all the dead would be difficult to hide. It was a busy night for the packs.

I'd sent my House back as well. I was sure the queen had exhausted her squads of rougarou at the riverboat, and my House would be more a hindrance than a help in this hunt.

The wetlands had reclaimed the night.

Owls cried, bullfrogs droned, mosquitos whined. Water dripped and leaves rustled. Treetops swayed in the easing winds. Dawn was coming, and the first bird calls pierced the cool air. There was nothing to tell me the queen was here.

The mud sucked at my boots as I climbed up a silted bank.

The storm had dragged a breath of the gulf up into the basin, stirred it in with cypress and moss, mud and decay, salt and pine and the great wheel of death. And underneath all that, like a snake slipping through the shallows, a most singular scent, one I had tracked through the remains of the night. Sweet pine and camphor. Eucalyptus and moss.

Stronger now.

The Queen of Diamonds was not far away.

My wounds were bleeding again. The saber cut along my chest, the deep tears of fangs in my belly, arms and legs. They all hurt in that sort of unfocused way that made me think I was borderline feverish. Even an Athanate should rest to heal.

Not yet. Close. She is so close.

She'd shielded herself magically. There were no trails of magic threaded through the early mists, no little pulse of power to fix on in the darkness.

I was shielded too. I'd seen what Kaothos had done to shield herself, *felt* in it my aura, and I'd copied that. My shield wasn't going to be as good as the queen's. She'd know when I got close. She must know now. And now, she might start second guessing. She might think I was tracking her by magic. How powerful was I, that I could sense her through her shield? Then she might wonder if I were deliberately giving myself away to distract her while the rest of my House crept up on her.

In truth, I couldn't shield all of them and hunt at the same time. That's why they weren't here, but she didn't know that.

Meanwhile, my wolfy sense of smell said she was less than fifty yards away. And this close, I could tell she was worried as well.

I rolled my shoulders and touched the hilts of both swords strapped to my back. Nekotsume over my right shoulder, Onibi over my left.

I felt under my tattered jacket, dipped my fingers in my blood and marked my face with it. Cheeks. Nose. Hard straight bars. The same as T-cat wore.

Then I emptied the water out of my boots, stamped my feet back into them and drew my swords.

Close. But where? Which direction?

I felt it when her aura stretched out to check for others in the area. She *did* think I had a team with me.

And now I knew where she was.

About thirty yards, right in front of me.

Her body was one root of a swamp cypress, her skin was bark, her hair a shadow. She knew the moment I saw her, but even when she moved, she looked more tree than human.

Beneath the disguise, she'd kept the face and body I'd last seen, the Chinese woman. Small, delicate...

Trick, Tara said. *She'll be stronger than she looks. And she's not tired. She hasn't been fighting rougarou.*

She also had swords. In her right hand, the Chinese jian, a long, straight, double-edged sword. In her left, a dao, smaller, slightly curved, cutlass style.

Her crouch, and the surefooted way she moved, indicated she knew about fighting, but I had no idea how good she was. Jian and dao together was... unusual, but there were probably as many Chinese martial art styles as the rest of the world put together. Bian had trained me briefly with both Chinese swords, but never together.

I'd start by assuming the queen was *very* good.

Our arena was a major factor. Rapid foot movements, especially backwards, would not work on the ground here. Too many roots to trip over, muddy patches to slide in. There was going to be much less maneuvering than in my fight against Cazenave. All the emphasis would be on a strong base for defense and attack.

The queen stopped. "Why?" she said. "Why bother to track me through the wetlands and confront me in my place of power?"

"It's not your place of power. That was the riverboat, and the power was stolen from the old gods. These are Louisiana wetlands. Even if this was where you made your home all those years ago, before the riverboat, they don't favor anyone. As for why I'm tracking you... you're still too powerful to go free."

She laughed. "But you're alone. Obviously, not everyone agrees with you. They think the riverboat was everything."

I smiled back. No, we had a disagreement about priorities, but let her figure that out, if she killed me.

I felt the shiver of a spell start. I didn't care what form it took. I leaped at her, Onibi raised.

She met the attack. She had to. Her spell dissipated.

Very difficult to fight and cast spells at the same time.

Our blades met in a pattern: left, right, left... three, five, seven times and then we parted, each stepping carefully back.

She was good.

In fact, I was sure she was better than I was.

"There's no need for you to die," the queen said. "We could work well together."

"We can't work together at all."

"But you can work with a person like Tucek. Interesting."

Sore point, but not something I was going to get into now.

I made a feint to keep her honest. She read my weight, knew it wasn't a real attack. She didn't bother to parry my blades.

"Not your normal weapons," the queen said. "But clearly you've worked with an expert. House Trang?"

"These are her swords."

"I'll take good care of them when I win. You know the katana has a spell?"

Onibi's blade was definitely glowing now. Not quite like Bryn's Valkyrie sword, which burst into flames when she fought, but a definite glow in the pre-dawn twilight.

It could be distracting, Tara said.

Not half as distracting as you, I replied.

I smiled at the thought of unleashing Tara at a critical point. But not yet. The queen hadn't beaten me yet. And she had to have a spirit animal as well, even if I couldn't see it. What if Tara had to fight a bear?

The queen stepped forward and we fought again. Nine strikes.

Both her swords were heavier than mine. Slower.

Trap. Trying to lure you in.

It would be *much* more dangerous to try the trick I'd used with Cazenave. Getting inside the arc of his saber had nearly gotten me skewered. Trying that against two swords, and against someone who wasn't fixated on competition fencing, would be a different order of risk.

"The katana will turn against you," she said. She was breathing freely. I was panting. "The spell is a very old spell. A Japanese Adept in the sixteenth century, I would guess. Almost certainly anti-paranormal."

Another pass. Eleven strikes.

I'd taken three hits. Just grazes, but there was more blood to join the sweat and blood soaking my side. My lungs were heaving.

"Why fight me with swords?" the queen asked. "Why don't you accept your magic and use that instead?"

"I accept it fine," I replied.

Another trap. Sword fighting didn't always go to the odds or the better stylist or the more experienced fighter. That was one reason why I'd always hated bladed weapons—as soon as there were sharp edges in a fight, shit happened.

This time, it might favor me. I might catch her off guard.

But I wouldn't do it using magic. Not even Blood magic, which burned in me, wanting me to use it. Not the Blood magic that T-cat whispered I should use. *That* would turn against me long before the sword would.

As if she heard what I thought, she said, "If you don't trust your magic, you could always try your god's."

Yes. I could channel T-cat and fry her where she stood. And then there would be a connection for him into the physical world. Much as I appreciated T-cat's help, I didn't want him here. I'd need an inch of his help, and he'd take the full mile. More.

I attacked as I replied, trying to catch her off guard. "The devil always takes back his gifts."

This time we fought across the width of the clearing. Back and forth. Every footfall treacherous. Every tiny step a risk.

Eleven blows. Fifteen. Twenty. Thirty...

And stop.

She stopped.

I'd slowed. She knew that. I'd lost the edge of speed from the lighter blades. I was too tired. I was bleeding from a dozen cuts, each felt like it was on fire. I couldn't get enough air into my lungs. My vision was narrowing. She could finish me now.

Why hasn't she?

There was still the hope that when Tara attacked, it would distract her just long enough for me to take advantage. If that failed, all I had left was that I'd take her with me.

Unless she took my head off.

She rolled her wrists and let the tips of her blades circle.

Distraction, just like I'd done with Cazenave.

"What is it you desire, Amber? People?"

Her face flickered; her features flowed. My father. Top. Melissa.

"They're dead. Speaking to your zombies doesn't bring them back."

"Riches? Honors? Answers? The meaning of life?"

I feinted, pretending my foot slipped, body tensed to drive Onibi up into her.

She ignored it. "No," she said thoughtfully. "You're genuinely the great idealist, aren't you? You want justice for all. You want the greatest good for the greatest number."

I got up just as she attacked again. I couldn't spare the breath to speak.

"Which is the same thing Altau says." Two strikes. "And Matlal." Two more. "And me."

My arms felt like they were on fire. I wasn't attacking, and I was parrying later and later.

"And this is where you begin to understand your attack was futile."

She slipped. Not enough for me to get through, but I managed to attack again.

"Even if you were to kill me, you would simply replace me with you."

Eleven more strikes. Finally she was slowing and panting. I had grazed her arms a couple of times. She didn't even notice, but she was at least tired enough that her sentences started to break up when she attacked again.

"You would start. With the best intentions. Like I did. Then one day. You'd be in an impossible situation. Altau's fault probably. And you'd use your discretion. Just that once."

We broke, stepped back.

"It never is once," I panted.

"And that nugget of wisdom wouldn't have protected you from becoming exactly what I am."

My vision was graying out, but through that I could see my katana's blade wasn't just glowing now. I could actually see blue-white flames rippling along it.

We're skimming the spirit world!

She'd distracted me and pulled us out of the physical world.

Tara manifested, in wolf form with flames.

Immediately the queen's spirit guide appeared. Snake! Huge, fast, venomous-looking. And as it moved, a shadowy mist moved with it. Tara dodged and darted, but she couldn't close without touching that mist, and we knew that was bad.

Which was another distraction, I realized as the queen launched another attack to drive me back.

Here, skimming the spirit world, she could fight physically and with magic at the same time. But when her magical strike came, it wasn't really a strike at all. She was probing, searching, locating one connection in my aura that she wanted.

She found it.

"Tezcatlipoca! Lord of the Night!" the queen called out, and I could feel the temple of night forming around me, sucking the gray of pre-dawn down into a lightless depth.

The fight had all been a ploy to get me here, on my knees. She was appealing to T-cat. She wanted a deal with him that would return her powers. She needed to show him she was the greater, more experienced fighter. The better candidate to be his priestess.

There would be no concerns from her about sacrifices to him.

The blade of the katana blazed. Tara dodged the spirit snake and shifted from wolf to jaguar. She was still clothed in flames and the light picked out echoes of her shape: jaguars, climbing the walls of the temple.

Was she saying I should call on T-cat instead?

Remind him how closely we were bound?

Blood calls to Blood.

I felt dizzy with a web of spirit connections. The feel of my spirit being in many places. I was here, in T-cat's temple of night. I was in the heart of the forest of ancient gods, by the banks of the Atchafalaya. I was in the gardens of de Socorro's mansion in El Paso. The riverside house of the Lafayette coven. The woods around Haven. Standing beside Ash, in the circle of trees around the cemetery in a tiny village in Ireland. With Jen's bank of larch and cypress at Manassah.

Blood calls to Blood.

I felt his presence in the temple.

The queen turned her aura to him with a wordless song of offering, full of rage and blood, of power and worship. Her vision of an avenue of death with its own awful beauty, leading out of this temple and across the unprepared world.

Whatever ideals she may have once held, nothing remained in the queen but the desire to *be* and the lust for power.

Blood calls to Blood.

I could have killed her right there, as her physical body lost the focus of her attention. I saw T-cat expect it. She would make a worthy sacrifice in his temple. Another step on his great path.

But Ash, tree of dreams, tree of life, soultree of the Threefold Spiral Coven, spoke to me.

Threefold thy acts return to thee, Ash said.

And Ash reached, channeling magic through me. I'd accepted I was a Blood Witch, with magic as dark as the temple of night, but my great ability was still channeling others' magic.

Ash reached through me and took me, and took the Queen of Diamonds, and her venomous spirit snake with its poisonous mist, and Tara. And reached again, through my spirit connections, up the Atchafalaya, to the sacred grove of the African gods.

All of us spirit jumped into the trees there.

We felt the stir of morning, from the promise of sun in the highest leaves of the highest branches, down into the depths of blind roots digging in the damp and lightless dark.

Perfect.

As she'd held them, they would hold her.

They were slow, full of the rhythms of seasons instead of heartbeats, a great wheel of time heedless of humanity's flickering concerns. Her hate and anger would slow to their cycles. She would weep from their leaves and be gathered by their roots. She would grow formless and lose the power of direction, in an unending song of being.

As Ash and I jumped back, a stream of tree-blessings flooded after us, and down into my spirit connections.

The gardens of de Socorro's mansion bloomed and spread, escaping the rigid geometry of pruning that had held them so long. The circle of the Threefold Spiral coven, Manassah's trees and Haven's woods burst with early spring growth.

And at the Lafayette coven's house by the river, where every structure and piece of furniture was old, dead wood, recycled from a thousand bits of timber, they woke again. Posts on their porch sank roots into the ground, beams turned, walls cracked, joined with the floor and pushed up through the roof to wait for the morning sun.

Entirely unintentional, but that would serve them right for summoning me like a demon.

Chapter 73

I couldn't go back to New Orleans immediately.

I was beyond exhausted, and yet hyper-aware of everything: dozens of wounds still bleeding, the rush of air in my lungs, the cold sweat, the pounding of my pulse, the blisters on my feet and hands, the ache of muscles.

Most of all, the scrabble of guilt.

The queen had struck me, and the deepest strike had been her comment about how I was willing to work with Mirela, but not with the queen.

I had two versions of Mirela in my head. The first was House Tucek, who worked for Vega Martine, the woman who'd killed Frank in front of me, had kept children in dungeons beneath the convent in Taos, had passed those children on to Matlal, whose team had failed to stop the degradation of children by Gálvez in Astilla de Luna. The second was Mirela, who'd given me an oath and kept it, who was funny and sexy and had trusted me to get us off the *Queen of Diamonds*, and who I *knew* wasn't like that other woman.

I could rationalize it in my head. That messing with aura in the spirit world had profound effects. We'd touched and twisted around each other, and it was easy to visualize that as the yin-yang of light and dark, with a spot of dark in the light and a matching spot of light in the dark.

But did it really work like that?

Was my aura strong enough to make Mirela change?

If that were so, had I changed by the same amount?

What had I done?

With my imagination still in turmoil from the spirit world, I visualized this disturbing confusion like an infection in my Blood, spreading through my body like fire.

I'd get back to New Orleans and my House and my obligations, but I had to work through this first.

I gathered the queen's jian and dao, tore strips from my tattered clothes and bound them to the sheaths of Onibi and Nekotsume. Then I started walking, holding the image of the little bay that formed the substantiation that T-cat had made for me.

And I was suddenly standing on the hill, looking down to the beach and the bay, where a group of naked women were having some kind of swimming competition.

I was male again, in the major's body, but still bleeding from all my wounds. Of course, I was naked except for the four swords strapped to my back. And my Blood warpaint on my face.

He had a sense of humor, did T-cat. This was my substantiation and I could probably change the rules about clothing, but I didn't have the energy at the moment.

The wind blew and chilled my sweat, but I still felt hot.

"Shit! Amber! What the hell?"

It was Mirela. Naked but for a beach towel over her shoulders.

She ran towards me and I had visions of her and Salar treating my wounds like they did last time.

"Stop!" I said, and held up my hands.

She came to an abrupt halt, frowning in confusion.

"Don't come any closer," I said. "Just leave me be. This is hard enough as it is."

Mirela snorted and her face took on a completely different look. Her gaze ran down my body and her eyelids lowered.

"I'm sure I could make it much, *much* harder," she murmured.

"Shut up, Mirela. We need to talk."

She stopped fluttering her eyelashes and spread the towel on the ground.

"Okay. Well, at least sit down."

I folded my legs and sank down gratefully on one half. She sat on the other.

"The queen?" she said.

"Dealt with." I was too tired to explain.

She nodded, as if she'd been expecting that.

"Good. Well done."

We were silent for a minute.

"We're all here," she said. "My whole House, twenty-two of us, and Donatienne of course." She paused for a long moment. "What are you going to do with us?"

"See? That there is why this is a serious conversation," I said. "A week ago, if I had the opportunity..." I clicked my fingers.

It wasn't exaggeration. Mirela's question showed she understood what power I had here. This was my substantiation. I could collapse it, and leave them trapped in the spirit world. Or I could just kill them all where they stood. I didn't know *how* exactly, but I was sure I could find out.

"I guess time has been passing differently," Mirela said. "You're meaning before we went for our ride on the *Queen of Diamonds*, but we've been here a couple of weeks." She nodded her head to indicate the rest of her House.

I blinked. "A month ago, then."

"I still don't believe it."

"What do you mean?"

"Even a month ago, before you really knew any of us other than what we'd done, you wouldn't kill us like that." She clicked her fingers. "I'm not suggesting you couldn't. Or you wouldn't have killed us face to face. I'm just saying you're not like that."

"Is this another way of saying I'm an appallingly naive boy scout?"

She laughed. "I did say that, didn't I? I guess I wouldn't use that description anymore."

She cocked her head and frowned, as if she found what she'd just said strange.

It was. And the longer I stayed in the spirit world, the stranger it seemed. Something wasn't right. Something you couldn't see while you were still inside. I needed to get out.

"Your whole House has changed, hasn't it?"

"Haven't you?" she asked.

"I think I have. A sort of yin-yang from the time we shared auras."

"A bit of me in you, a bit of you in me. Don't think it's so symmetrical. This substantiation is an extension of your aura." Her frown deepened. "It's kept working on me. I don't think there's a way back. Are you getting the feeling there are things you have done that you couldn't do now?"

This was starting to get like one of those conversations that Yelena and Vera had about Carpathian philosophy. It made me feel lightheaded. "I *am* wondering if I can do things that I wouldn't have before. I've accepted my magic is dark. Blood magic. Is whatever I've taken from your aura the cause of that? Is it going to make me slide down that slope?"

"I can't answer that."

This had become one of those dangling conversations, with a lot of silences between us. There were shouts and laughter from the beach. The hush of an onshore wind blowing. I should have felt cooled, but I was clammy.

"What are you going to do?" Mirela said finally.

"I don't know. There's something that isn't making sense," I said, getting up carefully. "It's things like this where the Agiagraphos kinda gets it right. I have a responsibility for you, but I don't know what to do about it."

I swayed.

"Are you all right?"

"No," I said, looking down at the beach where the rest of House Tucek were.

Their competition was over, and the team Donatienne had been on had evidently won. She and the others were celebrating with a group hug in the shallows, leaping up and down and splashing.

"Looks like Donatienne is fitting in well," I said.

"She is."

"Hold on. You said you'd been here for a couple of weeks..."

"Nearly three."

"What have you done about food and Blood?"

Mirela shrugged. "This substantiation is cool. Food appears in the huts and... ah, tourists wander along the beach and see us."

"How have you been—"

"We understand we're your guests, so we're handling them with kid gloves. A bit of distraction, a little feeding and blurring of memories, then we send them on their way. I guess they end up back in Hawaii, wondering if they dreamed about finding a naturists' beach that doesn't seem to be there the next time they look."

I grunted. "Good. I'll come back. I really need to go now. Need to go. Back."

Mirela was looking worriedly at me. She spoke, but already the substantiation was receding from me and I couldn't hear.

I was focused on where I wanted to go. I didn't want to return to the Hatch and wait for pickup, but then, I didn't need to. I was powerful, here in the spirit world. The power whispered to me.

I shook my head. Bad idea. Nearly fell over. Maybe I should stay here.

Yeah. Sure. Stay here and grow stronger. Build myself a riverboat, maybe.

In the same way Gabrielle had sought connection to travel back to New Orleans, I searched and sorted through them. They were like threads drifting out from my fingers into the darkness. Some felt fragile as a spider's silk strand. Some felt stronger than steel cables. There was one I was looking for, sure it would be there. The one I desperately needed.

It had a distinctive feel to it, and it was strong.

Diana was still in Louisiana. Not in New Orleans. She was out at Labastide's plantation house overlooking the Mississippi.

I was going to miss this capability to travel when I was back in the physical world.

Of course, I could always return to the spirit world.

I shuddered. Suddenly, in a moment of clarity, I wanted to spend as little time as possible in the spirit world.

I took Diana's thread and walked towards where it ended in a bedroom. We were in Talleyrand, the Labastide plantation house, overlooking the formal gardens in the front, with a distant view of the levee.

It was dawn.

The room was warm and humid. Full of scents.

I stood there, back in my own body and tattered, wet clothes, swords across my back. Still with dried blood on my face and fresh blood leaking from my wounds.

The visualization I'd had of that confusion spreading like fire in my veins hadn't gone away.

Maybe I just needed rest. Rest sounded so *good*.

In the growing light, I could see Diana wasn't alone in the bed. Solange Dupuis, Diakon Labastide, was with her.

Damn.

I couldn't creep out. I found I couldn't even move. Everything seemed so heavy.

"Amber?"

Diana sat up, eyes wide with shock and her hair draped around her shoulders like a shawl of the deepest black silk.

"Sorry," I mumbled.

The mattress reared up and struck me in the face.

I bounced.

The room spun around me.

I had a second to wonder why I was looking at the ceiling and then darkness claimed me.

Chapter 74

The fire in my Blood was poison, which, I learned, is a thing even for Athanate.

The queen hadn't used an ordinary poison. Oh, no. She'd smeared an Athanate-specific poison on the blade of her jian. A subtle thing, that used the prions, the Athanate protein strings in the Blood, to spread.

A mixture of being a hybrid and visiting the spirit world had given me enough time to get to Diana, and she saved my life. Again.

She bit me and sent her own bio-agents into my Blood to overwhelm the poison.

She cleaned and licked my wounds.

Held me while I shivered.

People visited me that morning and either merged into the fever dreams I had, or spoke to me in my moments of lucidity.

Gwen. Gabrielle was being cared for. Not recovered, but out of danger. Much like me, apparently.

Jen and Alex. My husband growling about what we'd do when we got back to Denver. My wife reminding me of a long list of promises I'd made to her in the shower that she had every intention of holding me to. But not right now. Diana sent them both away on the basis that their responsibilities in El Paso and DC were more important than watching me recover.

Felix and Cameron.

I wasn't sure whether that was the fever speaking or them in real life. They told me the ritual had been a spectacular success. Every halfy had changed. Every dubious member of every pack had ended the night confirmed and committed to their packs. Only a few dozen died. *Only*. But the other alphas were happy and the Gulf Coast all the way down to Florida was now solidly Southern League.

When they'd gone I wasn't entirely sure they'd been there—I was responsible for dozens of deaths and they were pleased with me?

Rita became a more or less permanent fixture in the room. She was upset she'd not been able to protect me when the riverboat came and didn't want to leave me, even in the safety of Labastide's well-guarded plantation mansion.

All my House who were still in Louisiana came up in ones and twos. All good. Their scent was soothing and it was like a beacon drawing me home when the fever returned.

Jo and Xavier came and massaged me, carefully avoiding my wounds. One of them massaging me had been wonderful. Two was incredible. I offered them positions in House Farrell and said I would fight Marguerite hand to hand for the privilege. They laughed and said I was still delirious. I wasn't.

I had the freedom of the House. As they finished the massage, they offered their Blood. I took it with such fever-enhanced pleasure I thought I was going to pass out. I might never get along with Marguerite and Solange, but I was just *fine* with some members of the House.

People kept visiting and re-visiting as the day wore on, and some stayed.

Tullah and Kaothos. They sat like twins, indistinguishable in the gloom, whispering to each other as I slipped down into sleep again.

My dreams had started out like I was skimming the surface of the spirit world, blown one way and then the other. Now they began to take direction, leaping and plunging like dolphins into the fevered memories of everything that had happened to me since we first spirit walked.

Gwen and Bryn came. They brought an easy chair for Gwen so that Bryn could manifest.

As night fell, I lay in bed, surrounded by them while I dreamed my way through encounters with T-cat, fighting the Queen of Diamonds and working with my enemy, Mirela Tucek. They all shared my dreams, even though I wasn't sure when I was lucid and when I wasn't.

The spirit world didn't sit solidly in memory, but Diana and the others patiently wove it all back together from the fraying fragments in my mind as I slipped in and out of sleep.

Around midnight, we ate from bowls of fruit that Nick and Ursula had brought with them when they joined us. After eating, Rita helped me with a shower and I returned to a freshly made bed feeling better than I had.

As she helped me back into bed, Rita broke the silence that had fallen over us in the room. "What *is* T-Cat? Exactly?"

She wasn't asking me, and no one hurried to pick it up.

Diana finally spoke. "Maybe the Carpathians have a neat explanation." She frowned. "A construct, like all the Lost Gods. The product of millions of minds and soul-energies that achieved an independence and sustained itself in the spirit world when the direct source faded."

"*Not* an actual god, though," Rita said.

"Walks like a duck, talks like a duck," Ursula muttered.

"Might as well think of Tezcatlipoca and Quetzalcoatl as they are depicted," Gwen said. "Lost Gods, enemies, trapped in the City, in a stalemate, and fighting to reconnect with the physical world to gain advantage. The way the world is now, their return would make them more powerful than they ever were, and they would devastate it."

"Unfortunately," Diana said, "Quetzalcoatl has found a path, through Matlal."

"We can't fight Quetzalcoatl yet," Kaothos said.

I felt their eyes all turn to me. We all knew there was a way Tezcatlipoca could remain on equal footing with his brother: through me.

"We can't risk it," Tullah said. "I'm not even going to start on the danger to Amber if we try and use her connection to T-cat. Face it, there's no certainty that two gods back in the physical world would cancel each other out somehow. We'd be in an even worse situation."

Nick nodded agreement. "This isn't like Amber using some of Ash's power and risking becoming tainted with the evil that created it. Or fighting the queen. T-cat's a whole level different."

The chill reached right through my fever. *My priestess,* he had called me.

"I've already started the process," I said. "I've used his power—"

"Or he made it seem like you were," Gwen said. "Don't just accept what he says."

That stopped us all for a minute. Their experience of what happened in the spirit world had come from them sharing eukori and sensing my aura as Diana had guided my 'dreams' back through my memories. We all knew that they were seeing things through my eyes, and my perceptions colored every event.

But in the same way, they knew, as I knew, I was the ehvasi of House Chrysos and tied by that into the very fabric of these particular gods.

And they also knew, as I knew, that my aura had been changed by the spirit world.

I'd used dark magic. Blood magic. As Nick and Flint and Kane had warned me, back in Denver at Christmas time, the first few times would be for the very best of reasons and with good intentions. And it would get easier to justify every time after that.

They all knew what I was thinking about. It was Diana who broke the silence finally. "If you weren't concerned, Amber, *then* I would be concerned."

"There's plenty to be concerned about," Gwen whispered.

"You are still you," Tullah said.

"But you're right," Bryn said. "You *have* taken an element of evil into yourself. Whether it came from Tezcatlipoca or the queen—"

"Or from Mirela, when you connected your auras to combat the queen," Kaothos said. "It still doesn't make you evil."

"But it *does* give Tezcatlipoca a huge potential connection," Diana said. "Every time you use your magic, he'll be there, offering to boost it."

"And you can't take up that offer without strengthening his connection to you," Tullah said.

"And the stronger the connection, the more he will be able to influence you," Gwen finished.

I didn't want to think about the whole situation, so I concentrated on one point Kaothos had made.

"Yes, about Mirela..." I started.

Tullah had experienced that last visit through me. She knew what was going through my head. "Your aura is stronger than hers. You had an influence on her," she said.

"Not that much." I shook my head. "I gave her my oath."

"You didn't mean to change her aura, any more than she meant to change yours," Gwen said. "Surely that's out of the scope of your damned Athanate oath?"

I kept shaking my head. "No. I'm not talking about the accidental exchange of fragments of aura when we had to combine to defend against the queen's aura. I'm talking about the substantiation I put her in."

"T-cat created it—" Tullah said.

"From my visualisation," I interrupted. None of them were seeing it yet. "I used his power to create my substantiation. I did it in a hurry. There's none of the thought I should have put into it. And the issue is, my aura isn't so wonderful that I've overcome all the evil in the whole of House Tucek with a wave of my hand."

Talking was making me feel weak again. Rita passed me some water to drink while they waited.

"So..." Tullah prompted.

"So that substantiation isn't some kind of safe place for them," I said. "It's a prison, and the only reason they're behaving the way they are is that they're all subject to a compulsion. *My* compulsion."

"My heart bleeds for them," Ursula said.

"Yes, but I gave my oath to Tucek I wouldn't do anything like that." I lay back and felt the fever stirring again. "If I break my oath and start compelling people, I'm no better than the queen."

"I see your point," Diana said, carefully avoiding saying she agreed with it. "We can't let them go, we can't keep them like that, and yet we need Tucek as a witness in the Assembly, and as a possible source for information when we come to attacking Vega Martine."

"Exactly."

No one had a solution.

Eventually Diana chased everybody else out except Rita, and I fell into a blessedly dreamless sleep between the two of them.

I woke in the morning when Pia came up to the room to hand my cell to Diana.

"What is it?" I asked sleepily.

"A message for you." Diana passed me the cell.

It was from Jacob Tosun, Skylur's temporary Head of Security—the man who'd been posted from House Elicott in Washington DC as a political move to placate the former Eastern Seaboard association.

It was curt to the point of rudeness, and simply said my presence in New York was urgently and immediately required. Not requested. *Required*.

"I was afraid of this," Diana said. "My guess is you've made a lasting enemy of Hecate Hinton."

www.ingramcontent.com/pod-product-compliance
Lightning Source LLC
Chambersburg PA
CBHW031944260626
47157CB00017B/2195

* 9 7 8 1 9 1 2 4 9 9 2 5 0 *